The Baby

Jennifer Aaron-Foster b
financial journalism. She later left the city o
London and moved to Dubai, where she worked as a correspondent for a local TV station. After finishing her novel; Jennifer, her husband, their three children, and their very precocious cat, eventually moved out of their shoebox home in East London, and settled in the countryside. Jennifer's debut novel can be found on major online bookstores, including: Waterstones, Amazon, Apple Books, Rakuten Kobo, Barnes & Noble and on Goodreads.

Visit www.littoralpublishing.co.uk for exclusive updates on The Baby Whisperer

Littoral Publishing Ltd

www.littoralpublishing.co.uk

First Published in Great Britain by Littoral Publishing Ltd 2024

Jennifer Aaron-Foster asserts the moral right to bc identified as the author of this work

ISBN- 978-1-0687512-0-2

Acknowledgements

I thank God, from whom all blessings flow.
I would also like to thank all those who believed in the project. My editor, Hope Bollinger, who had nothing but praise for the story idea. Sarah Vincent who gave a thorough assessment of the manuscript in its early stages. Liz & Dave Nunn; they never let me forget the relevance of this story. My mum and dad. Jean and Bill. My amazing brothers and sisters, who inspire me to be a better person every day. My adorable children, not forgetting my husband John, who is the most resourceful person on this planet! Hard-working, knowledgeable and kind, as well an eagle-eyed editor – nothing gets past him! And Amber for being an inspiration.
This novel is for you….

THE BABY WHISPERER

The most arduous journey ever undertaken by Humankind is the passage of birth. The unborn leaves one realm to enter another. And this one is like no other. It is earth. A mired place full of endless journeys...it is foretold after birth comes knowledge. But this is a grave oversight. For it is clear to see the innocent beheld knowledge long before the start…

***

Prologue

Siba

Before we delve into Christine's story, let me introduce myself. My name is Siba (which means rock in Arawak)
I was named after the mountainous terrain that surrounds the lands of my Ancestral home.
I am one of Christine's many Ancestors, and I am a nine-year-old girl. Well, I was when I roamed the earth almost a thousand years ago. And yes, I may be young, but please don't think me too precocious—I just happen to know a lot more than you right now, what with you being tied to the earth…
But I digress…I may be a million years ahead of my time, and often speak in poetry and rhyme (the language of the ethereal), but you will seldom hear me. For us spirits, we could talk about many things, but it's far more intriguing to listen instead. And that is what I do—I listen from the shadows.
But right now, extraordinary events take place on earth—and Christine's story is one of them.

However, you will soon discover much of what goes on in the world is none of my business. Although Christine is very much my business because she hails from my bloodline. But that's by no means the only reason why I comment. I do so, not to inform you, but rather to remind you of certain things—everything you read from here on, you already have knowledge of. You just don't remember you do. But more on that later…

My descendant, Christine Shore, has been given an amazing gift, but due to a horrible loss she is unwilling to unleash it. Like many, Christine walks around in a trance-like state, but she needs to wake up! Terrible things are happening with lingering consequences. So I will tell you her story, a bittersweet joy. Bitter, because it's life, and she's living it; and a joy because she's one of mine and she fights for it! And we are eternally bound by the blood, which I am forever grateful for, and now I am honoured to share Christine's journey with you all.

So I begin

Chapter One: Tilly's House

Christine

I had to try to keep up with Lydia. We emerged from the underground at Regent's Park Station and walked into a cul-de-sac with a short row of houses on either side. At the far end of the street was a pedestrian crossing, leading to one of London's oldest parks. Neither of us engaged in conversation—there was no need. All the introductions and pleasantries had exchanged on the tube ride. Instead, we sped past the grand white Georgian houses, which gleamed like blocks of salt against the purple night sky.

The streetlamps on both sides flickered on. That was when Lydia spoke to me. "Okay, we're almost there now." She pointed ahead. "It's four doors down, the one with the planters around the entrance."

I gave a brief nod and pulled level with my glamorous guide. Her name was Lydia 'Something-Something' she had politely informed me earlier. And Lydia 'something-something' looked about my age too… late twenties or early thirties, perhaps.

"Thanks for coming." Lydia nodded my way. "My cousin said you were a huge help to her and her partner—you saved them a ton of grief." Her plucked eyebrows raised as she said this.

I responded with an awkward smile. Making polite conversation was strenuous enough, let alone having to do it with conviction. However, I was spared this pointless charade as Lydia veered off the pavement and mounted the soaring white steps. I was less than a pace behind her. The front door arose ahead of us, gleaming like a boulder of onyx. On each side stood two brass lamp holders which shone into my eyes, obscuring my vision even after I had blinked a few times. *Drat!* I had forgotten the address I had scribbled down earlier. But of course there was nothing that could be done about that; I was here now.

Lydia rang the doorbell. The woman who answered was distressed. Her blond hair looked like it had been run through with a rake. Her eyes shifted between the two of us, then fell back onto her friend. "Hello, my darling—you came sooner than I expected." The woman received Lydia in a shower of coos and air kisses, then switched her focus back to me.

Lydia piped up, "Tilly, this is Christine…she's—"

"Hello, Christine—do come in. I hope this is not too much of a bother. I suppose Lydia has filled you in."

Before I could answer, the air was slashed by a scream, followed by a gurgling wail. A sound that could only be executed from the delicate lungs of a newborn.

Tilly rolled her eyes. "He's awake again." She sighed as she looked to the ceiling.

While the baby continued screaming, Tilly led us in the opposite direction. She guided us through a labyrinth of subtlety-painted corridors and checkered marble flooring. "We won't go to him just yet. My nanny Maria is with him, and besides, I would like a quick chat with you." She stole a glance my way as she said this. Tilly directed us down a short flight of steps into a bright and spacious living area. The baby's squeals had long since been lost within the dense fabric of the walls.

"Please, sit." Tilly waved her hand, "Would you like some tea, or—?"

"Tilly. You look terrible!" Lydia cut in, "Haven't you slept since the last time we spoke?"

"I have, but very little." She groaned. "If you think I look terrible, I suppose everyone else must think so too…"

While the two friends chatted away I took a closer look at the woman who paced up and down; rubbing her thin gold chain as though she was counting rosary beads. Tilly was not as young as I had thought. A wife of a foreign diplomat, didn't Lydia say something or the other? Although, there was no doubting Tilly was a new mother. The lack of sleep showed up in the crescent moons beneath her eyes, and judging by her heaving chest, she was still breastfeeding.

What am I doing? I tore my eyes away and cast them down to the ground. I didn't want to get caught staring and come off like some kind of nutjob. Besides, I was not in the business of reading minds. I was here for a different purpose.

"Christine?" The mentioning of my name ended my private analysis. "Ethan is two months old," Tilly said, weighing me up with a stare. "You might find this hard to believe or maybe not, considering your experience, but since the day Ethan was born, he has not slept for two hours straight. Something is interrupting his sleep." Tilly stopped talking and looked to her friend, Lydia, whose gentle nod urged her to continue. "I-I have no idea how this works, but please can you look at him? I understand this is what you do—help babies?"

I nodded. "Yes. It is what I do." I said this with a cheery smile to hide a sudden bout of self-consciousness.

"And if you don't mind me asking, do you have any children of your own?"

"No. I don't." My hand found a loose ringlet which I tucked behind my ear. It was the same one that always seemed to escape from my tightly secured bun. I cleared my throat. "Before I see him, I have some questions—nothing serious," I added, noting the discomfort on Tilly's face. "Are you the primary carer of Evan—Ethan, I mean?" *Too many names to remember.*

"Yes, but like I said, I do have a nanny, Maria, who helps out every so often. It's so that I can attend to my other duties, as you do. You know, they don't just get up and do themselves!" She said this with a nervous laugh. She stopped pacing and sat on the couch adjacent to us. "You see, Maria is new. She's only been with us for two weeks. I've had three nannies in the space of two months. The last two were *utterly* useless. Within a week, they handed in their resignations because they couldn't deal with the constant crying. Though, to be honest, they were well on their way to receiving their marching orders. I mean, seriously! How can anyone claim to be a professional if they cannot figure out why a three-week-old baby is crying his lungs out? What are they teaching these so-called specialists these days? Are they just giving these qualifications away?" Her eyes raged like the Baltic Sea. "I'm so sorry," Tilly pat her cheeks. "I didn't mean to raise my voice. Ethan is a beautiful baby—an absolute darling. He looks just like my father." She nodded; there was no disguising Tilly's pride. "He was a colonel in the Coldstream Guards, you know. He was a very fine man, passed away six years ago. When I look at my son, I see him. Bizarre, but I guess these things happen."

"Yes. Bizarre indeed," Lydia cut in. "But why not tell Christine a bit more about the problem?" She rolled her eyes.

"Of course." Tilly turned to face me. "Since birth, Ethan wakes up every two hours or so, howling as though he were in pain. His crying becomes more erratic in the early hours of the morning. We've taken him to the best doctors—they say there's nothing physically wrong with him, but there's something the matter with our son."

I nodded, encouraging her with a gentle smile. "Go on. Tell me as much as you can, I'm listening."
"I really thought I was prepared for parenthood." Tilly rubbed her eyes and sniffed. "But I didn't foresee any of this. Nothing has turned out the way I thought it would. I put on a brave face for everyone around me, even for my husband, but nobody knows how stressful this whole ordeal has been for me. Before I gave birth, I gained a horrendous amount of weight: puffy face, swollen ankles, varicose veins—the whole sodding lot. I hardly had any energy—it was torture! Then a week before Ethan arrived, I developed haemorrhoids. Can you imagine? And please don't get me started on the breastfeeding—it was an absolute nightmare! Ethan wasn't one of those babies who latched on right away. It felt like a piranha was suckling on my nipple. Now, all he has to do is yawn in my direction, and I break out in a cold sweat. I can't believe mothers go through this!" She looked around her in desperation. "And now my beautiful baby is here! But look at me. I haven't slept for weeks! I'm still fifteen pounds overweight; I have engagements to attend, commitments to fulfil, a husband who needs me, and a baby that consumes *every* waking moment of my life! Where does it end?" Tilly cried, "I don't think it does," she said answering her own question, "but who am I to complain? I have help for *god's sake!*"

"Tilly!" Lydia rushed to her friend's side, "You're just having a bad day, that's all. Why not take Christine to see the baby?"
Tilly responded with a pathetic nod. "Yes, of course." She paused. She took a deep gulp of air, then led the way.
As we ventured out into the foyer we were presented with a grand open stairwell which looked like it hailed straight out of a movie set. I took a sweeping glance at the fancy paintings; furnishings and frippery afforded by those who were not short of money. On one of the landings stood a life-sized photograph of Tilly—all smiles and big hair—posing with a famous hip-hop record producer. I swallowed my surprise. I couldn't stop and stare, I had a job to do. The two women swanned ahead of me, engaged in conversation like ballerinas at a recital. I wondered if they really were 'best friends forever' or just parading a kind of familiarity the bourgeoisie displayed with such disarming ease. Once upon a time I would have felt out of place in this showy display of wealth, but grief changed many things. No longer did I spend countless hours analysing who I was—or who I was with. I realised everyone had struggles, which was why I was turning corners in a mansion in Regents Park, and not sat in my north London, ex-council, one-bedroom flat, playing solitaire on my home computer.
"Maria's probably trying to lull him back to sleep again," Tilly whispered as we approached the nursery.

The door was slightly ajar. The soft murmurings of Spanish could be heard, but the baby, it seemed, was unimpressed as he carried on whining.

Tilly stepped into the room. "Maria, I've brought someone to look at Ethan." Whether it was the sound of his name, or the bright light which came flooding in from the landing, the baby howled at the sight of us. "Oh, no—there he goes again." Tilly took her child from the nanny, who did little to hide her irritation.

As soon as I stepped into the room, the sweet soft scent of baby cosmetics embraced me like a warm hug. Powders. Balms. Oils. Lotions. I was no stranger to these lovable fragrances. The nursery was adorned with pale-blue and powdery white apparels; it felt like I had floated onto a patch of unchartered sky. I paused to take it all in, and in that brief moment, I recalled a funny remark a newborn once made. He said to me: *'his mummy's arms was the only room he wanted to be in, and all the playground he would ever need…'* I absorbed my smile—this was not the time for humour. I hurried over to the middle of the nursery for there—in the midst of all that gorgeous, loveliness—was a red-faced, fair-headed baby refusing to be comforted.

"If it's alright with you, I'd like to be left alone with him." I didn't take my eyes off the wailing infant. "Is that okay?"

There was a moment's hesitation as my dark brown eyes connected with Tilly's pale blue ones. "Okay."

Tilly nodded. "We'll wait for you downstairs." She handed her son over to me. Caressing the soft bundle in my arms, I walked over to the rocking chair. I could hear their muffled voices as the two friends made their way back to the living area.

Fifteen minutes later, I emerged from the nursery. All was quiet. The baby was now in a deep sleep. I closed the door behind me and pondered my next move. There was no point in stalling—it had to be said. I walked onto the landing and retraced my steps back to the main room.

As I drew nearer, I could hear Lydia questioning her friend: "Have you taken Ethan to see a specialist, or what do you call them—a paediatrician? Something could be wrong with him on the inside?"

Tilly huffed. "Don't you think that's the first thing Rupert and I did? Don't laugh, Lydia, but I get the feeling Ethan is trying to tell me something…something I've overlooked or I'm not seeing…something is disturbing his sleep…"

I could no longer continue to linger in the hallway. I let out a shaky breath then stepped into the room. Without looking around, I made my way toward the marble fireplace. I felt awkward as their eyes slid toward me. I hated this part, speaking the truth whilst looking like a *complete* lunatic. Only a masochist would take on a role like this, but there was no one to blame for this predicament—it was my own doing. I was never really any good at saying *no* to anyone who needed help.

Taking a deep breath I leaned against the mantelpiece for support. "Th-these are Ethan's words not mine." I cleared my throat. "The champagne..." I paused and started again, this time without stopping. "I don't like the champagne. The bubbles in the breast milk give me indigestion. If you do insist on having a tipple in the evening, then might I suggest you have a glass of that Rioja you occasionally have. None of that 'New World' drivel as that gives me heartburn. But that Rioja is a very nice find. I had no idea my crying was causing you so much grief. So after tonight, I won't cry anymore, only when I'm hungry or feeling cold. However, if I do get indigestion, I'll indicate by lifting my legs and scratching my temples. Speaking of which, it's high time I had my nails filed down again, wouldn't you agree…?"

I watched the expression on their ridged faces as they gaped back at me. "Is this some kind of joke?" Lydia said in a blaze. She turned to her friend, whose creamy-white complexion took on a greyish hue.

"Yes—yes. It is good," Tilly said faintly. "It's 1982.""What's 1982?" Lydia looked about her as though everybody had gone raving mad.

"That Rioja." Tilly slowly turned her head around to look at me; her eyes wide with disbelief. Then she said, "Thank you." Her comment seemed to hang in the air for eternity.

It seemed like nobody moved for a time, then Tilly exhaled. I could almost see the tension drifting away from her like a spirit floating to the next world.

"Ethan—my father!" Tilly called out, suppressing a knowing smile. "He's here! He's right here!" She stared at me in a strange kind of wonder. "Oh my god…they're all here…"

Yes, Tilly, that is correct! As a roaming spirit I can boldly tell you, the world may think you're dim—but you're a lot quicker than most! For your father—our Ancestors—haven't completely left our lives, as many are led to believe. On the contrary, our Ancestors are very much alive; they have plenty to say, and the babies are in a prime position to say it! But who can hear their tiny voices? Well as it turns out, one specially selected soul, has this unique ability to do so…

"Did he say anything else?" Tilly's beaming eyes searched my face.

"Nothing I wish to repeat," I replied, apologetically, deadpan.

The smile froze on Tilly's lips.

For indeed, there is nothing cutesy about baby-whispering, as the world is about to witness. Nothing cutesy about it at all.

Chapter Two: The Girl

Christine

As a simple, care-free girl from Hackney Downs—East London, I remember an awful lot about my early years. I remember the day my mother called out to my father. My mother sounded somewhat distressed...

"Gerry!" she yelled. "Gerald Bartholomew-Shore. Come up this instant, or they'll be hell to pay!"

Still no answer.

"Ger-reeeeeeey." My mother's emphasis on the, *'reeeeeee'* made me laugh. My mother smiled down, shaking her head.

"Woman—I said I was coming!" Gerry replied. His voice bellowed all the way up from downstairs and left a vibration that continued long after he'd answered.

My mother was in no mood for jokes. "Your ma's going to be here any minute now, just have a look at me, will yer', and tell me how I look?" My mother's soft Irish accent did little to mar her growing angst.

I remember the rapid thuds on the stairs as my father took them two at a time. He bustled into the bedroom. "I said I was coming, Yvonne. I just had a quick look at the drinks cabinet." He strode over to where she stood and put his arms around her.

"Drinks cabinet?" She turned her head up to get a better look at him. "Are ye daft? It's your own

mother we're talking about. I'm the one who's supposed to be nervous here, don't you know."
Gerry laughed. "You've got nothing to be nervous about. I know my mother's going to love you, and our *lickal* princess, Christine." He smiled as he rocked us both. He crooned Marvin Gaye's hit song into her ear. *"Let's get it on. Oooow, baby. Let's get it on".*
Yvonne laughed and nodded. "Aye. She'll approve of us alright, but think her son is a few sandwiches short of a picnic." As she said this my mother's eyes wandered downward. He followed her gaze and saw that his flies were wide open, and the tail of his red shirt jutted out as though he were a frisky dog. At this, they both burst into hysterical laughter. I too, giggled out loud, so much so my sides began to hurt.
I remember...
I recalled the day my mother and father argued. He wanted to continue to live in the house they rented in Lower Clapton. It was a semi-detached with an overgrown garden at the front.
"It's close to where I work. Where else in Hackney are we going to get better with the salary I'm on?"
It was a bone of contention for many weeks in the *'O'Reilly-Shore'* household. I listened in carefully. There were so many different thoughts, feelings, opinions being expressed. But the ones that mattered the most to me, right then, were the voices of my parents.
I remember...

With varying degrees of repulsion, I recalled the taste of lukewarm boiled swede. I wanted to notify my mother, but then decided against it, which was by-the-by in the run-up to the events that followed…

There was a knock on the door. Two police officers stood outside.

"Good evening, ma'am. We would like to speak with Yvonne Shore."

"Yes, that's me," my mother answered. Immediately her heart dipped; her pale green eyes began to water from the acrid smell of trouble. The police. *The Garda.* Back home in Sligo, she didn't welcome the sight of them then, and they were still not welcome now.

The two officers gave each other peculiar looks. "You're Gerry Shore's wife?" The officer furrowed one of his brows as he posed the question.

"Yes, that's what I said. Is there a problem officer?" My mother was more acute than polite.

The police man shuffled, looking uncomfortable. "Could we come in?"

My mother nodded. She led them down the corridor to the living area. I felt a jolt, as if someone had kicked me in the stomach. I began to pay closer attention…

"I'm afraid to have to inform you…" The officer looked around the modest room, giving a scant inspection of the smiling portraits of the interracial couple. "Mr. Shore was involved in an accident on the site he was working on….He fell forty feet..."

The officer cleared his throat and looked down at his shoes. "I'm sorry. He fell forty feet….they rushed him to the hospital, but I'm afraid he didn't make it....Your husband was pronounced dead at 14.38 hours this afternoon."

My mother's hands flew to her stomach. She took in three gulps of air to steady her nerves. I looked up and felt her hand caress the top of my head.

I remember...

The funeral was held two weeks later. On that cold rainy day, there was a maelstrom of voices—weeping, singing, and jabbering. I recalled my mother's wretched state, still as severe as the day she had received the news of my father's death. My mother could hardly lift her eyes; they ached from the strain of producing so many tears. Nevertheless, the funeral forged ahead; through the weeping, through the singing, the jabbering, the noise….Then, I became aware of a sensation. But this time it was one of complete certainty…it was time for me to be present…time for me…to be born…

"Yvonne, are you alright, my love?"

"Aye! No!" Yvonne winced. She clasped the top of the chair to break her fall. "I think my waters just broke. Can somebody call an ambulance…?"

Three hours later, weighing less than a bag of sugar, I made my wonderful debut into the big wide world. The air was so cold, it felt like a thousand miniature icicles had pierced my delicate skin at the same time. I was many things—sleepy; disoriented, angry, thirsty.

However, the overwhelming desire to eat had eclipsed every startling sensation I was experiencing. And then, in a breath-taking shower of light, my mother peered down and kissed my forehead. I fought hard against the crushing desire to sleep but lost. My mother's smiling face drifted into darkness. From a young age I began to reflect on these events. And later I would realize I was different. Different, because unlike the millions of people before me, and the many that will come after, I did not forget my initial journey into this world. Oh, no. I remembered it all.

I remember...

***

Siba

As you can see, my descendant, Christine Shore, was born with a very special gift. She remembered her birth into the world. Me—on the other hand—I've almost forgotten what it feels like to be human, and what life was like on earth. However, the little bits I do remember, I didn't like very much. I found the human experience to be a restrictive one; a bit like being crammed into a jam jar with no connection with nature or the outer world, and the little space there was to manoeuvre was filled with too many questions and not enough answers. It was very suffocating for a nine-year-old, I cannot fathom what it would be like for the adults.

However, if you ask me what it feels like to be water? Now, that's a different story. It's absolutely AMAZING! The water and I are one, as we share the same life force. I can tell you right now, water likes being water, but I don't know if I can say the same for you humans. Anyway, that's how I remember life on earth. But in truth, that's not how it always was.

It's the same with my descendant, Christine. She remembered the first time she heard a baby talking out loud. It was a boy, and his name was Mason. She was twelve years old at the time, and the pair of them talked for days and days it seemed. He told her many interesting truths; they laughed a lot. Then, one day circumstances changed, and they had nothing else to talk about. That is how I remember it. Although, I very much assume my descendant would have a very different take on events, especially that of the 'life-altering-kind' which has a profound way of shaping humans quicker than a habit. Come to think about it, I suppose Christine did see it differently…

***

Christine

"I give up!" My mother's good friend, Ivy Wilkie, dumped the plastic spoon in the bowl. "I swear I would have more luck trying to soothe a rabid dog than getting him to eat. Seriously, Yvonne, why do babies act like little devils at times?"

My mother laughed. "My little one was always a good *'un*. Isn't that right, Christine?" My mother teased. "Most especially at mealtimes." She narrowed her eyes, which I understood to mean: I had to eat every scrap of food on my plate—or 'they'd be hell to pay!' I wondered if all twelve-year-olds had to comply with this silly rule, or if it was only me who had a mother who enjoyed giving their daughter a hard time!

That evening our next-door neighbour had come over for dinner with her eight-month-old-son. He was the mini-me of his mother; he had soft-locked brown hair and dreamy-blue eyes like deep puddles. From the few times I had met him, Mason was a well-behaved baby. But at that moment, he kept squirming around, and was making a terrible mess of things.

"What are you feeding him anyway?" my mother asked Ivy. Mason's sudden outbreak of tears disrupted the conversation. The baby continued to moan as his mother, again, mopped up clumps of orange-coloured mush which had gathered around his bowl like radioactive shrubs.

I was unfazed by the current kerfuffle. I had long since drowned out the noise with thoughts of school, when I heard a voice. It was as distinct as if it were me who had spoken out loud.

"I'm not hungry, Mummy. *Stop feeding meeeee!*"

I stopped chewing and turned a quizzical eye on the baby.

"Excuse me. Did you say something?" I asked, feeling a little anxious and foolish at the same time.
"Sorry, dear. Did you say something?" My mother stopped her conversation with Ivy to look my way.
"Errrr…no. I wasn't talking to you."
"I beg your pardon?"
"No. It's…errrrr…it's nothing." I turned my attention back to my half-eaten baked potato.
"Mummy! *Enough*!" the baby shrieked. "If you don't stop feeding me, I'm going to be sick. I mean it. I really am."
I jerked up. I looked straight at the baby who was staring right back at me with the same astonishment.
"You can hear me?" he said, or gurgled, rather.
My jaw fell open. "You're talking to me?" I gasped, clapping my hands over my mouth.
The baby dodged another spoonful and gave an answer. "Yes. I am talking to you. I can hear and

understand you—all of you—quite clearly." This time neither my mother nor Ivy broke away from their conversation; they probably assumed I was just teasing the baby.

"Please, could you tell mummy I'm going to be sick if she makes me eat another spoonful."

Obviously, I did not do as I was told. I just stood there gawping at him. I remained that way in complete silence before turning to Ivy, who, in the meantime, had managed to scoop another mound of mush onto the baby's spoon.

"Ivy…I think the baby's had enough." The words swam out of my mouth while my head was still reeling from the shock.

"Enough? Oh no, my dear—we've just gotten started." Ivy re-positioned the bowl in front of her child. "My Mason usually clears the plate, and we all know babies won't grow unless you feed them well." She turned to face her son. "Open up now, sweetie. Just one more *spoooonfuuul* -"

I edged back, which was a good thing, as in less than a minute the table; the floor, and Ivy's face was covered in bright orange gunk as Mason made good on his promise.

"*Arrgggh!* Quick! Get me a cloth!" Ivy screeched, as she strained to escape the sickly whiff of rotten fruit and eggs which had lodged itself onto her face. The pale orange-coloured vomit slid away from her chin; down to her neck, to form a small puddle at the base of her collar bone.

Oblivious to the mad dashes around me, I approached the baby in the highchair.
"Are you alright?" I asked.
"Yes, I am." Mason giggled. "I didn't mean to cause such a disruption. I may be small, but I'm not stupid. I know when I've had enough, and I've had enough of eating that slop!" He wagged his chubby finger at the bowl in front of him, "I have no idea what that is, but I can tell you right now—it is not roast beef and fresh vegetables."
I stared at him. "It isn't?"
"No. I don't think it is. It's more like something the cows have left behind on the ground."
"The cows…the ground…?" I was again reduced to stupefaction. "I-I can't believe you're talking to me right now!" "Who's talking to you?" my mother interrupted. "He's only a baby, Christine."
"Aww, leave her be." Ivy laughed. "You're just teasing the little cherub, aren't you dear?" She continued conversing with my mother.
I edged closer. "Why are you talking? What do you know about cows, beef—carrots, for that matter? How do you know these things?"
"How do I know these things?" Mason looked taken aback. Now it was his turn to look bemused. "Why? Are there things I don't know?"
Before I could reply Mason was hoisted over his mother's shoulder. "Listen, Christine. There's no time to explain right now, but please come and see

me—this is great! There are so many things we can talk about…"

And in the following weeks, the two of us did just that.

Much to the delight of my next-door neighbour, I volunteered to babysit Mason on the weekends. There, I asked him a litany of questions:

Why do babies cry?

Are they afraid of animals?

Are they sickened by the smell of their own poo?

What did they like to eat?

And (most notably)…

What do babies dream about?

"I can't speak for all babies, but I, for one, dream of *foooood!* Sometimes I'm sat overlooking a wide-open space, but instead of hilltops there are hundreds of bosoms. I have no idea which one belongs to my mummy, and quite frankly, it doesn't really matter to me." He laughed, "All I do is race from one nipple to the next, trying to fill myself up with as much milk as I can. Whenever I have that dream I wake up totally famished I...what's the matter with you?" Mason gave me a steely look, which made me laugh even harder.

"Oh. My. Goodness! Do you know how *crazy* that sounds, Mason? Just as well no one can hear what you're saying…hundreds of bosoms—I can't believe you said that?" My body shook from laughing.

"Okay, I'm done now!" I wiped my eyes, whilst trying to convey an air of seriousness. I was, after all, the grown-up one out of the two of us. "I'm not going to

laugh anymore, I'm still listening, Mason—carry on."
The baby looked at me with some reservation. "I do have bad dreams too, you know."
"Bad dreams?"
Mason nodded. "Yes. I'm in a place wMeanall alone, there's not a soul around. I'm crying out for my parents, but nobody comes to get me. Then it soon dawns on me that… nobody…will…" Mason's eyes spoke of a horror it seemed he had difficulty articulating. "To be left all alone is punishment—I fear it is even worse than death," he whispered. "You see death is only perceived as a nightmare since nobody knows the end. But isolation *is* the nightmare that has no end…to be shut out of the presence of love…the absence of hope…I don't think we were made for it, Christine…I don't think…we were..."
Mason stopped talking. He stared down at the carpet. At times, I got so caught up in what Mason said I sometimes forgot I was conversing with an eight-month-old. However, Mason was still only a baby all the same. I gathered him in my arms and gave him a gentle squeeze. "Mason, I'm here now," I said softly in the hope of erasing the fear that had crept over him. "You don't have to be afraid. I'm here." It seemed the gesture was enough to soothe his jangled nerves. He lavished me with a gummy grin, before making a grab for one of his toys.
"Any more—dreams?" I thought I'd ask since we were on the topic. I rolled back the ball he just passed to me.

"As a matter of fact, there is another dream…actually—it's not a dream." Mason didn't move.

I looked at him curiously. "You can tell me, Mason, I'm listening."

The baby hesitated. "It's not a dream, Christine…because…I'm not asleep…I've only just gone to another world, and its beauty goes far beyond your imagination and any apt description I could ever give it…it's…it's…" Mason let out a long sigh. "I don't know if you're aware of this fact, but it's a very precarious time for us newborns. A very strange and precarious time. For, although we are here—in the physical world—we babies are kind of suspended between two planes."

I frowned. "Two planes?"

"Yes, two planes." Mason gave me a quizzical look, "I'm starting to suspect you grown-ups don't know much at all. As I was saying, when we close our eyes, we are not always asleep as some of you are led to believe, we've only just gone back to the place that we came from…"

Mason no longer looked at me, and neither were his thoughts on the here and now. His clear, sparkling, blue eyes were immersed in whatever wonderland he was trying to describe. "And this world." He beamed. "Is a magical paradise filled with *unbelievable* things. A place where *love* is not a word—it's *alive!* And it moves around in a swirl of colourful sprinkles—through everything. Through the air; the plants, the trees, the waters, through creation. Yet, at the same time, it is also the *creator* of all these magnificent things."

Motioning with his little hands, Mason set about explaining this unique new world to me. "And there are many of us. Us—as in babies like me—and we're all having the time of our lives! We can roam everywhere, free from fear, violence, and decay. We get to walk with animals, converse with nature, and meet our great Ancestors from time passed. We are always learning new things, knowledgeable things—exciting things. Things of real value to us all. And somehow *joy* is laced in everything we consume. I can spend all day eating and drinking all the yummy delights that have been prepared for us. But there's just too much to do in one day, and too many delights for a hundred lifetimes! And to add to this, I'm surrounded by so many uplifting souls—it's pure bliss. The best feeling in the world, and the best place in the whole universe."

"Wow…." Was the only word I could come back with. "Sounds like you really love it there." Now, it was my turn to fall silent as I tried to imagine a world where there was no disappointment, sadness, or pain. A world, it seemed, where only babies lived.

I turned to Mason. "This place you describe sounds too good to be true. Seriously, why on earth do you come back here?"

"I don't know why? By all means, I really do want to stay there, but there's always something that calls me back. Or should I say someone…" Mason was a flurry of smiles again. He looked like how I felt every Christmas morning: happy and hopeful. "For some reason Christine, I'm always drawn back to the warm being with the wonderful light. I kind of like the feeling of being drawn in. It's like…not wanting to move until your favourite song has ended. No sooner do I run into their embrace—I wake up! I'm back in the world, and back in my little cot."

"What a strange dream," I said with mixed feelings. I didn't know why, but I shuddered. "I wonder what it means?"

"I don't know." Mason looked up at me, just as puzzled, "I feel as though I have a choice in this matter—whether to stay in this paradise or return back to earth, but I'm always drawn back to the world and to the warm being with the amazing light…"

The warm being…I stopped to ponder….

What my descendant didn't know at the time, was years from now she would experience its full meaning, and it's very context would crush her….But that was all much further down Christine's lifeline. For the moment, she busied herself with more pressing queries…

"Very well Mason," I continued with my subtle interrogation. "You still haven't explained to me why I am able to hear you?" I rummaged through the foiled package by my side and supplied Mason with another baby biscuit.

"I think you have a special ability that allows you to hear my deepest thoughts, and somehow you are able to translate it into language—or something to that effect." Mason stopped chewing. "I suppose, when you think about it, I won't be the only baby you can hear. You could possibly hear others talking—no matter their mother tongue. And who knows? You may even possess the ability to communicate with different life forms. How cool would that be?"

"Different life forms?" I paused. That was the last thing I wanted to do—speak with something that wasn't human. Come to think about it, I wasn't sure I wanted to be talking to babies either. None of this fitted with my understanding of life as I knew it. It was the late 80s, at this moment in time I was obsessed with growing my stash of *Smash Hits* magazines; begging my mum for the latest Timberland boots, and praying to get an invitation to one of those cool Pizza Hut parties. That was what my pre-teen ordered world was about, not listening to babies sounding off like adults. This didn't sit well with me at all.

"You know, we babies come from a very peaceful world." Mason cut through my thoughts. "But there is also a strange kind of battle taking place."

"A battle?"

"Yes, but don't worry Christine. It's more like a battle for our attention." Mason produced the biggest smile I'd seen all day. "For you see, our Ancestors want to be present: through you, through me, through us.

And they do this by imprinting their mark upon their offspring. And some of them leave quite deep ones, in a variety of forms such as: physical likeness; idiosyncrasies, character quirks—a whole manner of things. We adopt our Ancestor's characteristics in the same way that plants absorb sunlight. Mind you, it's not just the physical traits we take on, or the so-called good ones," Mason muttered. "We babies are free to choose whatever aspects of our Ancestors' personalities appeal to us. As such, no two people are the same, but all of us are a stunning mixture of humanity. I suppose it is that which makes us interesting individuals. Well, some of us." He giggled. "With a palette that versatile, it leaves more than enough room for a few oddballs!"

I chuckled alongside Mason, wondering if I could classify myself as an oddball. In my classroom there were brainiacs and athletes—and I was neither. And taking an honest look at myself, I could admit I was a world apart from perfect….I glanced over at Mason, who was sucking away on a soft toy.

I couldn't lie, I did enjoy my little chats with Mason. But I also found it a little bit unnerving, and I knew why…? I put the question to him again. "But, Mason. How is it you sound so…so...?"

"So what, Christine?"

"So wise!" I exclaimed irritably. "Something's not right about this. You're just a baby for crying out loud!"

"I suppose I am only a baby to you, but before I came into this world, I understood over six-thousand languages, now I can just about manage six…we babies are special, not because we are cute and cuddly and sometimes smell nice—okay, sometimes." He gave a fiendish laugh. "But I think we are special because we've been handed the best of both worlds."

"What do you mean?"

"Well, contrary to what you've been told, babies do not get distracted by the various colours of this world. We—unlike you lot—are able to see the best in things because our untainted sight allows us to do so." He nodded and smiled. "I'm starting to see you grown-ups are a strange breed. Your heart's cry out for many things, but you do not know what you ask for—and worse still, you do not see it when you receive it. That is why I say babies have the best of both worlds," he shrugged. "We have so much, because we can see what we have…"

I balked at his comment. "Honestly, Mason! All you do is talk in riddles." I turned away in disapproval. What did he mean? *'We have so much because we can see what we have…'* What could I see? Or what could I *not* see? At twelve years old, I didn't quite understand Mason's meaning, but ten years into the future, the precious wisdom in his words would never cease to make me smile...

"Christine. There's something else." Mason looked a little perturbed. "I'm very confused right now. It seems all we babies do is cry—when we're hurting;

play—when we're bored, and laugh insanely at life's many oddities. It all seems a bit too simplistic to me. This level of ignorance is of no use to anyone…although…" He peered up at me. "In order for you grown-ups to experience real joy in this lifetime, I guess there's no way around it! You'll need to start thinking more like us…"

"Ha! More like you lot?" I sniggered, but then I stopped to mull over what the baby had just said…

Mason looked up at me "Even so, I think there might be a problem with our growth. Something is not adding up. From the moment I was born, I know stairs are there to be climbed—but physically I am unable to do so. I know when someone means me harm—but I am unable to run away. I know fire burns. I know why the world is getting warmer, and why music is good for the soul. I guess, what I'm trying to say is that none of this is new to us babies. We understand so many things, much more than I can explain to you right now. But somehow, between now and entering childhood, something is lost or forgotten, and something else takes over. I don't know what that *thing* is and why it happens. But something is impeding our growth." Mason slowly shook his head. "You might struggle to believe this, but as I sit here, I can tell you on great authority that I have the ability to achieve whatever I want in this lifetime."

I raised a quizzical eyebrow.

"No—really, I do! All of us do! It's part of our general make-up. You see we are like gods. We were *deliberately* made this way. We, too, have the ability to make, break, and create—and there is much power in our words, but even with this knowledge so many of us will leave the world not having accomplished an iota of the good we set out to do. It's not supposed to be this way, Christine. Somewhere, something goes horribly wrong…."

Mason said no more but looked to his playpen. The forlorn expression on his face reminded me of those depressing billboard's advertisements, showcasing neglected toddlers. Mason seemed rueful. It was a look that didn't belong on any baby's face. I felt sorry for him, but I needed more answers. "Mason," I uttered in a child-like groan. "Why can I hear you? How is all this even possible?"

"I don't know! And in any case—does it even matter?" Mason's frown dissolved into a smile. "Although, I think you may be able to help us."

"Help…how?"

"The world we are born into…I think it's doing something to the babies. Many of us might need saving from ourselves." He paused. "Maybe that's where you can help?"

"And how exactly can I do that?"

"You have this ability for a reason. Maybe this might be the reason: to act as a kind of mediator between the babies and the adults. Between us—and our grown-up selves. That link reminding us of who we are—has been broken. Maybe you can fix it?"

I looked at him as though he had just grown a second head. "Fix it? Fix it?" I laughed. "Have you seen me at craftwork? I struggle to stick bits of paper together! I can't fix this thing! I'm just me, Christine! Okay!" I dismissed his comments with an angry wave. "I'm just Christine…"

I took a moment to process everything. All this talk of Ancestors; ambitions, abilities—was doing my head in! God knew I didn't need any of this! In a flash, I thought of my own culturally rich heritage: I was black and white, Irish and West Indian, Celtic and African. With my imagination for the dramatics, I envisioned a large gathering containing a multitude of people from all over the world. They came from different races and tribes, all shouting to be heard. They were stirring a gaping cauldron, and what was being mixed was the making of me…

I sighed, feeling awful about what I was going to do next. "I don't think I can do this Mason." I looked down at my hands. "I don't think…I can hear anymore…"

"What? You can't hear me?" Mason's innocent eyes scanned my face. "How about now?" He waited for an answer. "Can you hear me now?" I didn't make a sound, but continued to stare blankly at Mason. "What about now…?"

***

That was the last time I babysat for the Wilkies. Whenever Ivy popped over with her son, I made my excuses and left. To say I had developed a slight aversion to babies, put it mildly. If my mother noted a change in my behaviour she didn't say anything to the contrary. I fled back to my old life, but this time around I crammed it to the hilt with netball tournaments; *Pop* magazines, and a plethora of crushes which went no further than my overactive imagination. But this was normal to me, and normal felt—great! It was almost a year later before I mustered the courage to pay Mason a visit. I didn't outright admit it, but curiosity got the better of me. "How is little Mason doing?" I asked Ivy, who was in the kitchen seasoning a tray of lamb chops. "Oh, Christine my love. He's a dear, an absolute dear. It's so nice of you to come and see him. I know how busy you must be with homework and the rest. Go on in. He's in the living room crawling around in his playpen."

I slowly approached the ocean-themed apparatus. My heart did a tiny somersault in my chest. Mason had grown a great deal since the last time I saw him. His hair was thicker, and his limbs were longer. He appeared to be enjoying heaping multi-coloured bricks on top of each other, oblivious to the fact that others had entered the room.

"Mason," his mother called. "Look who's here to see you darling. We haven't seen Christine in a long while." Mason looked up at the mentioning of his name. He lifted himself off his bottom and stretched out his arms. "Mummy," he babbled with glee. He only had eyes for his mother. "Mummy, carry me.

Caw me, mummy. Carry me."

His mother picked him up and kissed him on his nose. He gurgled. "Look who's here Mason," she cooed at him. "Go and play with Christine. You remember Christine, don't you?" It was then Mason smiled at me.

"Hello, Mason," I said softly. I edged closer. "How are you little one?"

"Bah!" He answered, then what he said next was unintelligible…

"I've got to get back to the chops." Ivy placed Mason into my arms. "I won't be long."

I stared back at eyes that didn't seem to recognise me. Although, he did continue to smile sweetly up at me. Then he said: "Bah…Bah…BAAAAAAAH!"
A few years later I would learn that once babies uttered their first word, they lost the ability to communicate with me. Or was it me who lost the ability to speak with them…? I wasn't quite sure which. But with the utterance of their first word, there was a breaking of a bond, and a connection lost forever. Although, I noted whilst watching Mason struggling to reach for the bricks in the playpen, as babies matured they forgot, an awful lot...Mason was

right! Something did happen to the babies, and whatever that *thing* was, it had happened to us all…

Chapter Three: Tobey Daley and the Quiet Room

Siba

There are only three suites in the Special Care Baby Unit. The first one was the special care room—the safe room. In there, babies were granted liberal visitation rights as they were being prepped for their exodus from the hospital.

The second unit was often referred to as the precarious room. Here, behind the protective glass barrier, the newborns were given around-the-clock supervision, and were drip-fed all their vital vitamins. This room was also packed to the nines with the latest respiratory devices, in the case that the worst should happen...

And finally, there was the third cubicle. It was the last room at the end of the corridor. The glass partition on this front door was only several inches wide. It provided a small view to a tiny bed surrounded by a variety of clunky medical appliances. It was home to only one fragile resident. It was the room where little Tobey Daley, lay…

Conversations involving this name crackled with tension. But that didn't stop me from listening in….

"Nurse Eunice. Have you checked in on Tobey Daley?"

"No, Matron. The next check-up is due in thirty-five minutes."

"Is that what's written down on the chart?"

"Yes. The last check-up was carried out by nurse Lilly. She was accompanied by Dr Lawson."

"I see." The matron looked down at the chart. "And judging by the notes, they've also decided to increase the dosage...” She shook her head. The matron was about to say something else, but it seemed she changed her mind. Her eyes darted toward the end of the corridor, where little Tobey Daley lay in a bleak state of unconsciousness….

“When will his parents be coming back again?” the matron asked.

“I believe Mr. Daley has gone to work, but his wife has just popped down to the cafeteria. We urged her to get a cup of coffee and have a little rest. I don’t think she’ll be too long.”

An announcement was made over the intercom.

“Okay. That’ll be all.” The matron placed the file in the tray. “But just before you go, please notify me when the mother gets here. I’ll need to explain some of the changes that have been made in his report.” She took off her glasses and gave them a quick wipe. “Oh. And Nurse Eunice, try not to look so gloomy! I fear we greet the Daley’s with a look of utter hopelessness.”

“Yes, matron,” The young nurse hesitated.

“What is it Eunice?”

“The doctors. Why are they so baffled?”

“What do you mean?” The matron peered at the nurse. “You’ve come over from St Thomas’s. I know you’ve not been here long. You see, baby Toby has a rare form of *CMS*. From the moment he was born, he’s been on a respirator. I recall the last time they attempted to remove it; he could only breathe for fifteen minutes before they rushed him back onto it again. Ever since then the baby has had to undergo painful procedures and complex treatments to clear his lungs and keep his temperature down."

"But…" the nurse was defiant, "It's been almost a year now. How can any functioning human being endure all this—let alone a twelve-month-old baby?"

"Eunice! A nurse of your experience shouldn't be holding this kind of conversation, especially at this time. And you, and the others you consort with, would do well to refrain from talk that doesn't benefit anyone. The specialists are doing their best. That's all you need to know."

"I know." The nurse lowered her voice. "I just can't begin to imagine what the parents are going through, that's all."

"Eunice," the matron said softly. "We know things can't go on like this forever. I'm sure a decision will be made very soon. All we can do is pray it is the right one, and the best for all involved." She produced a small smile for the nurse. "But right now, we have to keep our spirits up, at least for the parents' sakes, okay?"

"Yes, Matron Graham. And thank you. I won't bring this up again."

The nurse turned to go, but before leaving she added, "That Tobey. You know, ever since I've started working here, I can honestly say, hand-on-heart, I haven't come across a more beautiful-looking baby. Despite the illness—he is such a cutie!"

Matron Graham gave a candid smile. "Absolutely." She watched as the young nurse scarpered off to her duties. "And what a shame," the matron murmured, as she took in the doctor's bleak notes; each line an angry scribble across the baby's medical chart.

***

Siba

As I said, I don't mind hospitals much. I suppose my slight preoccupation with these indomitable structures, is a lot like—I would presume—your interest in international airports. As you see from a comfortable distance, I watch human souls being ferried from one world to another. And I must say, I am riveted (and a little fearful) for everyone's unique journeys and destinations. As of this moment, I have ensconced myself at St Margaret's Hospital Trust. Although, the silence which surrounds this unit is never without interferences; the pulsating life support machines create a hypnotic rhythm of their own. But in spite of these slight intrusions, that is, the invariable hums, beeps and mechanical clicks, all are very much at home with the quiet…Occasionally, a baby's feeble wail can be heard over the noise of the machines. It is a blessed sound indeed—it signals life! A baby's cry is often like a beacon call. Nurses begin to rouse from their short-lived stupor: Quick! Someone needs them! There's work to be done!

The Unit hums with activity—the deathly silence is broken. The piercing call of a wailing baby, and the bustle that ensues is welcomed at St Margaret's Special Care Baby Unit, as invariably, the alternative is much worse... And that is why, to some measure, the workers on this ward are wary of the small room at the end of the hall. Where little Tobey Daley resides...

From the day he was born, Tobey never cried; he never whimpered, he never moved. And if things weren't grim enough for this helpless newborn, he couldn't breathe, either. Well, not without the aid of an advanced respiratory machine. His room was chillingly quiet. The only activity coming from there was the routine inspections carried out by the various health officials, nurses, doctors, and of course, the little boy's parents.

Tobey's case was interesting. Not only because it was rare, but because of the kind of reactions it elicited from those involved with the case. The nurses and medics on call hurried past the baby's room as if to outrun a curse; tutting and shaking their heads as they went by.

It appeared their apparent discomfort for the situation wasn't always so. In fact, in the early days, many of the staff members were upbeat. Some even dared to hope. This was, after all, St Margaret's Hospital Trust—the best hospital in the Southeast of England. The Daley's had a first-class team of experts on hand, working around the clock. But as the weeks turned into months, despair corroded their optimism like black ink over blotting paper.

Why couldn't they find a solution?

Was there a solution?

Who said there was a solution…?

The questions grew louder. But despite the scrambled quest for answers, the staff kept on working, and they kept on assisting. Meanwhile, Tobey Daley, who was lying in a soporific state, waited. He so desperately wanted to communicate with his parents, so he could tell them that he had made it through. Oh, how proud they would be of him if they knew…But now he had to wait. Somebody was coming to see him. He had been expecting this person for some time, and when that day would come, there would be much to do. But until then, in spite of the gripping pain, and sporadic calls for his death, Tobey would continue to wait. He had to. His well-being and the life of others depended on it…

Chapter Four: Dr Lawson

Richard

Dr Richard Lawson's pager vibrated; he didn't have to look down at it to know where he had to be. With the precision of a soldier he headed toward the Paediatric Intensive Care
Unit: "Imbecile…overweight…grotesque… degenerate…vile…I think not…"
These were just some of the words that flew into his head as he passed the crowds of people milling around the corridor. Not nice thoughts, but they were his truths, and he was thankful no one could hear them.
The doctor was a tall man by many people's standards—extending well over six feet. But instead of taking great big strides, he shuffled toward his destination. His grey-blue eyes zeroed in on the ground in front of him, as though analysing its very composition. His eyes darted to the left and to the right. If anyone planned to sneak up on him, they'd be sorely disappointed, as he'd be ready. He was that kind of person; prepared for any form of confrontation, but opposed to personal contact of any kind.
When Richard arrived at the unit, he reached for his access card which was clipped onto his belt. He didn't look up. He was very aware of the surveillance camera; its intrusive stare narrowed in on him like an ominous crow. The change from red to green took

only a matter of seconds, but it was still too long for Dr Lawson. Once cleared, he yanked the door open.

"Good afternoon, doctor," greeted the nurse on reception. She sounded out of breath.

"Hello, Dr Lawson," said another.

"Afternoon." He didn't look at them. He headed toward the end of the hallway where a small group of medics had assembled. They looked through a glass partition at a baby in an incubator and whispered amongst themselves.

"So, baby Lindsey has returned," he announced.

They all looked up at him. If they were shocked at his sudden appearance, they concealed it well. Some of the junior medics scanned his face for humour, but as always his eyes didn't connect with anyone in particular.

"The mother brought her in over an hour ago," one of his male colleagues volunteered. "The baby has developed a rather nasty-looking rash across her abdominal region. We're not sure what's brought this on."

Another one of his fellow workers, Dr Metcalfe, added her report, "Before the baby's release she appeared to be a healthy preemie. No problems other than the usual weight issues, of course."

"Could I have the notes?" They were handed over to him. "Okay, let's see what we have here…" He left the group and entered the room. He could feel their eyes on him as he asked the mother several questions.

A few moments later, he emerged. He turned to Dr Metcalfe. "Can somebody contact the Allergenic Specialist? We need to get the breast milk tested right away."

"The breast milk?"

"Yes, the breast milk. I believe the baby is undergoing an allergic reaction to her mother's milk."

It was a simple prognosis, but the strained expressions on his colleagues' faces revealed their complete chagrin for him. Not that their perceived reticence moved him the slightest. He was far too seasoned a medic to be smug over trivialities such as this. He handed the notes back to Dr Metcalfe. "As soon as it arrives, let me know the outcome of the test."

"Certainly," she replied. It looked like she wanted to say something else, but he had already surged past her.

Richard checked the time on his pager. He was due to see another preemie with eczema, but instead he wandered over to Tobey Daley's room. He peered through the glass partition. Other than the flaring of his nostrils, Richard remained rock-still. His metallic eyes honed on the silent bundle.

This baby is going to die!

It was a fact he could bet his thirty-three-year-old life on. As far as he was concerned, this pointless charade had gone on far too long. In his ten years in Paediatrics, he had never seen anything quite like it. After countless tests and examinations, the closest diagnosis given for the baby's disorder was: *Congenital Myasthenia Syndrome*—or *CMS*. Although there was a slight probability this was not *CMS*, granting, the symptoms did share many similarities with this chronic disease. Nevertheless, this was still by and large, the worst manifestation Richard had ever encountered, and one of the most challenging the department had ever had to deal with in its seventy-year history.

The hospital, himself included, had tried several complicated procedures, and one almost-fatal attempt to sustain the boy's respiration. But in time, they all had to concede the baby would not breathe unassisted. And in terms of medication—where could he begin? The much-heralded *Prostigmin* trials had turned out to be a complete disaster! He and his team were advised to switch the baby's medication to *3,4-DAP*—which almost killed the boy. Later it was agreed they would trial him on *Ephedrine,* since numerous reports had surfaced of its use with *CMS* patients. Still, there was little to no improvement, and judging from recent notes, it seemed the baby became a lot sicker on it as well. So, in god's name, what more could the department do? Moreover, in the last twelve months it seemed management had gone berserk on political correctness. All the departmental heads were being harangued to adhere to hospital policy. All this was happening because of this special case with Tobey Daley, which was being televised for the world to see.

The media partook in reckless reporting. They printed stories which did not hold a shred of truth, with some of the most distasteful headlines he ever had the displeasure of reading:

'Still no miracle from St Margaret'—heralded one newspaper.

'Award-winning hospital loses battle to save'—reported another.

And the least of his favourites…

'Doctor, Doctor. What do I have? We don't know! - That'll be £92m please: The real cost of NHS failings'

It was becoming obvious that the hospital, meaning—he, was still unable to resolve this clinical malaise. He couldn't ignore the gnawing sensation in his stomach. This did not look good; he never failed at anything. Richard was currently ranked among the top ten paediatricians in the country, and one of the most respected MDs at St Margaret's Hospital Trust. He had a pristine track record, and he needed it to stay that way. This had nothing to do with safeguarding the hospital's reputation, but with buttressing his own. Others watched him. Others more important than the stuffy members of the Trustee Board….

At least he could take some comfort in knowing this charade would soon draw to a close. He, and a select few, were due to attend a meeting later in the week. It was now time to begin proceedings to switch off Tobey Daley's life support machine. This time, he hoped there would be no objections. *As for the others who eyed him….*

All those years of research into the study of human genetics and nucleolus biology had not been for nothing. And all those years submitting countless articles for *The Quarterly Medical Review* had not gone unnoticed. He was now in the company of others who saw if there was success to be had, it would be found in stem cell research—the science of the future…

***

Siba

Forgive the intrusion but let me take a moment to tell you a little bit about Dr Richard Henry Lawson. Not many people know this about the young medic, but Richard is a highly accomplished obstetrician, paediatrician, and a gynaecologist—being one of the few on staff to hold qualifications in three medical disciplines. Richard could have easily carved out a fine career in genetics or microbiology, since from an early age Richard wanted nothing more than to become a medical inventor—a pioneer of sorts. Someone who would one day find a cure for all terminal illnesses or rid the body of every allergy known to humankind. From the start, Richard had a heartfelt desire to find cures for incurable diseases. But ever since he could remember, there was something that halted his progression: Richard was burdened with an insane fear of failure. It was a teeny, tiny personality defect, almost insignificant by worldly standards. But it would later turn out to be a huge stumbling block in Richard's journey. Whenever the doctor had undergone any such minor setbacks in his life, the experience had made him sick. So violent were the convulsions, he once burst a blood vessel in his right eye. As a consequence, Richard always chose the path with the least resistance. So although the doctor dreamed of finding cures, Richard would go on to excel in an altogether different area of study (I know it doesn't make any sense, but believe it or not, many of you human beings make similar decisions of this kind). In any case, Richard's dream had now undergone a slight modification, that would one day see the young doctor blossom into a fruit without a seed…of course, Richard could not see this; nobody could. This was only visible in the spirit realm, where mortals move around like beams of lights, and some of them are not switched on. But fortunately for human beings they are, amongst many things, soulful creatures. It was only a matter of time before Richard felt the stirrings of an unfulfilled heart. For no matter how hard he tried, he could not forsake his dream. That dream was a seed. And like all good dreams, it had been purposely planted there. And like all good seeds, it contained the making of him…

In time, Richard figured out the importance of realizing his dream; he knew it was somehow linked to his happiness. But the young medic was yet to make another blunder. I must point out there is something toxic about this mix: ambition and insecurity. It is a very bad coupling. Many times they share the same bed, but they do not belong together. It is not enough to have a dream; one still has to have the courage to own it—as so many people do. But Richard did not, instead covered it up like a dirty secret; choosing to pursue his dream in private and in the comfort of his own home. Night and day he toiled at it; working tirelessly away, far from public scrutiny as the doubtful often do. And this is where his dream had taken him so far...

***

Richard

Richard gathered the last of the bubble wrap and crammed it into the huge cardboard box, which was almost as tall as he was. Renovating his self-conceptualized laboratory had taken him longer than planned. He was already eight months over schedule—and still wasn't done with it yet.

When Richard began this undertaking, he started by gutting the attic room in his two-bedroom detached house (it had to be detached, he didn't want any interactions with nosey neighbours). All the pieces of equipment Richard installed—the anaerobic cabinets, microscopes, test-tubes, and calorimeters—all of them came hot off the production lines, from some of the finest bio-scientific manufacturers around the world.

When Richard ventured into his gleaming, white-walled territory, it was like stepping into his own private sanctuary. Albeit nowhere near the scope and comprehension of a professional-sized lab but he worked very hard on changing that.

It was clear for everyone to see that Richard had the zeal. He had the desire. He only lacked one thing. And fortuitously for him, that thing came to him when he least expected it...

***

In the autumn of 2002, which was almost two years ago, Richard travelled up to Edinburgh to attend a fundraising dinner. Many senior medical officials and scientists were invited to take part in a discussion about the advancement of stem cell research. It was a typical function full of fraternity members and old men in suits: the same people, same rules, and same tedious menu. But unlike most of the discussions, that night ended on a very promising note. Someone had been watching him…

Three days later, he received a call from Diligence. They informed him they were a well-known medical research and technology facility. They had affiliations with many of the world's leading pharmaceutical companies. Much to Richard's delight, they had read many of his old research papers and were very interested in his unique findings.

Two clandestine meetings later, money was discussed. Richard couldn't believe his good fortune. It seemed Diligence would become his real-life fairy godmother. They assured him there was nothing they couldn't do for him, which was true. They had the money, resources, power, and connections. Although for legal reasons, some of their human stem cell research needed to be conducted in an unconnected off-site laboratory. Diligence had been searching for some time for the ideal candidate. They didn't hesitate to let Richard know that he was the right man for the job.

Often, with most of these too-good-to-be-true deals, there was a catch. There was one thing Richard had to do for them…it was only one thing…

Chapter Five: The Assignment on Mallard Row

Lydia

"Tilly. You look amazing!" Lydia sat at the table overlooking Knightsbridge's busy high street. "I see you're back to your old self," she added with an extra layer of wry. Lydia had not planned on going out today, however, she was forced to make the journey to the trendy bar after receiving a hurried call from her friend to meet with her there.

"Thank you, darling," Tilly looked on approvingly at her attire. "You know beige really suits you. Is that Stella McCartney's latest range?"

Lydia smiled. "I take it you're referring to this blazer, and yes, it is by Stella—I love it!"

A waiter came to take their orders.

As soon as his back was turned, Tilly started chitchatting about the frivolities of her everyday life. It soon dawned on Lydia this was not a social call…

she let her friend talk for a few moments more before interrupting. "Tilly. You didn't invite me here to talk about Frieda Kahlo exhibiting at the Tate now, did you?"

If Tilly felt slighted by the remark, she didn't let it show. Instead, her bright eyes widened with her smile, and it seemed all her words came rushing out at once.

"Lydia! Lydia! You *must* give me Christine's contact details," she breathed. "My god! That girl has a gift that could benefit so many people!"

"What people?" Lydia responded with suspicion.

"My yoga class for new mothers for a start!" Tilly's smile descended into a scowl. "Oh, Lydia, darling, *pleazzze* just listen! It's for a childhood friend of mine—Hannah. She's in dire need of some help. It's her only child. Oh, please!"

"Look! I'm going to have to stop you there." Lydia glared at her. "Christine made me promise not to utter a word about her to anyone, and I as good as gave her my word." She sighed. "Tilly. I don't think it's something she wants out there."

"I don't see why not." Tilly scoffed. "She seems like a reasonable person. I'm sure if you tell her about—no hear me out!" she said over Lydia's attempt to cut her off. "It's just a small group of women I know. And believe me they will pay her handsomely for it."

"I hate to be blunt, but I don't think she'll be interested." Lydia shrugged and stood from her chair. "I'm sorry, Tilly. I can't help you. Now, if you'll excuse me, I have to use the ladies, and when I return, for the *love of god!* Let's talk about something else." She gave Tilly a quick smile, even though she felt her friend was not deserving of it. She picked up her clutch purse and went indoors.
Lydia made her way to the ladies' restroom. *Was she*

being rash in rejecting Tilly's proposal? Who was to say Christine wouldn't change her mind at the mention of money? Did the girl even know what she stood to gain from this? *Aaarghh!* Why the hell was she so concerned about this? She was no fan of the supernatural, quite simply because she wasn't silly enough to believe in it! Fortune-telling—was for the ill-advised, and tarot cards—for the *deluded!* She remembered her old school chum, Charlotte Ball, who was told all kinds of *gobbledygook* from a psychic she frequented. The so-called fortune-teller claimed to know all of her friends' deepest darkest secrets. Yet, as far as she understood it, her friend Charlotte was now living a life so far removed from the projections emanated from the crystal ball—*Pah!* So much for the predictions!

Lydia inspected her teeth in the large ornamented mirror. Once satisfied she turned on the faucet. *This is bonkers!* How did this woman work out what was troubling Tilly's son. And then to turn around and say the baby told her…? *That's insane!* But more shockingly, her friend believed every word…

Lydia had no choice. She would give this Christine Shore a call. Find out if she would be interested in doing—whatever it is she does—for a fee. God knows the dear girl might as well get paid for the hassle. Lydia thanked the washroom attendant and exited the restroom.

On her return, she saw Tilly had siphoned off a good measure of her Peach Bellini. She slid into her chair. Her mobile lay face-up on the table; she almost always left it face-down. The waiter appeared at that moment with their orders.

"I must say their seafood salad is to die for!" Tilly said with her head buried deep in the drinks menu. "Just look at it, so leafy and luscious—it's almost too pretty to eat. Have you tried the niçoise over at The Ivy?"

"I couldn't say that I have." Lydia inspected her plate. "Oh! And have you heard the news? Carlita's getting married."

"Who? Carlita Hulmes?"Tilly giggled.

"Yes, little Carlita, who slept her way through the rugby union at Exeter. Well, get this: she's set to marry a Russian gazillionaire—a crazy gazillionaire!"

"A gazillionaire?" Lydia laughed at her friends touch for the dramatics. "Oh, Tilly, I swear you're too funny."

"Yes, yes, but never mind all that. This time I'm more concerned about the crazy!"

Twinkling like fireflies, dainty little tealight holders were being placed on the tables being re-laid for the evening diners. Lydia and her friend were in no hurry. They picked at their salads, sipped their freshly poured Bellinis, as they mused on the frivolities of everyday life.

Christine

Sleep when baby sleeps, is one of many instructions given to new parents

But what if the baby is no longer there?

Despite the glare of the summer sun, Christine slept on

Old habits die hard...

I was awoken by the shrilling sound of my ringtone. Double-glazing failed to block out a conversation taking place outside my apartment block. Shedding my comfy duvet, I marched over to the window and peered through the curtain netting. I recognised the culprits right away. They were a couple of hipster lads who lived on the ground floor. Many times, they had accosted me in the hallway—inviting me over for cups of tea and a chat. Once, the pair of them jokingly threatened to commandeer my kitchen, so that they could whip me up a nice Sunday roast. They were being more than neighbourly; they were offering friendship.

Maybe I should think about taking them up on their offer…?

My gaze turned inward, toward the high set of pine drawers at the far end of my bedroom. The slight thrumming in my chest set about reminding me *not* to do—what I was about to do. But I ignored it as I always did. I approached the dresser and opened the top drawer. I took out the white-knitted shawl which was sewn with a pale blue underlining. I put my face to the comfy material and breathed in its delicate scent…*soft…like he was…*my eyes prickled in preparation toward a familiar pain.

My mobile sounded off again. The number which flashed before me was anonymous.
"Hello." The greetings were exchanged simultaneously.
"Am I speaking to Christine Shore?"
I cleared my throat. "Yes, you are."
"Hello, Christine, my name is Hannah Meade…" *That's a Sloaney accent. Where have I heard that recently?*
"A friend of mine gave me your number. I-I'm terribly sorry, but…I could really do with some help."
"A friend?" I swore under my breath. I would have slapped my forehead if I wasn't holding the handset.
"They told me not to say."
"How can I help you?" I already knew the answer to that.
"It's my baby girl. She's only six weeks old. I know babies are supposed to cry—I get that part! But there's something extraordinary going on here. I-I can't explain it…I've spoken to some specialists, but none of them can tell me what the matter is." There was a moment of silence. "Please! She's all we've got!"
It was a heartfelt plea, yet even with that I thought about hanging up. But what if this woman knew where I lived - or worse! Turned up at the building where I worked? I knew I couldn't put it off, I'd have to deal with this right away.
Once I came to terms with my ability, I often helped families who were more than happy to guard my

secret with their lives. I was discreet, so I had to be selective with whom I assisted. But against my better judgement I helped that desperate couple I happened upon last year in my local park. I remember the pair of them were sat a few benches away. Despite their best efforts to keep their voices down, they were bickering about something. It was over their baby boy who kept falling ill for no reason anyone could think of.

I believed my secret would be safe with Jillian and Matthew Simmons. And I guess, for a time, it was. But later, Jilly had shared her secret with her cousin, Lydia—*with the double-barrelled surname*—and of course Lydia had called up asking me to help her friend, Tilly. And now this request…

With a protracted sigh I shuffled over to my dresser. I picked up my notepad and pen. I was going to see this *Hannah Meade.* See if I could be of some assistance, but also find out who had supplied this woman with my details. I wasn't going to take any chances, I had to stem this tide before it broke the dam. I looked down, I was still holding the white and blue snuggle blanket in my hand. I brushed it against my cheek. I kissed it, then placed it back in the drawer.

A mad dash for their hearts,
One last breath, then it's dark.
So many times, too little, too late.
What did it matter?
A flood was coming…

Chapter Six: The Alpha Stem Cell Project

Richard

A month after Richard Lawson's twenty-first birthday he had submitted an article to:
The Quarterly Medical Review
The piece was titled: 'THE RESURGENT POWER OF FOETAL BLOOD'
Richard, along with many of his peers of that time, had developed an ardent interest in researching stem cells. During the 1990s, a raft of studies had been conducted on the beneficial properties of embryonic foetal and adult stem cells. However, the much younger Richard was drawn to the subject of foetal stem haematids. Early research had shown that foetal blood was a super-rich source of hematopoietic stem cells, which flourished more than those in embryonic or adult cells.
The study of foetal stem cells intrigued the young doctor to no end. Richard saw blood—foetal blood—as a fascinating multifarious cluster of ripened grapes; tiny individual cells bursting with a wealth of microscopic instructions.

'The older the grapes, the finer the wine…' He loved this area of study.
In his research paper the passionate doctor discussed finding more effective ways to obtain and test the potency of foetal blood. Unlike the leading experts of the day, Richard did not believe the emphasis should

be placed on studying the cells found in the umbilical cord or in the placenta. Although, he did concede, it was indeed easier and far safer to do so, biomedical science was overlooking a huge link by not finding more meticulous ways to study the blood of near-term foetuses…

His passionate writings conveyed his love for this area of study. The more he wrote, the bolder he became.

In Richard's second research paper; titled: 'FOETAL BLOOD: THE REWARDS AND THE RISKS,' the doctor went on the academic offensive. He claimed that leading cytologists and those in the industry wasted valuable time and resources on their persistence in the study of specimens that were less than twenty-four-weeks old. In his thesis he argued:

"Although the concentration of stem cells in foetal blood is higher than at any other time of life, only a third is left in the placenta once the foetus is delivered. Surely, the emphasis should be placed on studying the matter, which contains the remaining two-thirds of the stem cells? Certainly, the risks are greater when interfering with an older foetus, but with steady measures put in place, the overall outcome will justify the means."

Richard went on to say it would be in the researchers' best interest to study the stem cells of forty to forty-two-week-old foetuses. Not only because the blood was at its optimal richness, but because, once the foetus was delivered, the blood was unable to hold on to its potency.

Harking back to a study he recalled from his undergraduate classes, Richard highlighted that as soon as a baby drew its first breath, the lungs began to break down from their original cellular structure. This, in turn, had a knock-on effect on the baby's heart and blood pressure. As soon as the pressure increased, the previous vital units within the heart began to close down, thus, seeing an end to the old structure and the birth of a new respiratory system. However, Richard strongly contended that while this unique and very natural process was taking place, it was then the foetal stem cells lost much of its potency, ultimately, forfeiting any chance of anyone obtaining the blood specimen at its most dynamic. This particular article was not received warmly by some of the QMR's reviewers. In fact, it proved to be divisive with criticisms crashing in from all angles.

'So, Einstein. What do you suggest?'

Was there any need for sarcasm? He moved onto the next comment:

'Dr Lawson. You have no prior experience or qualifications in this field. I suggest you proceed with caution.'

'If you don't mind me asking, honourable colleague, are you an expectant father? If so, care to put your foetus up for experimentation?'

As the comments mounted Richard, who was fresh out of medical school, thought he was prepared for the criticisms, but the onslaught was unrelenting, as though he'd happened upon a swarm of killer bees. They could ridicule his choices, his demeanour…but his work? — His output? This was a bridge too far. Richard would never forget that stinging sensation... Nevertheless he continued with his own private research, but there was no blowing off course the encroaching clouds of depression which silently made their way toward him. The scathing criticisms had not only hurt him, but it had also unearthed not one; not two, but *three* glaring medical stumbling blocks. *They were right!*

To start with, where could he get his hands on a live foetus, one as close to its due date as possible? Secondly: how could he collect the stem cells before the baby's heart commenced with its natural reparative procedure? And last of all, how could he obtain this specimen without drawing attention? Richard's days became a brooding mix of panic and depression as he realized he could no longer continue with his precious research. There were far too many questions, and not one feasible answer.

The doctor spent many nights thinking up elaborate and often unrealistic methods. All futile.

Wallowing in semi-depression was the state Richard had arrived at before his chance meeting with Diligence. When Diligence came onto the scene, everything changed. The impossible became possible...

As it turned out the people at Diligence were also keen on the study of Human DNA. They too wanted to undertake further studies on foetal stem cells. But unlike Richard, they were better resourced and light-years ahead. They had foreseen the many challenges Richard now wrestled with and had found a way to iron out some of the potential hurdles. To say Richard was completely awe-struck was an understatement. It was as if Diligence had pre-empted his very arrival. His painstaking research was similar to the findings that Diligence had also conceptualized. This pharmaceutical giant had seen what Richard had guessed all along. If at any time he was looking for vindication, this day he had received it. Diligence not only welcomed him, but they also championed his ideas.

"Richard, you are on the brink of making medical history," the man from Diligence had said. *"I think you'll enjoy working with us. You should consider this arrangement more like a partnership. We are in this together"*

A partnership? Again Richard could not believe his good fortune. For every month he worked on this project, he would receive double his monthly salary. Richard came from a wealthy family. But like most of the world's rich, he had to admit there was nothing more satisfactory than accumulating more.

'The older the grapes, the finer the wine…' It was time to make his dream a reality.

After a series of discussions, Diligence said it was willing to facilitate him in any way they could. However, the company had one order—a very tall one. Diligence wanted the stem cells of no less than twenty live foetuses. This was more than Richard could ever dream of obtaining. They said he would need to select between twenty and twenty-five pregnant women, and all these candidates had to give birth at forty-two weeks. This part was non-negotiable.

Forty-two weeks? He was a medic - not a magician! How on earth could he control this colossal aspect of nature? The babies arrived when they were ready! Richard opened his mouth to protest, but it seemed the man from Diligence had anticipated this response. He said in a level voice: *"Richard. Listen carefully to me. We will provide all the necessary tools, and we will show you how to use them. But you have to do what we tell you. Believe me, we are on the same page here. If you follow our instructions, precisely, everything will go according to plan, you'll see. Now, Richard, are you ready to listen?"*

And listen Richard did.

The consultants at Diligence were very thorough. They understood what needed to be done.

Richard's new sponsors gave him a drug called *Miroplyome.* He had never seen anything quite like it. It was cool, clear, and untraceable. He was told it was a special drug the company had been working on with one of their many clients.

Miroplyome was similar to some of the well-known drugs on the market used to induce miscarriages. But unlike them, it did not actually carry out this function; it only mimicked the symptoms.

Richard needed to find expectant mothers who had never been vaccinated or hadn't received their jabs in a long period of time. This was because after the twenty-week' gestation period had passed, women who wished to be vaccinated against Tetanus, Diphtheria, or Pertussis were allowed to be given the Tdap vaccine.

This provided a perfect window for him. He mixed the drug with the Tdap vaccination, which he made sure to administer to the expectant mother in her thirtieth week of pregnancy. The women chosen for the task went into labour twelve weeks after.

"Richard…it is imperative that the foetus be born in the forty-second week—understood? Like us, you are aware that the foetal blood is at its most potent then. Once you have the stem cells in your possession, they should be stored and ready for pick-up. We'll show you how."

"Yes. I understand fully." Richard had heard how doctors liked to play god, which sounded like complete nonsense to him. But something about this quest made him feel…omniscient…omnipotent…as mind-blowing as when his rowing team beat the odds and won the 8s at Henley. Richard couldn't put it into words how it made him feel. *Was it the secrecy of others not knowing the power he had?* Whatever the case, there

was something about this level of control that hit him harder than the greatest high….
Once the forty-two weeks were up, the unsuspecting mother-to-be was rushed into the labour ward, where Richard waited on hand to collect his specimen. But as it was not a naturally induced labour, it was no ordinary affair...

'...it was a cataclysmic, gut-wrenching ordeal. Excruciating beyond words...'

The directive from Diligence had read.

All the same, there was very little the consultants at Diligence could do about it, as it was the effect brought on from the use of *Miroplyome*

'...as long as it did not lead to the death of the mother, it would just have to do in the interim...'

The report back from Diligence had concluded.

There was another drawback to this well-laid plan. For although the mother was able to avoid death, the baby's chances were a whole lot slimmer. This was another blip, which, those at Diligence were working to rectify. But until they found a solution the baby would just have to take its chances.
It had been a little over two years since this covert plan between Richard and Diligence had begun. And to date, they had collected seventeen specimens. And

of the seventeen, not one of the neonates had made it home…

The project soon neared its end. There were only three more specimens to go.

Richard was well-aware what he was doing, along with Diligence, was unethical—illegal, even. But if Richard subscribed to anything, it was the belief of the great thinkers that came before him: Darwin, Newton, and Einstein. They all demonstrated that as a matter of principle, man and science could create solutions for everything. And in the great scheme of things— *wasn't he doing just that?* One cure could save millions of lives. A person didn't have to be mathematician to see the genius in that…His right hand shot up to massage the smooth skin between his eyebrows. It only lasted a moment; an idiosyncrasy Richard had, ever since he could remember.

This simple gesture came from his great, great, grandfather—a Church of England bishop—and the second son of a noble family. This was spawned from this particular Ancestor. But this heinous plot to take the lives of unborn babies, just as they were preparing to enter into the world. Well…that was all Richard.

The doctor believed this project was his raison d'être, and this ardent belief empowered his every waking move. Richard continued to level his iron gaze at Tobey Daley. But just like his true thoughts and feelings, his smile, too, was carefully concealed from the world to see.

Christine

An hour later I found myself zipping through South Kensington's busy high street. I was looking for Mallard Row—*and this is where it should be!* If the directions I had clasped in my hands were to be believed.

Ahead of me loomed two expansive rows of houses with identical doors, I was ready to give up when one of them creaked opened. A woman with bright-red, waist-length hair, stood at the top of the steps. She waved me over, then wrapped her arms around her willowy frame. "Hello," Hannah said curtly as I approached her. "You must be Christine." There was no trace of the panicked voice that had greeted me earlier.

"I am, and you must be Hannah Meade." I notice my smile was not reciprocated.

Hannah gave a slight nod. "Thank you for coming. Follow me, please."

Before I had taken three full steps, I was accosted by two heavy-breathing English setters.

"Thatcher, Bailey—down boys!" Hannah gestured. "Over here." One of the dogs followed, while the other continued to sniff at my hand. I took an instant liking to the patchy-eyed dog. I made to pat the top of its head, but it growled at me.

A door opened at the far end of the corridor, followed by a sharp whistle. Both of the dogs darted in that direction.

"That is my husband, Seb. He is working from home today." Hannah led me into a dimly lit room. "This is my office," she announced as we stepped in. It was bright outside, yet the heavyset curtains remained partially drawn. It was difficult to see, I could faintly make out the walls were adorned with contemporary works of art. "I'm a gallery curator," Hannah stated as if reading my thoughts, or maybe the woman just felt the need to volunteer some information about herself. Hannah looked back at me, so I did the same.

"I'm a sub editor. I work for a publishing company."

"Do you have any children?"

"No. I don't. Errr…Hannah…Mrs Meade. How can I help you?" I tucked my ringlet behind my ear. I knew I could sometimes be a little short at times, maybe a little bit tetchy, but that was me. *What was this woman's excuse?*

"There's something the matter with Daisy." Fear crashed through her reticent façade. "Please. Just look at her and tell me what you think."

"I will. That's why I'm here." I sat on the chair that was offered to me. "If you can tell me a bit more about her behaviour."

Hannah looked down at her hands. She knotted them together then took a deep breath. "Our baby Daisy flies into these awful crying fits every night, at the same time. But when she cries it's not tears of hunger or frustration, it's something else…"

Hannah looked at me. Her eyes were wide, yet lucid. She peered down at her hands again. Her red hair slid over her face like a fiery drape. "It isn't just the crying. When she gets like that, she's inconsolable. I think Daisy's frightened."

"Where is she now?"

"She's with her nanny, but it will soon be time for her next feed."

"How long has she been like this?"

"Ever since we brought her home." Hannah paused. "On the day she arrived, we placed her in the big Moses basket right next to our bed. We thought it best she stay with us before transferring her to the nursery room. But on her first evening at home, at around 6 p.m., she started with this…this…excessive crying. We didn't know what to make of it. So we made the decision to move her into her cot, as it's much roomier than her basket. But she again, woke up in hysterics. This went on night after night until Seb and I made the decision to bring her into our own bed…" Hannah looked up at me, "I-I know it's not advised but the idea was to give her some kind of comfort, physical comfort from whatever it was that was tormenting her. It didn't make the slightest bit of difference, within a few minutes of putting her down, she'd wake up in a flood of tears and her clothes were soaked through with sweat. Good god, the sweat." Hannah's hand flew to her mouth, which was grey and trembling. "What could cause so much fear in someone to make them sweat so?" She took a moment to compose herself. "As soon as possible we arranged for somebody to come over and search the entire room. We wanted to find out whether there was a draft coming in from somewhere. Or a sound in the wall that was disturbing her sleep. But still nothing, the crying persisted." Hannah sighed. "The paediatrician said Daisy could be suffering from a severe form of colic, or was having difficulty adjusting to…" She petered off…

Colic? Colic? The big C of all newborn ailments. They were lame excuses—and both of these women knew it. But what could anyone say on this matter? Weird and wonderful occurrences happened all the time: An eight-year-old girl from Gibraltar has her period twice in a month. A middle-aged man from Nepal produced alcohol in his gut. Sometimes the body performed in ways which nobody understood. No 'human' body. Fortunately for you highly favoured beings—science, medicine, technology—are all there to help you understand how the human body works. I suppose only the creator knows—why?

There was a tap on the door.
"Come in," Hannah said. A blond woman with short-cropped hair stuck her head around the corner. "Mrs Mead. The nanny wants to know if you would like to feed Daisy or should she do it herself?"
"Thank you, Natalie, I will be up shortly."
Hannah switched on her desk lamp; it looked like it belonged in the 1920s. She flipped through some paperwork. "Daisy takes formula." Hannah lowered her eyes. "I was told I wasn't producing enough

milk." She said it quickly, but her words still hung in the air like guilt. I decided to bite my tongue. New mothers already had enough to deal with, let alone being made to feel guilty for the choices they were called to make. *Maybe I should try and encourage this conscious-stricken woman?* However, I didn't get the chance to, Hannah stood from her chair. My eyes grazed an ancient-looking tapestry, which hung on the wall behind her. It featured a lascivious goat wearing a bright red tunic dancing with three laughing women. I found I couldn't take my eyes off it.

"I collect all types of artwork." Hannah followed my gaze. "As you can see, in that corner I have a vast collection of gothic artefacts. And over there, books on witchcraft and various cabalistic practices.
Do any of these interest you?"

"Mildly." In truth, I didn't quite understand Hannah's meaning. Did she mean interested in reading about the occult, or practicing it? I could feel Hannah's expressionless eyes burning into me.

"There's an energy about you." Hannah paused. "It's palpable. I think you're a lot more gifted than you realize." She walked over to the door. "If you don't mind my asking, please wait for me here. I'm just going to give Daisy her bottle."

Hannah exited the room, leaving me all alone with my thoughts. But looking up at a Venetian mask that had black sockets for eyes, and a portrait of a grotesque face frozen in a scream, I was forced to contend I didn't, altogether, feel quite alone.

***

5.54 p.m.

As planned, Hannah led me into the nursery to inspect the sleeping baby. The curtains were drawn, and the lights were dimmed, but it was bright enough to see Daisy would one day grow up to possess the same colour hair as her mother. The baby looked pretty and rested.

5.57 p.m.

Although Daisy was still, I could hear a slight rush in the air as the baby took in breath.

5.59 p.m.

I didn't move, so I didn't see Hannah taking a further two steps back. On reflection, I would find it hard to believe that someone—so lost in sleep in one moment—could be howling with fright in the next. But that was what happened. Daisy was so overcome with fear, she didn't see the people around her as she screamed into action, her face matted with tears.

I looked to my side; Hannah was no longer there. She had retreated to the back of the room and bit down on her fist, as though to thwart her own cries.

I turned back to face the sobbing infant. "Daisy, Daisy, my darling. What's the matter, sweetheart? What's the matter?"

"It's so *cooold.*" Daisy bawled her eyes out. "But…they still want me to go with them."

"Who does?"

"My brothers…"

I paused for a second. I knew I wasn't going mad. There was nobody else in the bedroom except me, Daisy, and the baby's mother. I lifted the girl from the linen basket. I said my next question very carefully. "Daisy, where are they now?"

"They're playing over there," Daisy whimpered. Her eyes darted toward the end of the basket. "They want me to go with them inside the freezing light. I would if I could, but it's just too cold."

"What are they doing now?"

"That one." Daisy gestured with a steady finger. "Has just pulled the other one's hair. Now they're both laughing at each other."

"Are they now?" I smiled, "Do you find them funny?"

"Yes, they are very funny." She hiccupped.

"Do you like them?"

"Yes, I do."

"Okay, then. Daisy. Listen carefully. I want you to tell them something…"

***

Little Daisy dipped, then burrowed her soft silky head into the crook of my neck. The baby had fallen into a deep sleep, long before her tiny hands had unfurled. Cradling the weightless bundle in my arms, I allowed my mind to wander back to a time, where I was a different person to the one I had become now…

***

Through partially closed eyelids I observe the gorgeous eight-week-old balancing on my chest. He is so light, weighing nothing at all. I resist the urge to draw him to me, reserving that privilege 'til the end of the game. I am smiling, but I don't let it show. He leans forward and makes a clumsy attempt to grab the strings of my nightdress. My son is displaying an inquisitiveness well beyond his age. My eyelids begin to flicker. His pudgy hand zeroes in on a button, too big for his tiny fingers to grapple with. Unable to hold back any longer, I end my pretence with a dazzling smile…

***

We were back in Hannah's study now. In our absence someone had pulled apart the curtains and cracked open a window. Natural light now replaced the eerie glow from the arcane lampshade. I didn't feel as on edge as I did earlier. "I've not done anything like this before," I said in amazement. "I think Daisy had seen a ghost—maybe two of them." I turned to Hannah for some answers, and judging by the candid look on her face, I was about to get them.

"Three years ago I lost my twin boys. They were five months old. They died from carbon monoxide poisoning. When they found us—Seb and I—we had traces of the poison in our system. But the twins..." Hannah stared at the reed-like sculpture at the far end of the room, "I guess it was painless." I forced back the tears that rushed to my eyes. When I swallowed, it felt like I was taking down needles. With fierce determination, I ordered my body not to feel anything. I looked to Hannah whose sullen face was void of any painful expressions. I quietly commended her for her composure. As for myself to this day I refused to talk about it. I couldn't and I wouldn't. "I suppose you could say it was after the death of my twins that I began to take a real interest in spirituality." Hannah's eyes glanced over to the shelves heaving with books on the supernatural and the various faiths of the world. Something about Hannah had mellowed. There was no trace of the chill that had greeted me earlier. "I think I was searching for something. There had to be something

out there, some explanation for my loss...then I realized…it was I who was lost..."
"You don't have to explain it to me. I know how it is…you don't have to…"
Hannah shook her head; her eyes moistened with unshed tears. "I survived the only thing I thought would kill me: I survived the death of my children. I couldn't wish this on my worst enemy, and believe me, I have a few of those." She let her pale hands fall back in front of her. She continued to peer down at them. "When you experience that level of loss, I suppose there's a part of you that joins the deceased, and the rest of you comes back in a zombie-like state. I was told by several specialists I would have difficulty conceiving again. However Daisy came along. We were beside ourselves…but…I understood something…" Hannah spoke with a faraway look in her eyes. "I know it sounds a little odd to say this, but I realized Daisy was not a replacement. What I had in my arms was another life—another light. Because this is what Daisy is, what I believe we all are in fact: bright lights bringing clarity in a very dark world..."
Hannah spoke as though she'd come home. "If I didn't know it before, I know it now. We are all connected. And there is a common thread that connects us all, do you know what that is?"
I shook my head. "I don't know."
"It is our propensity to suffer." Hannah looked back at me. "Pain and suffering is part of the human condition. There is no running away from it—it is an

inevitability that plagues us all. What people don't realise is we suffer because of our separation from the source."

"The source?" Her comment elicited a frown from me.

"Yes, the source of our existence."

I nodded in pretence agreement: *What on earth is this woman going on about?* However, I continued to listen to Hannah, whose reticent smile warmed her features.

"I couldn't make sense of it before, but now I think I understand." She shook her head. "Suffering is not a place—it is only a state of mind. Likewise, separation is not infinite—it is only for a time…don't you see? Place and Time are *immaterial.* We can all be re-connected to the source if we *choose* to be. And today, *thank god!* I have received confirmation why I should. My boys are alive! My boys are alive!" Hannah gushed with a new light emanating from her eyes. "Do you think they'll come back to speak to Daisy again? Do you think they will?"

"I-I don't know." I was a little taken back by this sudden rush of enthusiasm. "I-I can't say for sure."

"What did you say to Daisy to make her calm down?"

I shook my head in an attempt to clear it. "I guess I said a number of things. First, I told her not to be afraid. I said she should tell her brothers all about me, and that I said that she was not allowed to go and play with them as her time had not yet come. However they shouldn't be too discouraged, as this is only a trial separation. One day the whole family will be together again. But in the meantime, their little sister will continue to think of them fondly but will remain obedient to her loved ones, *as should they!*" I imparted a short laugh with my affable caution. "Your daughter relayed this to her brothers; they both apologized for the commotion they had caused. Before departing, they hugged her and wished her well, so I guess…" I shrugged, turning to Hannah with a querying look on my face. "We'll just have to wait and see what happens next, but I get the strangest feeling you won't be having these problems with Daisy crying anymore."

I didn't recall Hannah saying much else after our brief discussion. Apart from the fact that Hannah tried to give me money, which I declined. And later, she tried to smuggle in more cash than the requested cab fare, which, again, I refused. What came next was a little out of character for the stoic redhead, but Hannah rushed forward and clung to me. "It's okay," I whispered, consoling a bruised soul very much like my own. "You don't have to be afraid, Hannah. It's going to be okay…" But with a heavy heart, I wondered how I was able to dole out this kind of advice, when I wasn't quite ready to accept it myself…

What could be more exceptional, more profound than my pain…?

A few months later I would receive an answer to that question, but not right then. Instead, I returned

Hannah's hug before climbing into my own waiting cab.
As the vehicle pulled away from the residence, I allowed myself to cry like I hadn't done in a long while. I didn't care whether the driver could hear me or not. I wailed for Hannah's loss, for the death of my own, and a world that allowed such terrible things to happen…*why do these things happen?*
Despite my own personal tragedy, I discovered there was much relief to be had in talking to babies.

Siba

Yes. My progeny was quite right; there was much relief to be had. But it would be of far greater benefit to the rest of the world, if my descendant let the babies, do more of the talking…

Christine

There were times I was especially grateful for my "thirty-two-inch" computer plasma screen. It made for a great barricade; shielding me from the prying eyes of my nosey work colleagues. They were talking loudly today, I wouldn't get reeled into their conversations. I leant forward and positioned my trusted cursor over a graphic. I zoomed in, scaling up to 100 percent. *Aha!* There it was! A scurrilous typo which stood out like a gruesome stain in the stand-first. I deleted it. This was the final proof. The editor-in-chief would have a *field* day if this landed on his desk to be signed/off. At the upmost *The Executive Education Review* was a compact business-to-business publication. What it lacked in size it more than made up for with its reputation in accuracy. Editorial errors were seldom tolerated.

"Are you working late tonight?" The query came from Kitty, the editor's assistant. She plucked her pink fluffy stole from the coat stand. Her voice was cheery but her eyes were veiled, as if guarding a secret. It was a look I had grown accustomed to as the months wore on. Ever since I came back from leave, nobody dared to talk to me about my time away. It seemed they had private conversations with each other, but never with me.

“No.” I responded, “I’m going to be leaving shortly; I’m just sorting out the templates for tomorrow. Have a good evening,

Kitty.” I didn’t look up. But I felt my colleague give me a sympathetic smile.

“You too, sweetheart—try not to stay too late.” She slipped through the sliding doorway.

Stay too late? I glanced around the partially empty room. *As if!*

My workstation was situated like a remote island in the middle of the open-plan office. Like many who worked in editorial, I did like my job, but I didn’t always enjoy it. Two out of five days there really wasn’t much to do, and even less to see. A quick glimpse at my computer screen informed me it was a lot later than I had thought. I let out a long sigh as one looking on a very untidy room. I made a scrambled attempt to close down the myriad ~~of~~ software programs on my desktop. My mobile rang. A little bit out of the ordinary I decided to take the call.

“Hello, Christine! It’s Lydia—Lydia Cartwright-Snowden.”

“Oh…hello, Lydia…” *It’s her again!*

“I remember who you are…how’s it going?”

“Errrr…it’s going well, thanks! I’ve just finished work. Not to say I’ve finished all my work—if you get my meaning, but I’ve reached my quota for today—there’s no more blood to give!” Lydia gave a short laugh and a cough. She cleared her throat.

A little bemused, I thought I'd agree with her, "Yes. I know what you mean. I find it hard to believe it's only Tuesday, yet it feels like I've worked a five-day week."

"Me too. And the thought of travelling through rush hour right now makes me break out in hives."

"Same here." I smiled. I was curious as to why Lydia was calling me and was a little taken aback by how I was falling in with this idle banter. God knew I didn't want to like her; I didn't need a friend.

"Best not beat around the bush," Lydia intervened. "I wanted to ask if you'd like to meet up?"

"Meet up?"

"Yes. There's something I would like to discuss with you, concerning your gift?"

"My gift? Oh, *that!*" I felt my heart quicken. I grimaced at the thought. "When did you have in mind?"

"Well, how are you for today?"

"…ahh…I guess we could meet later." I squeezed my eyes shut. Did I just agree to something I didn't plan to agree to? *What on earth is the matter with me?* Then a detestable thought crashed through my mind: Did Lydia have another mother lined up who needed my help…?

As if reading my thoughts Lydia responded, "It'll just be the two of us. There are no *damsel* mothers in distress this time. Well, not that I know of. We could meet for a coffee or a glass of wine, perhaps? Sorry! I didn't ask where you are?"

"I work at Keystone Publishing."

"Ah, you work there. I know where that is." Lydia seemed pleased, "You're in Canary Wharf, in that massive tower block."

"Yes, that's the one. They've got a few bars in the plaza. I think *Signatures* might be a good place to meet up?" I offered without thinking.

"Yes, I've heard of it. I should be there in half an hour. Is that okay for you?"

Is that okay for me? Of course it isn't! But there's no way I could get out of this.

"That's okay…"

"Good. I'll give you a call when I arrive."

"Okay…"

"Super! I'll see you later then." Lydia hung up.

I found myself staring into a blank phone. I glanced upward only to see that my computer had finished closing down, and without further warning, it had blinked itself into darkness. All the photocopying machines had ceased humming, and most of the lights in the open plan office were out too. I was the only person left in the whole department. *It'll just be a quick drink. I can handle that? 'Nothing either good or bad but thinking makes it so…' Unbelievable!* I had all but forgotten what I had for breakfast that morning, but here I was quoting 'A'-Level Shakespeare. How ominous. *This cannot be a good sign…*

***

Lydia

Lydia was in Canary Wharf. She trotted past the wine bars brimming with Docklands' high-powered professionals. She caught a glimpse of herself in her grey and purple designer suit. Her usual feathered hair was swept around her like a glittery shawl. All Lydia could hear was the tapping her heels made as they connected with the pavement. The rhythm helped to soothe her erratic thoughts as she wondered how in *god's name* she was going to explain to Christine what had just transpired!

Up until the phone call, everything seemed to be going to plan. She would meet with Christine and ask if she would like to be employed for her special communicating abilities. And no less than thirty minutes ago that was, supposedly, what she had planned to ask. But this was before she had answered the call. *Oh my god. The phone call!*

Lydia stepped off the footbridge and glanced up at the blocks of silver towers. As much as the snob in her disliked fraternizing away from her office in Mayfair, she had to admit she thought the developers had done quite an impressive job on the Wharf. It felt like she had disembarked at Singapore or New York, two of her favourite cities. She made her way toward the designated venue. The sleek black and white signage flashed ahead of her like a cabaret advertisement. "Good evening, Madam. Welcome to Signatures." The burly stubble-headed doorman gave a slight nod before opening the door for her.

"Thank you." Without a moment to lose she made her way into the smoke-free foyer. Lydia was right to assume all eyes would be on her, but the stares were of little importance. She scanned the area for Christine's whereabouts.

Should she tell Christine about the call? Of course she should. But how…? She tried to imagine how the conversation would play out:

'Look, Christine. You have an amazing talent. The women you helped are grateful for what you did for them, and they, too, have friends who could also do with your help. All of whom are willing to pay you handsomely for your trouble…oh… and by the way, you're likely to appear all over tomorrow's newspapers, as one of the grateful mothers I just mentioned, has tipped the media about what you do. And less than half an hour ago a producer from Six Live called, asking how they could score an interview with you…'

Silence…

'So what do you say to that glass of wine…?' Lydia bit on her lip. *So much for discretion!*

With one hand holding the brass railing Lydia descended to the seating area on the lower landing. She spotted Christine right away. She looked like the last time they had met. Her dark brown hair was pulled back into a glossy bun, which highlighted her slender neck and delicate features. But despite the apparent appeal there was no concealing her obvious discomfort. Lydia wondered what the matter was. She made her way toward her. The girl was dealing with something, and whatever it was, it overshadowed everything else.

"Hi, Christine." Lydia offered her hand.

"Oh. I didn't see you come down." Christine awkwardly shook it, but her smile seemed genuine enough.

The waitress darted to their table. "Can I get you a drink, madam?" Lydia looked over at Christine.

"I'm drinking the house special—it's a Merlot." Christine shrugged.

"Then, I'll have the same, actually. Let's make that a bottle, shall we? If that's okay with you?"

Christine nodded. "That's fine."

Lydia wasn't one for awkward silences. She took her seat. "Since the start of the week, the only liquid I seem to be taking down is red wine." She chuckled as she shrugged out of her blazer. "Heading up a small PR firm has its advantages. I mean, take today for example. For lunch I ordered roasted quail, which was served in a red wine reduction. It was suggested I have their vintage Bordeaux to accompany the meal, which I could not refuse. I politely passed up on the sweet course but accepted a small glass of red as my dessert. If they cut me open right now, I think I'd bleed the bleeding stuff!" Lydia looked down at herself, laughing. Christine cracked a dry smile, Lydia glimpsed, which was better than nothing. "Is your office far from here? I love what they've done with this part of the city."

"No. I'm only a few minutes away. Lydia…you said you wanted to talk to me about my gift. I'm not quite ready to share this with other people if that's why you've asked me here?"

Lydia swallowed. "Christine, as a matter of fact, oh! Mind your head, darling, here comes the waiter."

Christine shifted in her chair to accommodate their order. She drained the remnants of her wine before accepting a top-up from the waiter, who, much to Lydia's relief, had appeared at the most fortuitous time.

A song began to play in the background.

"WHEEEERE'S YOOOOOUR HEEEEAD AAAAAAT....WHERE'S YOUR HEAD AT? WHERE'S YOUR HEAD AT?"

The lyrics spurred the listeners, and the beat was undeniable.

"Basement Jaxx!" They both called out simultaneously then collapsed into laughter, "Where were you when you first heard this song?" Christine didn't answer straight way. "I believe it was around Christmas time, 2001" she smiled somewhat reminiscently. "I was out clubbing with Andreas…he…errr...it was a good night…" Christine broke off. Lydia noticed. "Why? Where were you?" Christine shot back.

"I was at Homelands. I attended the 2002 festival." Lydia looked her over with curiosity. "Albeit, I was one of the late ones. All my friends were raving about House music yonks ago! I hardly attend any of these events, unless it's to do with work. And besides, most of my chums are busy getting married or divorced and trying to get married again." She paused. There was something in Christine's eyes that stopped her in her tracks. She wondered if she had said something wrong. She looked down at Christine's left hand, and just as she thought, there was no ring. *So why the hesitation?*

"I…was married once." Christine took another sip from her glass. "I know what you're thinking, and yes, we were quite young. I was twenty-two years old at the time. His name was Andreas Chairo. He was half-Greek and half-British, and from the moment we met, we were crazy about each other…"

Lydia slowly placed her wine glass back on the table. It seemed Christine was ready to talk, and she began to speak to her.

"You see, Andreas was born over here, but he spent the majority of his childhood in Athens. He moved back to the UK to study Public Administration. That's where we met, at Portsmouth University. He was part of the international set. We had a nice group of friends who came from all over the world. If I have to be honest, I didn't feel like I quite fitted in, you know, being the only one in our group coming from a gritty London borough in East End. It was a world away from my life at Clapton Girls. Anyway, I don't know what possessed us. We got married after we graduated. I guess we thought we were going to be together forever," Christine said with muted eyes and a voice tinged with sarcasm. "How does that saying go? Marry in haste and repent at leisure. Well, that was us all the way. We soon realised we were very different. He was an idealist, me…not so much. What can I tell you? I lost my father before I was born, and my mother was a widow from Southern Ireland raising a mixed-race child on her own. Trust me, I had to get with the programme quite early in life, seeing how things don't always turn out the way you expect them to."

She looked down at her glass. Lydia didn't say a word; this was Christine's time to talk.

I didn't accomplish anything I planned to do when I left Uni. Instead, I wasted a lot of time and energy trying to make my failing marriage work."

"Ah, you poor thing," Lydia said. It sounded a little dispassionate to her ears, but she meant it in earnest.

"There's no need to feel sorry for me, Lydia." Christine dispensed a humourless smile. "I can admit now we were both very naive. When Andreas's dream to work for an NGO didn't quite plan out for him, he became very resentful. I watched as his racing enthusiasm crashed and burned and saw a more calculating man emerge. Not long after Andreas went off to work for a major asset manager, that's when things really took a turn for the worst. Success came fast for Andreas, and sure enough, the women came faster."

"Oh, did they now?"

Christine smiled but continued in all seriousness. "Of course, Andreas denied everything. But one day he decided he wanted out. He said he could no longer live in a sham marriage. He said he was doing me a favour; can you believe that?" Christine wore a haunted look on her face, as though she could still see that heavy day unravelling before her eyes. The waiter appeared in front of their table. He uncorked another bottle of red wine and placed a small dish of tempura on the table. "Wow." Lydia popped one into her mouth. "These look absolutely divine." It was she who suggested they eat something to soak up the alcohol. She saw Christine barely gave the tray a look in. Instead she necked her drink and continued with the next part of her story….

"I think I kind of envy you," Lydia said a little later into the evening. The venue had begun to empty out. The waiters busied themselves cleaning up the bar top. "I don't think I've ever been in love before. Well, not in that kind of way that draws you back to the person as though your very existence depended on them." Lydia sighed. Her silvery-green eyes lit up as she romanticized the drama in her head.

"Admittedly." She paused to take another pull on her drink. "I've had tons of infatuations, but this thing called love..." She let the word hang in the air like poetry. "Love has too many layers for me; I like to keep things light and simple like my Donna Karan shirts." Lydia laughed at Christine's surprised expression. "Honestly Christine that is my idea of comfort." She finished her drink. "So if you don't mind me asking, where is this ass — excuse me, Andreas, now?"

Christine didn't answer right away. She looked down at the empty space on her ring finger. "After I agreed to the divorce, I discovered I was pregnant. Andreas didn't want anything to do with me or the baby. It didn't quite fit in with his plans I was told. I said the pregnancy didn't have to change anything, I guess it didn't…he left." She kept her eyes on the table, "I didn't plan to be a single mother. No matter what they say, it is always the woman who is made to feel guilty about these things." Her cheeks burned. She fixed her gaze on the elaborate light fittings around the ceiling beams, before letting them fall back on her surroundings. "I'm not crazy, Lydia. All my life I've been made to feel ashamed about my gift. I don't know why I can hear what babies are saying, as though they were speaking to me in plain English. It doesn't matter where they hail from, be it male or female; black or white—I can hear them all! But here's the biggest irony, I couldn't hear my own son. You know, like how I can with all the other babies. I just couldn't hear him. I guess hearing him or not, wouldn't have made the slightest bit of difference."

Lydia didn't move. She stared at the sparkling unshed tears that swirled around in Christine's eyes. Lydia didn't want to ask the next question. Somehow the answer was obvious, but she knew she had to. "Where is he now? Where is your son?"

Christine met her gaze. "He's not with me anymore." Her tears streamed like melting wax.
"He was only four months old…they said it was cot death…" She closed her eyes.
Lydia felt an intense rush of guilt, almost as if she'd had some part to play in the death of Christine's baby. This was awkward. How could she relate to this? How could she even begin to try…? She looked down at the ground feeling like a real numpty.
Christine wasn't sad; she was broken. And yet the woman who sat to have a drink with her, was much stronger than she was, and far braver than she could ever be. Babies talking, babies dying. These were matters way over her head and out of her jurisdiction. In that moment she realised their meeting was not about having casual drinks in a bar, to see if two like-minded women could become friends. Without venturing into the realms of psychobabble, Lydia felt this was happening for a reason…
She didn't get around to asking Christine whether she would want to counsel distressed mothers for a fee. In the wake of what was revealed to her, it just seemed a little insensitive to put out there. And whilst giving Christine a gentle hug, before seeing her off in a cab, Lydia also realized she hadn't warned Christine about the intrusion from the national press. By god, she wished she had! The poor girl didn't need that kind of attention. Not now. Talking to the press would be the last thing anyone in her situation would want to do.

Great stuff!

After the car turned a corner Lydia climbed into her own waiting cab. The driver peered at her through his rear-view mirror. "Good evening, Miss. Where would you like to go?" She gave him the address then reclined into the leather seat. She peered out into the glittering night. The crowded city streets were ablaze with twenty-four-hour convenience stores, and clubbers revelling in winding queues, while the buses pulling up beside her seemed as preoccupied at night, as they were in the daytime. *Does this city ever sleep!*

"So you're off to Chelsea, are ya?" the cabbie called out in his cheery voice. "Oh, let's see! There are major road works taking place on Commercial Road, but I should be able to avoid them by cutting through Mile End, if you don't mind me taking that route?"

"No, not at all." Lydia shook her head. In all fairness she didn't care how long it took, just as long as she got there. She was dog-tired.

"Not many people know this fact, but at this time of night going through Mile End and Whitechapel will get you to that side of town a whole lot quicker, 'cos you avoid the tailback up on East India Dock Road. But does anyone take note of this?" He huffed and nodded to himself. "I'm certain even my daughter knows this, and she's not even a year-old yet."

"You have a daughter?" Lydia said a little too quickly. A few weeks ago she would not have asked this question. But her perception of babies had become a little altered, somewhat.

"Yes. As a matter of fact I have two of 'em. One is ten months, and the other is three years old." He gave her a lingering look. "If you don't mind me asking, do you have any kids of your own?"

"Oh, god no!"

"For or a young lady like yourself, there's no real rush. I 'ere women are having babies well into their thirties these days."

"I am in my thirties."

"Really? Ahhh, well. Like I said, there's no real rush. In fact, I hear women are 'aving babies well into their forties these days, like that Madonna, for example. But honestly, I'll tell ya something. I'll give anything to work out what my little angels' gabber on about, especially my ten-month-old. She's giving the missus a right ol' hard time, she won't go in the kitchen and seems to be very wary of anything in the colour blue. God only knows what goes through that little head of hers!" He growled in jest.

"Yes, only god knows."

And Christine Shore, a woman with a very extraordinary gift indeed.

What else did she have yet to discover about life or the afterlife, for that matter? *Were there any more surprises?*

The cool blast from the car's air-conditioning felt like a revitalizing balm on her warm skin, yet Lydia was far from relaxed. Everything she knew or thought she knew about life, was being challenged. *Babies were alive before they had lives? It can't be! Why was she not told about this? Should she have known…? In short: what did she understand about the meaning of her existence…?* She took a moment to ponder on this statement. As far as she was concerned, she had not lived a sheltered life, no matter how it looked to others. She had dealt with her fair share of drama. Her favourite cousin had died from a drug overdose; her titled mother had never been faithful to her father. And once upon a time, she did think about becoming a local radio presenter—but she couldn't do that to her dear papa. And now sat in the car whisking through the city at night, her life stories seem to pale in comparison to the growing knowledge of the unknown. *What is the meaning of life?* She was at the right end of thirty—*why was she asking herself this question?*

A safety net, is pulled away. A grand narrative, disintegrates. In a word: there was nothing pleasantly surprising about that. I guess that was why she queried her existence, she surmised...But more worryingly, why was she so perturbed by this question…?

Chapter Eight: Who Is Henrietta?

Henrietta

There were not many people who would describe Dr Henrietta Metcalfe as the oblivious sort—or so she prided herself on this matter. Although, Henrietta had begun to doubt many things about herself. This sudden courtship with despair was all very new to her, and quite frankly she did not care for it, one jot! Henrietta had decided to embark on a relationship with a certain individual she had liked for quite some time. But instead of losing herself in the sweet harmonious flutter of butterflies, she found they lay grounded at the bottom of her stomach, as though made of lead. Henrietta could not force them to fly, no more than she could continue to fool herself: she was no longer in control of the dalliance she had got herself embroiled in…

Around 7 p.m. that evening, Henrietta had made plans to meet with two of her female co-workers for dinner at a new restaurant in Wapping. But a text she had just received, ended the arrangement. The message read:

"Hello…"

And that was all.

Her face warmed as a flood of blood rushed to her head. *It's him.* Her heart pounded so hard, it drowned out the noise coming from the TV. Henrietta took a moment to compose herself before texting back:

"Hi…how are you?"

It would be half an hour later before she would get a response. In that time, she had: cancelled her dinner arrangement, vacuumed her living room…twice, scattered her wardrobe and brushed her hair…not necessarily in that order.

She was now sat back in front of the TV. Henrietta wasn't watching it though; her thoughts were fully rooted on…*him*

He still hadn't replied to her text message. Her body felt as taut as an over-tuned guitar. All this wreaked havoc on her nerves. She couldn't wait any longer. Henrietta grabbed her phone and tapped on the keypad.

'How was work today?' She made to follow it up with another question but paused. She wanted to message something interesting, informative—yet leading…what should she say?

'Did you get the email I sent this afternoon? Vinopolis is holding a wine-tasting event. It's on tomorrow evening.'

As soon as she sent it, she winced. For *frick's sake!* She didn't want him to think she was some kind of a lush. That was the last thing she wanted to project.

Her phone buzzed back.

'Yes, I did…I'll call you in ten minutes.'

That was all it took to whisk Henrietta from a state of gloom, to a place of glee! She was well-aware she'd behaved like a giddy schoolgirl with a crush, but she couldn't help it! She was beside herself; utterly consumed, totally besotted, with Dr Richard

Lawson—the most sought-after medic at St Margaret's Hospital Trust.

The phone rang. She took in a deep breath then went to answer it.

"Etta." That was the name he preferred to call her by.

"Hello, Richard."

"Yes. I did get that email," he responded with little enthusiasm. "By the way, did you receive the BMJ case study report I sent?" He paused. "I emailed it to everyone this afternoon."

She shivered. Every word he uttered was sheathed in leadership and refinement; it floored her whenever he spoke. *Was she the only one reduced to a quivering wreck from the sheer magnetism in Richard's voice?* "Yes…I did get it...mmm…thank you. I haven't had the chance to read it in full, but I will do—" She was about to say, 'later tonight.' However she hoped to do something else later. Preferably with him…

"Actually, I came across some interesting findings…" Without taking a pause, Richard proceeded to list them to her.

Henrietta tried to pay attention but she was only half-listening. The other half thought about this affair, and how it all began. Of course nobody knew her and Dr Lawson got together, occasionally...

***

"I think it's best nobody knows about…our…err…meetings…" Richard had said at the time. "Do you agree?" It wasn't a question. "You know there really is no need to make this..." He waved his free hand. "…office fodder…"

"Yes. Of course."

To be honest she couldn't talk to anyone about it even if she wanted to. There really wasn't anything to say. *What were they doing?* She asked herself many times over the ensuing weeks. They weren't dating, as dating consisted of outings, laughter, shared confidences, dinners…

Dinner…

She recalled one evening with Richard. They had both finished working the late shift. They spotted each other as they left the premises. Somewhere down the line a late aperitif was suggested.

The Old Italian restaurant a few streets away was the nearest establishment that sprung to mind. When they entered the building, soft music played in the background and scented candles were placed on every table. Perfect for Henrietta.

After the first round of drinks, she suggested they get something to eat. It had been four hours since she'd last taken anything down; it had been that busy a day.

"Okay." Richard steadily replied. An air of awkwardness had set in. One, which no amount of banter on her part, could be dissipated.

"It's nice in here," she said conversationally.

Richard gave a scant inspection of the room. "I do hope they hurry up with our orders, this is a terrible waste of time. I have some important things to be getting on with." Henrietta realised that Richard had let her know - in his own offhand way - that whatever she thought they were doing—it wasn't what he was thinking. This was no date, and they *certainly* weren't dating!

Richard didn't smile when he spoke to her, but Henrietta couldn't shake the uncomfortable feeling that he was. She peered around the largely empty room, then down at her meal which had just arrived. Avocado mousse, salmon tartare, and caviar. Every delicate morsel was arranged and plated to perfection. She sensed Richard still watched her. *This was not a man wanting to be in a loving relationship.* Henrietta received this news like a hearty kick in the stomach. Alarm bells went off in her head. *What am I doing? What am I playing at?* Henrietta picked up her fork. She may as well have been feasting on unseasoned tofu. They ate the rest of the meal in rigid silence. Not long after that, they left the restaurant without dessert.

In due time Henrietta found she had nothing more to look forward to, other than the promise of casual hook-ups, which, much to her chagrin was not as frequent as she would have liked. *Is there another woman—there has to be? Damn the man for his control!*

One day Henrietta made the onerous mistake of calling him to arrange one of their meetings. To her dismay he refused to see her and gave no reasons for his actions.

A few weeks later he had a change of heart. But then the questions came…

'Has anyone ever said anything about you being a little controlling?' he once asked. He didn't even look at her as he posed the question. On another occasion, he mentioned he didn't like pushy women. Richard then proceeded to give his unique observations on some of the female medics on the ward. He later made it known he didn't like women who were: docile, giddy, unresponsive, chatty, gregarious, loose…the list went on.

Henrietta was confused. She had indeed made a mental note to check herself against these failings. But she soon gave up, or gave in! She didn't know which. One thing Henrietta did know for certain; Richard took great delight in inflicting emotional pain. She likened the feeling to bursting a pimple: the discomfort was short-lived, but each onslaught brought out his nicer side.

Nevertheless, despite these brief inconsistencies, Richard was indeed a fine catch. She was lucky to be with him, and others would think so too, if they knew….

Henrietta was no one's fool, and no one's prisoner! She was as free as a bird, as she made the point of reminding herself many times over. She could always get herself out of whatever sticky situation she was in. This was her choice, and she was more than happy with it. For the moment, Henrietta would stay put.

Things would work out. Richard just needed to get to know her better.
“Are you free tonight?” Henrietta blurted just as Richard finished his sentence. Maybe he sensed the need in her voice, or he didn’t quite care for her forwardness. Whatever the reason, he paused.
“Ermmm…not tonight, Etta. I think I’ll have an early one.” The rebuff was viscerally felt. Henrietta knew very well he had contacted her for the contrary. “You don’t mind, do you?”
“No…That’s okay,” she muttered the quiet lie, “no worries at all.”
“Very well, I better shoot off then,” Richard said with all the cheer in the world. “Have a good evening, and I’ll see you tomorrow.”
“Goodnight,” she spoke softly into the phone.
He hung up.
Henrietta half-collapsed onto the sofa behind her, “Free as a bird,” she scoffed at her own remark. “Birds have wings. Where the heck are yours?” ***

Chapter Nine: The Secret Is Out

Christine

I was hung over— and it showed. My hair looked a fright, but I would soon bring it to heel: with half a tub of gel and a fifty-pence scrunchie. *Grim*. But that was all the love I could afford to give toward my grooming efforts right now.

I didn't spare a glance at my featureless bathroom, which looked the same way it did the day I had acquired the property. When I moved in a year ago, the floorboards were already laid down, the kitchen was tiled, and the walls throughout the entire apartment were painted in a pale-green hue. It gave my home the feel of an old classroom, or public library, for all the lustre it failed to bring to the fore. No complaints, this suited me fine. My apartment also came installed with built-in shelving units and a mirrored cabinet in the bathroom. What more could I ask for? I wouldn't get bogged down with any fussy decorating, that would be too much like nesting, and I wouldn't be re-visiting that again…

My toothbrush clinked against the enamel cup-holder. I returned back to my bedroom. A mishmash of books and beauty products sprawled across my chest of drawers. At least my bed was made up and the curtains drawn apart. The unwashed cereal bowl languished at the bottom of the kitchen sink. It would just have to remain that way until I got back in from work. I didn't want to be late today and incur unwanted stares with eyes asking questions I wasn't

quite ready to answer...my colleagues queried after my well-being, as though I didn't know my office was filled with busybodies who drooled over new gossip like it were hot slices of pizza. They were not going to get a thing from me. *Am I being a little critical of my work colleagues?* No. I did them a favour. What good could I share with anyone right now - my odd gift? My shame? My grief...? I was far from comfortable in my own skin, to just let anyone in...quick thought: *I should call the office. Maybe they'll let me work from home today. There's no harm in asking. Maybe they will...*
On my way to Manor House Tube Station, I narrowly escaped being flattened by a white transit van. Although, on the flipside, a young man held the door open as I entered my local newsagent.
Ahead of me a heavyset eastern European man stood at the front of the queue. He asked the shop owner for directions; neither listened to the other. I put my head down and made my way toward the freezer section. My gaze soon fell upon a popular tabloid yelling this morning's must-read news:
'Commons Powder Attack on Blair...'
Within seconds I had submersed myself into the story about the Prime Minister being pelted with purple paint in the House of Commons.
"Good morning," beamed the shopkeeper. "Do you want the paper too?"
I had been served by him so many times I didn't have to look up to see that he wore the same grandad-style jumper over a mauve shirt. He was used to seeing me

too, dipping my hand into the same beaten-up blue leather purse.

Carrying the same emotional baggage

"I'm sorry. Just the water and orange juice for me, thanks." I returned the newspaper to the top of the counter; as such, I missed the story about a real-life baby-whisperer resolving dilemmas across the city of London. The story went on to say the full identity of the woman had not yet been disclosed, but this was only a matter of time…I popped the bottles into my tote bag and continued with my journey into work.

Brian Henderson was the first person to greet me that morning. He handed me a cup of tea, in a coffee-branded mug, "There you go!" He winked. "Tea, milk, and no sugar. Did you get in okay?"

"Yes, fine, thank you, Brian." I dumped my bag on top of my desk and fitted my body-warmer around the back of my chair. He hovered behind me, "How about you?" I knew his response was going to be anything but short.

"It was okay," He said as he puffed his cheeks out. "Although for a minute there, I thought I left my travel card in my other coat pocket..."

All in all, Brian was quite a cool guy. He was the magazine's junior sub-editor, and a lanky bespectacled foreign-language graduate with brown shoulder-length hair, and a passion for *'real'* music—or so he professed. I looked on as Brian began, with much animation, to regale the office about his *mis*adventure into work. "You see, men don't carry handbags so there aren't many places to look, are there?" He gestured, shoulders hunched, palms out wide. "They weren't in the back of my jeans, and I checked my coat pockets as well. I realized I had to turn back home." He paused to suck in a lengthy breath of air before continuing, "Now…at this point, I was *fuuuuming…*"

I didn't hear the end of his story, my phone rang. A woman with a crisp Scottish accent spoke up,

"Hullo. Am I speaking to Christine Shore?"

"Speaking."

"Miss Shore. My name is Silvia Moore. I'm a producer at *Six Live*. Do you have a moment to talk?"

Six Live? I recalled the well-known Breakfast show.

"Yes, I have a moment. How can I help you?"

"I understand you have a very special ability to communicate with babies..."

I froze.

"I know you might not want to discuss this at the moment," the voice rushed on. "I understand the circumstances, but I was wondering if we can meet up today or to—

"Sorry…I…have to stop you there! I don't know where you got this number from bu—"

"You understand what babies are saying! This is mind-blowing stuff! Don't you want to…?"

"I think you've got the wrong information. I can't help you, sorry!" My apology signalled the end of the conversation. I hung up in haste.

"…And that was how I was able to get into work on time," Brian concluded. He flashed his youthful grin at his semi-captive audience. There were a few *aahhhs* and stilted laughter, as everybody swivelled their chairs back toward their workstations.

I stared at my jam-packed computer screen. A TV producer wanted to talk to me. *Oh my god! They know about me!* I looked around the office. My heart began to pound against my ribcage as though it perceived my need for flight. And there, in the midst of my personal turmoil, I recalled events from my past…

I remembered it like it was yesterday. I had only been thirteen years old when I told my mother everything. Much to my surprise, not only did my mother believe me, but she also encouraged me to keep talking to as many babies as possible…

"So, you don't think there's something wrong with me, or anything like that?"

"Something wrong with you, child? Don't be daft!" My mother couldn't conceal her joy. "The Lord gives us many blessings, and that's what you are, Christine—a blessing to your generation…"

With that said, my mother didn't waste any time. She confided all to her dearest cousin, Kelly O'Reilly, my pushy aunt. Who went on to tell Father Michael, the parish priest. And somehow, whispers got around the church about a young girl with a special gift that allowed her to hear what babies said to the world, and to each other. People talked. Pondered. Listened. But the interesting thing about people, and special phenomena, was they did not really have it in their hearts to believe…or those who told, as much as those who listened, it simmered in the back of their minds. The sneaky suspicion: Was she really doing this? Was this some kind of stunt? But no matter the assurance of the truth a niggle of doubt disrupted the peace, like a pebble knocking around in a shoe. Despite myself I began to feel very special about my new abilities, but my heightened sense of security didn't last; a friendly conversation between three pre-teenagers soon put an end to that.

"Have you heard? There's a girl in our school who can actually hear what babies are saying!" It was Tamara Mitchell who started this discussion.

"Yeah. I heard something like that," Sara Fox gave a gruff response. "My mum was talking to my dad about it the other week."

"I heard that too." 'Big' Darrell roared with laughter. He was the only boy in our group. "But if you ask me, that ain't right, that. That's just dead freaky! I also hear the girl's a little bit 'loops."

Darrell made a point of winding his index finger around his head. "Every night she has sex with the devil, and that's where she gets her special powers from."

"No way!" The two girls giggled. "So, she's getting it on with the devil, is she?"

"Yep! That's right!" Darrell spared no details. "If someone possesses a supernatural gift, it's because they've done some kind of deal with the devil. No doubt about it, that girl is a wrong 'un!"

"A wrong 'un?" The two girls laughed harder.

Darrell tossed his empty soda can into the refuse bin before replying them. "You see, all the devil wants to do is use and abuse. And that girl, my friends, is definitely being ABUSED!"

"Use and abuse? And where is that bit in the Bible?" Sara gave him an accusatory stare.

"Uh…it's there somewhere. I've just said it differently, that's all!"

Tamara eyeballed him. "If she's being abused, Darrell, shouldn't we at least be feeling sorry for her?"

"Sorry for her? Nah! That's her own fault. Why should we feel sorry for her?" He awarded them with a sharp look. "Listen. Take it from me, she is doing something wrong—that's why she's all wrong. The girl is in the wrong—SHE'S WRONG!" He probably hoped it would put an end to it all. And much to my dismay, it did. My other two friends nodded. They did not care enough to challenge Darrell's moronic assertion. It felt as though I saw my friends for the first time. What was wrong with them all? How can they be so pathetic!

"Do you know what? I think I know who they're talking about," Sara said. "I think it's Sharon Robson, in Miss James's class."

"What? Sharon 'Nob-son' haaaaaa!" Darrell laughed as though it was the funniest joke he'd heard all year. "Yes, her hair looks like burnt shepherd's pie! But, nah! I don't think she's the one…" He paused. "To be honest I heard she was in our year. What do you think, Christine? You've been awfully quiet." The three of them turned to look my way.

"Emm…yeah…probably…our year," I mumbled. My apparent lack of engagement drew puzzled looks from my friends.

Tamara stood up, "Okay, guys." She ground her cigarette into the concrete wall. "Let's change the subject. Stuff like this gives me the creeps..."

That ridiculous discussion with my schoolmates on our lunchbreak shook me up harder than I cared to admit. In under an hour, I had learnt some of life's toughest lessons. The first one being; doing something different, even for good, could transform a person into an object of ridicule and fear. To me the reasoning was unjust, but it seemed there was nothing anyone could do to change that. And the second lesson was that, many people were ruled by fear - and I found I was no different! As soon as I returned home that afternoon, I swore to never communicate with babies again. Neither would I listen to their ridiculous plans they had for the future. I was done with it all, absolutely done! And this time I meant it! I chose to keep quiet …but it turned out I had a heart after all. As I matured I grew bolder. And every so often I would venture out of my safe zone to help parents in distress. Although I did try, I couldn't altogether ignore the thing that made me special….

***

But at this moment it seemed it had caught up with me, and the timing couldn't be worse! I peered around the office. Try as I may, I was unable to drown out those childish taunts from my past, chanting in adult voices: *'She is doing something wrong—that's why she's all wrong. The woman's in the wrong—SHE'S WRONG!'*

An emulsion consisting of this morning's breakfast made an uncomfortable U-turn in my stomach. I sought out the wastepaper basket, just in case I was about to spew all over the office floor.

"Are you alright?" Brian stood in front of me with a handful of printouts. It looked like he was going to say something else, but then thought better of it. A colleague had warned him once; *'If she appears to be a little distant at times, you should leave her be….'*

Brian plonked himself down at his desk and pretended not to notice as I slipped out of the office and headed in the direction of the toilets.
The cool water streaming down my face did little to quell the growing tsunami within. *Come on, Christine!* I tried to will myself stronger. *You've come through tougher situations.*
At least my colleagues were still in the dark. I dabbed my face with the coarse hand tissue, straightened myself up and left the toilets.
As soon as I stepped back into the office, a cloak of silence descended on the room. I realised everyone knew. Gossip really does travel faster than the speed of light. I tried not to look directly at anyone. I got to my desk and went for my mobile. After two rings, my mother picked up.
"Christine," my mother's voice was fraught with tension, "they were talking about you on the breakfast show. I think the press are heading over to your office, you better hurry up and get out of there."

"I'm leaving now…Mum, can you meet me at Carchicco's café? It's a stop away from here, we visited there a few weeks back?"
"I remember the one. I'll see you there…leave now!"
I looked up. My editor, who always seemed to dress like an antiquated stockbroker, stood in front of me with a newspaper in his hand. "Christine, do you have a moment?"
"Niall…I don't feel very well. Can I be excused for the rest of the day?"
I caught him off-guard with my response. He sputtered, "Yes. Of course, Christine. If there's anything I, or the department can do, just give me a call. Let me know how you feel tomorrow…"
I could see he was bursting with questions, I didn't give him the chance to ask them. I gathered my belongings. "Thank you Niall, I am so sorry. I will call…" I didn't complete my sentence; I rushed toward the exit. *Could this day get any worse?*

***

I was so relieved to see my mother waiting for me when I arrived at the café. She must have left as soon as I ended the call.

"Mum…I can't believe I've been *so* stupid." I put my face in my hands and scrubbed my cheeks as though the very act could erase the past. Classical music flowed from the radio as patrons tended to their Italian coffees. "I helped some posh woman who was very desperate. Her name was Tilly Reed. And also her friend, Hannah. I think more people have come forward since. What am I going to do?"

My mother sighed. "You have quite a gifting there, Christine. What did you think you were going to do—bury it?" She tapped my hand. My mother's eyes narrowed. "Excuse me, can I help you?" She asked the man on the table adjacent to us who was taking notes. He looked up. "I umm…I work in the office two floors down from her." He pointed at me, whilst keeping my mother's gaze. "You know *The Docklands Gazette*. I got the tip; I followed her here. If I could just have a quick word with *the baby-whisperer*, I just need to clarify some facts?"

My mother looked on the young man as though he were a rabid rat. "You lot better stay away from my daughter! All of you, I mean it! She's already been through enough. Come on, Christine, let's get out of here…"

***

"Are you sure you don't want me to come with you?" my mother asked while we waited for the tube to arrive, "I could rearrange my doctor's appointment for another day." Even though my mum spoke in a calm manner, she was unable to conceal the worry in her eyes. She sighed, "Thankfully my dear, not everybody live their lives glued to the TV set. Don't worry darling, this will be old news by tomorrow."

How I really wish that were true!

I helped my mother onto the carriage and waved her off, then I looked down at the newspaper which the street vendor had slid it into my hand as we entered the underground. It seemed he didn't make the connection between me, and the large full-coloured photo of myself splashed across the front page. I remembered when that picture was taken; it was ten years ago. I was in the student union bar; young, care-free, posing with a *Bacardi Breezer* in hand. Someone from my past must have handed that in.
The gall of some people!
There was no hiding from this! My old school friends. The couple downstairs. My local shopkeeper. The people at my office…they would all know who I was.
And who am I, exactly…?
Already there were claims circulating in other news outlets stating that this so-called: *'baby-whisperer'* was a fraudster, despite the barrage of testimonials that had since come flooding in. When I stepped onto the carriage I was forced to stand facing the sliding

doors. Like literature-guzzling zombies, everybody's eyes honed on the free newspaper they held in their hands. I started counting down the number of stops before I could make a swift exit from the carriage. Before arriving home that evening, I had managed to burrow myself into a very dark space, where I toyed with thoughts of suicide. *Maybe I could jump off the A1's Suicide Bridge, or step in front of a racing car?* Of course, they were meaningless notions—not seriously considered at all. But sat on my sofa with the curtains drawn, I fed my melancholy with vitriolic delight. And placed by my side was my habitual steaming hot drink: brandy, whiskey—a cup of hot Lemsip. It was all the same to me. None of them hot enough to char my pain, so in time I just settled for tea….Someone buzzed the intercom downstairs. I already knew who it was going to be. Taking a deep breath, I walked over to the receiver by the front door.

"Hello. Am I speaking to Christine Shore?" The female voice posed the question.

"What do you want?"

"Hello, Christine. I'm Mandy Rogers," the reporter spoke in haste, probably sensing she was not going to be granted an audience with me. "Please, can I have a moment of your time? *The Daily News* has already broken the story—it's all over the evening papers. If you could just give me a moment, I'll write up a really good story, your story. Don't you want to be heard?"

"No, I don't." I wanted to disappear. I felt a little sorry for this young woman; coming up all this way, working out of hours just so she could nail the story, most likely to be the biggest one of her career—*but I wasn't going to be it!*

That was how I would handle all of them, I decided right then. Let them come pointing their dictaphones, cameras and flashlights, with no words they cannot write! *They'll soon tire and leave me alone.* The absolute worse had happened. I had been outed as *'The Baby Whisperer,'* and yet, I was still here.... I took a moment to absorb this terrifying truth. Sadly, the world did not come to an end when a travesty occurred. For some, this is when it begins. The fire blazing within propelled me to action. *Why should I be made to hide from this?* I was not a criminal, I had done nothing wrong! Why should I hide?

This girl is a wrong-un!

I AM NOT A WRONG-UN!

I didn't ask for any of this. I cannot apologize for something created outside of myself. *I will no longer hide from this!* Embracing the fire in my belly, I hung up the receiver and marched back to my sofa. A decision had been made. I could stare down the shame of being different, *I'm ready. I could do that.* But lying further in the emotional abyss was another burden I carried around with me, which I could not discard like a coat out of season.

How I wish it was as easy as that...When it hurts. When it's over. When you're done. The only consolation for grief is a well-meaning: 'Oh dear' Then you're urged to get back onto the saddle again...Why must we carry on...?

I curled myself up at the far end of my sofa. As soon as I placed my head onto the cushion, a wave of calmness swept over me. Only then, in that safe foetal-like position, could I allow myself to get lost in the precious memories of a loved-one gone too soon…

***

'Breathe!' I cried. His perfectly formed face was blue…and I knew… 'Let him breathe!' I screamed a request. The biggest I would ask and would ever ask again. But in my darkest hour I was met with a stony silence, which is quite commonplace when there is only one person, in a room, all alone, by themselves….

He can't be gone—it's too soon! Where did he go? He was in my charge. He was my responsibility! 'LET HIM BREATHE…' But in that moment I realised from that day onward, I would have to coexist with my grief. I would have to share a space with an unwanted tenant, who would not leave the premises, not unless I left it first….the rage. The loss. The sadness. To coexist with these afflictions? This was unfair! Unjust! Unacceptable! But…not impossible…Making it for me the gravest cruelty of it all…

***

Siba

Meanwhile, here I am, seven miles away in London's busy Docklands, watching a certain couple with much interest…a man sits on a beige and cream couch. He faces the television set, but he isn't watching it. A woman paces up and down the room; talking as she goes along. She is blond, of medium height. Tired, and unhappy. She holds a newspaper in her hand. She shakes it as she speaks. She Stops pacing and looks to the man. He wears a shirt, which seems a little too big for him. His collars lie on his jumper like crumpled petals, and his grief hangs off him with the same panache. The woman resumes talking and stops again. The man turns his attention back to her face. He shakes his head. He rolls his eyes but utters a response: "If this is what you want, Kelly, then we will find her." Kelly, the woman pacing up and down the room, carries on talking. She seems unfazed by what the man had just said. I guess in some ways it didn't really matter at all. She had already made the decision to do what needed to be done on behalf of them both. You see, it is not a matter of difference, but one of accord. After all, there's no end to what a desperate mother will do to save the life of her dying baby, is there?

Chapter Ten: Mission Impossible

Christine

It had never mattered where I was at the time. Whether shopping with my mother, taking the bus, standing in a queue, the babies couldn't help themselves; they told me their incredible stories. I remembered attending mass, I was fourteen years old. There was a little one who kept looking at me over her mother's shoulder. "My mummy makes me laugh." Megan gurgled as she bounced up and down on her mother's knee.

"Megan. Stay still!" her mother commanded, but Megan wasn't having a bar of it.

"As I was saying, my mummy makes me laugh. She went away and when she came back her hair looked different. It's bright yellow and very fluffy now! *Ha, ha, ha!* It's so fuuuuny. It makes her look like a Neecon."

"What's a Neecon?" I whispered.

Father Michael had just led the church into The Lord's Prayer. With my eyes downcast I could very well be reciting the prayer, like the rest of the congregation, but of course I wasn't. I was chatting with an eleven-month-old girl.
"What's a Neecon?" I repeated.
"A Neecon looks a lot like a horse, but it's not quite a horse. They have long necks and flowing yellow hair,

a bit like mummy's." Recounting her observation set off more peals of laughter.

"Where did you see this Neecon?" I smiled and tapped her little nose. The girl looked cute in her pink and white dress. Megan didn't answer right away. She crumpled her face into a frown. "I don't quite remember…it seems like such a long time ago, in a faraway place…but I've definitely seen a Neecon before!" She nodded.

I did not doubt her. Ever since I was able to hear them, I had been told a number of interesting things. It almost seemed as though these babies had come from another world, just like what baby Mason had tried to explain to me a few years back. A world, it seemed, where all their wants and needs were gratified. Which would go some way in explaining why newborns cried their lungs out when things didn't go their way. It seemed as though they were protesting against the constant adjustments and delays they had to contend with in their new environment. And it would appear this special world they came from was quite a fortified place, as babies were quite bold in nature. It was as if they believed they could do, or achieve, anything, before suffering injuries told them otherwise.

Megan then made a comment which I understood and knew I would never forget. "I like your melody," she said in a sing-song manner. "It's full of colours…it sounds so beautiful. All babies born in…" She frowned. "1972—the Year of the Flute—

they all have this same distinct sound. It is so beautiful. The sweetest melody you'll ever hear…."
Then Megan muttered more to herself, "…but every day, it seems I forget what gift goes with each year..."
Typical of most babies Megan became distracted with something else. She soon caught sight of her mother's hair and laughed again.
I sat dead-still with my mouth wide open. I couldn't believe this infant knew the year of my birth. *She said she liked my melody…it was full of colour...what did she mean by that…?*
I would later learn babies were a lot like cars - or was it that cars were a lot like babies? For instead of serial numbers, babies who were born in the same year had signature qualities which set them apart from those born at a different time…*wow!* I was blown away by what I'd just discovered. This was biological engineering of a celestial kind. But I could go no further in trying to make sense of it all. How could I examine something bigger than my imagination…? *How long was a piece of string…?* Nevertheless there was a small part of me that relished the idea of being born in *The Year of the Flute* Did this mean I had a heart of an artist? And if I had a sound, wouldn't that mean someone could hear it? *Hello, out there. Who is listening? Can anyone hear me…?*

***

Lydia

Lydia groaned like somebody who had been deprived of sleep. She put down the newspaper. It appeared another person had come forward to talk about *The Baby Whisperer.* She had only just found out Tilly had gone through her phone to get Christine's number. Why the *heck* Tilly would blab to the media about it, was beyond her? But then again, her friend wasn't known for her subtlety, neither did it help that Tilly's cousin was the managing editor of a major tabloid newspaper.

Friends in powerful places, can place you in prickly spaces! Aaaarghh!

Lydia scrolled through her phone book to retrieve Christine's number. She wouldn't blame the girl if she refused to take her call. After the third ring Christine answered.

"Lydia. I was about to call you."

"You were?"

"Yes…I…wanted to thank you for the other night."

"Thank me? The other night? Oh—that! No problem…as a matter of fact, I called to see how you were doing...you know, with everything…?"

"I'm okay, Lydia. I don't want to talk about it."

"Look. I am so sorry—"

"I said I'd rather not talk about it…"

Lydia paused. This prolonged silence was beyond excruciating. She realized she'd have to do more than apologize.

"Christine…I know its short notice, but as it's the weekend, do you want to come out for a spot of lunch? Please, it's on me! It's the least I can do, and believe it when I do manage to shut up, I'm actually quite a good listener."
Christine let out a long sigh. Lydia hoped this meant she was too tired to think up an excuse not to go.
"Okay," Christine said, "but I haven't been out in a long while. I have no idea what is trendy in London right now, so if you don't mind I'll leave the suggestions to you."
"Don't worry!" Lydia said with high spirits. "London is my town! Says *moi* from a teeny village in Oxfordshire." She could sense Christine smiling down the phone. A friendship which ends in betrayal? Don't they all? Lydia smiled wryly. This may not always be the case. And besides, it's not the end yet…

***

Christine

A few hours later, I was stood on Borough High Street on the cusp of the city. The sunshine in its wonderful way made everything anew, which was why I detested it sometimes. But earlier that morning I promised myself I would make an effort.
The summer heat rose from the pavement and suffused the air, warming me from all sides like sliced bread in a toaster. The occasional jeer and bouts of

laughter came pouring out from the surrounding pubs, while it seemed the motorists on the high road cruised toward London Bridge, as if they had all the time in the world. It was a stark contrast from the usual hustle and bustle of the working week.
I spotted Lydia on the other side of the road.
"Thanks for getting me out today." I approached the *Boho-chic* attired female, who was also responsible for disrupting my steady routine. "I didn't have anything planned today. Actually, I had planned to do nothing."
Lydia gave a dismissive wave. "Don't worry about it." She slipped her travel-card into her fringed purse. "I'm just glad you agreed to come out. For a minute there, I thought you were going to say no…." Lydia took a moment to study Christine. "To be honest, I feel dreadful. If I hadn't called you, you wouldn't have met Tilly, and if Tilly had never met you, she wouldn't have had anything to blab to the press about. I can't believe she went through my phone to get your number. Just you wait 'till I get my hands on her!"
"Please, no bloodshed on my account!" I laughed. "It's true, I do possess this gift, and as I'm beginning to suspect, the truth always has a way of getting out in the end."
A rusty-looking Morris Minor pulled into the street we were about to cross over to. We both stopped walking.

I looked ahead. "Is Borough Market at the approaching crossing, or do we take a turning on the next right? I've been here a few times, but I always seem to forget."

"It's the next turning, over there." Lydia pointed. "I hope you don't mind my suggesting Borough Market. I absolutely love what they sell in there. They have some of the best local cheeses around, plus, it's close to the river, and I thought it would be quite easy for both of us to get to."

I noted the simmering excitement in Lydia's voice. It was the sort of thing I was used to hearing when conversing with people who were not born and raised in the capital, like I had been. I had to admit I loved London, because I hadn't really been anywhere else, but I could see Lydia, and people like her, loved the city because they had.

"So?" Lydia approached the matter dead-on. "What are you going to do, now that the whole country knows what it is that you do?"

"Good question." I pulled a face. "Right now, I don't think I'm ready to let the whole world in. I have no idea what to tell them. I've got some kind of impairment otherwise everyone would be able to do it—wouldn't they?" My scowl deepened. "Seriously! I don't know how or why this is happening? It's just so hard for me to stand by and do nothing. Especially when I can hear their little voices. I mean, what would you do?"

Lydia shook her head. "I couldn't begin to fathom what I would do if I were in your shoes."

I kept my eyes on the dusty pavement. "I can't pretend I don't understand all the anxieties that go along with being a parent. I know how it is—was. I was once a mother myself…" I fell silent and looked to the road. "But this time I mean it, Lydia. My hearing days are over with. It's not the kind of life any sane person would want for themselves. And even when it mattered, I was unable to hear my own baby…imagine that? Possessing this strange gift that allows me to hear everyone else's but my own! That's not a gift; it's a curse." I kissed my teeth. "Every parent has their own problems to deal with, and if they can't handle them, then…they really have no business being parents!"

I couldn't stop the words from flying out, but when they did they targeted my own heart. I lowered my head. I didn't mean to say what I'd just said, I was only venting. But in that fleeting moment, I understood all too well why it is said: *'When one is angry, then one is still wrong,'* as I felt now.

"Lydia. I don't know what the heck is wrong with me. I'm not very good a letting things go, especially when it comes to my emotions." I laughed with pity. "I remember when I was four years old, my nursery teacher gave me a right telling off for sticking my finger in the patio doorway. So I cried for days afterwards. I don't know if I was embarrassed, or just so upset I'd made her angry. All I know was I was *extremely* cut up by it, you know—just devastated…and when I was ten years old—I can't believe I still remember this—I had a massive crush on a boy at school." I chuckled. "Very quickly he told me where to get off. Lydia, I think my heart exploded into a hundred pieces, for it seemed it took that many days for me to get over it. Imagine? Something as trivial as that could set me back, but it did. I just can't seem to shrug things off the way normal people do. It's not the way I'm wired. So when I lost Jerry…" I looked down at the ground. "I know I'm not the first person to have lost a child to SIDS. People somehow get over these things, or so I've been told. Personally I don't know how they do it, because Lydia, I don't know how to..."

My son was gone, I stung with questions that would torment me for the rest of my life:

His milk - did I give him too much? Too quickly?
Maybe I should have let him sleep on his front—not on his back?
Should I have checked in on him one last time before going to bed?
Did I do this to my baby?
Did someone do this to me?

The two of us stepped out of the midday sun and into the hustle and bustle of Borough Market. The exchange was situated under the overpass. Every so often the air would stir, as a train rumbled down the tracks, causing everything to vibrate. It made such a tremendous racket, but nobody seemed to mind. The scent of grilled meats and fresh fruit streamed through the air, followed by the occasional murmur of soured milk which drifted over from the counters that sold lumps of cheeses. It seemed everywhere we turned some form of produce was being chopped, blended, or seared. I glanced up at the wafts of white smoke. The tendrils swerved around the billowing canvas like a phantom dragon. I continued to follow its movements as it petered out into the midday sky. Sometimes I wished I could do that; just float up high above my anger, disappointment, and pain. Out of my body—away from my mind.

I thought of heaven and my total lack of belief in it. *Is there really much else to look forward to?* After all, I have had my hearty fill of love and hate and was left drained by the pair of them. What was the point of it all? *Why am I still here?*

"Do you know, they've filmed quite a few movies on this location?" Lydia's random observation scampered my wandering thoughts. "And this strip of the market," Lydia indicated with her free hand, "where we are standing now was featured in *Bridget Jones' Diary*, and also in *Harry Potter*. Not sure which one, though." She straightened herself and bent her head to the side. "*Mmmm* can you smell that?"

I whirled around. "Yes, I can. It smells delicious. Where's that coming from?"

The two of us closed in on the stall that produced this wonderful aroma. A small group of people had already gathered around it; they ogled the array of baked goods on display.

"If I eat one of these now there won't be any room for lunch later." Lydia laughed. "I must resist! I must resist!"

"MUMMY, LOOK AT ME! I'm down here, please look at me!" The command came from a little boy who was squirming around in his pushchair. The baby's cries went unnoticed by his mother whose attention was firmly placed elsewhere.

"MUMMY, LOOK AT MEEEE! I'm down here, please look at MEEEEE..."

The woman still didn't glance at her son, but I did.

"What's the matter, little fella?" The boy didn't look older than eight months to me. He was of East Asian descent and wore a red and white striped shirt. He poked his little head up to take a better look at me. He seemed taken aback by the question I had just asked him. His big brown eyes narrowed in on me. It was as if he was looking for something…maybe…sensing something, perhaps. He took his time before answering. "Nothing," he said with a disgruntled pout. The frown was still on his face. "I want Mummy to look at me. She hasn't bent down to look at me in a long while. I just want to see her face, that's all."

"Oh, I see. You do know that your mummy is looking at some of those delicious treats over there.

She could be selecting one for you." I smiled at him, then looked up to see his mother giving me a queer look. "H-he's very cute," I stammered.

"Thank you," the mother said curtly.

"Are you going to look at me *now*?" the baby demanded as his mother began to steer the pushchair away. Then, as if by some telepathic instinct, the woman bent down to smooth over his outer garment and stroked her son's cheeks. After a moment, she straightened herself up and plunged, pram first, into the sea of shoppers. I could just make out the baby's whoops of delight before his voice blended in with all the other noises in the busy marketplace.

"Here." Lydia handed me a brown paper bag. "I guess I couldn't resist after all. I hope you like your fancy-looking tart? I'm going to have mine after we've had our lunch."

I accepted it. "Thanks, you shouldn't have." I took a peek inside the bag. "Yum! Now that's what I call a work—" My ringing phone interrupted me. It was a withheld number.

Lydia noted the hesitation. "Do you want to answer that?" I shook my head. I did not want to speak to another member of the press, least of all today.

After ignoring the first few rings I thought I was ready to let the call slide to voicemail. But on the sixth and final ring, I relented. I could barely hear the voice down the other end; there was too much going on around us. "Sorry…can you speak up? I can't hear you."

"Christine…"

The voice was male, but that was the only thing I was able to make out. I wasn't going to get anywhere with this conversation unless I moved away from where we stood. "Please. One moment..."

I followed Lydia's lead. We exited the marketplace and crossed over to a narrow-cobbled pathway. All the shops that lined this street were closed. It was quieter and cooler too.

"Hello. I'm Robert Daley. I'm sorry to intrude like this. Someone gave me your number—I need your help! I'm not sure if you've been following the news, but I'm the father of Tobey Daley..."

As soon as he mentioned the name, images of the distressed couple flashed through my mind. I saw the pair of them facing a panel of reporters at a press conference. I didn't follow the story then, but later, I had read up on it in one of the nationals. Their story was truly heart-breaking. "Yes. I have heard about you and your family. I'm so sorry for your ordeal."

I looked over at Lydia whose hazel-green eyes danced with many questions.

"As I said," Robert Daley continued, "I'm very sorry to invade your privacy like this. The doctors—they don't seem to have a clue! They don't know where to start! It's hard to explain, but my wife, actually, we both feel—believe, our son wants to communicate with us, somehow. Don't ask me how we know this; we just know." He paused. "And money is not a problem we can pay you—"

I cringed, "Mr. Daley. Please. That won't be necessary. If I can help, I will. I just don't see how I can?" *This is beyond baffling!* Communicate with a comatose baby? Whatever next? I was certain I had never spoken to one before, or ever recalled hearing from one, for that matter. That said, I had never been in a situation that called for it either.

"Yes, you can help me!" Robert Daley cried. He paused before adopting a gentler tone. "Believe me, if somebody had said a few weeks ago that I would be consulting some kind of medium—*a baby whisperer*—about the progress of my son's health I would have laughed in their face. I'm not the type of person who believes in this kind of thing." His voice petered off.

I understood his contacting me was more on his wife's prompting, than his own, which made me feel even sorrier for the guy.

Taking a deep breath I looked across the exchange. It teemed with lively market porters, traders and tourists, all chatting away whilst chomping down on their expertly wrapped delicacies. It seemed everyone around me was just getting on with their regular, drama-free, lives. Their uncluttered minds far removed from thoughts of dead children and ill babies.

But not me

"I know this is none of your business," Mr. Daley said, as if reading my thoughts. "I understand if you don't want to get involved, but if you do change your mind, you can meet me—and my wife Kelly. We're at

St Margaret's Hospital Trust in Whitechapel. We are there most of the time. I won't tell anyone about this conversation, you have my word." He sighed. "Thank you for listening."

"That's okay." Then the line went dead.

"What was all that about?" Lydia stared intently at me, "What are you going to do?"

I drew in a lengthy breath. "Well Lydia, I guess I'm going to head down to St Margaret's Hospital Trust to try and communicate with a comatose baby, who has never opened his mouth before, let alone made any use of his lungs, and who is—might I also add—hooked up to a life support machine."

Lydia's smile widened. "You've had one crazy week, Miss Shore, and I fear it's going to get crazier still!"

"I know. Do you want to come with me?"

"Do you have to ask?" Lydia gave a little girl grin, "Now what's the quickest route to east London from here?"

Chapter Eleven: Sleeping Cutie

<u>Tobey</u>

I am awake and asleep
I am lost to be found
I am light, and it's dark
I am long, and I'm round
I am here, then I'm gone
I am alive, and I'm dead
I am screaming with no sound
I am brave, and I'm scared
Like a star, I fell from my Ancestral Tree
Look! Behold! There's a baby
And the baby is me
When they whisper my name, they call me, 'Sleeping Cutie'
But that is not the sign that was given to me, from the sagacious old roots of my Ancestral Tree…

Tobey was no longer Tobey. He was still Tobey Daley; the ill, unfortunate, catatonic baby, holed up at St Margaret's Hospital Trust. But things were very different now. Very different indeed…

For now, Tobey could stand straight if he wanted to, swing his arms above his head, touch his toes, or take to the skies—as he did now. He wasn't just happy; he was ecstatic! Forget the grey and rainy skies of London, he was now in a special dwelling place; a world of true unlimited, unadulterated, splendour!

In this abode, his body not only worked as it ought, but it also gave off a subtle glow. And the bright blue sky which was rolled out as far as the eye could see, was dotted with every kind of precious stone: diamonds, rubies, sapphires, amber, and emeralds. Each, emanating their own distinctive hues and twinkling like disco lights at night. Except, in this case, it wasn't night, and this was no longer earth…

In the distance Tobey could hear the rapturous roar of rushing water, and everywhere he looked there were flowers—trees and plants of every description, colour, and size. And when the wind blew, as it did now, the petals chimed. For flowers in this place did not only release their scent, but melodies as well. This was not unusual—nothing here was. There was harmony in everything, especially in the air, which ebbed and flowed as it swirled around its glorious setting.

Today, Tobey headed toward Second Heaven Cliff to meet his friends. They had all agreed to gather at this destination point on his last visit here.

"Tobey…Tobey…" the female voice sang his name; it was wrapped up in the wind.

Tobey smiled. "Yes, I'm here. I've just arrived." Hearing that voice made him glad, he knew what came next.

"Tobey. Someone is waiting for you by the tree."

Nothing more needed to be said. In this place much was communicated, but words were seldom used. Tobey found that messages that were meant for him, made their way to him somehow.

A gigantic tree emerged appearing both majestic and ethereal in stature. The long, furry-green branches looked like they were in the process of melting but had stopped in mid-flow. And sat below it, in a large comfy chair, was a middle-aged man.

As far as Tobey was aware, there were no adults roaming around in this paradise. Except the Creator of Love, which, wasn't quite an adult, but it wasn't one of them, either.

Everyone knew the Creator very well, and just referred to it as Love. But besides that there were no grownups. Not even children. Only babies, like him.

Tobey's heart raced. This was another Wisdom Call from one of his Ancestors.

He approached the man sitting under the tree. The meeting with his friends would just have to wait a little while longer.

"Hello, Tobey," said the man. Tobey smiled. The voice sounded pleased to see him. "My name is Espen Aagaare. It is an absolute honour to be here, and to see you face-to-face." The man grinned and continued to bob his head, as though he still couldn't believe his good fortune.

"I'm happy to meet you too, Espen Aagaare." Tobey observed his Ancestor's appearance.

In the past, Tobey had seen all sorts of people; all members of his family—his Ancestry. This particular Ancestor had white-blond hair, and eyes the colour of the ocean. But just like all the other visits, his Ancestor's appearance started to alter. It was very slow and ever-so slight, but Espen Aagaare's bold features aged. The lines on his forehead cracked into fine ridges, and his cheeks started to thin away. He became a very old man, right before Tobey's eyes. Then, just like that, the aging process started to reverse on itself. Espen's eyes grew wider and brighter, and the hair on his head thickened. He was a young man, a sprightly lad, a lanky adolescent, then a little boy again. This transformation process was slow and deliberate. As such, the vacillation from young to old continued without impeding on their conversation.

"Although Espen is my birth name," his Ancestor furrowed his brows, "for some reason my family ended up calling me Baldur. It was the name of one of my uncles, who was a magnificent warrior, another great Ancestor of yours. Not that I'm saying I'm great, or anything like that." He chuckled. "But like any of your Ancestors would profess, once upon a time, I did live a great life or rather, a life worthy of greatness….mmm, I never know which one pertains to me as such…" Espen trailed off; he took a moment to contemplate. He gave a dismissive wave of his hand. Espen was all smiles again. "Oh, my son. Forgive the ramblings of an old man. But let me tell you, Tobey Daley," he announced with renewed focus. "Aagaare used to be your family name a long, long, long time ago. I know right now it might not be all that paramount that you know this. But at the same time, it is very important that you do." Espen shook his index finger to stress his point. "Do you understand what I'm saying, son?"

Tobey hadn't the foggiest, but he wasn't about to reveal the contrary.

Espen continued, "To be honest, when you enter the *Third Realm*, you won't remember much of our time together. This will all be a bit of a haze to you." He leaned in closer, inspecting his face. "You are aware of this, aren't you, Tobey?"

"Yes. I am aware." He was a little relieved that he at least understood one thing, so far.

There was something about his Ancestor's appearance which fascinated Tobey to no end. Whenever Espen looked to the left or to the right, his greyish-blue eyes lit up like bits of flint. It reminded Tobey of the many times he had sat at the edge of the waterfront, watching groups of fish coursing through the freshwater lakes. Their skin glistened under the sun's rays, and then suddenly, there'd be a flash, which was unusual and unexpected. Just like what Espen's eyes did at that moment.

"Tobey. As you are here, and I am here." Espen made himself comfortable in his chair. "We might as well enjoy the little time we have together. And I would like to spend that time talking to you about me—not about you, but about me." He then brought forth a resounding laugh, which, Tobey really liked the sound of. So much so, he decided to collect that for himself…

"I know that sounds mighty selfish of me, son." Espen smiled. "But this is definitely the time for *you* to listen to everything I have to say. You'll have plenty of time to talk much later."
And so, Espen began to relate tales of his life as a young boy growing up in nineteenth Century Europe…

***

The young Espen Aaagaare was born and lived in a busy shipping town in Norway. He had lost two of his eldest brothers to the great North Sea, but that did little to diminish his family's love for the waves. The warrior in their blood needed to hunt, and the object of their pursuit was now the capturing of cod. They, meaning Espen and his father, had docked in Britain in Liverpool's industrious port, brimming with commerce and trade. Espen and his father spent most of their time disposing of their netted goods, stocking up on supplies, and mending damages to their weather-beaten boat. This took between three to five months. But this was far too long for the young Espen Aagaare. For him, the days were cold and miserable, and the nights, noisy and unsettled. Espen longed to be back on the great high seas, where each conquered wave brought them closer to home.
It was on Espen's fifth visit to Liverpool that his father was taken ill, and later died.

The loss filled the young Espen Aagaare with a biting sorrow that no future loving—or good fortune, would ever overturn. However, despite Espen's crushing grief, he lived on. And sometimes—he lived well.

How does one find happiness in sadness?

It was a paradox which baffled him throughout his life. But in the afterlife, Espen would learn it was for this very reason the Ancestors fought so hard to be heard...

Fourteen-years-old and stranded on foreign land, Espen was now on his own. Having lost his mother as an infant, he didn't have a family to go back to. He was reunited with Andreassen Brevik, one of his townsmen who had docked in Liverpool a few years prior. Andreassen had married a local girl, then went about expanding his warehousing business.

Andreassen and his wife bought Espen into their home. They welcomed his labour, but they couldn't find it in their hearts to love him like a son. Just like a donkey, Espen was put to work.

"I was at an age where I wasn't permitted to laugh and could get a huge walloping for crying. Such was the new life I had awoken to," Espen said with a degree of nonchalance.

"I couldn't tell you if I remember asking to be born? But if I was one of those eager nippers who did, I was regretting that decision now—I can tell yer!"

When Espen wasn't toiling away, he could be found milling around the docks or chasing rats into the sea. He didn't have meals—he had scraps. He yearned for

his childhood, but those days were far behind him now.
But in spite of the hardship, Espen made some good friends. They were a group of young lads who, like him, hung around the shipyards during the day, and skulked through the windy city at night. And just like true jesters, these boys found a joke in everything. Espen soon found he could laugh again. And this group would have a significant impact on the rest of his life on earth…

"Although we cackled all day like a bunch of hyenas, deep down, we believed the things we saw in the eyes of the townspeople: that we were hopeless, a bunch of unlovable nobodies. As such, we jumped off broken roofs, and swam out way too far from land. Each of us would have gladly died on any given day, but was happy to see another tomorrow, if you know what I mean. That was how little we thought of our lives, dear Tobey. But I tell yer now, it's no way for a young person to live..."

Turning to face his descendant Espen said, "In your lifetime many young people will live like this: riddled with self-doubt and self-loathing. They will give up before they even get started."
"In my lifetime?" Tobey couldn't believe what he was hearing. He looked back with disbelief and disgust.
"Yep!" Espen nodded. "In your lifetime. Along with that: unacceptable levels of waste, mass poverty, and the gross distribution of wealth…come to think

about it—I guess not much change there!" He gave a heavy shrug and continued with his storytelling... *"Samuel was the leader of our group. He had us all believing the women who worked the public houses were condescending and charged way too much for their wares. So we took advantage, as, and whenever the urge took us. What can I tell you? Assaulting the weak was less challenging than attacking a fierce defender. One, was an easy win. And god knows we wanted to win..."*

What ensued were years of criminal activity: a little robbery here, a spot of fencing there. Many now saw Espen as a gruesome thug, which didn't bother him at all, at least they noticed him now. Espen would have kept up with his life of crime, but the eventual hanging of one of his closest friends ended this lifestyle. In truth, he wasn't sad to see it end.

"There was something about my life, young Tobey, which was mathematical in the most bizarre sense. The more I added to my conquests, the less of a man I became. Toward the end, there wasn't much of a difference between me and those rabid dogs that fought each other night after night in the baiting pits. I believed taking up a life of crime was my only choice. But once that was taken away from me, I saw that there were indeed other choices. Even if I chose to do nothing—it was still a decision. I had a choice…why didn't I see this before? What had I been doing all along?"

Without putting too fine a point on it, Espen started over. And so the next chapter of his life began….

At the age of twenty-three Espen became an apprentice to a skilled carpenter. He soon married the daughter of a local baker.

"You know, Tobey, there really is no shame in poverty," Espen said with a knowing glint in his eye, *"only for those who seek to make others impoverished. But as a man of the earth, I didn't understand this simple truth. Poverty to me was like a debilitating disease—it was cruel and undignified. I hated it!"*

With a painful awakening, Espen realised even if he worked every hour that was given to him - no matter how much timber he could square off, or how quickly he smoothed over the boards, he - and his loved ones - were still going to die in poverty. He knew this truth like the back of his own hand. This grim reality was a stone-cold certainty for many of those in Espen's community. He tried hard to fight it, but it ate at his resolve and eventually drove him to drink.

His wife of five years died giving birth to their third child. Espen did not stay widowed for long. He married again, but this time to a woman he really liked.

"On earth, everything you see is beautiful, believe it or not—everything! The fattened slug, the curl of a dung, the fins of a Roosterfish—it's all beautiful!" Espen roared with laughter at the haughty expression on Tobey's face.

"But the extraordinary thing about beauty is that; it is not what you see that is beautiful, but rather how it makes you feel when you see it…how best can I describe my feelings for my

new wife? Only to say, there was something about her that was so easy to hold; she had fresh features that never waned in my sight, and a laughter that made me laugh whenever I heard it." Sarah Ward was her name, and she bore him two children. Sarah later became pregnant with his sixth child. But that year, Espen fell ill and died on a stormy afternoon. It was February 17, 1903. Espen Aagaare was thirty-three years old and was buried in the local Methodist Church, the only place that would have him.

The child his second wife was carrying was Tobey's great, great, grandmother, Veronica Staunton.

Through changing seasons and melodies, Espen Aagaare went on to tell Tobey about the varied stories of his life: the happy, the sad, the fun, and the regretful. Espen went on for days and days, it would seem. But in this paradise, the conversation was actually quite short, and expressed in no more than a few poetic verses. As time—unlike earthly matter—could not be accounted for in the spiritual realm…

***

Tobey soon discovered there were no morals to be found in each of his Ancestors' stories. They didn't come to moralize. In fact, they did the opposite. Their experiences were laid bare for all their descendants to see. The weak and the strong, the beautiful and the brutal, all told in the same sanguine-like manner.

***

Siba

As I mentioned before, I never did live long enough to see myself grow into a woman. My uncle lured our clan to a new dwelling place, and it was there where I met my gruesome end. However, after my transitioning, it was lovely to be given the opportunity to see what I would have become. I tell you now people, I changed DRASTICALLY from the days of my youth. Good god! I cannot believe it. But I am happy to report that in spite of the years, not an iota of my essence had been altered. Not one jot! I can attest, there is much more to us than flesh and bone—indeed! At any rate, whilst Tobey is engrossed in his Ancestor call, I would like to share something with you all—if I may? It is the same information Tobey, and all the other little ones will be absorbing during their visits with their Ancestors.

As of now, nothing gives me greater pleasure than to walk and talk with my descendants, many of whom have funny ideas about their journey to earth. But it's all a joy, really! The Ancestors are only too happy to tell their stories, as the world has the exceptional memory of a goldfish! It seldom remembers those that came before them. Let alone, their true heroes. Such people, the world forgets, and history is even more unforgiving; omitting the names, the dates, the battles—and most scandalously—the deeds of the just…

Although the world may forget, the descendants do not. They hear the stories, and it is up to them, the little ones, to take away what they want from it. The descendants are free to choose, without prejudice, what they think is wise, beneficial, favourable, or cautionary to them. And whatever they take away would be used as tools in the next realm, earth. The ultimate testing ground…

Tobey, like all the other babies in this realm, was endowed with an acute perception of the truth. They understood the Ancestors had a palpable desire—or wish, rather—for their descendants to prosper on earth. Charged with this undertaking, the Ancestors—with every passing generation—thought up more elaborate ways to equip their offspring with the best of whatever they had to offer. Be it: knowledge, particular physical attributes, or special abilities…anything, they hoped would give their progeny a feasible chance at success on earth. But if their descendants could not succeed, then, the overriding objective was for them to at least aim… 'To do well…'

'Do well…?' How does one, 'Do well' you ask? And moreover, what does 'Do well' mean…?

This is another answer Tobey, like all the other babies in this paradise, had learnt sometime before they were born. For it went without saying, the world is a living and breathing organism, which has some unwieldy conditions of its own…

At the start, humankind was bequeathed with a special prize which was not given to the rest of creation. And that prize was the gift of choice. As such, the very survival of creation depended, not on choice, but on the rules, and these rules governed every living thing on the planet. If the rules were broken then, there were consequences. And consequences meant the course of every action did not disappear into the ether, like humanity thought—or in some cases, had hoped. Instead, the repercussions of the Ancestors live on, and they are also passed down. Not only this, but they are free to swirl around in the celestial family gene pool, like snowflakes after a blizzard.

Tiny distillations of actions passed. And these abstractions are free to settle on anyone on that tree—without prior thought or design. So in essence, a good person could receive an ominous repercussion. Likewise, a bad person could be the recipient of good fortune. Because despite the general makeup of the world, there are repercussions; either good or bad. And the descendants do inherit them…both the good…and the bad…

As a rule, the babies were made to understand life on earth was far from futile. Whatever took place there, had a profound impact on everyone on their Ancestral Tree. Therefore, it was important for the little ones to strive to do well. 'Do well,' to create rich blessings for their descendants—and not the reverse. Ensuring they do the best with the tools they are given, and leaving the rest…to take care of itself…

That was as much as Tobey and the other little ones understood about the current mystery to their existence…

***

Tobey

Then, in a blink of an eye! Tobey's Wisdom Call was over. It ended like all the others, with the Ancestor placing a farewell kiss on his forehead.

Before he left, Espen said, "As you know, I dwell in another dimension, Tobey, a place you cannot go to right now. One day I might see you there." He smiled. "Which, isn't altogether a bad thing, but we're all hoping you'll aim much higher, son, much higher."

With that, Espen sighed and reclined back into his chair. The chair then entered the tree, and the tree drew away from Tobey, before disappearing into nothing…

Chapter Twelve: Life in Paradise [Part 1]

Tobey

Tobey didn't want to be late to meet his friends. He decided to make use of the orange-coloured trees that were embedded all over the paradise like pins across a naval map.

He soared over shimmering grasslands, pathways and streams, to land on the nearest tree that came within his sights. It seemed he was able to clear about seven to eight miles in a matter of minutes.

On one of the trees Tobey bumped into Bright-Night: a white-feathered eagle owl who was a resident of the paradise and was almost twice the size of him.

"Hello Tobey," the owl called out with excitement. "Are you staying with us long, or just passing by?"

"Oh, hello, Bright-Night. I didn't see you there." Tobey laughed. He always remembered the names of everyone he had met in this world. Unlike when he was back on earth, where he still struggled to recall the name of the helper who changed his sheets.

Oh, what was the assistant's name again? He'd heard it so many times before…

"No. I'm only here for a short while," Tobey answered the owl's question. He gazed off into the distance. "I'm on my way to Seventh Heaven Cliff." He made preparations for the next leap.

"Seventh Heaven Cliff?! Why? I'm going that way myself. I'll come along with you, if you don't mind?" The owl's enormous dazzling white wings unfurled like an exotic flower. All Tobey could do was stare at the exquisiteness perched before him.

"You think I look amazing?" Bright-Night chuckled. "But it is you, dear boy, who is, in fact, the wonder here. On the way, I want you to tell me all about your travels to earth."

In unison, they sprung from one orange tree to the next, as Tobey relayed as much as he could about his experiences on earth.

"Tobey. Look around you. You are very special indeed. It is rare to see someone as mature as you in this realm."

"I know, Bright-Night" Tobey nodded, "but for some reason I keep coming back here. I don't know how it must look to the others. I really do want to stay and take part in the journey, but when I get there the pain I'm under is so *excruciating*. I don't know why that is? And I don't know how much more of it I can take…"

The owl looked back at him. She cleared her throat. "Tobey. Did anyone tell you about the natural order of things?"

"Do you mean how the world is arranged?"

"Yes." The owl answered, "But most notably, how *this* world is arranged,"

"No. But I do know when babies get to earth, they don't come back here."

"You are quite right in saying so." Bright-Night chuckled. Her steely feathers bristled like a strong breeze swishing through a glade. "But Tobey, there's more…approximately two months before you are all due to enter the world, you begin to pop up all over this paradise like flowers in spring. It is such a wonderful sight to see. It's an even greater honour that we get to know you all, personally, before you set off on your magnificent journeys to earth. But this is by far, not the best part of your journey."

Tobey's eyes widened. "It isn't?"

"No. Some babies, as you will find out, lose their lives shortly after arriving on earth. These babies are referred to as the *wee ones.* Do you know what happens to these precious souls? They go onto the most beautiful paradise ever known to us all! It is called *The Island of Lights*. It is the best place I've ever seen, and the best place ever created."

"You've been there?" Tobey was shocked. He didn't know there were other lands in the Spirit Realm.

"There are other realms in this spiritual kingdom. With special permission, we who reside here can visit all the realms in this universe, but only for a short time. In fact, there are realms which you humans go to once you have completed your life's work on earth. I'm not sure if you're aware of this, but earth is just another stage of your journey. It is the penultimate plane. What happens there determines where you go next."

"Wait a minute. I thought earth was the end of our journey? If we're going someplace else, shouldn't we be more concerned about where we'll end up?"

The owl nodded. "Good question, and I see where you're going with it. But I can tell you first hand there are no worries in the end realm. I suppose it is because there is nowhere else to go. You are, where you are, and wherever that is—it's final." Bright-Night's luminescent eyes were fixed on him. "So it appears all those anxieties and concerns you humans have only take place during your time on earth." She paused. "Yet in spite of all the worries and concerns, earth is still the only place in the whole wide universe where the inhabitants have been given their *full* independence. Do you know what that means, Tobey?" The owl's eyes blazed like bits of burning sulphur. "All of you have been given *complete* autonomy. Whatever you create on earth, or whatever happens there will have a direct impact—not only on yourselves, but on the whole human race. I cannot begin to fathom that amount of power and responsibility, and why it was given to you humans? What on earth did you do right—or wrong," she said with smiling eyes, "—to be charged with such an almighty undertaking? I suppose. Love…really does love you..." The owl was quiet for a moment. "You do know the universe is governed by rules—or should I say guidelines. You humans have many of them, which allows you to live in freedom."

Tobey frowned, "How can rules bring you freedom?"

The owl chuckled, "I guess that's one of life's many wonderful riddles, which you'll come to understand in time. Every day, for you humans, is a new dawn -

oh, most fortunate beings! Although Tobey, your journey on earth could prove to be a… little…problematic…"

"How so?"

"Well, the life handed to humans is like a double-edged sword: you have privilege and opportunity—which is both a blessing and a curse. But Tobey, never let it be forgotten you wield a *mighty* weapon," the owl shuddered, "and I look at you all, all itching to get your hands on them."

Tobey laughed. "I guess we are all raring to go, but we can't help it! We just want to get on with the journey, and luckily some of us… can…" He couldn't disguise his hurt.

Bright-Night eyes softened. "I can see why you are all in a rush to get there," the owl said. "The world is truly an amazing place, home to both humans and beasts. The beasts are of little worry to you humans, as the power bestowed on you allows you to live in peace with them. It is living with humans that will prove to be the real challenge. While on earth you can choose to love each other or hate each other, but in that sphere you are immutably stuck with each other—thus, making earth the most *electrifying* place in the whole universe." With eyes swathed in pity the owl looked him over. "Sadly, I hear you all have the temperament of a pudica plant; easily shaken, caving in at the slightest touch. Lightning is a thrill to look at, little one, but you do not want to get burnt..."

"But I won't get burnt!" Tobey asserted. "I'll avoid all the pitfalls; I'll take good care—I know I will. I just want my chance Bright-Night, I just want my chance."

"Oh Tobey. I know it's hard for you now. I'm sure there's a good reason why you keep coming back here. Do you know what's even better?" She said cheerily, "There's nothing that pushes determination further than experiencing a few setbacks in the beginning. It's the stuff that builds character. And believe me, little one, you'll need plenty of that where you're going to. But when you make your mark on the earth, you are going to be a real contender—truly unstoppable!" She gave him a friendly nudge.

"I hope so." Tobey allowed himself to relax at the owl's assurances. "That's all I want to do: have my turn. Take part. And be a great light on my Ancestral Tree…"

At that moment they both looked ahead. They saw the White Mountains emerging from the clouds.

"Fear not, Tobey. At least there's some consolation." Bright-Night blinked at the magnificent spectacle that lay before them. "You won't be going to *The Fears*. I believe you've safely passed that timeline." The owl was unable to conceal her reservations for the place everyone in the paradise referred to as: *The Fears,* "Today I saw five more babies making their way… toward…that…place."

"Really? That is quite a high number, don't you think?" Tobey also tried to hide his apprehension. He fell silent as his thoughts flew to another part of this habitat. An area, which seemed a little out of place in this peaceful paradise. It was the territory where *The Fears* resided…

***

Siba

The Fears…what can anyone say about The Fears? Other than to say it is a huge, dark, gaping hole, situated at the furthest part of the paradise. Although this pit was monumental in size, it was neither frightening nor dangerous. In fact, it was a place that held much wonder and intrigue. Babies wanted to venture toward the dark hole. But what halted their tracks were the guardians of the hole. And these guardians were what everyone referred to as: The Fears

There were three of them: one, was a hefty beast, of sorts, with large sharp gnarly teeth. Its grisly mouth was smeared with saliva, and it spat and growled at anyone who dared to look in its direction…but that was as far as its aggression went...

The second, was a human skull, which was ten times the size of a person's head. It hovered above the ground, and faded and reappeared like a chilling hologram. The skull was a crude reminder that underneath their resplendent bodies was a grey crusty matter which was subject to decay. For some reason, this particular fear disturbed Tobey the most.

And last of all, there was Fear number three. It appeared to be a person. It could have been a male or female, but nobody could tell. It wore a cloak of many colours, which was drab and void of any radiance. This, however, wasn't exactly menacing, but

the mask it wore—was! In fact it was gruesome! And that was not all. A loud and sinister sound could be heard emerging from the masked being. It could have been quite musical, except, the chords were broken, which made all the babies shudder whenever they heard it. All the babies held a universal revulsion and distrust for these three 'Fears' And quite tellingly, when babies make their way to earth, many of the little ones carry these eerie reservations with them, still…
As it so happens, occasionally, a baby would leave the colony of babies and head toward the place where The Fears resided. The baby would then approach The Fears, and—as if some implicit conversation had taken place prior to anyone's knowledge—The Fears would step aside and let the baby go into the dark hole. No one knew why that baby was permitted to go in, or how The Fears knew which baby to let in. Only, that the baby that went in, no longer had their special glow…

Bright-Night must have read his thoughts, "I don't think anyone knows where those babies go to." The owl shook her head. Tobey needed answers,

"I don't understand it. Why are some babies selected to go there?"

"I don't know," Bright-Night answered, "My concern is that *The Birth Trail*—the realm you are currently in—is the last stop before you make your grand entrance into the world." Bright-Night stopped talking. Tobey realized the owl wasn't contemplating what she was going to say, but rather how she would say it. "I don't understand it myself. How can you win a race if you don't take part...? Those babies never got the chance to light up their Ancestral Tree or shape the destinies of their descendants. To see this opportunity snatched so close to the starting line…I think it would have been better if they had not arrived here at all…."

In that instant Tobey's mind raced to the boy he once saw disappear into the black hole after *The Fears* had let him through.
Bright-Night cleared her throat. "I can only presume those babies have gone to a good place," she looked doubtful, "I guess it just happens to be a place that none of us has any knowledge of. What we do know for certain is that those babies are never seen again…."
The two of them approached a cluster of trees and prepared themselves for another landing.

"Thank you for travelling with me." Tobey grabbed hold of a branch and secured his footing.

Bright-Night eyes twinkled back. "There's no need to thank me, Tobey. To be honest, it is I who should be thanking you—and apologizing."

"Apologizing?"

"Yes, Tobey. I know you have many questions, and I'm sorry I couldn't answer them all. I sense you're experiencing a great deal of pain on your trips to earth. I'm so sorry little one. Like you, we are all watching and waiting. We truly believe all this is happening for a reason. In the meantime, may *Love* continue to light up your path and keep you out of harm's way."

Tobey nodded. "Thank you, Bright-Night,"

The owl stretched out her gigantic wings. She turned to him. "I do hope I get to see you again, dear Tobey. I really enjoy hearing about your time on earth, and the interesting people in your life. However, I know this cannot go on forever. One day your journey will have to begin and end like everyone else's. But until then, take courage young one. Remember, everything happens for a reason. It could be a good reason, but only you can make it so..."

Bright-Night then took to the skies. She soared past the swaying multi-coloured trees; and the tiny jewels in the sky which twinkled like stars at night. Higher and higher the owl climbed until she was only a speck in Tobey's eye.

After a moment, Tobey approached the glade. He could see babies playing by the multitude. It seemed there were millions of them, all shining in a beautiful array of colours. All of them appeared to be oblivious to his presence—and rightly so—as Tobey was just another fun-loving baby, playing in their midst. The babies continued in their merrymaking, all, except six of them. As Tobey approached the gathering, six beings—who were scattered in and amongst the crowd—pulled away from the masses and made their way toward him. This manoeuvre was as fluid and as natural as breathing. The group of six, gradually making their way over to where he stood, did not need to be called. They were all Toby Daley's soul mates….

***

Siba

Now you're probably wondering: 'What is a soul mate?' Well, there's no need to ponder on this—I'll quickly answer that for you. Soul mates are people born into the world—who could end up living anywhere in the world. Sometimes you find them. Sometimes you don't. Hey! That's life! And life goes on. But if you do happen to find each other, the affinity is magical and everlasting…

Plain and simple: a soul mate is a kindred spirit, a forceful soul. Someone who has such an incredible impact on your life path, they literally light up your world! They are your teacher, your friend, your confidante, your helper, a person you understand like no other, and who you yearn to be around—and vice-versa. When you do happen to come across such a compelling being, the chances are, they stem from the same soul group as yourself…

Before we go any further with Christine's story, let me introduce you to this sprightly bunch of babies, who also happen to be members of Tobey's' soul group…

First up is Victoria Shine: 'Tori'—as she'll affectionately be called by her loved ones—will be born in Sydney, New South Wales, Australia. Victoria has no idea that one of her English Ancestors discovered the very place her family now calls home. And like her famous globetrotting Ancestor, she, too, will explore new territories, fend off gruesome predators (of the human kind), and set up home in a remote province somewhere in the Arabian Peninsula…

Thabo Mokhonoana is Tobey's second soul mate. Thabo comes from a long line of fighters. His Ancestors fought for possessions, for freedom, and—at one time—they even fought as a form of entertainment. Whether Thabo will continue with that fighting spirit is anyone's guess, as Thabo is destined for a life of unmeasurable privilege. He is set to be born to extremely wealthy parents, in a private hospital somewhere in North America. As it turns out, sometime in the future, Thabo will also have to fight (not the physical kind) to save his showbiz career. And there's no guessing where his ability to fight would have come from…

Number three, in this soul group, is Husna Begum: in terms of appearance, Husna is a real stunner! She hails from a long line of exceedingly beautiful women. Husna also possesses a gentle spirit and a kind heart. She still has some way to go, but when

her time comes, she will be born in a well-known hospital in London's East End…
Next up is Albert Simon, who is soul mate number four: Albert's Ancestors are well-travelled. They've been all over the world, including the Middle East, Central Europe, and North Africa. However their plight was not spurred by good events—but one of persecution. Albert's family would settle in the poverty-stricken districts of east London. The family acquired a good name, and great standing with the local people which they never traded in, not even when their finances began to improve. Remnants of the Simon's clan still live in the East End and are still practicing Ashkenazi Jews. And just like some of his soul mates, Albert will coincidentally be born in a large hospital somewhere near to where Tobey's parents live….
Then, there is Nnenna Ochuko, who is the fifth soul mate. Her skin is the colour of terracotta, and her luscious hair will grow thick and unruly, like the trees that surround her secluded village. Nnenna's lineage was one of the longest purebloods on the planet! But alas, a tribe of giants from the Levant, made their way to the Southeast of modern-day, Nigeria. And what was beautifully untainted, became wonderfully diluted.
Nnenna's Ancestors may have stayed put, but her parents did not. As a result, Miss Nnenna Amaka Ochuko will be born some four-hundred kilometres away, in a booming leafy suburb in the city of Lagos, Nigeria.
Li Wei, from the Far East, is soul mate number six. Just like Nnenna, he is also from a prominent lineage, but his Ancestral pedigree is not as stellar. As it stands, Li Wei's genealogy is punctured with so many acts of bloodshed and violence, it would have made Genghis Khan blush like a schoolgirl. But

fortunately for humankind, the past does not have a bigger bearing than the future. Choices alter many outcomes. And luckily for Li Wei, many of his kin had made some wonderful ones, which has thus overturned some disastrous repercussions that were due to fall on the House of Wei. Although Li Wei's family hail from mainland China, Li will be born in Hong Kong, in the same hospital as his father, and grandfather before him. He will also be born a twin. But his brother does not reside in this soul group, often the case with twin births.

Last of all there is Tobey Daley. The seventh and final soul mate….

There are only seven unique beings which make up a soul group. And soul mates are a tremendous benefit to the human race. Possessing these symbiotic connections, is a lot like having seven invisible energy-enhancing cords being attached to one's essence. And these cords release a hearty dose of good cheer, or—in other words—they supply an organic 'feel-good' factor to the soul. The members do not have to meet each other to experience this warm bond of well-being. Their very existence is a light, which illuminates the lives of the others. And when the soul group remains intact, the more fortified and rewarding that member's experience of life will be.

There are only seven people in each soul group, but not everyone on earth will finish up with as many. The loss of a soul mate is a frequent occurrence, and it is every bit like losing a limb. For although there are many types of prosthetics, a prosthetic can never take the place of a natural limb, and the same is said of a soul group member...

The loss of a soul mate is another one of life's many great misfortunes, but at the same time, it doesn't spell the end of things…life still goes on…

As you can see, soul groups are made up of members from all over the world. And although they are formed in the same soul bubble, it doesn't mean they will all be born at the same time. Some will make their entrance many years before or after, their soul mates. As fate would have it, a high proportion of Tobey's soul group will be born, not only on the same island—referred to as the United Kingdom, but also in the same part of the city as well. My friends, this is not an accident. Nothing ever is. This has occurred for a reason, and the reason, is of course, why this story is being told to you in the first place. Lest we forget, I am still in the middle of telling it, so I continue...Tobey is an extremely lucky boy, for he has seven wonderful soul mates. And the soul group all have each other for now…or so I believe…

Chapter Thirteen: Life in Paradise [Part II]

Tobey

Tobey sat smiling like a proud parent. He loved being back here, listening to his friends laugh and swap stories on their many adventures.

"What should we go and see today?" Thabo's playful voice echoed across the clearing. He rested on top of a nearby tree and was splayed out on a purple leaf which resembled a large velvety cushion.

"Thabo, come and join us." Husna waved him down with her free hand. "I know what we can all do today. Let's head over to Colton's River. I hear there are many weird and wonderful creatures moving about in the waters."

"No. Not Colton's River." Li Wei groaned. It was a trait most of his group had grown accustomed to as the time wore on. "We went there on our last visit. And please don't mention Kwan Bay either. I've been there twice already."

"What about Salm Gardens?" Everyone turned around to look at Albert. "I was told the place is teeming with interesting life forms. There are *flying trickeets*, *musical letters,* and *Neecons*—big and small ones!"

Nnenna's eyes widened. "*Neecons*? *Nah, wa!* That creature *no be small o*! When it moves, I swear it blocks out the seven suns."

Albert laughed. "Yes, they are a bit on the big side. On my last visit I was introduced to a family of sunflowers." He looked around the group with a mixture of awe and dread. "I'm not sure what to make of them. I think they're cheeky tricksters. Whenever you play hide-and-seek around them, they always give away your hiding position."

The group members exchanged looks.

"No they don't." Victoria frowned.

"Yes, they do." Albert disagreed. "They act like they're just standing there minding their own business, but then you hear a; *'psst,' 'psst,'* then the sunflower points in the direction where one of us can be found." Despite himself Albert broke into a crafty laugh. "It's quite funny, but not so much when it is *you* they are telling on."

"They've never done that to me before." Victoria looked at him with suspicion. "Maybe you were heading somewhere you weren't supposed to go?"

"Or," Thabo weighed in with a pensive stare, "it's payback for the times you've fobbed them off whenever they've tried to get you to dance with them. You do know how much they love to *Muchongoyo*?" he said in his native tongue, which got them all laughing at their friend.

Victoria grinned. "Knowing you Albert, that's probably it. They love it when you take a moment to dance with them, even if it's only for a short while." To demonstrate her point, Victoria sprang to her feet and danced on the spot. "See. Look what I've learnt so far?" She leapt and bopped to a catchy beat that only the group could hear. A luminescent pink dragonfly flew up beside her and proceeded to mirror Victoria's dance moves, which elicited a big chuckle from the group.

"I do dance with them!" Albert protested. "It's just that…I can't keep up…besides, you do know we're only here for a short while, and as fun as it is, I don't want to spend the whole time dancing with sunflowers. I just think it's best to avoid it—them, altogether, if you know what I mean." His voice was drowned out by peals of laughter erupting from a pack of troublemakers, who also happened to be his soul mates.

Tobey decided to give an answer. "Okay, Albert. This time we'll watch out for you. One of us will step in before you spend the whole time dancing the day away. Are we all agreed?"

"Agreed!" The members responded with great big smiles on their faces. It was still early on in the day, but every one of them knew they were in for a good one. Today's plan was to head to Salm Gardens. It was the ultimate playground, there was no other woodland like it.

One by one the babies climbed—and occasionally flew—over the paradise's many districts.

In no time at all, they stood in front of a large cave. To get to Salm Gardens, they all had to climb through it, which they did in quick succession. After a brief spell in the darkness, they emerged on the other side full of joy and ready for an adventure. However, it took a brief moment for their eyes to adjust to the dazzling brightness. They were indeed back outside again, but it was very different from the paradise they had left behind. They were now in Salm Gardens, and in this wonderland, every living thing was tinted in shades of yellow. The trees were yellow—including the bark—the grass and the sky were yellow. Even the very air was a sweet kiss to their nasal senses. If yellow had a fragrance, then this was it, and the babies blissfully breathed it in.

Tobey was the last one to climb out of the cave, it was Husna who helped him up.

"Every time I see you, it looks like you're getting bigger." Her warm brown eyes keenly observed him. "Do you have any idea why this is happening to you?"

"No. I'm still none the wiser." Tobey made a move to take her hand. "I wish I could tell you more…but…"

"Oh! Don't worry about it. It's probably not that big a deal, or anything like that." She was flippant, but that did little to mask her obvious concern.

Tobey knew Husna, like the rest of the group, was apprehensive about what was happening to him. And quite rightly so, they were all members of the same soul group: physical bonds were no match for spiritual ties. It went without saying, Tobey needed to be alright for them all to feel…alright…

Husna hugged him. "*Thikache chele!* It's okay Tobey. Let's go play hide-and-seek."

***

Later in the day Tobey and Husna broke away from the rest of their group. They sat at the edge of a sprawling lake, where babies from other soul groups played on the waterfront.

"I hear you had an Ancestor call today." Husna sat crossed legged on the grass and twisted a small clump of cloud around her wrist. She attempted to tie it in a knot, but after some time, she released it. She watched as it glided upward to re-join whatever puff of cloud it had come from.

"Yes, I did, it was really interesting. How about yourself?" He smiled back.
Husna was a true definition of a cherub. She had a potbelly and ruddy cheeks, and when she smiled—as she did at that moment—two dimples the size of pennies appeared on either side of her face. "I had one too." She laughed. "It was epic! But also very sad as well."
"Sad?" Tobey frowned. "What happened?"
"No! You tell me yours first"
"It's okay, you go first," Tobey knew Husna couldn't wait to tell all. And just as he guessed, without missing a beat, Husna ploughed right in.
"When I arrive on earth, I will be of Asian descent; the offspring of two Bangladeshi parents, who are also from a long line of Bangladeshis." She smiled proudly. "However, the woman who came to see me today existed long before the birth of our nation…she was the youngest daughter of Chandragupta Maurya. Her name was Durdhara..."

According to Durdhara, she grew up surrounded by wealth, beauty and the respect of her loving subjects. Durdhara didn't want for anything. How could she? Her father was Chandragupta Maurya, commander of the greatest battalion in the East, whose very name instilled terror amongst the armies of Alexander the Great.

Durdhara was often referred to as the 'Doel' of the region, as her long hair was black and shiny, like the ubiquitous silent bird that visited the area. But Durdhara was far from subdued. She had a beautiful singing voice, and it lured one of the emperor's loyal generals to the private garden where she sang.

The young officer, General Sutta, hid amongst the trees, listening to her ballads. He stood there with his head in the air and eyes closed, whilst Durdhara's sweet-sounding songs softened the man within…

Husna continued.

A chanced meeting evolved into a fevered affair. It was the kind of fierce passion that propelled the two of them to run away together. They crossed high mountains, brittle fields, and icy terrains, to try to find a place they could both be safe to love. It took the emperor's royal army six months, two weeks, and three days to find them. She was spotted bathing in the river. The soldiers shielded their eyes until she had finished. Then they came for them both.

The emperor's daughter was welcomed back into the royal fold. She was with child, but it didn't seem to matter. Of course, neither Durdhara nor Sutta could ever be together again. Sutta took an oath and withdrew from public duties. He began a fast. It was a fast to the death...

"It wasn't for nothing," Husna added cheerfully, "he died without shame." She acknowledged the ancient Jain ritual.

As for Durdhara, she, too, died after childbirth. She had given the Great Maurya a male heir—just what the emperor had prayed for Durdhara's son was a natural-born ruler. He later went on to have many daughters, but no sons—each of them rebellious in their own way.

Smiling coyly Husna added, "And I don't think it will stop with me either." She descended into a fit of giggles. "But jokes aside. The babies and young children of my Ancestors have had to deal with so much unnecessary suffering and pain, and many times, it seemed they went without guidance." Husna looked to Tobey. "I've decided when I get to earth and I grow up, I want to be of help to the young ones. Maybe I'll teach or become a mentor of some kind. I can't think of anything more rewarding than to nurture and take care of as many of my people as I can."

"That sounds like a lovely ambition, Husna."

Tobey admired his friend's compassion. He spent a moment basking in her wonderful glow.

"…Although…" He pulled away from her. "I wouldn't want you as my teacher."

Husna looked aghast. "Why not?"

"Because all you'll do is tease and play horrible tricks on the little children until you'll drive them all *craaaaaa*—" Tobey didn't finish his sentence. Husna lunged after him—just as he'd planned.

"Tobey! How dare you!"
"Ha, ha, catch me if you can!" Tobey scrambled, then took flight to get away from Husna's playful wrath. *And just like the babies they were, Husna and Tobey were back in play mode. Always play mode. This was paradise, after all.*

***

"Come on you lot, let's go see *The Fears* again," Thabo said with a maniacal grin, which made the group laugh whenever he did this. He was, of course, projecting more bravado than he felt.

"What? Now?" Albert looked very uncomfortable.

"Why not?" Are you afraid something might happen?"
"Is something going to happen?" Nnenna blinked back at Thabo
"I don't know," Thabo laughed at his friends' facial expressions. "But we won't know until we go and see. Oh come on guys, you know you all want to."
Tobey smiled. Thabo was right of course. They all wanted to have a glimpse of the dark hole. All of them were well-aware *The Fears* were not a physical threat to anyone. Yet, that did little to quell the pure exhilaration and stark dread that came over them at the mere mentioning of the name.
Looking courageous and resolute Victoria clapped her hands. "Okay, mate! Let's have a *Captain Cook!* We better set off now as there are a lot of distractions

along the way. But if we link our hands together—" she grabbed the nearest pair to her—"and keep them linked, then we should be able to get there a whole lot quicker."

The members did as instructed. "Are we all set?" Victoria asked. "Let's go!"

By late afternoon they had arrived at *Fears Bay*. The dazzling enclosures, colossal palaces and pathways, all appeared to be gilded in molten silver. A visual feast for Tobey's eyes. Even the fragrance in the air left him enthralled. It was a chore to keep his heart from leaping out of his body to be at one with the scent in the sky…furthermore, in this part of the region, the soul group were free to partake in one of their all-time favourite pastimes: Angel-Spotting. For just like magnificent, rare birds, angels could only be observed from a distance. With blazing wings of fire, they were either seen to be descending on certain parts of the paradise or soaring to some far-off place…

Later on that day Tobey and his group stopped by a soft grassy area referred to as Flurries Glen. While there, they ate all the delicious food that had been laid out for them. After they had had their fill, and of course, a little nap, they were ready to seek out *The Fears*, which, Tobey conceded, wasn't really much of a search at all. *The Fears* were where they had always been stationed: in front of a large black hole in the atmosphere….

And there they were again: The Beast, The Skull, and The Phantom in the Mask.

"Uh oh, I think they've seen us!" Victoria ducked behind the hill where the rest of the group hid.

"Told you I should have gone to inspect. I would have been more discreet." Albert rolled his eyes.

"It doesn't matter who went first," Husna addressed them all. "No matter what we do *The Fears* will always detect our presence. Their sense of awareness is higher than all of ours, can't you see that?" The babies nodded. Husna was right.

Li Wei scrambled forward to get a better look. "What are they? And why do they guard that hole?"

Before anyone could think of an answer, an eerie silence descended around them. They all felt it at once.

"Look over there!" Nnenna cried.

There was a baby boy. He was making his way towards the dark hole, ergo—*The Fears*…The infants would have called out, shouted out—anything, to try and arouse the poor baby from its stupor, but they had all become transfixed on the little boy's appearance.

Tobey shivered.

I understand for human beings, glowing bodies are imaginings of a celestial kind—or at best—the stuff of fantasy fiction. But in this paradise every living thing glowed. The Force which gave it life and resided in all things was on display for everyone to see. However, the baby making his way toward The Fears had no radiance to speak of. His eyes were bleak, as though something had crawled in to cage his warmth…it was unkind…unnatural…a lot like death, I suppose.

Nnenna was the first to speak up. "We should do something!" At once they all started to call out to the little boy

"Hey!"

"Don't go there!"

"Where are you going?"

"Come back!"

But the infant took no notice of their commands. He kept moving ever-nearer toward the hole where the three apparitions swayed in the distance.

Thabo jumped out from behind the hill. He ran toward the baby boy. Tobey followed. If they thought they could hold him back, they were mistaken. This was not a physical world. The baby breezed right through them and continued on his way. Thabo and Tobey raced ahead of him, but something soon stilled their motion. The two of them began to pour with sweat. It was so excessive, it spewed out of them as though they were melting. They had never experienced anything like it before.

"W-what's happening to us?" Tobey cried, turning to Thabo. They were still making a beeline toward *The Fears*, but the boys no longer saw *fear* ahead of them, but felt it welling up like a miasma from within. *It was coming from within!* And it proceeded to speak in a noxious hiss: *'Do not come any closer! Can you feel that?*

Good! I'm sure you can. For I am the fear of: Abandonment. Rejection, and Pain. I am
FAR worse than any FEAR you will ever see…'
And for Thabo and Tobey, it was indeed a lot worse. For the nearer they drew toward *The Fears*, the more unbearable the sensation became. They both came to a halt. *Mental Fear* had eventually brought them to a standstill…
In no time at all the baby soon bypassed them, and was stood in front of *The Fears* It almost looked like the snarling beast was going to swallow him whole, but a moment passed, then *The Fears* stepped aside to let the boy through.
"No!" Tobey cried, but it did no good. Just before the baby disappeared through the hole, his little body crumbled and dissipated like powder in a wind. Never to be seen again...
After the boy's exit into the abyss, Albert was the first to speak up. "If we make a move now," he drew out the last word, as though he wasn't quite sure it was the right time to speak, "we can catch a glimpse of the swirling night dragons before they begin the show…" His oddly timed suggestion broke the group's temporary paralysis. It was true. There was nothing anyone could do to change what had just taken place.
"Come on, guys." Tobey took in a deep breath. "I think we've seen enough of *The Fears* for one visit." He turned to smile at the rest of his group hoping to erase the look of uncertainty on their faces. It

worked, everyone relaxed. But the repose was brief. Husna looked up, "Tobey…" Her eyes were not focused on him. "Look over there." Tobey followed her gaze over to a red shadowy manifestation floating high in the sky. It was a sign Tobey was all too familiar with, as were the rest of his soul group. It was a reminder that before the end of tomorrow, he would have returned back to earth. That sign always appeared a day before his departure from the paradise. At one time, seeing this caused Tobey a great deal of distress. But now, he welcomed it, as it allowed him to prepare for his leaving.

"Oh, well," Albert said. "At least this time around you'll get to see the swirling night dragons before, you know...you…pop off." Some of the group members sighed, Albert's timing was the stuff of legends. "Hey! What did I say?" He frowned, searching their faces. "What did I say?"

Tobey laughed. "Come on, guys. Race you all to the waters."

***

In this beautiful paradise, the nightfall was even more exhilarating than the daytime—or so Tobey came to this conclusion. The expansive darkening horizon became an electrifying canvas where hundreds of dancing dragons lit up the skyline.

They appeared in every colour of the rainbow—and some which did not feature on the human spectrum. All the while, the heavens above showered the little inhabitants with the sweetest melodies ever heard by the living. It was super. Serene. Sublime. Nothing less than magical from the music made by angels….Tobey could feel his body preparing to fall into a peaceful slumber. He absolutely adored this sensation. He wished he could sleep forever….

The morning began as the night ended: in glorious consummate tranquillity. Smiling to himself Tobey opened his eyes and peered around. His soul group were all around him, or so it seemed. He immediately felt a discordance in his soul. It was as acute as a syringe puncturing the wrong vein (and boy, did he know what that felt like!)
His soul group gathered around him. But all were silent and looking at the same thing. They looked at Husna, and with good reason. Poor Husna's ever-present glow had gone. And her eyes were muted; they communicated nothing.
They all knew what this meant.
Tobey didn't get the chance to react. The red shadowy manifestation in the sky chose that very

opportune moment to claim him. It was time for Tobey to return home. He was engulfed in a rush of red mist.

However, just before Tobey, and any other visitor to the paradise were whisked back to the world, they were always given the opportunity to take a brief stop in the ether. What is this ether—you ask? Don't worry, I will answer that for you: the ether is an opening, and Tobey was presented with two of them. One, led back to his bed, his parents, and earth—which was usually the one he reluctantly went down.
While the other opening led to The Corridor of Revelations...when Tobey first began taking these ethereal trips between the dimensions, he was often advised to make a quick stop at The Corridor of Revelations. 'You never know what might be revealed to you,' a voice chimed from the distant unknown, 'Bearing in mind you still remember what you've seen…' Whether it was the combination of travelling between two realms, babies often tended to forget, or they only remembered snippets of what had been revealed to them. But right now, Tobey needed answers. He decided to do something he had never done before; he flew down the entrance leading to The Corridor of Revelations....

Tobey stepped in—or he stepped out. He couldn't explain what he did. All he knew was that he was now in a different place. It felt like he had entered into a vast amphitheatre, and displayed across the far-reaching walls was his earthly world in motion…

Tobey saw his mother. She talked to somebody on the phone. His father was in another room. He washed his hands with lilac soap. But wait! There was more…much more...what could he see? He observed a man in a white coat. He knew who he was, it was Dr Lawson. He wanted him dead. But wait…there was more. The man in the white coat had a plan. A plan, which would see the death of some of the members of his soul group, and many other innocents. He witnessed what the doctor had been doing all along….and still…there was more...there was a young woman—from *The Year of the Flute*. She was not like the others; she was gifted. She could see, hear, and feel the presence of others. Her name was Christine Shore. She was coming to the hospital, to see him.

Tobey realized he needed to return back to earth *immediately* so that when this special lady arrived, he would tell her as much as he could. She was the only one who could stop this Dr Lawson. Tobey headed toward the exit, leaving *The Corridor of Revelations* behind him.

***

As always for Tobey the journey back to the world was an excruciating one. The air he breathed in became thick and heavy and set his tiny lungs on fire. It felt like he inhaled harmful contaminants.

Tobey was, in fact, taking in oxygen, one of the natural elements that surrounded the earth's atmosphere.
Then, with a rude awakening, Toby became aware of his own saliva. It tasted like he had sucked on old pennies. Not that he knew what that tasted like. All the same it was nauseating but he found he was just too weak to vomit.
'Aaaarrgghh!' Tobey groaned out loud. Did someone crush every bone in his body and leave him for dead? There wasn't a part of him that didn't succumb to the agony of it all. And to further add to matters, he was icy-cold and desperately hungry.
Tobey could hear the periodic beeps of his ventilator machine, and the all-too-real sound of silence. He was back at the hospital.
"Husna." His heart raced. He recalled his visit to baby paradise. "No! Please…not Husna!"
No longer was Tobey Daley the able-bodied baby, who, at a moment's notice, could take to the skies when he wanted to. Instead he now convalesced in a sterile room, waiting for help to arrive. Each breath was a fight to live, but at that moment, all Tobey wanted to do was die. But he couldn't do that either. He had to wait. He couldn't say which felt worse.

Siba

A woman is placed on a gurney. Her screams are unbearable, almost too much for the assistants to take, and they have heard the worst of them. They were well-aware that labour was a grisly affair, but there was something woeful about this one. This had happened before, and the results had been far from favourable…

The attendants quicken their pace, crashing through plastic sheeted doors as they rush toward the emergency ward. The woman's husband tries his best to hold onto her, but it's not an easy task. She thrashes and grabs hold of him at the same time. Throughout the whole ordeal, he offers sweet words of comfort. His tears do not go unnoticed by the helpers. They stream down his cheeks and run into his beard. All the while, he keeps up his assurances.

The obstetrician arrives. Relief lightens the room like a gust of fresh air. But the woman is still crying, she does not want to let go. She screams out:

"My baby! My baby! Please save my baby…"

She lets out a wail so piercing, her husband's tears trickle like sweat. Amidst the commotion the obstetrician remains composed. To everyone around him, he looks like a man who has a job to do. Which is quite right, although, he has not one—but two jobs to carry out…the doctor makes provisions for the baby's arrival. The midwife, the nurse, the husband—look at the woman in distress; they make great efforts to try and reassure her. Nobody sees what the doctor is doing. He appears to be doing his job, and on one hand—he is doing just that, but with the other, he is claiming his prize...

The woman is urged to keep on pushing. She does so. She strains with all her might. Then, as if by magic, the crown of the baby's head appears. The woman is asked to push one more time; she growls like a doomed animal. The newborn flows outward with such tremendous force, as if freed from a snag.

Relief is felt by everyone.

The workers move into action. One, reaches for the trolley where the appliances are kept; the other rushes forward, to position the baby onto its mother's chest, while the doctor—at the centre of it all—places something into his coat pocket…

All this fussing took only a matter of seconds. But that was how long the baby girl had to live. She only breathed in once, and it was her last. Baby Husna lay dead on her mother's chest.

It was one of many semi-stillbirths taking place in one of the largest paediatric units in Europe. In a hospital that overshadowed half the skyline of London's East End….

Siba

When I lived on earth I was known as Siba. But now that I am a spirit of the universe, there is no name for what I am and what I do. Neither, as it stands, do I see things in black or white. There are just truths and untruths, and along with that a never-ending list of questions from all you precious human beings.

The questions make me smile. But I'll tell you something; all I ever hear everybody talk about is: the sins of the father! The sins of the father! Well, what about the sins of the mother? I dare ask? This is an interesting concept, which so happens to involve one of the little ones in Tobey's circle…

As mentioned earlier, Albert Simon—a member of Tobey's soul group—was from a very worthy lineage. A genealogy studded with hard work and good deeds.

In 1930, one of Albert's Ancestors helped build several chevras—or small synagogues—as they were referred to back then. These dwellings were set up to provide welfare for the impoverished Jewish community of London's East End, and doubled up as a place of worship. Albert's Ancestor did not charge any money for his labour and volunteered his services without reserve or reward.

'Adonai Yireh,' Albert's Ancestor would say with a happy grin. Adonai Yireh meaning: 'The Lord will provide…'

This dedicated man seemed more concerned with his community's well-being, than the amount of change he had rolling around in his pocket.

Due to Albert's family's honourable deeds, many of the descendants have been the lucky recipients of good fortune. But, in spite of all these blessings, there was one aspect the family couldn't overturn. And that, it seemed, was the dreaded curse of poverty.

Yes, poverty lay over this family like a dark shadow looming on the horizon. No matter what took place, it was always there. But alas…it wasn't always so...

Like everyone else, Albert's Ancestors began their journey with a clean slate. They were bequeathed with two almighty legacies: the gift of will and the gift of choice. And both of these intriguing dynamics would produce fascinating results—or consequences as it goes.

Good choices meant favourable fortuities, which were distributed on the family's descendants. And bad choices—well. Let me tell you about one of Albert's Ancestors.

Albert's great, great, great, great, grandmother—or somewhere thereof—was an obscenely wealthy woman. Her name was Zipporah; she had married a man even wealthier than herself.

As in life, an interesting situation presented itself. Zipporah needed to make an important decision. She had to decide whether to have her baby brother murdered, so that her son could inherit the family's fortune. Indeed, this sacrifice would mean her dynasty would be assured throughout the ages. My, oh my! The short-sighted vision of the human mind.

Nevertheless, Zipporah made her choice without delay

Zipporah only lived a further seven years, but as she had hoped, her family enjoyed a hundred years of wealth. Wealth, which was acquired off the back of her cunning decision.

On the surface, this family was extremely rich. But what the family did not know, was that it had, ironically, inherited wealth—but not prosperity…and these two are not the same, you know...

As decades became centuries, the gushing flow of wealth receded to a trickle as though someone had turned off the tap of good fortune.

Then a time came when everything stopped.

This is not to say there were no more riches to speak of. Some of Albert's Ancestors, in fact, were able to carve out quite good livelihoods for themselves. It was just that whenever the funds did arrive, it appeared to seep into the ether. Just like dry riverbanks absorbing rain—there was no accounting for its presence…in the same way, all the family's long-term investments resulted in rack and ruin. When it involved riches, it was a case of, here today, gone tomorrow! An aphorism sorely felt by those stemming from this Ancestral Tree.

And so far, no number of good deeds have been able to overturn this outcome. And this is how it continues to be to this very day...now, many of you are thinking that a life-long sentence of poverty is a tad harsh. Especially, when it was caused by one person, and one person alone. But in this world, where we are all connected, there is no such thing as alone…the Ancestors all have a part to play in the stirring of you and I...

Nevertheless, on a less depressing note, the definition of poverty in Albert's case hasn't always been absolute in its entirety. For you see, many of his Ancestors became diligent workers. It was as though they saw hard work as the ideal stick to fend off the onslaught of poverty. And from such assiduity, they were able to obtain slight reprieves. Moreover, many of Albert's

Ancestors were oblivious to this protrusive default in their lineage. After all, in those times, people were either rich or poor; there was no middle ground. Hence, their circumstances appeared to be no different from everyone else around them. But of course, they were. For Albert's kin were not merely stuck in a financial rut. They were being constrained by an Ancestral curse...

My former fellow beings—never forget: consequence is no coincidence! A fact, and a truth! Which is quite interesting, as you don't often get many of those…plain talking: our consequences have shaped all our Ancestral Trees, and with that, the history of the world! It is bewildering to think one small flame can start a forest fire, yet a simple action in time has the power to change…time...

To that end, although human beings are bound by the choices they make, their genealogies are free to roam and intertwine. And over the ages they have done just that! Things are no longer black and white. Our bloodlines carry lineal blessings and curses. All, working alongside and against each other. All, vying to overlap, nullify or counteract the other. And when this occurs, the results can be quite encouraging, as in the case with Albert's mother and father.

As it so happens, the curse of poverty derives from Albert's father's genealogical tree. However, Albert's mother's family—The Blumstein's—are an auspicious lot and have been for quite some time now. In jest, it has often been said; if any one of them should happen to fall into a river, they would come up with a salmon in their mouth. On the flipside, although very hard-working, Albert's father was a broke, self-employed, accountant. Yes! You heard correctly. It seems highly inconceivable, but people with plush careers and meagre funds do exist, as I can clearly see.

But as fate would have it, the affable but notably cash-strapped, Ben Simon, met and married Zoe Blumstein, who hails from a private banking family.

An accountant. A bank. I say no more…

Moving forward, Albert's offspring will feel the sting of poverty pinching at their heels. But the blessing of affluence which follows Zoe's lot, could very well provide the salve that soothes the wound.

*Our fascinating Ancestry is a swirling pot of goodness, madness and sadness, and who's to say, in any case, what the outcome will be? Some blessings cover a multitude of curses, and some curses overshadow a band of blessings. But all families under the sun have a generous share of them both…*all *families under the sun…*

And that is the poetry that rustles the great leaves of our Ancestral Trees.

Just before I continue with Christine's story, I would like to answer some queries, if I may? I hear these floating around all the time. What exactly are the Ancestors saying to their descendants? And why should anyone have to take on the sins of the father?

In answer to the first question, I will say some people do hear whisperings. And these are the voices of the Ancestors calling out to their kin. Although they speak from the past, they do not want their descendants to go back there! Oh, no! Quite the contrary. The Ancestors want their offspring to look upward (for that is where the help is), march onward, proceed forward, and liberate themselves from all the fears that once held them

back. The Ancestors' whisperings are an instinctive call…to remember…
Remember: you are the luscious green earth; it is rooted to your veins,
You are the cool, crushing water; it is calling out your name,
There is a fire that burns in you, yet, you are not at odds,
You were made to do all things,
Don't you know? Ye are gods,
Remember…

***

This brings me onto the second question. Why should anyone have to take on the sins of the father? This is a very good question, and I must say, not an easy one to explain. However, it is important that I do, as it weighs on the human soul. It was also the same question I asked right after I died and saw the world in its true form. I was given the answer then, and I'll tell it to you now…

What if I told you this cause-and-effect relationship was consciously set up—not to hinder, but to enrich life on earth? Take agriculture, for example; when a person tills the land, something happens, something grows. Here, is a brief illustration of a cause (someone working on the land) ending with an enriching denouement (someone reaping from the land). And I continue: from the love of two, will spring a love for many (children). And when we help a neighbour, it gives birth to a community, a place from which nations are formed…

This cause-and-effect relationship was established as a rewarding indication. A blueprint for how the world was intended to be. But as we can see, it doesn't always work as it

should. Not to say the mechanism is flawed, but rather, it can only be a tool of positivity, when positivity is applied. When the reverse happens. Well, I guess we call that life…
Lest we overlook, this relational structure is the superior mark of a creative intelligence, showcasing the wonderful symbiotic code to our creation. And that is: you can't have one, without the other, and one is always the result of the other…this intricate balance was set in place, so the world would understand it is in a relationship, hence, it does not work alone…
So then. If this dependency is the reason why we have consequences, why is goodness rewarded, you ask?
Earlier, I said my life on earth held too many questions and not enough answers. Please forgive me; it was an oversimplification. If you listen in carefully, of course you are able to obtain the answers you seek—I didn't say you would like them, though. But since you asked, I will answer you this: if the reward for 'goodness' isn't evidence of the 'divine,' then by Jove! I don't know what is! But lest I digress, let's get back to Christine's story.

Chapter Sixteen: Name that Tune

Christine

I approached the two nurses on reception. I hadn't thought through what I would say, I just knew I couldn't turn around now. "Hi there," I greeted the nurse nearest to me.

"Good afternoon. How can I help you?"

"I'm here to see Tobey Daley, his parents are expecting me."

"Tobey Daley?" The nurse drew a blank. She looked over to her colleague, who was probably the senior of the two as she replied my query. "Oh. You mean *sleeping cu*—Tobey. Have you been here before?"

"No…ermm…it's the first time…" I felt awkward. "Robert and Kelly Dal…" Before I could finish my sentence the security doors at the far end of the corridor issued a warning signal. Then the great big metal doors opened.

A woman stepped out. I recognized her from the papers, she was the mother of Tobey Daley.

At the same time Lydia joined me at the helpdesk. She had rushed back from her quick jaunt to the restroom.

"Kelly?" I called out to the woman heading toward the exit. This halted her in her tracks. She looked up.

"Are you Christine?" She sounded hopeful.

"Yes, I am. I spoke to your husband earlier. He asked me to come."

Kelly placed her hands over her heart as she thanked me for coming. "I really appreciate you making the journey. I hope I am not inconveniencing you in any way."

I shook my head. "Please don't apologize. I-I really don't know what it is I can do."

"It's alright, Christine. I'm not expecting miracles, I'm just so glad that you're here."

I made the introductions. "This is Lydia. Is it okay if she comes with us?"

"Of course, it's not a problem." Kelly smiled at Lydia. "He's in room 412. I'll take you to him now."

***

Just as I thought I didn't know what to expect. On either side of the hallway there were white-walled rooms with smaller-than-average babies lying in huge glass incubators. Some of the newborns napped under fluorescent blue lighting, while others shuffled and twitched as they absorbed the rays. It was so quiet. The only sound I could hear were the machines beeping in the background, and people talking in hushed tones. I soon realised it wasn't the grownups who were whispering, but it was in fact the premature babies whispering to their loved ones. Their voices were low, because some of the newborns were underweight, while others were just too feeble to speak up. I tried my best not to eavesdrop, it was only fair. After all they spoke about matters which did not involve me.

We soon arrived at Tobey's room. Kelly turned around to face us. "Just before we go in, I think I should prepare you. Tobey is very small and is unable to move because of his condition. He can't breathe, so he is on a ventilator. The tubes you see are the ones feeding him, helping him to breathe—keeping him alive," she sighed, "because of his fragility, he is also susceptible to germs, so we ask first-time visitors to wear a face mask. It's not compulsory, only if you feel you might have something which could be passed onto him, you know, like a cough or cold."

Kelly produced two synthetic mouth pieces from a fixture on the wall. Lydia and I accepted them without hesitation.

"We also ask that visitors sanitize their hands before going in, if you don't mind doing so."

We nodded.

"That's fine."

"That's okay."

I was overcome with immense pity. I could see Kelly was beyond exhausted; her pale skin was blotchy and lacked lustre, but the biggest giveaway were her eyes. They were so dim, I had to look three times to ascertain they were blue, as I had thought.

"Since the day he was born there have only been a handful of times where he's shown some kind of response to his environment." Kelly sighed again and smiled weakly. "On one occasion, after I sang to him,

I saw him blink a few times. I know he heard me. I think he liked the song." She looked to me. "I get the weirdest sensation that he knows *exactly* what's going on. I feel he wants to share something with me. I don't know how I know this—*I just know!* But the doctors say he's getting worse, not better. He grows weaker by the day…" She broke off. Her eyes watered. She looked back me. "I saw you mentioned in the papers…and…I just thought…I'd appreciate anything you do.

Please, just let me know if there's any way I can assist."

I followed Kelly into the ward while Lydia trailed a few paces behind us. The baby's room was brightly lit and warmed above room temperature. The area was bathed in disinfectant.

Kelly and Lydia dropped a further few paces back; leaving me to approach the bed where little Tobey Daley lay.

There were so many wires around the baby. He looked like a delicate rose nestled in a bed of thorns. I put down my bag and gripped onto the side handles around his bed. I took in his pale complexion and mousy brown hair, which was shiny for a baby of his age. Every strand of his hair groomed by his parents, no doubt. As expected, Tobey's eyes were closed. The laboured pull of the ventilation machine made me uneasy. I wondered how the parents coped seeing their little boy in this way. It was deathly quiet. Tobey appeared lifeless in his special bed. I didn't know what say. I began to feel the familiar waves of panic rising from the pit of my stomach. I looked back at Lydia.

“Are you okay?” she mouthed

I nodded. “I’m fine…I...errr…I can’t hear anything.”

Lydia stared back at me in bewilderment. “You can’t hear anything? Maybe try getting a bit closer?” The expression on her face said it all: if I didn’t have a clue, they didn’t have a hope! I pulled up a chair and leaned in, yet the silence remained.

The gift of hearing I found over the years, wasn’t something I could just switch on or off like an electric kettle. Receiving signals was like watching a person conversing with someone on the phone, and then finding that the distant voice on the other end had become louder. Until I was able to hear that voice just as clearly as the person taking the call. Only, in reality, the speaker has no idea that the baby—the one on the receiving end—was responding to everything that had been said to them. When a parent stares lovingly down at their newborn and tells them they love them, ninety-nine-point nine percent of the time, the baby always says it back. Nevertheless, in my experience there was still-like silence, and silence like death. And Tobey’s life was coasting toward the latter…

“Tobey. Tobey,” I softly called his name. “Can you hear me?”

Nothing.

I thought about waving his mother over but changed my mind. What if she came over and still—nothing? At this point, I didn't know who would feel worse: me for failing so quickly, or his mother for trying so hard.

Lydia noted the perplexity on my face. She looked to Kelly, who, without being told, rushed over to my side, "Is there anything I can do? Would you like to hold him?"

"Yes that might help." I got up from my chair and stopped. "Wait. Hold on a minute." I sat back down and reached for Tobey. Then I lifted him up, and rolled him onto his side, as though I were appraising a small antique vase. I then separated the Velcro buttons on his onesie, and stroked his pale back. For all the heat in the room, it was still not enough to warm Tobey's little body. His tiny left cheek was resting in the palm of my hand, which had a strange waxy coolness to it. I kept up with the strokes. Suddenly I felt something. A warm sensation flowed through my head. I continued to glide my hand up and down his body. I heard a slight rustling in the air. Different from the sucking sounds coming from the ventilator. Ever so gently the baby began to take in breath; it was only audible to me. My smile widened.

"Christine…" Tobey said. His voice was weak, but to me it was as welcoming as birds tweeting on a sunny morning.

"Yes, Tobey, it's me, sweetie…I'm here…" My gentle strokes imparted the words from my mind.

"Tobey, are you okay? How are you? How are you feeling?"
"I feel tired…so tired…my body aches all over. I-I don't like the drugs they're giving me, and they keep stabbing the bottom of my foot with something…sharp. It's so painful."
I fought back tears. "I'm so sorry Tobey," I cried. "They're doing this to keep you alive. Everybody wants you to live. Your parents want you to live!"
"I know." The corner of his mouth twitched. "I know they do. Their love for me has been my lifeline. I can't begin to describe to you just how *glorious* it feels! Oh, Christine. Please thank them for their love."
I gulped, touched by the urgency in his voice. "I will Tobey."
At that moment I remembered there were others in the room who had no idea what was going on and could not take part. "Tobey, hang on. I'll be right back!" I brought my strokes to an end and turned to face the others. "Kelly, Lydia!" My wide smile said it all, "I've made contact with Tobey. He can hear me! He can hear all of us!"
Kelly rushed over to the bed, "What did he say? Is he alright? Can he hear me now?" Tears of joy streamed down her face. Lydia looked relieved.
"This might be an odd request." I turned to the two women in front of me. "But would I be able to have a few moments with him alone? Don't take it the wrong way, I'm just thinking there's no need for the

pair of you to be hanging around, watching me looking at Tobey in relative silence, so to speak." I averted my attention back to Lydia. "I know how busy you are Lydia, but I also know you're too considerate to remind me," I said with a grateful smile.

"Very true." Lydia gave a short laugh and shrugged. "I suppose this is the part where I jump off, but if you need anything don't hesitate to call or text—I'll be over like a rocket!" I knew she meant every word. Lydia turned to Kelly. "Although it was brief, it was nice meeting you."

Kelly nodded.

"Your son's in good hands," Lydia said with a sympathetic smile, "I just hope going forward you get the answers you're looking for."

Following Lydia's departure, Kelly's phone rang. "It's Robert. I'm going to pop out and tell him the good news," She slipped on her cardigan. "We've also got some hospital matters to discuss, so I might be a while. Can I get you some tea or coffee?"

"No, I'm fine, thank you. Just take your time. I'll see you when you get back."

Kelly shut the door behind her. All was quiet again. I dashed back into my seat. I stretched out my hand and resumed stroking Tobey's small cotton-clad body. "Tobey. Can you hear me, sweetie? You can talk to me now; I'm here." The warm sensation permeated through my head again. And just like before, I could hear him straining to breathe. And then he did something amazing. He opened his eyes, not too wide, but enough to take me by surprise. I thought about calling out to his mother, I didn't know if he'd done this before.

"Hello, Christine. You came back," Tobey said through laboured breaths. I could hear the smile in his voice, but then his tone changed. "Christine. I have something to tell you. It's so awful! I don't know how to explain it!"

"I'm listening." I drew him closer to me.

"There's something going on in this hospital. Someone is doing something they shouldn't. The babies, they disappear."

"Disappear...?" I didn't get the chance to process what had just been said, for at that moment, the door swung open. One nurse and two male assistants bustled into the room. "Oh. Hello there," the only female amongst them voiced a greeting. "You're not Mrs Daley."

"No, I'm not. I'm a visitor. I came to see Tobey." I wasn't sure whether I should get up or stay put.

"Well." The nurse looked around the room. "It's time for the baby to be suctioned. His mother's usually around for this procedure."

"Ermm…I believe she's on an important call. She might not be able to make it back in time—can it wait?"

"Wait! Most certainly not! Left any longer the baby could choke to death on his own saliva. This procedure needs to be carried out on the hour, every hour. Mrs Daley is well aware of this fact."

Her response did not strike me as genuine concern, but I was ready to accept whatever the nurse had to say. "Very well." I moved out of their way. "I'll stay here with him." The nurse shot me a wry look.

"Are you sure about this?" She hesitated, "some people may find the procedure…a little…uncomfortable to watch."

"I'm sure it is," I swallowed my growing annoyance, "As I'm sure it's very uncomfortable for Tobey. So, if it's all the same to you, I think I'll stay." Before leaving Tobey's side, I reached out to stroke him again. "Would you like me to sing to you?" I asked, not knowing why I did so.

"Yes." His voice was shaky with tears. "Can you sing: 'Wheels on the Bus'? Do you know it?"

"Yes, I do." I smiled, recalling Jerry's gurgles as I sang it to him. "Is this the song your mummy sings to you?"

"It is. It's my favourite tune."

"Okay, I will sing it. I'll be right back, Tobey."

I was forced to make way as the attendants went to work. Throughout the whole ordeal, Tobey laid lifeless in the nurses' hands. He didn't utter a single sound. Well, not one anyone could hear.

Richard

Richard surveyed the small conference room, one of the few still in use at the sprawling hospital. He fixed his scornful gaze on the tall, grey-suited practitioner, whose curly hair clung to his scalp like a silvery woolly rug. He then peered ahead at the pot-bellied, olive-skinned physician, who was picking his nose and paying little attention to the ream of notes spread out in front of him. Then Richard cast his eye over to the right, where a clean-shaven platinum-haired consultant was taking sips from his cup as though it were vermouth on ice. *Maybe he wishes it was.* And there were many others in the room all pretending not to notice him, looking at them.

At this moment Richard had their full attention, which was just the way he wanted it.

It was the third time that year that this particular group had assembled. The first time was to discuss Tobey Daley's crippling condition. They had all agreed the baby was born with a rare form of *CMS*. One, the hospital had never encountered in all its history.

The second time was to discuss the introduction of palliative care. Heated debates were the norm of the day as they tried to find the best way to work with the boys' parents, who were desperate for answers—answers the specialists was finding difficult to provide. And now today, Richard pushed for another matter entirely. It was time to carry out the inevitable....

Highly sensitive cases such as Tobey Daley's, always involved outsiders descending on the hospital like vultures to an open carcass. These medical bureaucrats crunched through piles of laborious guidelines and legal documentation for no reason, Richard could perceive, other than to justify their asinine existence. Although, to be fair, it wasn't so much the duty they had to do which aggravated him so, but rather the type of morons they sent out to do it.

Nevertheless, Richard was confident he had the hospital's full support. Paul Healey, the administrator, was an insecure drunk. There wasn't anything the hapless man could suggest that Richard could not overturn. In time Paul became a smarter man; choosing to make Richard a useful ally, rather than a career-destroying foe. For Richard, Paul Healey proved to be the easiest person to get onside on all matters...

Susan Graham, on the other hand, was a little harder to persuade. She was the matron - or clinical nurse, as it referred to these days. She was a very hard person to please. But for reasons only known to herself, she was willing to end the charade and put the baby out of his misery.

As far as Richard was concerned, all those of importance to this case agreed. But now he had to rouse enough patience in himself to listen to these outsiders mull over and challenge his authority on this matter.

"For the fifth time, I am well aware of *The European Convention of Human Rights.*" Richard emphasized to the visitor on his left-hand side. "Nevertheless we believe stopping further treatment would not be a breach of his right to life." *Didn't they read the report?* "For baby TB to exist, he will first and foremost need to be able to carry out some basic functions, wouldn't you agree? Such as: coughing, reacting to stimuli, and breathing. The last, and most crucial of which, he is unable to perform without assistance. Over the last year, the baby has failed to exercise any one of these fundamental functions. And lest I add..." Richard impressed upon his audience. "Over the last few months, the baby has undergone a series of muscle biopsies and genetic testing, all of which have come up inconclusive."

"What about the use of Prostigmin?" It was a brave or foolish MD, to ask this kind of question while he was putting forward his findings. The visitor continued, "It's not the first time it's been proposed, and we cannot deny it has been used to treat *CMS* patients, albeit, not as young as this candidate, but overall the results were quite positive."

"Dr Birhmani, have you been reading your notes?" Richard cut in. Some of the visitors shuffled at his marked abruptness. "As I said earlier, the baby did not respond well to Prostigmin. As soon as we saw signs of distress, we discontinued use. We witnessed

similar reactions with the application of *Ephedrine* and *3,4-DAP*. Again, both trials had to be discontinued, and please!" he said without the slightest hint of humility, "no more talk of subjecting the patient to a tracheotomy, as some of you have mentioned. I believe the drilling of holes in the hope of facilitating breathing is at best an absurd fantasy made to give the parents nothing but a false sense of hope, and worse, a profound insult to our profession."
"An insult?" One of the specialists raised an eyebrow. "That's a tad bit harsh, don't you think? We're just having a discussion Dr Lawson, just a discussion."
Richard leaned back in his chair. "Look." He implored, feeling very much like the lawyer he gratefully did not become. "Our job is to prolong life, not to prolong death, and under the circumstances we're doing a bad job of both! Not that I care in the slightest what the media has to say on this matter, but our failings are starting to be an embarrassment to the hospital. Deep down, I believe the parents are under no illusions of their son's mortality. It is now up to us, the voices of medical reason, to stand firm and united on this matter. It is only then his parents will be confident in their private convictions and agree for us to take the necessary steps." Everybody nodded. He levelled his gaze at the varied team of medical professionals. "And the necessary steps need no further introduction. I believe we all know what they are…" He let the silence do the talking. "Right then, as soon as possible we will let the parents know

of our intentions to take Tobey Daley off the ventilator." Nobody said a word. "Once we have their full cooperation, we therefore request the motion for palliative sedation. We believe it's the best course of action in this particular incident."

Richard closed his folder. As usual he had won his case. Twenty minutes later, the discussion would draw to a close. And fifteen minutes after that, Richard would fall head-over-heels in lust for an auburn-haired beauty he spied roaming the hospital's hallways. Richard wasn't one to collect phone numbers, but that didn't stop him from staring. He watched as she gracefully moved around until she found herself a seat in the visitor's canteen area…

***

Lydia

For some unknown reason, Lydia didn't feel quite right about leaving the hospital. It wasn't a sense of foreboding that had blighted her mood, but more like the feeling she had left something of significance behind her…She looked ahead at the hospital's main revolving doors, which led out of the building and toward the busy intersections. As Christine pointed out it was the weekend, there was so much more she could be doing with her time. But ever since their meeting in Canary Wharf, she had made a promise to herself. She wanted to help Christine in any way she could. God knew the girl was going to need it—the world would think her crazy! Who would believe her? *Did she even believe her?* But the hardened cynic within had nothing to come back with. Christine was many things but crazy wasn't one of them. Although, the girl was extremely sentimental; most evident in the way she held that sick baby. *Oh, Christine, what are you like?*

Hospitals. Babies. Bereavement. Was not her idea of fun, especially, grappling with such weighty matters on a Saturday night. She had already missed a few calls from her circle of friends wanting to know if she would attend Tarquin's annual wine reception. The event always received a sizeable spread in the *Tatler.* At some point today she would have to get back to them, and her answer would be— *no!*

There were just some matters of true importance, and this situation just happened to be one of them. Before she could talk herself out of it, Lydia spun back around and headed toward the refectory. As soon as she found herself a seat, she texted Christine to let her know that she was waiting for her…

***

Christine

"The wheels on the bus go round and round, round and round, round and round, The wheels on the bus go round and round, all through the town..."

The suction machine choked and spluttered as it carried out its gruelling task. I had to remind myself the appliance was there to preserve life —and was not doing the opposite. Honouring Tobey's request, I sang the old nursery rhyme as sweetly as I could. I never faltered. Not once. Not even when it became too distressing to watch. No one who was fully in charge of their capabilities would be able to withstand the apparatus' violent intrusion. Tobey remained silent. His small arms flopped up and down as the machine went to work.

"There! All done!" the nurse announced. The two attendants connected Tobey back up to the ventilator. "His doctor should be dropping by later this afternoon to take a blood sample," the nurse smiled, "I see his mum has not returned. Do let her know about the doctor coming by, just in case she has some questions to ask him. It's always best to talk to the experts whenever you can catch them."

"Okay. I'll pass on the message." I drummed my foot on the floor, wishing they'd hurry up and leave, but it looked like the nurse wouldn't exit the room anytime soon. She potted around Tobey's bed. "Oh. And just a quick reminder." The nurse peered down at her watch.

"Weekend visiting times are shorter I'm afraid. Visiting hours are from 2.30 p.m. to 6.00 p.m. We'll be sending out a reminder around…quarter to..."

"Okay. Thank you." I nodded. *Now hurry up and leave!*

The nurse put a few things away in the drawers before exiting the room. I remained at Tobey's side until the door was closed behind them, then I pulled up a chair and caressed the back of Tobey's head. Just like before, I couldn't hear anything at first. I kept up with the strokes, humming a light tune as I went along. Then, ever so softly, I heard the scratchy feeble sounds of Tobey taking in breath. But that was all. It occurred to me that the baby had drifted off to sleep.

I sighed but remained seated at his side. I stroked him until his mother later joined us in the room.

"How's he doing?"

So absorbed in my own thoughts, I didn't realise how the time had flown. "Oh my god, it's five to six!" I gasped as I glimpsed the clock on the wall. I sprung up from my chair. "I guess I should be leaving now—*ow!*" My back groaned from the strain of crouching over Tobey's bed. "Kelly, I'm so sorry. I didn't get much time with him. Not long after you left the nurse came to give him his suction. After that…I think...he's fallen asleep, or so I believe…"

"That's alright." Kelly sighed. She gathered some items from the side table and placed them into her

bag. "To be honest, I prefer it when he sleeps. At least, then I know he's at peace…"
We walked toward the exit of the neonatal ward.
"Tobey says he's in a lot of pain," I gave Kelly a truthful update. "He also doesn't like the drugs they're giving him, and he *absolutely* abhors having his blood taken, it's—" I didn't finish my sentence.
Kelly's hands flew to her mouth.
"I know! I knew it! I could feel it! But what are we to do?" she cried. "We don't know what to do."
My heart sank. The worst part of being a parent, I recalled, was dealing with these sporadic episodes of helplessness. There were times when you just couldn't provide the assistance your child needed.
Say something positive.
I swallowed, "Kelly…Tobey loves you both so very much. He said when you hold him, he can feel the love—it's been his lifeline." Kelly's tears ran down her dry cheeks. I continued, "Just before the suction began, I asked him if he would like me to sing to him? He said yes. He wanted me to sing: 'The Wheels on the Bus.' He said you sing it to him. It's his favourite."
"Yes, that's right." Kelly burst into a smile. "That was the song I was singing to him when I saw him blink. Oh, my son! You really spoke to my son…"
I had already decided not to tell Kelly about the other matter. About there being: *'something wrong at the hospital'* I didn't want to worry her. And besides, if The Daley's allowed it, I would come back again at

least to find out what Tobey meant when he said: *'Someone is doing something they shouldn't…'* I didn't like the sounds of that. Come to think about it, I didn't like the sounds of most things, but when had that ever stopped events from happening…

On my way out of the hospital I paused to check my phone. I saw Lydia's text message and smiled. It took me longer than I estimated to find Lydia's whereabouts. I glimpsed her through the sea of diners, she had found herself a seat by the window at the back of the canteen. I selected a few items from the chiller, then made my way toward the check-out. "Now, Christine," Lydia said as soon as I sat in the seat adjacent to her, "Don't laugh, but last night I had a very strange dream. Do you think you'll be able to explain it to me?" Before I could refuse, Lydia launched straight into it, "I was looking up at a billboard, just randomly glancing…when…I heard a voice from behind me. I turned around. There was a man standing there. Now…this is the weird part. He said: *'try harder,'* he repeated this three times. The man was…honestly, I couldn't describe him to you, only suffice to say I have never laid eyes on him before in my life," she paused. "...well, I don't think I have…Anyway, he was far from menacing—if you catch my meaning. It was just…really…weird…a very bizarre dream. What do you make of it?" She broke out of her deep thoughts to face me.

"Sounds like a regular dream to me." I shrugged. I didn't know what else to add. I felt the urge to fight off laughter.

"Oh…so that's it? Thanks a bunch!" I looked on with amusement. Lydia chuckled. I was glad I wasn't the only one who found it funny.

"What did you expect me to say, Lydia? I'm not a psychic or a soothsayer or a mind-reader—or whatever the papers are calling me these days! *Who knows what I am?*"

"That's true." Lydia glanced down at the table. "What was I thinking?" Her long eyelashes fanned her cheekbones. She then looked up solemnly at me. "Actually…there is something I haven't told you…"

I noted the change and waited for Lydia to continue.

"I…didn't get around to telling you this before, but I'm related to someone…quite famous...."

"Famous?" I couldn't hide my puzzlement.

"Yes. My sister is Stephanie Downes…" Lydia paused, waiting for the information to sink in.

"Stephanie Downes, Stephanie Downes?" I repeated, at least to ascertain that Lydia wasn't mistaken and was indeed referring to: '*The*' Stephanie Downes—A-list celebrity, humanitarian crusader, wife of Oscar-winning director, Charles Lintz—'*Stephanie Downes*'

Before Lydia had finished nodding, my eyes widened as the realization hit me. *But of course!* I wasn't seeing Lydia for the first time. I'd spotted a face uncannily similar to Lydia's before: beaming from TV sets—splashed across magazines, accepting awards…

"Oh my god! She's your sister!"
"I know. That's what I said."
"W-what? Why didn't you tell me this before?"
"I-I don't know! It sounds silly, but I just forgot to mention it. I guess there were more important things going on." She gave a dismissive wave. We both smiled at each other now.
Well, it wasn't entirely implausible. I guess I did have other matters to contend with. But this piece of news was a little bit *out there*, and I thought I knew a thing or two about surreal situations. "Wow! So you have a famous sibling."
"I do indeed." Lydia gathered the tangerine peelings that were scattered like petals across the tabletop. She piled them into her empty Styrofoam cup.
"Although," she added with a surreptitious grin, "she is in fact my older sister and *'Stephanie Downes'* is her stage name. Her real name is Sophia, but she prefers Stephanie now." Lydia paused. "You are aware my sister is expecting, right? It's all the *bloody* tabloids talk about these days…*ahhhh,*" Her eyes lit up as though she was having a *'Eureka'* moment.
"Yes. Your sister's pregnancy." I gave a sly look at the obvious parallels. "I do believe I read that somewhere. I expect you'll be wanting me to have a chat with the baby as soon as it arrives. You know, ask if he or she had a comfortable journey, and how do they take their milk—that kind of thing?"
Our wayward laughter drew disapproving looks from the family seated nearby.

"I don't think that would be necessary, thank you very much!" Lydia giggled, wiping her eyes. "Why do I always tear up when I laugh? I look pathetic..."

I was glad Lydia had stayed behind. Seeing Tobey earlier, lying lifeless in his bed shook me more than I cared to let on. Right now I felt a little uplifted, so much so, I almost forgot to say what I wanted to share with her. "Lydia, the baby told me something!" All traces of humour had left my voice. "Just before he had his suction, he said there was something wrong at the hospital. Something about babies disappearing." I paused. "I don't know, but I get the feeling he was very frightened."

"Babies? Disappearing?" Lydia pulled a face. "That doesn't sound too good."

"I know. Tobey's mum said I could come back again to speak to him. I think I will."

Lydia sounded a little wary. "Are you sure you're up for this?"

"Yes...it is a bit...difficult..." I mumbled, "But, if there is something wrong, I guess here is where I can be of help."

It was gradually growing darker outside, yet, the two of us remained seated in the emptying canteen. We sipped our hot beverages and indulged in the odd bit of celebrity gossip.

"It's not gossip, Christine, if one's own sister offers clarification on matters." Lydia guffawed at my gaping expression of surprise. "Yes, my dear. This is what happens behind closed doors, and that is how it has always been…"

Chapter Eighteen: Diligence Pharmaceuticals

Siba

From my many sojourns around the globe, I could confidently tell you that large pharmaceutical companies, tend to be tucked away in highly secured compounds. Although, I see the executives at Diligence Biopharmaceuticals have chosen something, altogether a little different for themselves. It seems this company has no desire to make their presence known to the general public, well, not in a visual sense…Diligence, as they are referred to, is a covert establishment. And like most elite circles, the power behind such secrecy is astonishing.

Headquartered in picturesque Geneva, Diligence draws little attention to itself, and even fewer visitors. There were no guards on lookout, only one senior citizen ready to assist individuals waiting to enter the luscious country grounds. In truth, the red-bricked estate, was more like a residence than an Institution. However, its façade sheltered one of the most advanced laboratories ever built in the twentieth century. Inside the facility, rows and rows of anaerobic cabinets gleamed and shone like toy soldiers made of steel.

Despite the spacious surroundings, there were not that many employees who worked on the site. The international mix of biotechnologists, chemical engineers, biologists, and geneticists were all sectioned into small groups and confined to various parts of the building.

The great minds who worked for Diligence had very little to complain about. They were paid well for the job that they did and worked in very agreeable conditions. There were no synthetic communal green areas for these bright minds. Oh, no!

The nature that surrounded them was authentic. Every day, as the employees glanced out of their expansive screen windows, they were gifted with the cool serenity of The Lake Geneva, and the snow-dusted caps of the great Swiss Alps. Professor Florian—the owner of this prestigious Institution—wanted it no other way. Facing his colleague, and his wife of forty years, the Professor placed his coffee cup down in front of him and picked up his diamond-studded fountain pen.

"Just before we get started, what news is there of our *Alpha Stem Cell Study?"* The Professor directed the question to his colleague, Bernard, who was a decade younger than his sixty-eight years. Bernard shifted in his chair, "Yes…about that…" he replied with a hint of a German accent. "I was going to bring this up. One of our operatives in London, Richard Lawson, is a little uncomfortable with the media attention his hospital is attracting." He slowed down.

"Naturally, this could shine a spotlight on the work he's doing for us, he—"

"I do believe the candidates we selected were well-aware of the risks," the Professor cut in. "If my memory serves me—all, but one, said they were equal to the task. Tell me Bernard, your fellow in London isn't getting cold feet now, is he? Not when we're nearing our target." The Professor levelled his piercing blue eyes at his colleague. They were clear for a man of his advancing years. "A physician of his, said, capabilities should be able to work well under pressure, whatever that may be. What is it, Bernard? Is it more money he's after?"

"No. I don't think that is the issue here…" Bernard stared into his half-drunken espresso. "Anyway, let us not worry about this for now. I'll be travelling to London at the end of the week. I'll have a chat with him then, and maybe a little look around." He downed the last dregs of his coffee and lifted his notes from his briefcase.

The Professor looked over at his colleague. "I'm glad you're making this trip. I must say, this bit of news has put me at ease. *The Alpha Stem Cell Study* is an important one for the company, it may even supersede the findings from the *ERS report*—our greatest achievement yet. Most surely the biomedical breakthrough of the century. Wouldn't you agree, Bernard?"

Following a brief pause Bernard nodded. "Yes, that is correct. But if I may add, the *ERS* report was a success only because the world's largest Food and Beverage Company had acquired the patent for it. I agree, the report did unearth some interesting findings, many of which we had suspected all along. But to call it the biomedical breakthrough of this century…?" He grinned. "I don't believe it is; they'll be more interesting findings to come."

The Professor looked back at him; there was a creak of a smile. "You are quite right Bernard. I don't know what has gotten into me. I think I am getting impatient in my old age." All of them, including the Professor's wife, laughed at this comment. They knew it was far from true; the Professor had *always* been an impatient man.

Bernard ground out his slender cigar and continued with the run-down from the list he was reading off. "Just to inform you, we've received the results back from our HIV vaccination field trials in DRC. It turns out this batch is more dynamic than the Lockland Cure of '98," Bernard paused, "but Elias," he said slyly, referring to the Professor by his first name, "you knew it would be."

"Yes. But we're going to have to put a lid on it for now. We don't need this getting out, since we've just patented the latest batch of antiretroviral."

"No problem. And what about the test results from our cancer research trials? Again, they were very positive. Full recovery estimated within two weeks from the detection of the disease."

"Bury it!" The Professor's response was gruff and precise. "As we speak, our advanced chemo treatments are being shipped to the four corners of the world. We can't afford to let this one slip by like some of the others." His eyes, calculating events, were fixed on the recently shorn grass. "We need to leave enough time to formulate a solid financial strategy." The Professor sat up and clicked his fingers. "After this meeting, get Clive on the phone. We'll need to brief him and the rest of the board. But for now…no popping the champagne corks, nothing gets out until further notice."

Bernard leant forward, he tip-tapped on his keyboard. The Professor added. "Before I forget, do you remember that health official who was sticking his nose in where it wasn't wanted?"
"The man from The WHO?"
The Professor nodded. "Yes. That busybody. We deployed our prototype radioactive agent on the subject. It was quite a messy affair, as you will remember. However, the resulting brain tumour was 100 percent inoperable." The Professor grinned. "But here's the good part; not only did it bring an end to his irritating investigation, following our live field tests last week, we were given the greenlight from the boys in the lab to commercialize the agent. I'm due to talk to some of our government agency partners in the week."
"This is great news, Elias."
"I know. This brings us up to how many orders so far? I think we're exceeding our targets set for this year."
"Speaking of partners." Bernard narrowed his eyes as he skim-read the document on his laptop. "We have another order from our friends from the East. Can you believe they are asking for more Ferronium?"
"More? What in heavens do you suppose they're doing with it?"
"I don't know. Something to do with energy, I think. But I could always find out."

The Professor shrugged and looked away. "What is Ferronium? If not a tonic with less healing properties than tap water." He chuckled.

"But it's cheaper to harvest than tap water."

"That it is, Bernard. That it is. So without further delay, let us put this order through. Also, inform them there is going to be a 30 percent increase in the price due to import taxes and the rest. Don't worry, they'll pay. They always do." The Professor cleared his throat. "I guess this brings us to the end of today's round-up. We will meet again in a fortnight."

"Why the grin, Elias?" Bernard looked curiously back at him.

The Professor leaned back and wagged his finger. "I've just got a really good feeling about The Alpha Stem Cell Study. I think it's the one we've been waiting on."

"Good thing I'm off to see our contact in London. He will need to explain to us what the delay is all about."

"Yes, I trust you'll take care of matters in London. Enjoy your trip, Bernard."

"Thank you. I always do."

"Ah, yes. I remember Dr Lawson," the Professor's wife said with a purr. She had been silent for most of the discussion. She gave her husband a lingering smile. "Isn't he the rather dashing, albeit mildly-manic-depressed medic who has developed quite a liking for painkillers?"

"Yes, he's the one." The Professor smiled off his jealousy.

"Highly driven, extremely gifted…but…a little unbalanced."

"Unbalanced!" Her eyebrows shot up. "That's putting it mildly. In Italy we call them *svitato,* darling. But you are quite right, he is one of a kind. The best of them always are." She turned her perfectly coiffed, dyed-red hair, to take in the grounds around her. She laughed softly, as if milling over a private joke. "The best of them always are…"

The woman's gentle laughter emanated across the clearing, and around a large, marble statue, which loomed over the premises. It was of the great Swiss social activist, Jean Henri Dunant. His presence on the grounds was by no means a coincidence, as Dunant was the well-known Ancestor of the Professor, himself. As it was only a statue, it could not hear the woman's playful laughter. But Jean Henri Dunant was no statue—he is all spirit now, and he can clearly see events. Not that it made a difference, mind. He can only look on, as all Ancestors do…

Chapter Nineteen: Another Trip. Another Story…

Christine

I was sat up in my bed facing my small TV set, which my mother had gifted me a few Christmases ago. The television presenter wore brightly coloured clothing, and seemed to be talking at a hundred miles per minute. He interviewed a celebrity hotshot that evening. I laughed at some of the gags being delivered; it had been a while since I had felt this relaxed.

Something has shifted.

I knew I was a long way off from being healed, but as thinly as it was, a salve had been applied to the wound.

'You should go and see a counsellor—it's free! And it'll do you some good.'
'Yes…but counselling won't bring my son back.'
'No. it won't, Christine…but in time…it could bring you back…'

The closing credits rolled to a fade. I lowered the volume and padded barefoot into the kitchen. My mission: to rescue a box of half-eaten cherries from decomposing in the fridge. It was one of the few edible items I had left in there.
I peered into the refrigerator and knew my mother had been in it. There were Tupperware dishes crammed full of food, with packets of crap I had no desire to cook. My mother's plan to fatten me up was dying a slow death, but my mother had the spare key

to my flat, and so she persisted with this pointless replenishing exercise.
My considerable weight loss disturbed my mother greatly. What could I say? Grief had many faces—and it appeared it did whatever it liked to the body…I thought of Jerry's father then…Andreas Chairo…

At first, when I heard the news, he was coming to the funeral, I was unsettled. To me, the damage had already been done. Andreas had abandoned the marriage and had no desire to raise his child. Hence, to hear that he wanted to pay his respects, when there wasn't any to start with, felt like a heavy-handed slap in my face. In his own angry words, he had said marriage was: 'A social construct…a pointless act…' So in my opinion, how was a funeral any different…?

I felt bereft all over again. I didn't want to face him. But it turned out his presence at the burial held more significance than I realized…
On the day of the funeral, I saw Andreas in all his glory. Except, on that day, I noticed that he didn't have any. Seeing Andreas through grief-stricken eyes had somehow worn the sheen off him a bit. Andreas no longer stood out like he was the last man on earth. On that day, he shuffled around in the background, not in control of himself—or any situation. When Humphrey Bogart said in the movie, Casablanca*: 'It doesn't take much to see that the problems of three little people don't amount to a hill of beans in this crazy world'—I felt our situation was even smaller than that. The once-almighty Andreas had become one, amongst a small group of men. And I grasped that I too had now become one, amongst a few. Just a*

person in despair. No longer his woman. No longer his tears…from a distance we watched each other without staring, both seeing that our love bond was no more. It had combusted and dispersed like a shower of confetti. We were no longer bound to the love we once shared. We were free to move on, as it were, or at least, move away, both knowing that we could meet up a hundred times afterwards, but that very moment, that very day, marked the end of our short-lived love affair.

And that was that! I was free to talk about my doomed marriage with all the zeal of a stoic, and the experience of the wretched. Like all star-struck lovers, we had our time. And now…I didn't feel like eating cherries anymore. I closed the fridge door and headed for bed.

Before drifting off my last thoughts were of Tobey Daley. I recalled his soft skin; his cute voice, and his amazing head of hair, which smelled of jasmine and orange flower. Tobey seemed a lot worldlier than some of the babies I had conversed with. I was looking forward to seeing him again. In the meantime I could only hope the dangers he spoke of were more imagined than real.

***

Tobey

On the other side of the universe Tobey awoke to warm kisses on his forehead, and the sweet symphonic sounds of baby paradise. '*Yay!*' He was back in the land of Love…

On his previous travels, Tobey had learnt that there were three stages of babyhood, and thus, three wonderful realms which babies resided in…

The first realm was called: *The Primary Path.* A paradise

far away from where he was now—or so he had been informed. He was told humans in their early post-conceptions stages, lived there. He also learnt the babies living in *The Primary Path* participated in plenty of Wisdom Calls, much like what they were experiencing in the *Birth Trail.* Those babies also decided what their names would be when they arrived on earth. Once agreed the names were sent out like freshly released doves to the world and to their intended parents.

Whispered in the mind…engraved in their hearts…

To this day, many guardians labour under the mistaken belief that they choose their babies' names. But of course, this is not the case. It is the babies who decide, along with a little help from members of their family tree…

The next paradise was *The Birth Trail.* Where Tobey and his soul mates resided *(in medical terms, this period is referred to as the third trimester)* Tobey was told that the paradise he was in was the most anxiety-ridden stage of them all. It was the penultimate plane. After here, those who were fortunate would enter earth, where they'd be given the chance to carve out their names on their *Ancestral Tree*, or failing that, they ended up facing *The Fears…*

However, Tobey later learnt that some babies did neither. Instead, they went onto another stage referred to as the *Island of Lights…* Tobey was never told why some babies were permitted to go directly to this plane. But he understood all too well why they wanted to be there. This stage was the best of them all!

According to various reports, the paradise was nothing short of spectacular! It was a place reserved for babies and very young children who had lived on earth, but only for a short while. Those young ones were given the best in everything. It was never spoken, but this place was revered in the highest esteem, because it was the place where *The Creator of Love* spent most of its time…

There were other realms Tobey was later told about, but these were places where people went to after they had passed childhood, and had completed their journey on earth. It seemed, everyone Tobey met knew very little about these other dimensions, including the Ancestors who came to visit him. Tobey supposed, like the rest of the babies, when their time came, they would just have to experience it for themselves.

Tobey was called to the tree again. He flew toward it as fast as his newly charged body could carry him.

A beautiful woman sat on the throne-like chair. Her skin was as smooth and as shiny as a freshly earthed chestnut. Also, he noted his Ancestor's hair did not lie flat but rose from her head like soft billows of brown smoke. "Hello, Tobey." She smiled as she examined him. "How are you, little one? It's so good to finally meet you."

Tobey, feeling at ease, let his happiness pour through his smile. He sat at her feet. Whenever his Ancestor spoke, a gust of air soared up inside him. It felt as though he had awoken into a dream.

"My name is Kaori of the Manami family. I was born in Togo in West Africa, in a village not too far from the capital." She grinned at him. "Although Kaori is my birth name in later years I would be called Elizabeth Johnson..."

Tobey was enamoured with Kaori's voice; it was like listening to a live orchestra—there were so many different levels at play. His Ancestor wore a robe which glistened with all the colours of the rainbow, and placed on her head was a majestic crown that dazzled like a vibrant city. Of all his Ancestors' glorious features, Kaori had the most captivating brown eyes: pure, and all-knowing, the best he had ever seen! He listened intently as his Ancestor continued with her storytelling, "My dear son, a lot happened to me, or rather, a lot took place before the changing of my name." Kaori paused, then smiled again at him, "Are you ready, Tobey?"

"Yes, I am Kaori," he replied without a moment's hesitation. He sat still as he absorbed the rich tones in her voice, and the force radiating from her eyes. Kaori Manami began to relate the tale of her life as a farmer's daughter…

***

The year was 1824. Kaori was considered one of the most blessed girls in her village. After all, her family owned some of the most productive lands in the district, which, in those times, was akin to owning the world! The soil glowed red with richness, and year after year, their crops never failed nor faltered. To those around them, it was nothing short of miraculous! It was with little surprise that her clan drew envious stares from distant family members and villagers alike...

'You have the full blessings of your Ancestors behind you,' many would say to Kaori's father whenever they glimpsed his bounteous harvest. Kaori chuckled. 'And do you know what, Tobey?' she said with an arching smile. 'It turns out they were not too wide off the mark.' She laughed before continuing with her story. 'Through trading with the local merchants, my family soon came to own some of the finest things in the whole village. We exchanged our crops for many exquisite items; instruments made out of pure bronze,

copper, gold and other shiny metals. We were given pots of many sizes, some for cooking, and others for storage. And the women in our family received hordes of pretty beads, shells, and precious stones. Things, our unsated eyes had never seen, as they were mined in neighbouring countries or came from far off shores. Little did my people know, that I'd be venturing there myself one day...'

Kaori told Tobey about the time when some of her father's enemies broke into his compound. They approached when all the men had gone off into the bush. They dragged Kaori away, along with other women and children from her kin. They took them to a stately wooden mansion by the sea...

'I had heard about this place before. It was a two-story building where merchants and some white traders met to conduct their businesses.' Kaori knew she would never return home. She had heard that those who were dragged into that mansion never were freed. Kaori feared for her life, but more so for the young children who wailed all around her. She was later grateful that none of the little ones from her village had survived the journey to the other lands. The hardship waiting for them there, was the source of Kaori's nightmares right up until the very end…Kaori looked bigger than her twelve years, but every night she cried like a baby. She was now locked in a darkened room and chained to its floor, wishing she could turn back time. She longed for her life in the village; the abundance of trees, the women

singing as they cooked, the men pressing palm kernels with the soles of their feet, and the scent of moist roots in the air, which reeked with all the life that lurked in the riverbeds. If Kaori could only be allowed to return home, she would never again curse the stench of rotting fruit or gutted fish, which she used to deride with such childish disdain. Kaori would never abhor these odours again, for the smell of hopelessness and despair was far too harrowing to describe, but from that day onwards, her young senses would be forced to comprehend. *'I was subjected to a strange and powerful law, Tobey. A law that said my kind was not human…we all listened to this law, which proclaimed to know all…"* She smiled and shook her head, as though she were watching children fight over small toys. *'But how wrong they all were, Tobey. How wrong they all were. They did not know the first thing about love… '* With a light sigh Kaori turned away from the memory and continued: *'No sooner did my feet touch Barbados' clean shores, people started to call me Elizabeth. I didn't fight it. A new name was more than apt for this new life I had entered into. You see, above all else, my time in Saint Lucy was a lonely one. Many of the other slaves were gathered from the same region, and thus shared the same mother tongue. They did not speak the ancient language of Ewe, the only one I knew and longed to hear.'*

As a result, many of the inhabitants were free to comfort each other during some of the most harrowing times. But when such events befell the likes of Kaori, she would sing. She sung to the mothers, who were separated from their children; to the injured, and at times to herself, especially, when she lost two of her babies in infancy—and later their father to fever. Her name spread amongst the neighbouring plantations.

'Ironically Tobey, I became the sweet voice of tortured souls. The pain in my heart never sounded so sweeter in rhyme.'

Kaori was called to sing in front of everyone: lords and ladies, governors, merchants and their wives. She was even called to sing to the sick, and of course, the dying…

In 1834, freedom came to the little island in the West Indies. Kaori had planned to leave the plantation, but her singing abilities were in demand. She soon found she was able to keep afloat by working as a part-time singer and a general house maid. But just as destiny took her to foreign shores, so would love. Her intended-husband-to-be, Percival Johnson, was an ambitious African sailor. He wanted to travel to the UK. He had heard there were numerous jobs springing up on Cardiff's busy shipping ports.

Whilst at sea, Kaori was reminded of the journey she had made over fifteen years ago.
'My birthplace became like a dream to me. And just like a dream, when I woke up, I was unable to go back to it....I don't know why I felt that way, but the feeling never changed....I never did find my way back home...'

On her passage across the choppy Atlantic Ocean, Kaori developed a severe case of seasickness. *'It was the*

most distressing of ailments, which would stay with me for the rest of my life.'
Many of her descendants would also be afflicted with this dreaded condition...

Kaori was taken in by Cardiff Bay. Although it was, somewhat, disorderly and bitterly cold, it was far better than the horror she had painted in her mind's eye. It was a stark contrast from the warm and sunny climes of Barbados, but she didn't mind it too much, in fact, she was grateful for the change.

That night, she hugged her betrothed even tighter. A decision had been made. This was the place she would start over, have children, and live out the rest of her days.

And just as she said, the children came. And her children had children. And their children had children. Naturally, Kaori did not meet them all. Not on earth.

In her later years, Kaori learnt to read music. She became a respected music teacher. Respected, more so, for some of the good decisions she made. For it happened that out of her meagre means, Kaori made it a mission to teach the poor about the joy of music. No financial demands were placed upon anyone who showed up at her door with only the simple desire to learn.

After life, Kaori would hear the fate of some of the pupils she had taught. And what she saw filled her with jubilation. Through her life's work, many of her students and their offspring, were able to create a positive impact on the world's stage. Some were good; some did well, and some were even successful. But all of them bestowed honour on their Ancestral Trees...

Kaori was seventy-one-years old when she died—three years after the death of her husband. Her children gave her a small burial, just as she had requested. She was dressed in her favourite navy-blue Sunday gown. And in her hand, someone had placed a string bracelet made up of tiny shells and exotic beads. They had belonged to Kaori, and now they were buried with her, just as she had requested....

Kaori Manami had three strapping sons. They later settled down with the local women of the city, and produced offspring. These children married locals too. And what was once distant and exotic, appeared white again.

***

Tobey burst with questions. "Kaori! Kaori! When I enter the world I want to sing just like you!"
Kaori laughed her special laugh. "If you want it, Tobey—then it's yours, my darling! Everything I have is yours, and only you can make it so. Through the ages, the story of my family was somehow lost. But as you enter the world, just like the many that had come before you, your skin will be as white as any of those from our Nordic brethren. But those brown eyes you have decided to take on, they are not

just brown eyes," she said with a knowing smile, "they are *my* brown eyes."

"I know," Tobey beamed. He couldn't disguise his immense pride, "If I can see the world the way you saw it, and yet remain all the more stronger and dignified, then I'll be a great survivor, just like you."

"Oh Tobey! You really are a wise one," Kaori said with delight, "I wish you a great journey ahead. May you be richly rewarded, as I have been."

Tobey remained by the tree long after his Ancestor had ended the *Wisdom Call*. He wrestled with the idea, but he eventually made the decision to take the disorientating trip through *The Corridor of Revelations* He wanted to refresh his memory on what the doctor at the hospital was up to.

Also, as is often the case with babies, Tobey had forgotten a huge majority of what he had seen. However, Tobey was not to know this, but he was yet to face another obstacle when he resumed his talks with Christine. As it goes, the names of all the newborns could only be mentioned in this realm alone. No baby could utter the name of others, including themselves, until they had fully entered the world, and had been given their names by their rightful guardians…But that was a quandary scheduled for later down the line. For the moment, Tobey was in paradise. And while there, he would enjoy the little peace he had left until the red shadowy manifestation in the sky came to claim him, once again…

Chapter Twenty: Tobey Tells All…

Richard

Before noon Richard had overseen; nine ventouse deliveries, seven eco-pregnancies, five forceps, four breach-births, and two C-sections. By the end of his shift, those figures had almost doubled. Richard was glad to get to the end of the day. He drove home as fast as the limits would allow and headed straight for the shower.

It took him awhile to relax. His mobile rang, he saw right away it was not a work call. The German accent that greeted him got straight down to business. Seconds passed as Richard listened to what the caller had to say. He nodded a few times, although there was no one around to witness it.

Ten minutes later the call was over. The time was now 8.pm; his M&S dinner for one was humming away in the microwave. Richard surveyed his surroundings, everything was going to plan. Just one more thing. He headed toward the back of the kitchen. He rustled around in one of the cupboards until he found what he was looking for. It was a small glass bottle of CNS depressants. He gulped down two pills with his orange juice and walked over to the kitchen window.

The blinds were drawn but he could still see outside very clearly. Then, just as he was expecting, a silver Mercedes SLK crunched its way onto the drive. It was Dr Henrietta Metcalfe. Richard continued to study her through the blinds. He smiled. He was glad to see she had made an effort for him. Her hair, which shone, was the colour of coal and was pulled in a high chignon—just the way he liked it. And her face appeared flushed with make-up. He grinned again. He liked the way this young medic took hints and was desperate to please, much like a pup with a new owner. Sometimes he found himself looking forward to their little encounters. It gave him the opportunity to air his observations on some of his favourite topics, naturally; stem cell research and the complexities of bioengineering.

Richard didn't have many friends, but even if he had, he wouldn't have said anything to them. He found it easier to talk to the women who shared his bed. Although, with Henrietta he had to admit he was taken back by her inquisitiveness. Not only pertaining to work, but also matters outside of medicine. Etta was much more than a pretty face, he saw, all the more reason why he had to be more guarded when he was around her. She was indeed a very intelligent girl, but still no match for him.

Just before she was about to ring the doorbell, Richard opened the front door. He looked on at her surprised expression, "What have you done to your hair?" he coolly remarked.

Etta didn't reply with words, if it were possible, the smile she responded with almost outshone the lights at the front door. He spoke again. "Well, are you just going to stand there or are you going to come in?"

“I’m coming,” she gave a nervous giggle and entered the hallway, “Mmmm, something smells nice. Did you make us dinner? Really, Richard, you shouldn’t have...”

Christine

Ping!

I had just received the message I had been waiting all week for. The Daley's had invited me back to speak with their son again—I didn't have to be asked twice!

Forty minutes later I was stood outside St Margaret's Hospital Trust. I thrust myself into the crowded lift. It looked like I wasn't the only one in a hurry; a rather tall and stoic-faced medic brushed passed me and exited the premises.

Four floors up, I approached Tobey's bed. He was rock-still. It was hard to believe this little body held life, but it did as I was very well-aware of.

Today, Tobey wore a blazing-red onesie covered in big bright yellow spots. *Loud and cheerful clothing for a depressing situation!* I couldn't blame his parents, if Tobey was my child I'd do the same. I drew up a chair, leaned in and stroked Tobey's fragile back. Moving very gradually, I caressed the top of his head then worked my way back down again. I noticed his breathing was much more laboured than the last time I saw him.

"Hello, Christine. You came," he whispered. "Thanks for coming to see me."

"That's okay, sweetie. How are you feeling today?"

"I feel wonderful," he croaked, "besides the ever-present taste of poison in my mouth, the skins of my feet feeling like they've been doused in fire, and having painfully hard tubes being inserted, and re-inserted into my body. But besides all that—I feel great!" We both softly chuckled. I knew he was only making light of his most obvious discomfort.

"Tobey. I'm here to listen to whatever you have to tell me. You said something about danger..."

To the best of his ability Tobey told me all about his life in the outer world.

"You see, no one leaves and comes back again," he said of his special status in paradise, "It seems I'm the only one of my age taking these amazing trips between these two realms."

"And in this other world? Are you all floating around like spirits, or do you possess the bodies you have now?"

"No. We are not spirits. At least, I don't think we are. But we are able to move around easily and venture into different spheres, like *The Corridor of Revelations*. It was there I saw a man. He's a doctor here at the hospital." Tobey paused. "He's doing something, but I don't understand what. All I can tell you is that he sits at the entrance of those coming into the world, and that entrance leads to their death. Some of these little ones end up dead at his hands, and it's no accident! He's killing them. He's already killed…" Tobey stopped talking, his voice was too shaky to go on.

We were interrupted by Tobey's father who came in to ask if I wanted a hot drink. I declined.

"I'm heading back to work now," Robert said. "Kelly should be along shortly. Are y—"

"Don't worry, I'll be fine with him. And Robert, he's doing okay today. He says he loves you both."
Tobey's father looked back at me with a tearful smile before leaving the room.
"Christine. Does the Creator of Love roam around here, on earth?" Tobey asked.
I detected the merriment in his voice. To say I was a little thrown by the question was putting it mildly. When it came to the matter of religion, I didn't quite know where to place myself.
"I-I think...it's a little different over here..." I hesitated, but then I decided to answer truthfully, "Tobey. I don't think this Creator you talk of could live here on earth. I don't think it could...not the way we live…"
"That's odd," Tobey sounded a little befuddled. "The Creator of Love said we could find it everywhere and, in all things, even on earth. There isn't any place the Creator cannot venture to—it can go anywhere and believe me Christine—" The joy had returned back to his voice. "You are happier than the happiest when it's nearest to you!" His laughter sounded as though he floated on a raft of bubbles, "I've heard while they are asleep some of the wee ones go and visit the Creator of Love. Did you know that?"
"No, I didn't," I smiled, of course I didn't know this. On speaking with Tobey I realized there were many things I didn't know. However, I felt myself become still. I began to breathe ever so slightly. It was the kind of calmness that comes over a person when they

know they're about to hear something of great importance to them.

"Sometimes the wee ones are permitted to visit *The Island of Lights*. I hear all the babies that visit want to stay there, and occasionally some of the babies are allowed to…can you believe that?" Tobey gasped.

"Unlike the rest of us, these little ones didn't have to undergo the earth journey, but they still ended up in the best place of them all! How lucky are they?"

There was silence.

"Christine…Are you still there…? Are you...smiling?" He sounded a little bemused.

"I am, Tobey." My teardrops ran with such a force they soaked through the collars of my blouse. I dabbed the sides of my face with a scanty pocket tissue, "I'm smiling for Jerry, that's all. I'm just smiling for Jerry…"

"But why?"

I breathed in, "Because my dear, my son has gone to the only place I guess everyone else is dying to be…"

"Oh…" Tobey fell silent. He took a moment to bask in Christine's peace. "I hope I get to meet your son one day," He perked up. "I suppose that all depends on how my journey pans out. But at this moment: I have a life, I have a purpose, and I'm excited about fulfilling it."

"Excited?" I looked around the sterile room, "I can't see why, Tobey? This is it! This is life!" *This is YOUR life!* I yelled, although, I didn't dare say it out loud.

"Aren't you scared?"

"Scared? No. We babies are fearless! We already know the truth about this world."

"And that is?"

"Everything is a lie…"

I stared at him in disbelief. "Everything is a lie…well, that's a fine way to begin your journey on earth."

"No—no! I don't mean to sound pessimistic," Tobey responded, but my Ancestors said when you understand this simple truth, you are better placed to find love. For you see, in paradise it is all around you, but here we have to look for it, and we have to find it, because we need it. We need it like we need air. It's strange, but it seems we forget what love is and what it looks like."

"Love? And what exactly is that anyway?"

"It's mercy, Christine. Love is mercy. It's doing the unexpected - or more than the expected, because you have the ability, and it's within your power to do so. The question is: can you do so?"

"Can I do so?" I blinked. My eyes narrowed like bits of flint, "Can I show mercy? Tobey…" I couldn't keep the bitterness from seeping out of my voice. "I am not some godlike being, why should I extend mercy?"

"Godlike? No, Christine—you mean *'Love-like.'* In this world, in your life, and in your everyday thinking, you will always be in a position to extend mercy, because that is what love is, and that is what love does…" He paused to take in a raspy breath. "Christine, the act of mercy is a formidable power; a tremendous contribution to this world, and a wonderful fulfilment of our purpose in life."

"Mercy?" My face crumpled into a sneer. "Do you mean like forgiving someone who has *deliberately* set out to destroy you? How's that mercy? That's not mercy, Tobey—that's unfair! If love is all about mercy, then I'm better off without it!"

What had gotten into me today? Inside, I was a swirling vortex of anger, bitterness, and pain. If the baby couldn't see the hopelessness of his situation—*then by god! At least I'll feel it for him!* I couldn't help it. Tobey's situation was beyond tragic, and here he was banging on about mercy.

"Oh, Christine! Love has not forgotten you, but you have certainly forgotten who you are. Is this what happens to us then?" He sounded all but defeated. "Now that I'm on this journey I've got to be where Love is. I've just got to be! No matter what happens or what I face, I hope I never forget that." He paused. "If you remembered, Christine, you wouldn't want to be anywhere else."

I let my eyes rest on the baby's bleached cotton sheets. "How can I be where Love is?"

"By being it," Tobey replied. .He suddenly began to choke. I flew into panic mode. The sound of someone fighting for breath is never pleasant, especially coming from one so young.

"It's happening again," Tobey said in between gasps for air. "Call for help!"

I made a mad dash for the emergency button. A few seconds later a female nurse and two male attendants flew into the room.

"Is everything okay?"

"Quick! Quick! Do something!" I cried. "He needs help!"

The three attendants turned to the motionless lump lying on the bed. They looked back to face me. I couldn't understand the delay.

"Well...that's obvious," the nurse drawled.

"No. I mean—he's struggling to breathe!" I almost screamed at the woman. The nurse continued to glance at me but the expression on her face had turned to one of impatience. It looked like she was about to say something when one of the helpers spoke up.

"Oh, look! It's coming up to the hour." He pointed to the clock on the side table. "It's almost time for the baby to be suctioned. It's a good job we're here now." He circled around the ventilator to get to the top of the bed.

"Yes! Yes! That must be it!" My relief was audible. "Go quickly! He really is struggling to breathe." The nurse shot me another wry look but said no more. She began to make preparations for the task ahead.

I paced up and down the room. The helpers' pedestrian movements grated on my nerves to no end.

But who could blame them? After all they couldn't see what was going on in Tobey's world, neither could they hear his stifled cries as he fought for air.

It would be half an hour later before I would sit to talk with Tobey again. "Are you alright, sweetie?"
"Yes, that's so much better." Tobey sounded like a two-pack-a-day chain-smoker. Yet, he was still determined to talk to me. "Where was I? That was it. I was telling you about a doctor in this hospital. From what I can remember his name is...Dr...More-son. No! That doesn't sound quite right. Wait…Let me think..." Tobey was silent for a moment. "That's it…I believe it's...Lawson. Yes! That's what I heard. His name is Dr Lawson. This doctor has killed many! *Blembub, blembub...*" He paused.
"…*blembub*…*blembub....blemblub*. Oh, no!" Tobey sounded mortified.
"What is it?"
"Christine...I-I can't pronounce their names. The names of the babies he's killed. I-I can't pronounce them."
"That's okay." I had to think quickly. "How many? Were they boys? Or girls?"
"*Blembub* was a boy...and *blembub* was a girl." Tobey explained in this way until he had listed all the deceased.
"So in total eleven boys and seven girls have been murdered in a space of almost two years?" My wide

eyes reflected the horror I felt inside. "That can't be right…."

"Yes. That is correct. *Blembub's* passing was hard on me," Tobey said with the weight of the world on his shoulders. "*Blembub* was one of my soul mates you see..."

I fell silent. I was trying to make sense of what I'd just been told. I didn't know what to think, but I had to say something. "Tobey. I'm going to have a look around to find out what's been going on. I don't want you to worry about this, okay?" The hands on the clock let me know it was coming up to closing time. "I'll be back tomorrow; we'll get to the bottom of this. Please try and stay strong."

"I know you can help us." Tobey was unable to conceal his sadness. "See you tomorrow...."

I rose from the chair; I was still holding onto his hand.

"One more thing," Tobey called out. "Don't forget to tell my parents I love them."

"I won't forget, Tobey." I hated leaving him all alone with his pain. I kissed his little hand and placed it back by his side, "I'll come back tomorrow, Tobey. I promise I'll come back…"

I closed the door as I exited the room. My mind spun with a million questions: who was this Dr Lawson? What was he up to? Moreover, the issue I wrestled with right then was whether I should be discreet with my investigation, or confront the said-medic in question?

<u>Siba</u>

As one of Christine's Ancestors, I am in the prime position to tell you where each of these choices will lead. The former will get her nowhere—fast! But will only serve to allow the continuous slaying of these helpless newborns. While the latter, will result in the conscientious planning of her murder…I guess you could say, on this note, it is indeed a very small mercy the people of this world have no idea just how grim their choices are…

***

Chapter Twenty-One: Things You Didn't Know about Diligence…

For a rather reclusive establishment, Diligence has made quite a few impressive biological advancements. Over the years the company has invested decades of meticulous research into the study of genomics, and the complex structure of human DNA. For leading scientists and experts of the day, understanding how cells work—both their strengths and weaknesses—could be the key to solving some of humanity's most debilitating diseases. Thus, carving out a world where cancer can be cured, AIDS understood, and malaria contained. Before the start of the twenty-first century, Diligence had found cures for all of the above. And, at present, it was in the final stages of formulating preventative drugs for the aforementioned diseases.

Running through a hypothetical checklist of medical breakthroughs, Diligence would have scored an A+ in all categories. But when it comes to perfectionism, much like the sort Diligence had over the years grown accustomed to, landing an A+ is just the starting point…

Through studies and the stringent isolation of genes, experts at Diligence deciphered the profound workings of human DNA. With further ground-breaking research, the company was able to zero in on some of the many strengths and weaknesses prevalent in all human genomes; both gender and ethnic specific. The bright minds at Diligence did not stop there. Further probing showed that these strength and weak particles, could not only be extracted, but they could also be distilled. And when an element can be distilled, it could also be stored, and later introduced into another component...it was only a matter of time for those working at Diligence to see that a genetic wonder, could be turned into an exquisite weapon…

Of course for Diligence, this was nowhere near the end of the research project. For reasons still unknown to the company, it was only able to locate and isolate the 'weak' gene. Which in turn, was what the experts at Diligence had poured all their energies into. The technicians worked around the clock studying this miniscule matter. Strands of this inexplicable material were drawn out, and synthesised into a component, which, at the end of undergoing a specialized process took on a soluble, salt-like, consistency. This component, that looked a lot like sodium, could be mixed into and added to other elements. When this happened—well, who knew how far things could go?

Imagine, for example, baking a loaf of bread contaminated with this salt-like molecule. A salt, manufactured to bring on early dementia in women—and only women….

And likewise, imagine a mouthwash, which, when used over time could reduce the sterility of Asian men, let's say, or trigger cancerous tumours within certain groups of society. Or even make a nation of people lose their wits just from having frosting over flakes or munching on a bag of salty crisps. Imagine such a weapon engineered to attack its enemies based solely on their genetic code…imagine...no more accidental mishaps. Once targeted, everything in the spectrum becomes a casualty...

Now, if this compound should happen to fall into the wrong hands—the results could be catastrophic! But the interesting thing about Diligence is they are more than happy to place it into anyone's hands, at the right price…

Given this revelation, one needn't despair. It is of some consolation to know it is only governments who can afford Diligence's extortionate asking price. Consolation, perhaps, depending on the mind-set of one's government, I would presume...

Just the same, Diligence is a shrewd operator—working in an even shrewder world. The executives of this company have made their choice; it strives to be the best! But not the worthiest. Though, sometimes in this world, the best is judged the worthiest, and the worthy, not the best. When this happens, what happens next, I ask? I ask you, for I already know the answer to this, but I cannot comment as it is not my place, and more pressingly—it is none of my business.

Although, I will say this, in the world of jungle politics, Diligence is as insidious as the crocodile. For when this reptile sinks its teeth into its prey, it's impossible to extract the doomed creature from its locked jaw. It is the same type of possessiveness Diligence extends over all of its ongoing research projects. If the company happens to encounter a problem along the way, and is presented with the option to either discard the project, or the problem? Ah, well, the answer is simple. The only thing one needs to remember is that when dealing with Diligence, under no circumstances do you want to be...the problem.

***

Lydia

It seemed as though she was talking to somebody on speed, as she listened to Christine run through—and then go back over—the story of a homicidal baby-doctor running amok in St Margaret's Hospital Trust.

"So let me get this straight. According to Tobey, this doctor—Dr Lawson is snuffing the life out of these babies a few seconds after they're born. Right under the mothers' noses? A doctor doing this...?" Lydia could feel the blood drain from her face. "Christine. This is the vilest thing I've ever heard."

"I know, Lydia! But this is exactly what he is doing?" Lydia rose from her bed; her free hand smoothed over her throat. "It's a good thing I'm lying down because I'm starting to feel a little queasy. Oh my god, this is diabolical! This is disgusting! This is insane! What do you plan to do? How are you going to find this man? Even if you did—would you confront him? What would you say?"

"I don't know!" Christine said full of despair. "I'm not sure. Maybe I should find out, if I can talk to the hospital's administrators. I could ask them if there have been any suspicions surrounding the deaths of these newborns...oh, Lydia! I don't know what to do! What would you do in this instance?"

"What would I do?" There was no hesitation on her part. "You know me, I think you should confront the bastard! Get him to tell the truth. Tell him you can hear what babies are saying, and that Tobey has explained everything!" She paused. "And if he doesn't stop what he's doing, right away! You'll have him arrested quicker than he can say *'ob-stee-ri-tion'* or however way you pronounce that blasted word they go by!"

"But what about the babies he's already killed?"

Lydia sighed. Her head throbbed in line with the tapping her fingertips made against her mobile. "I don't know, Christine. I don't know how you'll be able to explain this to anyone, let alone trying to seek out justice in a courtroom. There might be nothing you can do for those who have gone before, but going forward, you can only try and stop him from killing anymore."

"I hear what you're saying Lydia, but we just can't charge in like that. We need evidence. There must be someone we can talk—"

"Christine, don't you see? Every minute we sit on this, a baby could die. I'm a pragmatic person, as you know, but right now we don't have time on our side. We need to broadcast these deaths—the raised suspicion alone should buy us some time, then, we will show them the evidence. Everyone knows there's no smoke without fire, so let us light a match…" Lydia breathed out heavily. She could so do with one of her cigarettes right now. This is not how she would go about handling a situation, but she faced a very unusual circumstance. Somehow Christine had spoken to Tilly's baby, and now Christine was communicating with Tobey Daley. If she had read about this in a newspaper, she wouldn't have believed it, but the problem is, she hadn't. All this happened in front of her very eyes. Christine could very-well be a little traumatized, as would anyone dealing with what she had gone through, but that didn't explain the phenomenon she herself had witnessed on these occasions. She would not act as rationally as she could. Something awry was going on at the hospital, and she was going to get to the bottom of it.

"Look. I'm going to come with you," she sensed Christine's reservation, "you don't have to face this drama on your own."

"Lydia. This isn't *Sherlock Holmes*. This might prove to be a little...problematic. There aren't many people who would take too kindly to being accused of murder. Especially by a baby who can't speak, or should I say who is clinically dead in the eyes of the masses."

Lydia massaged her temples. "Yes, I do understand." *This situation was beyond surreal!* Her eyes centred on the glass chandelier above her bed then trailed over toward the end of her bedroom where the last rays of daylight spliced through her patio windows. In the distance, she could see The London Eye glittering like a gigantic Swarovski bracelet suspended in the sky. "Look, Christine—I'm not going to pretend. I still can't get my head around how you are able to do, what you do, but somehow you're doing it. I know I do not have to get involved with what you're facing, but now that I know you I can't pretend you don't exist. And even if I had a choice I wouldn't want to." She leaned forward to pick at a speck of lint on her bedding, which, on closer inspection, she saw was non-existent. "Christine, I know you think I'm the privileged sort, more concerned with the latest handbags and hangouts, but that's not what I'm about. I think I can help here. And besides, I can already see your mind's made up. You want to help this baby, don't you?"

"Yes, I do."

"So there we have it! There's nothing more to discuss. I'm coming with you, and we're going to move forward as planned."

"Yes, Sergeant!" Christine laughed. "Are you sure you weren't a governess in your former life, or something to that effect?"

"Me? A governess? Oh, that! My being forthright and whatnot? That's just how the women in my family are. I guess we are a bit gutsy, and I've inherited it by the tractor-load."

"Well, that's a good thing because I hate confrontation. I'm just going to quietly go in and ask a few questions—"

"My dear, you're going to have to say a whole lot more if you want to help this baby…a whole lot more..." Lydia could hear the resignation in Christine's voice.

"Lydia. There's no way around it. I can hear Tobey, therefore, I have to help him. In the end we have to do what we were born to do, isn't that right?"

"Do we really?" Lydia's voice dripped in mock-contempt. "Do we really have to do what we were born to do, I wonder? Because sometimes, darling, I'm not so sure. I'm being told I look *ah-mazing*." She laughed. "So I suppose I was born to make everyone else feel bad."

Christine lightened up, "Don't mind me, I guess. I'm just being dramatic."

"Speaking of drama, have you received any more annoying calls from the press?"

"No." Christine answered "That's died down. But honestly Lydia, it's so awful to be shoved in the spotlight like that. I can't think why anybody would want that for themselves. If I had known you had a famous sister beforehand, I would have asked for tips on how to deal with this sort of thing."

"Tips?" Lydia roared with laughter. "Don't you know anything about celebrity? All of them are fighting for attention, not trying to shy away from it my dear. Listen. The only advice my sister is likely to give: is to remind you to avoid wearing unflattering colours at all times and cut out carbs where necessary."

"Give up carbs?" Christine scoffed. "In a pig's eye!"

Not one to pass up on a barb, Lydia responded, "That's protein-rich, so I believe that one is allowed."

They both chuckled into their phones.

Lydia sighed, "Let's just hope a semblance of a plan materialises soon,"

"Maybe in a dream, perhaps," Christine groaned, "You are a godsend. Thanks for listening to all of this. Night, Lydia."

Siba

Even though Christine and Lydia had ended the call, I could see that neither of the two were able to switch off. How in the world were they going to make sense of all this…? It was the burning question they asked themselves, as they prepared for bed, under the bright night stars. Meanwhile, Tobey Daley, along with many others sleeping babies, was only awaiting permission, to venture beyond them…

Chapter Twenty-Two: Fate and Reason

Siba

Sometimes fate is stronger than reason. Now, before you say—what do I mean? Just take a moment to think about it...Why is it some people happen to seize the right opportunity, at the right moment, at the right time? In the same way, some people get lumbered with the reverse?

There comes a time when one has to admit that some momentous acts in life do not, quite, come together by accident, wouldn't you agree? As we all know, Christine and Tobey was the reason why Lydia Cartwright-Snowden was at that very moment, roaming the high-ceiling hallways of one of the oldest hospitals in the country. Meanwhile, fate, however, is what happened next...

***

Lydia

Lydia knocked on the door; she didn't wait for an answer before venturing into the Patient Services Department. "Hello. I'm looking for Mrs Graham. I was told she is the matron on the neonatal ward."

The woman on reception eased herself further into her chair. She gave off unhelpful vibes. "Yes, that is correct. But I'm afraid you've just missed her. I think she's been called back to the ward."

"Back to the ward?" Next to strawberry blancmange and playing croquet, Lydia hated being given the run-around, which was all she had encountered ever since she stepped foot into this blasted building! "So, you're telling me I have to make my way back to the end of the corridor; find the lifts, go up three levels, and cross over the bridge again?" It wasn't a question, which was probably why the assistant shrugged and offered a sarcastic smile. Lydia swallowed the rich insult that came to her lips. She closed the door and left the unhelpful cretin to her bidding.

Five minutes later she was still wandering around on the same floor. *Could this day get any worse?* The area swarmed with people, but none willing to establish eye contact with a person obviously in need of direction. But then, the right words came… at the right moment…at the right time….

"Excuse me. Can I help you?"

Lydia turned toward the voice with the aim of launching straight into her query. But it didn't quite happen. Her words had stalled like the rest of her.

To the ears of everyone around it was a simple assembly of words: '....excuse me. Can I help you?' But for the two people facing each other it felt as though they had been submerged into a private space, floating several feet below the surface. And whilst everything else was blotted out, just like the initial consciousness of Adam and Eve, they could see and hear each other clearly… 'It really is just the two of us here, isn't it...what do we do now…?'

They were in a place where all potential lovers find themselves, lost within the folds of this outer-worldly connection…it was a deep breath in a short time.

Then they were back.

"I-I'm looking for Matron Graham," Lydia stammered. "I-I mean...please, do you know where I can find the lifts?"
Dr Lawson leaned in. "Have I seen you before?"
"No. I don't think we've met." Lydia was drawn like a magnet and rooted to the spot. A rather bizarre synchronicity. She couldn't stop staring into his eyes—and he just let her, appearing unfazed by this intimate intrusion. The rush of blood to her head warmed her face. She was relieved when he told her where she could find the lifts.
"Thank you." The words were all too quiet to her ears. Maybe she hadn't said them at all. *Does it matter to him?* She wasn't to know; he had gone just as quickly as he had appeared.

***

"The matron will be along shortly. Why don't you take a seat?" The warden pointed to the designated seating area.
"Thank you." Lydia sat with her eyes transfixed on the posters of smiling babies and messages of advice

for new mothers. She shuddered. She was glad she was not a mother and had no desire to be one anytime soon.

A tall-ish-looking woman with glasses appeared at the helpdesk. Lydia knew right away this was the matron. She got up and went over to introduce herself.

"Hello, are you Matron Graham?"

"Yes. That is correct. I hear you want to talk to me." She cast a brief nod to the nurse on reception.

"Yes, I do. My name is Lydia Cartwright Snowden—Lydia." She offered her hand. "I take it you are aware of the story: the plight of baby Daley?"

"Yes. We are aware of the reports." The matron regarded her suspiciously. Her eyes narrowed, "I'm sorry. How does this concern you?"

"As a matter of fact, I'm here about another story that has appeared all over the tabloids. I'm not sure if you've heard about Christine Shore—the baby whisperer?" She wasn't expecting the matron to acknowledge the fact, so was quite surprised when she nodded.

"Yes. I read something about her in the papers. Again, how does this concern us?"

"I'm not sure if you are aware, but Tobey's parents have allowed Christine to talk with their son." Lydia registered the disapproval on the matron's face, but she continued talking. "It appears Tobey has told Christine some rather interesting things...but..." She paused, thinking about what she was going to say next "…something has been worrying the baby. He said there is some kind of malpractice taking place in the hospital."

"Malpractice!" The matron spat out the word as though poison would have fared better. "I beg your pardon?"

"I'm afraid it's a lot graver than that…I think it would be a good idea if you met with Christine, she's with Tobey now."

"What?" The matron looked back at her incredulously. "She's in the room with him, now?"

"Yes, I believe she's been talking to him as we speak...Matron Graham—

"You can call me Susan."

"Thank you, Susan. I think Christine would be in the best position to explain all this to you. Do you think you could spare a few minutes to talk with her? Or at least, listen to what she has to say?"

It looked like the matron was going to do more than refuse. "And the parents? They're happy to have this Christine woman around their son?"

Lydia nodded.

The matron didn't say anything more, she just sized her up from the corner of her eye.

"Very well," She looked over at the nurse on reception, "Some supplies should be arriving shortly, please see to it that the boxes are handed over to the ward supervisor; he'll know what to do with them. If anyone needs me, I'll be in room 412." The matron took off her glasses, "Although, I shan't be long." She gave them a slow wipe then looked her way.

"Right then, Lydia. You have my full attention. Let's go see baby Daley."

***

Christine

"Lydia!" I cried, as Lydia and the matron stepped into the room. The expression on my face brought the two of them to an immediate stand-still. "He hasn't stopped crying. He's scared. He's frantic. Something's happened!"

"What is it?" Lydia rushed to my side.

"It's Dr Lawson. He's doing it again. Right now as we speak, he's doing it again!" I blubbered, unaware I mirrored the baby's apparent hysteria.
The matron's sharpened eyes darted to Tobey then back to me. "Dr Lawson? What about Dr Lawson?"
"We don't know him," Lydia answered. "We were hoping you'd be able to tell us something."
I looked to Lydia and the matron, "Tobey said something about a glow not being there…they've gone to *The Fears*…now…that baby...has…gone..."
A silence fell over the room.
"Lydia, we've got to do something, we have to help him."
With her gaze fixed on me the matron shook her head. "I-I really don't know what on earth is going on here," she said looking like a passenger lost at sea. "But...I think there's something you both need to

know as I'm sure you're bound to find out soon, no doubt. You see, Mr. and Mrs. Daley have been called into a meeting. There is no helping Tobey…not now..." The matron's gaze fell back on the motionless bundle in my arms. "Not unless he makes a miraculous turnaround in the next seven days..."

***

Tobey

Seven days!

Tobey understood implicitly what had just been said. If he thought the electrifying pain shooting through his head was bad enough, it was nothing compared to the anguish he felt at the possibility of being separated from his parents, and not being able to take part in the life journey. *What kind of cruel place is this?* From the moment he was born, pain had hijacked his body—now it ravished his heart. In this realm there appeared to be no relenting; no escaping, no retrieval from pain. It was scattered all around him and lay dormant in all things…*I hate this world!* He growled with an anger he didn't know he possessed, and yet, the thought of leaving it filled him with even greater dread…

The sheer callousness that someone would dare to extinguish his life—*his light!* As though he didn't matter, as though the dark world had no need for candles….

Like a small animal caught in a well-placed trap, Tobey could smell the corrosive scent of doom. *Who am I kidding?* He could not stand up to this crushing blow of defeat... *Why me?* He never lived—now he was going to die! He couldn't understand it. *Why me?*

Unfortunately, no one could hear Tobey's outcry, in the same way that no one can hear the torment of a flower being torn from its roots, or the earth's fierce protest as it absorbs spilt blood. No one could hear him. But Tobey wept bitter tears for the unkind hand it seemed that fate had so cruelly dealt him.

Chapter Twenty-Three: Richard and the Matron

Richard

No sooner had Richard sat down at his work desk, his pager flew into a convulsive fit. He ignored it. He would make the rounds when he was good and ready. He popped a pill and ran through his inbox. He was surprised to see a message from Susan, the matron. He hardly got any emails from her. He suspected she didn't like him very much, which suited him fine. He didn't need anything from her anyway. It was a very short email:

Dr Lawson,
Let me know when you have a minute.
I need to talk to you about something.

His mind flew over to the bothersome case with Tobey Daley. He hoped this silly woman wasn't thinking about overturning the decision. In any case, it was too late for all of that. Last Friday the Daley's had both given their full consent. He stood aside as he watched man and wife battle it out with each other. It wasn't his place to get involved with their emotional wrangling. He was only contented when they produced the answer he waited on.
Re-positioning his keyboard Richard typed out his reply:
I'm down for the late shift.
(He wasn't going to make this easy for her)
If you catch me before I start, you're free to talk to me then.

Richard allowed himself to relax. Thankfully the media circus was drawing to a close. Once this matter with baby Tobey cleared up, he would be free to continue with his work without the added pressure of getting caught. His pager vibrated again. He switched off the alert and dropped it back into his coat pocket. And just like an officer on parade, he went about his working duties.

***

Christine

"Hello…am I speaking to Christine Shore?" It was the voice of a stranger. *Not again! It's too early in the morning for this!*

I thought about hanging up but the female voice quickly fired, "Hello, Christine. If this is you, please hear me out." There was a pause. I knew what was coming next. "I need your help. There is something the matter with my baby..." I went to wrack my brain but I had to admit, I had never said no to anyone who needed help.

Yep! I'm a sad case

***

To be fair, I rather liked the assignment I had agreed to take on. Angelo Beharry, who was five months old, was a real cutie and his mother, Ashley, was just as sweet. "I feel like such a dummy!" The baby's mother slammed the palm of her hand on her forehead. "I had no idea I had the volume up *too* loud, giving my little Angelo these *awful* headaches." She tut-tutted while she peered down at her son, who now dozed in his jungle-themed swing chair. "Would you like some more ginger tea?"

I looked down at my half-empty cup. "Yes, please, it's really refreshing. Thank you." I smiled.

"If you don't mind me asking—how do you do it? How can you understand them? Is my son a grown-up, living in a baby's body?"

I couldn't hold back my laughter. "No! It's not like that. Babies are babies. However, they are quite different from us. When they arrive on earth, they are more determined to survive than I think we give them credit for. Believe me, Ashley, these little ones already have an agenda. They're no accident. They know an awful lot."

"What do you mean?"

"I don't know where to begin…babies have a very bizarre belief system. They believe one can live, yet be dying inside. Or one can die, and yet, they can live…to be honest, I'm still trying to get my head around it."

The mother smiled. "You sound very wise, Christine. I guess you've learnt a lot talking to these babies. Who would have thought there was so much wisdom coming from ones so young?"

I nodded. "I guess I have…"

"Do you plan to have children of your own someday? Sorry…did I say something wrong?"
"No. No, you didn't." I looked on at the sleeping child in front of me. "I had a son. His name was Jerry. He died when he was a few months old."
"I-I am so sorry." The colour drained from her cheeks. "I didn't mean to—I..."
"It's okay, Ashley." I breathed out, "We had four amazing months together. My son loved his rest. I guess, like most of us…"
Ashley offered me more ginger tea. In a moment of exceptional wholeness, I accepted it. It would be the start of many moments to come…

***

Pat-a-cake, pat-a-cake, baker's man,
Bake me a cake as fast as you can,
Roll it, pat it and mark it with B,
And put it in the oven for baby and me

***

Richard

"Excuse me. Can you repeat that?" Richard said to the matron, looking at her incredulously. Richard hoped to catch a glimpse of some mischief-making on her part, but the matron's impassive stare showed there was none to be had.

Her reply was as level as always. "As I said, earlier today two young women came to pay Tobey Daley a visit. One of them is said to be a *baby whisperer*, I believe, something like a *horse-whisperer*, only, she communicates with babies. Her name is Christine Shore. The parents have given her permission to speak with their son."

"How could you allow this?! I mean of all the ridiculous things—"

"If you let me finish. I am as shocked and as appalled as you are. A woman who can speak with babies?" She turned away. "Now I know I've heard it all! I also met her companion, Lydia 'something-something,' she had a rather posh-sounding surname and looked quite familiar to me. By the by, I followed her to Tobey's room and encountered a rather odd scenario…" She paused. "I was hoping you might be able to explain this to me…for you see this woman, Christine Shore, was supposedly having a conversation with the baby when we entered the room. And right there in front of me, she said there was a doctor in the hospital, who was, at that very moment taking the life of a baby as it was being delivered…sorry—are you okay, Doctor?" The matron peered at Richard over the top of her glasses.

"Y-yes, I'm fine. Just slight indigestion, please continue..."

"The baby said this doctor was in the very act of committing this deed as we were all gathered in the room." The matron was silent for a moment.

"Christine, or albeit, Tobey mentioned the name of this doctor. They referred to a…Dr Lawson…" She said no more. The doctor cleared his throat. "This is some kind of joke, isn't it?" He coughed. Richard's thoughts raced to Diligence

Who the hell is this baby whisperer? What on earth does she know?

He rubbed his temples and laughed. "This is a media stunt of some kind. Didn't I say this case was attracting the wrong kind of attention? Didn't I say that? And now it seems we have a pair of hoaxers to contend with. I swear the decision to end his life couldn't have come soon enough!"

Susan turned away from his insensitive remark.

"Why? What do you think this is, matron?" Richard calmly looked back at her.

"I'm not sure what to make of it, Dr Lawson."

"I think I should meet with these women. What do you think? I'm sure this is some kind of misunderstanding, nothing that a simple discussion couldn't iron out."

He leaned back into his chair and swivelled around to face his computer, signalling the end of the conversation.

The matron made steps to leave the office.

"So…when do you think these women will be coming back again?" His voice rose from behind the chair.

"According to the mother her son loves having this baby-whisperer around. I don't think it'll be too long before she makes an appearance. Are you down for next week?"

"I am."

"You might catch her then."
"Okay. Thank you."
She nodded and left the work area.

***

The Matron

What the—? Something was awry. After the two women had left she had made a quick detour to the ward's shift board. And as she had suspected, Dr Lawson had been on duty. In fact, he had been in the delivery room at the same time they were all in Tobey's room together. She later learnt there were two mortalities on the ward. One occurred five hours after the birth. While the other…well...the other was a little confusing…it seemed the baby was semi-stillborn. The details were a little bit hazy, but according to the notes, the baby was breathing—post-delivery—but died almost immediately after.…*What on earth is going on?* Sometimes Susan was particularly grateful she was a member of the spectacles-wearing-society, for this meant that she was not as easy to read. Her glasses, the lenses, the frames, somewhat obscured what prying eyes tried so desperately hard to see: the truth of the matter. But for Susan there were no such obstructions. Thanks to her 5.6 x magnification lenses she was able to see everything in razor-sharp definition. She barely missed a thing. Although it was as quick as a blink, she didn't miss that all important, tell-tale, blink. *He was hiding something.* A deep sense of unease crept over her. She was fond of Tobey Daley and his parents. They were the sweetest couple—young enough to be her children. Over the last few months, all she could do was stand by and watch as The Daley's were dragged through the pits of hell, and back again. She didn't have the sharpest vision but her intuition was second-to-none. Starting from today, she would keep a closer eye on Tobey Daley…and everything else concerning him.

Chapter Twenty-Four: The Gift

Christine

My mum and I turned off Clapton's busy high street. We walked up a long stretch of road leading to my mother's Victorian-conversion, two-bedroom, maisonette. It was the home I had grown up in.

"From everything you've told me so far, I doubt Tobey's parents would agree to switch off the ventilator." My mother said with a defiant look in her eye. "I know you said his situation is beyond tragic, but as a parent you'll do anything to save the life of your child. I don't think they'll do it, Christine, so don't give up on them. You can help him."

"Mum. I'm not so sure."

"Sure about what? You don't think Tobey has a right to life?"

"He's in pain, Mum. He's fighting with everything he's got, but he wants to help others."

My mother smiled encouragingly, "Then, my darling, help him to do so."

"Mum…I know I always ask you this, but do I remind you of my father?" The question was as surprising to my ears, as it would have been to my mother's no doubt.

"Your father?" My mother's eyes shone. "You don't have to be sorry, dear. It's good you still ask questions. It's even better than good. All those questions are a reminder that you're your father's child; he had such an enquiring mind!" My mother laughed and brought out her key to open the front door. "What's the reasoning behind all this?"

I shrugged, realising I hadn't done this since childhood. "I don't know. I've just been thinking about so many irrelevant things lately."

Who am I? What happens to us when we die…?

I sighed and turned to face my mother. "Not too long ago I spoke to a mother of a six-week-old baby. She said all of us are beacons of light."

"Beacons of light?"

"Yes," I nodded, "she said it was bright because this is the colour of our souls…And did you know there are over seven billion people in the world and sixty-six million of those live in the UK?" My mother pulled a face. I chuckled. "Mum, don't ask me where I get these random facts from. The point I'm making here is: the world is crammed full of people, *so* many people. And I guess, deep down, I started to believe we were insignificant…expendable…replaceable, even. You know, a lot like those tealight candles you find in church: when one is snuffed out another one springs up in its place…" I stared at my mother's recently washed floorboards. "It has only just occurred to me…what if there *is* no replacement, no replacing any one of us? And somehow, somewhere, this really matters…? What if, in the great scheme of things, each of us is significant, yet so infinitely delicate…shaky…finite…like candles in the wind. Wouldn't that be tragic and even more cause for concern?" I turned to face my mother. "I remember learning in primary school something about the world not being static, but is spinning around as though it were chasing something—or running away from something. I'm beginning to think it does so to get away from the dark. Our world is a beautiful void surrounded by an encroaching darkness, and it's everywhere! I think our lives is a light for humanity. We are like immutable lighthouses, casting our rays across the choppy waters, across the shadowy face of this earth. As such, there is something uniquely precious about our light. For as long as it continues to flicker, it unable to be one with the darkness, it can only shine in defiance against it —oh my word!" I paused, "I think I know what we are..." I rotated back to face my mother. "It's starting to make sense to me now…we are gifts…."

Outside the reverberant purr of a powerful engine swept up the main road, then it was deathly quiet again. We were stood in the kitchen. At the centre there was a small rickety dining table for three. "Have you been talking to the wee ones again, bonny?" My mother raised her eyebrows.

"Yes, I have," I half-laughed, "but it's only now that it's starting to make sense to me…you see, whatever devised humanity did so with the intention of making us a gift…maybe even a gift to itself, perhaps?"

"A gift…?"

I nodded as I walked over to the sink. I turned on the cold tap and let it run for a few seconds, "Think about it. Deep down we are all driven by this innate desire and ability to please—albeit, mainly ourselves—but the specific need to please, is ingrained in us all. This is why we find ourselves doing so many interesting things with our time, with our lives. All, with the aim to increase or extend our pleasure…when I refer to us as being gifts, what is the purpose of a gift if not to *please* something or someone special?"

"Okay, so let's say I agree with you on this." My mother's judicious stare failed to stop me in my tracks. "We are gifts, and we were made to *'please'* something special. Is there a point to this?"

I responded with an excited nod. "If humanity was created to be a gift that would mean our innate purpose is to gift everything we come into contact with. Don't you get it? We have to be what we were created to be. We are to be a gift to everything around us. A gift to nature, to the land, the sea, the air, creation, to the creator—to each other. To everything we come in contact with, we are gifts! Wow!" I released a satisfying sigh at receiving some clarity for a change. "Now it all makes sense, because *we* make sense." I took a few sips of my water then poured the remainder down the plughole. "But what if we are not fulfilling our purpose, or living as nature intended?"

"What do you mean, as nature intended?"

I pivoted around to place the tube of salt in the overhead cabinet. I caught the look of confusion on my mother's face. "What if, there are some actions we are taking that go against the grain—that works against our natural ability to function as a gift?" I fell silent as I ordered my thoughts, "What is the opposite of a gift?" My mum quickly gave an answer, "I guess the opposite of a gift would be a penalty of some sorts, to have something taken away. Or to put it another way; to receive a gift is to receive a blessing, so I suppose the opposite of a blessing is a curse…Oh my Lord!" My mother's face fell into a mild mix of shock and horror. "A curse…I've never looked at it that way before. So in essence, if we are no longer gifting, then, we will be doing the opposite: taking away…penalizing…cursing…*Sweet Jesus, Mary and Joseph!"* The look of awe on my mother's face deepened. "Imagine that, a world full of walking curses, breathing curses. Ultimately, what we will be witnessing is the eventual malfunctioning of humanity… how in heaven's name do you suppose we've come to do that?"

I didn't get the chance to answer my mother's query, my mobile rang. "Hold that thought Mum, I'll take it in the living room." I headed in that direction.

"Hello, Christine. It's Kelly."

"Hi, Kelly. How are you? How's Robert?"

"We are well I guess, considering the circumstances." Kelly took a deep breath. "Christine I'm so sorry we missed you on Friday, we were in a meeting. Were you able to talk with Tobey?"

"Yes, I did," I picked up one of the cushions and slid into my favourite armchair. "Kelly, I'm so sorry.

Tobey still struggles with his breathing. He told me he doesn't like the taste of the current medication the doctors have got him on. And he *absolutely* abhors the suction pro—"

"We know that! That's the thing. That's the reason why we missed you on Friday. Robert and I were in a meeting. We were talking with some specialists about Tobey's case."

"I heard…" I could feel a strange beating in the pit of my stomach.

That's too low, that's not where my heart should be.

"And is it true, Kelly?"

Kelly was silent. "Robert and I both agree with the specialists. It's time to take Tobey off his medication, he suffers too much."

"Take him off?" I stood up from my chair. "Why? Is this what the hospital wants you to do? If it is you don't have to accept it—you can fight it! You can take it to the courts. You don't have to—"

"No. It has nothing to do with the hospital, or anyone else. It's our decision, Christine. *It's our decision!*" Kelly wailed in between sobs. "R-Robert and I have both decided this is what's best for our baby. Y-you can't imagine just how hard this has been for the both of us. Y-you don't know. H-he's lying there. He doesn't move, but I know he's in pain, Christine. *I know!* We love him so much; he's our little boy, but we can no longer bear to see him like this! They will take him off the ventilator. If he breathes, he breathes. If he doesn't…" She let the silence do the talking.

I was caught in a new dichotomy. Just like everyone else, I too could see Tobey's pale lifeless body. But I could also hear his lively voice. He was very much alive—*he was alive!* But how could I get them to see this?

"Kelly. Please, listen to me. Right now Tobey is helping others. He isn't just fighting for himself, he's fighting for others. There's something terribly wrong going on at the hospital. I can't explain it all now, but I will do."

"He's helping others?"

"Yes. I'll come in tomorrow. I'll explain it to you then. But in the meantime, if you can, please delay your decision."

"Christine, I appreciate your care. We both do. But please don't ask this of us..."

I fixed my eyes on my mother's light beige carpet. I could hear the seconds ticking away from the clock that lived on top of the huge oak cabinet. My mother had said that it had been in her family for over a generation. I wondered how much sad news had been delivered in the face of that grand old clock. The strange fluttering sensation in the pit of my stomach had ceased. Although it wasn't any better; there was now a painful bulbous throbbing in my chest.

"I understand," I could scarcely get my words out, I swallowed back tears. "You're right. I can't imagine what you and Robert have been going through. I'm so sorry for you both…." I rubbed my forehead. "So I will see you tomorrow. Thank you for letting me know."

"Thank you for being there," Kelly whispered before ending the call.

"Is everything alright?" My mother made her way toward me. I fell back into my chair. It felt as though my insides had turned to jelly. "Oh, Mum. Why does he have to die? Why was he even born? I don't get it!" I cried with eyes full of angry tears. I wiped my cheeks and looked to her. "For all its power and purpose, this gift of life is too fragile a thing." My face was empty of reason; my confusion—apparent, seeing I was still nowhere close to understanding the great mystery of life. "Mum…it's too fragile a thing…"

Through blurry eyes, I took in the grainy wrinkly hand that was rubbing my arm in loving sweeps. At that moment, I thought of my mother's mortality. My mother had been there for every milestone, *but she won't be here forever...*The cold truth reduced me to silence. My mother let out a momentary sigh. "A gift is beautiful, therefore a gift is precious. We cannot change what we are darling, we can only be..."

Chapter Twenty-Five: Richard. Lydia. And Everything in Between

Siba

From where I am standing, it appeared Dr Lawson was having a rather difficult conversation with his contact from Diligence.

"Richard. Do we look like an organisation that deals in hoaxes?" Bernard asked in his clipped accent. "I assure you hoaxes are the least things Diligence pays mind to."

It was fortunate for Richard that he could not see his contact on the other end, as Bernard had just struck out his name with his golden pen.

Bernard was regretting his choice of agent. In all his time working for Diligence and before then, at the European Commission, he had never made a bad decision. But there was a first time for everything, and this was it! He could see Richard was going to be a problem, which was a massive shame as the doctor performed superbly in other areas. This medic lacked one vital characteristic; the one Bernard deemed the most important of all: self-control. *Richard was a drug addict!* If the doctor couldn't control his habit, how was he going to navigate obstacles when they arose? Bernard was sceptical. Nevertheless, he continued the conversation in a calm manner. "I know we've been through this before, but are you certain your notes are in a safe place and your passwords have not been compromised?"

"To the best of my knowledge, everything is secure."

"Then, I'm going to have to report back to central office. They're going to be very much intrigued to hear about this woman who can read the minds of little babies."

"Wait!" Richard didn't miss the sneer in Bernard's voice. "Let's just wait a minute here." He could feel himself perspire.

Why didn't he take a pill before starting this conversation?

Timing can be a blessed thing. At that exact moment an email appeared in his inbox. It was a message from the matron. Richard opened it. There were only six words typed in the body of the email. It was enough:

`She's back. She's with him now`

"Bernard! I've got to go, she's here! She's in the hospital!" He scrambled to get a hold of his jacket.

"Please wait. It might not be a good idea to bother the Professor with this, just yet. Not until I've spoken to her. I'll call you back later."

"See that you do." Bernard hung up.

***

Christine

Christine: Hi. I'm going to see BT later
Lydia: What time?
Christine: @2.30 p.m
Lydia: Great! My meeting ends then. I'll c u there! :-D
Christine: Thx Lyds – ur a star!

I pressed the send button, then got myself ready to face the office. Today, I made the decision to work through my lunchbreak so that I could arrive at St Margaret's hospital at the promised time….

***

I slowly approached Tobey's bed. He wore a gorgeous royal-blue and white onesie. I had bought a similar-looking one for Jerry, although it was no longer in my possession. I recalled seeing it in the cardboard box my mother had donated to The Lullaby Trust.

I massaged Tobey's back and feet, humming a light tune as I went along. Tobey was asleep when I had crept in earlier, and it appeared he was still in that restful place now. "I hope you're enjoying your time there, Tobey." I whispered. His lips were lined in a faint smile, "Take all the time you need little fella. When you wake up, I'll be right here…waiting."

***

Siba

The Birth Trail is a luscious place of eternal beauty. But despite the ethereal wonder of this glorious habitat, there were indeed other eye-catching effects that added to its natural charm...

For you see, everywhere you turned the landscape overflowed with mind blowing creations of every description. There were sweeping structures that lit up the horizon, humongous screens that spun around in the sky breath taking costumes and designs, and brightly coloured machines that could fly. There was an abundance of remarkably constructed things. Things, which the eye could not describe but the mind had conceived. But The Creator of Love did not put them there. Oh, no! In this utopia, it was the babies that did all of the creating. As such, this magnificent realm was a wonderful manifestation of their tiny creative minds…

During their time in the Birth Trail, the babies were free to enjoy each other's exquisite handiwork. They had the most fun showcasing their performances, appliances, devices and designs. No matter how bizarre, big, or small, all were welcome, and everything was acceptable.

On occasions, soul members came together to create a monumental thing of wonder. While at other times, they joined forces with neighbouring soul groups to usher some outstanding thing into existence. Although this beautiful haven was a glorious place of rest, it was also a thriving hub of creativity. What else did you think these little ones did with their time? But of course, the babies had plenty of fun creating, just as The Creator intended. However, it behoves me to report that during the babies' journeys on earth, only a few would get to see their

greatest talents come to fruition. Sorry! I exaggerate. Maybe more than a few, but still far too little compared to the wealth of inventiveness on display in this stunning paradise. But why, Siba? What is the world doing to these little ones that are curbing their natural-given talents?
This is a good question—to which there are many good answers, not that the newborns are taking notes at this stage. They are far too preoccupied with trying to enter the race, just like how I was when I came into the world. They are going to see to it that none of their Ancestors' tales are wasted on them! The babies are well-aware the world is like an exotic beast: beautiful, but cruel. To get anything from it, they would have to fight for it! But for how long? And against what? The babies had no idea of knowing. Neither did they not know, that they would have to fight…to hold onto that fight… How terribly exhausting it all must be for the newborns. The earth journey is paved with never-ending stumbling blocks, and a tirade of interferences prohibiting these little ones to just be. So in my humblest opinion, if there is anyone out there in the world who, in spite of all these hindrances, is still able to create. Then by all means I say—LET THEM CREATE!

***

Tobey

"Well done!" Thabo smiled into the faces of all his soul group members. "We did it! We thrilled them with our music!" There was a rush of cheers again, they all congratulated each other on their hard work. Putting together the musical score was Thabo's idea, and with the help of his soul group, one of many of Thabo's inspirational dreams was brought into existence.

"What should we make next?" Victoria put the question to the group.

"Let's create a maze," someone suggested.
"How about a castle?" said another.
"What about a submarine?" Everyone turned to look at Li Wei.
"Yes! A submarine!" They all agreed.
"And I have a couple of suggestions," Li couldn't suppress his shy smile. "It's something I've been dreaming about for quite some time now…"

***

For Tobey, it seemed like days and days had gone by—and he was having the time of his life! He and his good friend Albert worked on a very important project that would manifest into a stupendous submarine.
"How was your time away?" Albert knew Tobey's jaunts to earth proved to be a little hard on him.
"It's a lot better now. I've made a friend. She's the only one who can hear me."
"She can hear you? That's awesome! Did you tell her about this place and all of us here?"
"I've tried." Tobey fell silent. "Albert…earth is a… weird place. Don't get me wrong—it's amazing!

Everything you've ever dreamed it would be, and more. But…you know the feeling you get? The one when you're close to *The Fears*?"

"Yes. That uncomfortable feeling."

"Well, on earth it appears that feeling is with you all of the time."

Albert looked aghast. "All of the time?"

"Yes…but…magnify that sensation by ten…"

Albert said nothing, but his eyes grew as much. "What? That's insane! How do people on earth cope? How is it possible to do anything with that…that feeling around you, all of the time?"

"I don't know but they do. Many grownups live their lives in fear; they feel lonely and unloved but they just get on with it."

Albert winced. "What an onerous burden to carry through life." His face contorted as he pondered on the grim and the ugly. "All the same Tobey, I'm still looking forward to going there. Whatever trials and challenges lay ahead, I plan to overcome them all!" Albert paused to flex his underdeveloped muscles. He laughed, as did Tobey, with him and at him—naturally. "I've decided when I get to earth, I'm going to be a caretaker of animals—you name it: horses, dolphins, gorillas, bears—that's what I'm going to do." He glanced across the valleys and plains which surrounded them like a pantheon of lights. "Tobey. Look around us. I love all the magnificent creatures we have over here, and I'll love them just the same when I arrive over there."

Tobey had nothing but the utmost admiration for all his friends' passionate life plans. "Albert, I think you've got the right kind of attitude. Although…" He displayed his confusion. "It seems, in the world, time is a lot shorter than the length of our plans. They'll be much to learn; much to teach, in short, there we will be much to do. I hope you'll be able to do it all, in the time that has been given to you." Tobey lowered his head, "I just wish I wasn't born into so much pain..."

"Oh, Tobey…" Albert flew down to give his friend a much-needed, spirit-filled, hug. "I'm so sorry for what you're going through. Maybe your path is a little different from everyone else's. But that doesn't mean it's not as important. Remember#

Loves' decree? Everything works out for good in the end…everything always does..."

Tobey froze.

"What is it, Tobey?"

"I know it's a weird question to ask…but…where are you from?"

Albert looked back at him. "Indeed, that is a strange question. Like you, I'm from all over the world."

Tobey tutted. "I know that…I just meant…your most recent Ancestors—where did they hail from?"

"*Ahhh,* let me think…the other day I met one of my uncles from generations back. He was full of sad tales but had quite a happy ending...oh, yes! My grandmother, my father's mother. She paid me a visit not too long ago. She said she had passed on quite recently."

"And where was she from?"

"I think my gran said she was from a city called London. From the East End, I believe." He glanced back at Tobey. "Why? Do you know where that is?"

Tobey recalled earth and the private conversations going on around him…

'This is the best place for him! We're not moving out of east London!' His father had said in a firm voice.

'I've come all the way from North London to see you,' Christine conveyed in a whisper.

'My goodness…I swear this place must take up most of the East End,' Lydia had remarked.

"Do you think you might be born somewhere in East London?" Tobey put the question to Albert.

"I wouldn't rule it out," Albert shrugged. "From the little my grandmother said, and bearing in mind many of my recently deceased relatives also seemed to hail from that region. So, yes. It's looking likely. Why? Is there a problem?"

"Albert...do you remember Husna?"

Albert looked puzzled. "Husna? Who's Husna…?"

Now, just before you conclude that all babies are emotionally detached, or fickle, or have the memory of a sieve—this couldn't be further from the truth! For you see once a member of a soul group is lost to The Fears, *the impact resonates amongst the other surviving members, and this concurrence is everlasting…even during their brief stint in the world, that pain does not up and disappear. Instead, it wavers in the background, like the distant sounds of the sea: a sweet longing, a sharp deficiency, an existential grief, which the mortal bodies they receive on earth are unable to nullify. Moreover, that soul groups' celestial resolve becomes ever-so slightly diminished, much like the dimming of old gold. But alas, the memory of that precious member is no more. After all in paradise there can be no pain. So what more for the stinging reminder of loss…*

Nonetheless Tobey Daley was no ordinary soul mate. He could still remember everything..."Husna was once a member of our group." He noted his friend's apparent confusion. "Never mind…Albert. I believe your time is nearly due. I'm…a little concerned about your journey to earth…" Concerned was putting it mildly, Tobey was petrified.

"Am I going to *The Fears*?" Albert cried. He looked back at Tobey in horror.

"No! No, of course not!" Tobey reassured him. It wasn't a lie. There must be more than one hospital in the East End. What were the chances that Albert would be born in the hospital where death was waiting? And even if he was, who was to say it was there to claim him? Although the chances were slim Tobey had lived long enough to know there were no coincidences. He took a deep breath and looked to the spray of colours in the sky. His sleeping days were well and truly over. He had to get back to earth - to Christine! Time travel…infinite pain…sleepless nights...this was a job for a superhero. Maybe this was the job he was born to do.

***

Henrietta

"Richard...Richard..." Henrietta breathlessly called out, speeding up her efforts to keep up with him.

"Oh," Richard spun around. He slowed down. "Yes, Dr Metcalfe, what is it?" He looked impatiently down the hallway.

"Errrr…I'm sorry. I was just wondering if we're still on for tonight? You said you were going to call me yesterday, but…"

"Oh, yes. That."

Henrietta could see Richard was distracted. This was unusual of him.

"Yes, about tonight. I won't be able to…actually…if you're free…do come over…"She was half-expecting him to say no, but it seemed he had had a sudden change of heart. Henrietta was indeed free and very delighted. "Same time?" She smiled.

"Yes. Same time. We'll talk later."

Richard continued marching down the hallway, he had a peculiar look on his face. A look, which did not go unnoticed by Dr Metcalfe.

What is up with him?

Henrietta proceeded to watch as Richard advanced further down the corridor. He headed toward the quiet room where that extremely sick baby was holed up. As soon as Richard approached the door, he didn't enter the vicinity. Instead, he peered through the glass partition. He was contemplating something. He kept taking quick glances through the meshed screen window in the middle of the doorway.

What on earth is he doing?

Henrietta was intrigued

***

Meanwhile....

Tobey

"Are you there? Are you there, Christine?" Tobey was awake, and he was ready to talk.

"Yes, I'm here, Tobey. Talk to me...."

***

Henrietta

Henrietta stood in the distance. What was Richard contemplating? She was due to return back to the ward but decided that whatever was going on there would just have to wait. She continued to watch Richard, observing whatever thing had snared his interest. Then, without further warning, Richard straightened

himself up and stepped into the room.
As always curiosity had gotten the better of Henrietta. She rushed toward the end of the corridor. She too, wanted to get a look at the thing which had so got hold of Richard's attention.

***

Christine

I looked up. A rather tall and attractive-looking man had entered the room. He wore a white coat.

He appeared to be a medic. I suspended stroking Tobey. The doctor looked at me with a degree of surprise, then he cleared his throat. "Who are you?" he asked.

"Who are you?"

"I'm Dr Lawson."

I swallowed.
"What is it, Christine?" Tobey whispered, "That's him, isn't it?"
"Yes," I replied Tobey.
The doctor stood still. He looked like he was weighing up something. "I've been told you have quite an extraordinary gift." He took a few steps further into the room. His eyes never left my face. He stopped walking and produced a tight smile. "Where are you getting your information from?"

I flew into alert mode. I drew Tobey closer to me. "I've been speaking to Tobey—he's told me many things." I couldn't stop the words from tumbling out. "You're doing something you shouldn't be doing, Dr Lawson. You've killed ten boys and seven girls in furtherance of some private experiment you're conducting." I paused. "But your exploration is not complete. It just so happens some of the lives you have taken, and plan on taking, are very close to Tobey."

The doctor looked like he was about to erupt, but he said with an air of menace, "Look. I don't know what all this is about, you better quit now or you're going to find yourself in a lot of trouble."

"Trouble? Is that a threat Dr Lawson, or can I call you Richard?" Lydia's silky voice interrupted proceedings at the most opportune moment.

Neither Dr Lawson nor I had heard the door open. Lydia stood in the centre of the room looking every inch like a snow queen. With her plum red shoulder bag; designer mac, and hair swept loosely on top of her head—who knew salvation could be so stylish? Lydia's eyes clashed with the doctor. It seemed they had met before. Richard looked at me then back at Lydia. "That was not a threat," he simply said. Lydia and Richard stared at each other like two people fascinated with their own reflections. The conversation was now between these two, I gathered. I breathed a sigh of relief. Very little sigh…even smaller relief…

Richard cleared his voice, "Who are you?"
"My name is Lydia Cartwright-Snowden." Lydia tilted her head back to get a better look at him. "You didn't give me an answer to my question—can I call you Richard?"
Richard looked at her and smiled, "I think we should all sit somewhere and have a proper chat." He opened his hands, seemly as a friendly gesture "Wouldn't you agree? This room is probably not the appropriate place for this."

***

Henrietta

While this fiasco was going on, Henrietta had placed herself outside Tobey's room. She had seen and heard everything up to a point, and buzzed with curiosity. But then, just as swiftly, that spirited sensation had turned to rot. Everything came to an immediate standstill as soon as that woman brushed passed and stepped into the room. It was as if Richard had come alive when he saw her. There was something in his eyes that made Henrietta pour scorn over the many times he had glanced at her. For in whatever way it was, it certainly wasn't in the way she was seeing now...They were making plans to exit the room. Henrietta had to quickly get out of the way.

"My department is on the mezzanine level. It's not too far from here," she overheard Richard saying to the two women. They walked a few paces behind him.

"Is everything alright?"

Henrietta jumped. It was Susan, the matron.

"Yes—I'm fine."

"I mean is everything alright with baby Tobey?" the matron frowned. "Didn't you just come out of that room?"

"No...errrr. I was just on my way to the staff room. In fact, I'm running a bit late..."

A beeping sound went off in the distance.

"Ah. It's time for his procedure." The matron nodded in Tobey's direction. "Okay, Doctor, I better not keep you."

"Susan." Henrietta sidled up to the matron's side, her lightly made-up face was all awash with concern. "What is the current situation with Tobey?"

The matron gave her a slow piercing once-over. "Do you have a minute?"

"Yes, I do," Henrietta lied.

"Then follow me please. Today I'm overseeing the suction routine."

There was no objection from her side. Henrietta accompanied the matron into the room, where Tobey Daley was slowly being primed for his painstaking procedure.

Chapter Twenty-Six: Henrietta Goes to Work

Siba

Oh! To be a fly on the wall right now. As a matter of fact, I am a lot closer than that! My vision is fixed on every spinning plate. I am a spirit—I can do that. Richard Lawson is a very canny character, indeed…

The doctor led Christine and Lydia to the mezzanine level, as he said he would. But he had no intention of taking them to his assessment area. Instead they walked a little further down the hallway until they came to another department.

Richard spoke to the assistant who met them at the door. "Tell Mr Healey I'm here. There are some people who wish to have a chat with him."

Anyone wanting to speak with the hospital's administrator would have to book an appointment, but as it was Dr Lawson, the assistant went off to check on Mr Healey's availability.

She tapped on the door before entering. "Excuse me, Mr Healey. Dr Lawson is here with two women. I don't know if you know anything about this?"

Paul Healey's head emerged from the side of his computer. "Oh, yes. Thank you. Please let them in. There's no need to be surprised, Hazel. I was expecting them."

Indeed, Dr Lawson had contacted him earlier about some hoaxers who were bothering The Daley's and their sick child. And as Richard had rightly pointed out, it was up to his department to sort out matters.

If there were going to be any media stunts at this hospital, it was not going to happen under his watch. That much was for certain!
Paul Healey straightened himself up. He pocketed his pen and cleared his throat. Oh, yes. He was more than ready for them...

Christine

Lydia and I were led into an ornate-looking reception area. The place was decked in heavyset curtains, with rows of medical journals lined-up behind glass cabinets. Large stately portraits of the hospital's preceding patrons peered down on us from either sides of the walls. This was a revelation for me. Other than the hospital wards, the waiting areas, and the public toilets, I had never been inside any other room in a hospital before.
The doctor motioned for us to sit. The administrator appeared from around the corner. Lydia stood up but Richard quickly cut in. "Ladies. I have brought you to the attention of Paul Healey, a very important person here at St Margaret's Hospital. He is the administrator. If any of you have any pressing grievances or concerns, they will need to be taken up with him, and him alone."
Lydia tried to intervene, but Richard continued. "For various reasons, I am not required to be present at this meeting, as I am sure you can understand. I

am also on-call and juggling what could only be described as an exceedingly demanding work schedule. So if you'll excuse me…"

"But wait!" Lydia shot out, her request fell on deaf ears.

"And if there is indeed anything to investigate," he threw Paul a look of mock-exhaustion, "I believe this will be taken up through the right channels. I'm sure you both can respect the hospital's policy in regard to this matter. Have a good day all. Paul?" He nodded to the administrator, who nodded right back. Then without further ado Richard left the room.

"He needs to be here!" Lydia turned around to face the administrator. "Why did you let him go? Listen. We are not going to be fobbed off! I know how this must look to you, Mr Healey, but this is not a hoax, I can assure you." Lydia's eyes shone like an angry tiger. Paul let out a long sigh and looked at his watch.

"I'm glad you're both seated. I've asked for Tobey's parents to join us. They should be along any minute now. I understand it was them who sought out…Christine Shore?" He looked from me to Lydia. The bored expression on his face made it very apparent he had no intention of taking anything we had to say seriously. He shrugged. "Let me tell you, ladies. Right now you're in one of the oldest hospitals in the capital. The services we have provided span over a hundred years and is a rival to none. It is everyone's continuous hard work and commitment that has taken this hospital to this level thus far." He stopped to glance our way, before continuing, "We set extremely high standards here at St Margaret's Hospital Trust. I am sure you can appreciate the amount of pressure our staff are under daily. As the hospital's chief administrator it is my job to cultivate an environment where they can meet with their targets, free from any hassle, violence or *harassment* of any kind."

"Oh, please, Mr Healey! Spare us the corporate spiel! Babies are mysteriously dying at this hospital, or have these colossal incidences somehow escaped your notice?" Lydia leaned forward. "If you stuck your head out from under the parapet and did some research, you might find that something rather suspicious has been going on here." She laughed with disdain. "Please, do tell me, Mr Healey, just what exactly are you shovelling to the parents who've lost their babies? Are you saying these deaths are natural?" Her eyes flashed. "You think this is a hoax? I suggest you start making some major enquiries or it is you—and not those who *you* claim to look after—who might find himself under immense pressure."

"What? Are you going to take this to the papers or something? I hate to remind you ladies, but people are extremely busy. I'm sure journalists hear stories like the ones you're fabricating every day, and to no avail."

"Ah, but you see, Mr Healey, being the younger sister of Stephanie Downes—yes, you heard correctly, the movie actress. Garnering the right kind of press attention will not be a problem for me. I'm not talking about a side column in a local newspaper; think more like the top bulletin on the *Six O'clock News.*" Lydia was, of course, bluffing. She said she had never used her sister's celebrity status to obtain anything. But maybe this occasion might prove to be the exception.

"I see." Mr Healey fixed his uncaring eyes on her. "And tell me, Stephanie Downes' little sister. Where is your evidence?"

"Like I said, why don't you do some research of your own? Some of these newborns did not die from natural causes. Dr Lawson is conducting some kind of experiment—right here, under your noses—and you don't seem to care!"

The administrator straightened up. "Let me correct you there, I care about everything that happens in this hospital—that's my job!"

"Then please do it!"

"I am," he said, clearly ruffled. "And just as formalities dictate, if you have any grievances I'll be more than happy to give it its due consideration, if you could kindly get it all down in…writing…" His rigid smile said it all. Lydia looked like she never wanted to swipe the smile of someone's face as much as she wanted to do so now. There was a knock at the door. Kelly and Robert were escorted into the room.

"Good afternoon Mr and Mrs Daley. Glad you could make it." He ushered them into their seats. "I'm

really sorry to have to call you in today, but this has only just been brought to my attention. You see I understand you have given these women visitation rights to your baby?"
"Yes. We have," Kelly answered. "Is there something the matter?"
"It appears they have a grievance with one of our senior medics on staff. And going by formalities, we must suspend any further visitations by Ms Shore and Ms *Downes* effectively from today, so we can look into this matter."
Lydia gave the administrator a simmering look.
"We will have to follow this through." Paul Healey kept his eyes on the couple. "At least, until this issue has been cleared up. As we know this won't be too long, since concurrently, Tobey will be taken off his medication at the end of this week."
I turned to face the couple. "Kelly! Didn't you say anything? Can't you delay—?"
It was Robert who answered. "Christine. Our son is on his last legs. I know you can see that. We can't do this anymore. *He* can't do this anymore. It's been hard for us to face this, but we must let him go."
"It's not what he wants."
"Even if it isn't. Although he is in here, we haven't stopped being his parents. We must do what's best for him…"
Nobody spoke. The room was filled with silence but no peace. I looked up at the administrator. "Believe me, Mr Healey, my friend really does have the clout

to take this to a whole new level. But…I don't want this to be the case." I sighed. "Since Tobey will not be with us for much longer, I don't want to waste precious time dealing with this. So I say right now, no more will be said in regard to Dr Lawson." My hand shot up to fend Lydia's protests. "Please, overlook everything that has just been said."

"I'm not sure that—"

"Mr Healey. If you can overlook. We can overlook."

The administrator paused. This was not his idea of a truce, but at least he didn't lose face. Paul Healey didn't quite say yes to my request, and he didn't quite say no either. Therefore as no official line of action had been drawn up, we were free to keep on seeing the baby as the parents so wished.

Before allowing us to leave the administrator made sure to collect our full contact details. He also assured us he would be in touch, just as soon as he had convened with the other officiating members on the board. And that was the end of that murky episode! But it looked like as far as Paul Healy was concerned his meeting with members of the board couldn't come soon enough.

***

Richard

Richard raced out of the hospital grounds like a dispatcher responding to an A&E on a Saturday night. He was over the driving limit—*but to hell with the speeding ticket!*

Richard had planned to make a brief stop at Paul Healey's office, to ask him how his meeting with the hoaxers went. But he didn't do that. Neither did he make his scheduled call to Diligence. At that moment, Richard was more concerned about sitting within the four walls of his home, preferably in his lab, so he could think long and hard about his next move…

There was only one more specimen to collect, and it was due in this Thursday. He needed to be there to do that! With a clenched jaw and sweat creeping down his temples, Richard recalled a conversation from the past…

'Now, tell us, Doctor, just how much time do you need?'

Richard, who had been dreaming about this meeting from the moment he woke up that morning, gave a rough estimation.

'You do understand,' he went on to explain to the voice down the line, 'to avoid suspicion, these mortalities need to happen few and far between. Everything must be done to eliminate my culpability.'

'Yes. I understand,' replied the voice on the other end. 'We will go along with the best timeframe for you. Just let us know when you're ready to begin, so we can start making the necessary arrangements.'

On that occasion, Richard did not speak to his usual contact, Bernard. The voice on the other end claimed to be a bio-technician, also assigned to the project. There was no reason for Richard to doubt this, as the person did impart some vital knowledge on the subject area. But there was an air to his voice...Richard suspected he was talking to the brains of this entire operation.

Nevertheless the order was simple: Diligence had requested the stem cells of twenty live foetuses. No more. No less. And no further explanation was given—and who was he to argue?
The study they were involved in was bigger than them all. The results found in the testing of these stem cells could very well lead to the discovery of the century. Richard had invested a huge amount of time and effort into this project. Likewise the same could be said of Diligence. He'd be a fool to walk away from it now. There was no way he could do that. He had a job to do, it was within his sights—he could do it! And the money…?
The doctor wiped his mouth as he went over the figure in his head. Ever since he was assigned to the project, every month a steady flow of cash was deposited into his bank account, just as Diligence had promised. And of course he dove into it; filtering the money into the international stock markets and financing his costly laboratory. Now, two years on - and here he was - two days away from finalizing his side of the deal. And now this pernicious

accusation…no doubt the spotlight would be turned on him. Under these circumstances, it would be reckless of him to continue with this project. In fact, it would be pure folly. If investigated he could stand to lose everything—not only his medical license, but his freedom too. As fickle as the general public could be at times, he was certain they wouldn't take too kindly to a baby-killer. Not even if everything that had been carried out, had been done in the name of progress. *What do people really believe—that we share the genetic make-up of a rabbit? Give me strength!* There was no way around it. Human beings would need to be experimented on, and the industry has always found stealthy ways to do this. *It is not ideal but that's life! And life is not fair—it never has been!* And Richard could fully attest to this, being someone who at the age of thirteen, had lost his three-month-old brother to SIDS, and nine months later, his grieving mother to breast cancer. Those losses needed: Answers. Remedies. Cures. Human trials and experimentation would allow for this. *Why should the most progressive in society be blamed for finding solutions?* Richard was sick to death of hearing from the moralist brigade. *The strong dominate and the wise win! Scientists should not be dragged over the coals for doing their duty; no more than a manager for following the whims of the director, or the director for obeying the CEO's protocols. If things are placed in order, everything had to work for the good of that order. Where one happened to appear in that hierarchal order was anyone's guess—he didn't make the rules.* There would always be big fishes that ate little fishes, and yet, the ocean will always have creatures of every size. That was the way of the world, and he had made his peace with that. Yet, Richard remained flustered. He looked down at his hands, which were now folded together like an old-fashioned steeple. *Why did he sit here trying to justify his actions?* Of course he wasn't going to abort the mission. This was his goal, *his dream!* And he was just too close to walk away from it now. And even if he wanted to, he couldn't just stop. Diligence didn't look like the kind of operation that would accept an apology. There would be serious repercussions if he did not hold up to his end of the bargain. Serious repercussions...but this situation with the baby-whisperer? This woman was bound to draw more attention, if not now, then after he made his final collection when another mortality was announced… The sweat cooled on his forehead, but Richard was still nowhere near to sorting out this quandary. He had to think fast. *What should I do?*

Henrietta

Henrietta was feeling confident today, not because she looked better than her usual best. But because she knew something, and Richard did not know that she knew…Yes. She bordered on the ridiculous, realising she was being empowered by something as minute as gossip. But Henrietta felt good, and she was not about to spend all day beating herself up over it. She teetered toward Richard's front door as quickly as her heels would allow. On one of her rare visits, Richard had taken her to a large clearance space in the attic. From the way the area was arranged, it looked like a self-made laboratory. There was fluorescent panel lighting on the ceiling, and futuristic scientific appliances stationed in every part of the room. Seeing this made Henrietta smile. She was finally getting a glimpse of the man behind his reticent façade. Henrietta could see his work—his research, meant a great deal to Richard, even though he did his best not to let it show. During these rare trips to his special office/lab, Richard would talk about aspects of their jobs, and ask her questions on the latest research papers. Much to Henrietta's annoyance she found it was always work with Richard. Whether he was bitching about decisions by the board of trustees, or the ordering of new office appliances. His focus was on the work. But this was not his only passion, Henrietta soon discovered. This self-made laboratory of his conveyed much more of his persona. Henrietta perceived Richard saw himself as a medical pioneer—an expert of sorts. It was a side of him she didn't quite mind; she liked ambitious men. Although right now, Henrietta could see Richard was not himself this evening. There was no quick trip to his lab. No discussions about work. And no bottle of wine chilling in the refrigerator. Instead, they ate their meal in relative silence.

"I'm going to have a bath later," Richard announced, as they were getting ready for bed.

"Would you like me to join you?"

"No. Not tonight. And no need to wait up for me either. I'll be gone awhile."

"More like an hour," she said in a playful strop. "You take ages when you have a bath. What do you do in there?"

"I catch up on my reading." He didn't look at her. "You know. Zone out for a bit."

"I bet you do." Henrietta recalled the bottle of pills she had spied in the medicine cabinet. However, the next time she had a snoop around, they had been removed.

"You can join me next time, Etta, I promise." He tossed his towel over his shoulder and left the room.

After ten minutes had passed, Henrietta crept out of the bed and tiptoed toward the doorway. She caught a glimpse of herself in the long-mirrored wardrobe. She wore her soft peach-coloured negligee; it was a recent purchase. Ever since being invited to stay over at Richard's, she had never repeated her night clothes. Another aching reminder that she was only his guest, and not his girlfriend. She wondered if this would ever change...

The door was opened; wide enough for Henrietta to slip her slender frame through.

The bathroom was situated next to the flight of stairs leading to the attic. Henrietta had to be very careful; she hoped to god there were no creaking steps. She couldn't imagine what she would do if the bathroom door swung open, and there was Richard catching her in the very act of sneaking toward his special lab. She would quite literally die of embarrassment....

On the landing by the oak bookcase stood an immaculate *Bechstein* shining in all its glory. It beckoned her to come over and play. Henrietta had yet to hear Richard perform, she imagined he'd be very good; he was quite astute at pointing out her imperfections.

She broke away and turned toward the stairwell. The winding staircase led straight to the only room at the top: Richard's pristinely maintained self-made laboratory.

As soon as Henrietta stepped into the attic beams of light flooded the area. It appeared the lab was installed with a sensor light switch. Henrietta hadn't noticed that before. She looked behind her. All was quiet. Feeling like a kid in a petting zoo, she surveyed the appliances, not knowing what exhibit to inspect first. Displayed in front of her were three large work counters. On top of them were petri dishes, thermometers, and microscopes of various sizes, and a scattering of paper which had been scrunched up into balls. She turned to her right. Across the room stood an industrial-sized water cooler, and beside it was a lone anaerobic cabinet with a razor-red beam of light that winked away in silence.

What is Richard conducting here?

Soon enough, Henrietta's eyes fell upon Richard's computer. Judging from the humming sound, it was still on. She stood still and listened. It was very quiet. She allowed herself to breathe again. Richard would still be in the bath; he hadn't been gone that long. With great ease, she pulled up the black-leather swivel chair and sat in front of his workstation. Richard had quite an interesting screensaver. Beaming back at her was an image of a middle-aged woman who was smiling; she held a newborn in her arms. There was no doubting who the woman was—Richard was the spit of his mother. But there was no way Richard was the baby nestled in her arms. There was something about the resolution…*the photo wasn't taken that long ago?* Henrietta didn't have time to ponder. She scanned the keyboard then struck a key. It gave way to Richard's jam-packed desktop. She double-clicked on the envelope icon. Instantly, rows and rows of emails filed across the screen. They all appeared to be from the same company: *Diligence.*

Who are they? There was no point in gawping at it. She read from the top. Henrietta was a very adept skim-reader, and that evening she used it to her fullest capability. She jumped from one correspondent to the next—there was too much for her to take in—every one giving more engrossing details about what Richard had been up to over the last two years.

This is explosive! And it explained everything. She needed evidence of this….
It was a silly idea or so Henrietta thought, but she decided to head back down to the bedroom, she needed to get to her handbag. Inside it there was a floppy disc which didn't hold much data, except a copy of her CV and some research articles, but as a graduate and ever since, she had never left home without it.
What am I doing? What if Richard cuts his bath short? What if he comes up straight to his lab? What if? What if would get her nowhere—she just had to do it!
Henrietta slid out of the chair and made her way back down the winding stairwell. A few moments ago when she had tiptoed up them, she was only intrigued with Richard's preoccupation with this so called *'baby-whisperer.'*
But things were very different now. What she had just read had nothing to do with another woman—*this was much worse!*
Her heart thumped so hard it shook the flimsy garment she wore. Richard was not the aspiring medical pioneer Henrietta had believed him to be. Richard had quite simply lost his mind! He couldn't be all-there. How could he be? What he was doing or being asked to do, was beyond horrifying! Let alone the criminal and moral ramifications involved in this entire project! What kind of a person would do this? *Someone without a heart, Henrietta, and you should know…*

As soon as Henrietta entered the bedroom, she seized her bag. She rummaged through each compartment until her hand fell upon her floppy blue and white disc. With the jagged four corners placed firmly in her grasp she ventured back out onto the landing. And there…she waited for a while...

Did she have enough time to copy everything onto her disc? Or should she just climb back into bed and wait for another opportunity to present itself?

Again, Henrietta wasn't quite sure what to do. But she knew she couldn't confront Richard about this, not until she had the evidence in her possession. Yet, if she waited it could be two or three weeks before he'd extend an invitation for her to spend the night. She couldn't wait that long, she needed to talk to him about this—*now!*

Her underarms were slippery with perspiration, and her negligee clung to her like a second skin. Henrietta breathed out and ventured back up the winding staircase, but this time she did everything in haste. By the time she sat in front of the computer, she knew she had made the right decision.

With her ears cocked and eyes darting from the entrance back to the screen, Henrietta copied and pasted as much as she was able…

Five minutes after Henrietta had climbed back into bed, Richard sauntered into the bedroom. She could hear the chaffing sound the towel made as it rubbed against his athletic build. The enticing scent of oud and lavender pervaded through the air. Henrietta breathed him in. She couldn't help it; her body betrayed her. Although pleasing to her senses, her stomach churned with everything she had just discovered about the man. But despite her better judgement she planned to reason with him. To hear him out. Maybe she could help him somehow - to stop this madness! This was not who he was. At least, she didn't think he was.

Oh my god, Henrietta, you're sleeping with a mass murderer!

She continued to listen to Richard readying himself for bed. Henrietta appeared as though she were fast asleep, but that was the last thing she could do. She didn't move. Not even when he leaned in for whatever reason, to take a good long hard look at her. She laid still, but kept up with her timely breathing. Her eyes were sealed, but her mind was far from asleep, and Henrietta would stay that way until the sun came up…

Once Richard had finished putting on his night clothes, he slipped out of the room and went up to his special lab. Henrietta held her breath...

Chapter Twenty-Seven: All's Fair in Love and War

Lydia

Lydia: I got the day off, were you able to do the same?
Christine: I called in sick.
Lydia: fantastic! Shall we meet - 11ish?
Christine: OK! c u den. Thx Lyds!
Lydia: no worries darling - we're going 2 get him!

Lydia prepared to return to the hospital. This time, she had a plan or something resembling one, she hoped. Her mind wandered back to her short confrontation with Dr Lawson, and the heated discussion she had with Paul Healey, the administrator. She smiled. Neither of them had seen the worst of her yet; she was just getting started.
Note: must call Stephanie!
Amidst the excitement of the last few days she had almost forgotten that her sister's due date fast approached. It was hard to believe that in a few weeks' time, she was going to be an aunt. It seemed like only yesterday she was seven—and her sister—twelve, and they were out in the sunny North Fields of Didcot dissecting insects together. But now they were both women, and she was going to be responsible - or at least partly responsible - for another human being. The thought filled her with dread. In her experience babies were nothing, if not a huge inconvenience. They dribbled, flopped around, and puked all over you with little-to-no provocation.

Well, the babies she'd had the dreaded misfortune of holding, did just that. Perish the thought her friends knew her true feelings about their little bundle of pride and joy. But she couldn't pretend. *Yuck!* Babies were much more of a hassle than any demanding job could ever be!

But babies are real. They are not an occupation. They are you. You are them. And they say something about us....

Do they? Lydia shrugged. She didn't have time to be philosophical right now. She closed her front door and made her way to the underground car park.

***

Christine

Tobey's little body had turned a darker shade of grey. He looked like someone who was dying, and when I called out to him the weight of his condition bore down on his voice. "Christine...I'm worried about *Blembub.*" Tobey couldn't hide his trepidation. "He's my best friend. He's going to be arriving any day now. What if he comes here?"

"Please Tobey, try not to worry about this. We're going to put a stop to whatever Dr Lawson is doing. I promise you, we will!" I was desperate, so I knew I would have to find an answer. "Please, just try to concentrate on you for the moment..."

Tobey continued with his toilsome fight to draw breath. It was pure torture to my ears; it chilled me to the bone. But I could not drown out Tobey's feeble attempts to breathe, being privy to both his thoughts and his struggle.

"Christine. I wish I had met your son Jerry."

I smiled through my tears. "I wish he had met you too. I think you would have been friends; you do remind me of him, you know."

"Really?" Tobey's voice scaled up a notch. "Why? Did he ask you random questions and bored you silly with his dry wit?"

"Ha! I'm sure he would have," I let my laughter warm me. I looked down at Tobey's tiny fingers and began to caress them. "Tobey, my dear. You don't have to be sorry about anything. I love hearing from you. It's been the biggest revelation of my life so far. Always feel free to ask me anything you want."

Tobey grew quiet. "Am I going to die?"

I said nothing.

"It's okay. You don't have to answer that. Did you tell my parents I will always love them?"

"I did." I began to weep.

Tobey spoke candidly, "I feel really sorry for them, you know. Where I am going to is a lot better than earth, in so many ways. For starters, I'll be free from this wearisome burden of loss, which people drag around like a bag of cement. I cannot even begin to describe to you just how crushing that feeling is to the human spirit. It really takes its toll on you…Oh, my poor parents!" Tobey exclaimed, seeing the dire situation, "I really hope, regardless of what happens,

they are going to be okay; they are going to carry on, and they are going to *do well!*" he said in a blazing panic, "Remember, it is important they do. I know I am their son...but…they are also my people, if you get my meaning…"
To my surprise I found that I was trembling; I was unable to take in a steady breath, "Christine. I know how you're feeling. I can feel it. But you must understand something: hurt people hurt. It's understandable, but I'm afraid it's not excusable." He paused. "Christine, you have to let go of your hurt."
"I don't know how to." I gulped.
"You have to," he said with force.
I lowered my voice. "When you meet this Creator, this Creator of Love. Please ask it to heal your parents' wounds. I suppose, if you must go, then…that's all I could really ask for."
"I will do," he replied. "And I'll ask the same for you too."

***

Lydia

Lydia left Christine in the room with Tobey. It was time to do some searching of her own.
Soon enough she happened upon the section she had set out to find. She caught him just as he was preparing to leave the area.
"What are you doing here?" Richard asked. There was no heat in his voice. "I…don't know…" It was

an honest reply. She had been looking for him, but she didn't know why?
Other than flying in the face of polite behaviour, Lydia wondered if it was natural for two people to stare at each other, without speaking, for a lengthy period of time. It had only just occurred to her that she was looking at an incredibly handsome man…*incredibly handsome*…and one she had begun to warm to, in spite of herself.
She had many questions: What was he doing? What was it all in aid of? What a shame! What a waste! Why did it even matter to her what he was…? In no uncertain terms was there going to be an opportunity for them to get to know each other better. There was going to be no ski trips to the Alps. No cabin cruises in the wild. No holding hands as they stared in amazement at the Northern Lights, which seemed to shine down only on them. No dancing together, no glasses clinking in celebration. No dining out. No dating. No - nothing. There was not going to be any of that. Although, there was something momentous growing between them. Lydia could feel it as one feels sunlight spilling into an empty room. But this light wasn't without its shadows. It was being eclipsed by a simple question that put paid to everything else:
How could anything good ever come from this…?
Lydia saw a stirring in his eyes.
What is he thinking?

"You caught me on my way out to lunch. Lydia…that is your name, right? Is it okay if I call you Lydia?"
"That's okay."
"Would you mind taking a walk with me?"
"A walk?" She had to think quickly. Before launching into battle even generals at war met up to discuss terms, so going for a walk shouldn't be too perilous a task, or so she reasoned. Lydia responded with a quick nod. She didn't quite trust herself to speak, just yet.
Richard fell by her side. He steered her out of the ward and onto the lobby, and later down a few flights of stairs. They didn't use the communal lifts. Lydia had planned to ask him outright: what he was up to, and more importantly, why he was doing it? She had the strangest notion that he would tell her everything if she all but asked. But Lydia never did seize the moment. Instead she became distracted by the questions he now put to her, and it had nothing to do with the matter at hand.
"I didn't really know anything about this part of London, not until I started working here," Richard said unexpectedly. "Obviously, I'd heard about The famous Kray Twins, and how the East End was bombed to smithereens during the Second World War. But other than that, I couldn't really say I knew much else. How about yourself?"
They had left the neonatal wing. It seemed he was leading her out of the building and onto the grounds.

Lydia had no objections. Many times, she caught Richard staring at the crowds of people moving in and around the hospital. He looked at them as though they were laboratory specimens or vermin, even. *Who does that?* More's the point…*who the hell does he think he is, looking at people in this manner?* Bristling with fury Lydia was primed to unleash it. But nothing materialized. Instead, she found herself handling Richard's odd proclivity, as one handles their own shortcomings: with lashings of pity and swift forgiveness...

"I had no idea East London had such a rich history," Lydia replied. "I recently took a tour of The Museum of Childhood in Bethnal Green, and The Docklands Museum in Canary Wharf. People always refer to the violent gangsters, but did you know a great many social reformists hailed from this part of the city?" She peered up at him, "Doctor Barnardo's, Sylvia Pankhurst, William and Catherine Booth. In short, I find there's something nostalgic, yet, quintessentially British about this side of London."

Richard nodded. It seemed he wanted her to keep on talking, so she did so. Hence, they walked and talked with no destination in mind. From the outside they were just two people strolling around the hospital's quiet green spaces. Richard came to a halt by a large bronze statue. In the distance a speckled dove broke through the trees and took flight. There was barely any noise around. It was forecasted to rain, but there they were enjoying a sunny afternoon. Lydia was

bemused by this sudden turn of events, yet fully engaged in this beguiling dance.
"This is Saint Margaret." Richard looked up at the statue. "I was told she was the patron saint of the destitute, insane, and falsely accused. She was later canonized by Pope Benedict XIII in 1728. She accomplished a great deal in her lifetime; setting up hospitals for the sick and the impoverished."
He was looking up at the statue, but she studied him. "You seem to know a lot about her life."
Richard half-smiled, "As a matter of fact, I'm more interested in the legacies pioneers like her, leave behind." He scrutinized something in the sky. The sun dipped behind a cloud, bringing a sudden coolness. "According to history, St Margaret had a son who grew up without a father; he was found murdered in the woods when the boy was just a child."
"I couldn't fathom how heart-breaking that would be." Lydia honestly couldn't imagine how she would respond to such grave news.
"A loss of a loved one... is…." Richard swallowed, he straightened himself up. "So, what do you like to do?" He smiled at her. He looked like a teenage boy receiving a trophy for his team. She noticed he changed the subject.
"What do I like to do?" Lydia gave a self-conscious laugh, "Well, besides my nine-to-five, I like to buy things. Nice things. Clothing, accessories, artworks, furnishings…" She petered off. *Now comes the*

judgement part. It always comes.
"You like to buy things?" He seemed pleased. "So do I. I bet your home must be filled with interesting items."
"My home?" Lydia double-took. "Hold on a minute, didn't you just mention your father bought you back some beautiful iron carvings from Zambia, where he runs a health clinic for the blind? No, Richard, I'm very certain it is your home that is filled with interesting things."
"My home?" Richard smiled. "No, only my mind." His Adam's apple bobbed as he laughed. The intense look he gave made her blush. Their identical smiles came naturally, and conveyed more than words.

***

Henrietta

Dr Metcalfe was heading toward the hospital's main entrance. *Did her eyes deceive her or was that Richard in the distance?* It looked like he was having an intimate discussion with a very attractive-looking female. *It was! It was her!* That woman who had stormed into Tobey Daley's room the other day. He was talking to her. *But why…?*
Henrietta didn't want to be seen, she darted toward the entryway. As soon as she stepped into the air-conditioned building, she hovered by the window, hoping to get a better glimpse of the two of them. There they were again. Chattering away like lovebirds.

Henrietta winced. She and Richard were both down for the late shift today. She hoped to have a gentle discussion with him about his project with Diligence. *Gentle discussion!* Her insides curdled. As if Richard warranted anything gentle from her! Richard barely looked at her in public, but there he was swanning around with a woman he barely knew. *He's gone too far this time!* There was only so much she could take. When she caught up with him later she was not going to have a kind discussion with him. She was going to confront him with everything she knew about his shady dealings with Diligence. As soon as the bitter thought flew into her mind, Henrietta began to feel a little better. She managed to tear her eyes away from the detestable pair. They appeared to be making their way back to the hospital. *Yes!* She was going to confront him. She was not going to be made a fool of. Henrietta took a moment to compose herself, then headed toward the lifts. She had to move quickly; there were only a few minutes left before her shift began.

***

The Matron

"So…" Paul Healey looked at the matron with apparent apprehension. "What do we have here?" His hands were clasped together as if in prayer, and from the look that Susan gave him, he would more than likely be making one soon.

"I've called you into the surveillance room because there's something I think you need to see."

Paul looked over at Roger who was head of security at the hospital. "You said this was about Dr Lawson," he whispered. "A senior medic on the ward. Are you sure we can't discuss this…in private?" He looked uncomfortably over at the security guard.

"No. I don't think we can, Paul." Susan shook her head. "From the looks of things, this might be a lot more serious than we thought, and possibly a matter for security." She turned to Roger. "Please, if you don't mind, could you run the tape again?"

Black and white video footage of the hospital grounds blinked onto the screen. A large white estate car pulled into the premises. On one side it read: T-Code: Blood Urgent.

The driver was the only person in the vehicle. The car remained stationary for a few minutes, then someone exited the hospital and approached the driver. It was Dr Lawson.

No words were exchanged, or none that was caught on camera. Then the doctor handed something over to the driver and returned to the hospital.

"This footage was taken four weeks ago." Roger looked over at Paul. "Matron Graham then gave me some more dates to look over. She asked me to search through the backlog, which I did as you can see here. He clicked the mouse and another window opened. It was the footage of the same view, taken from the same surveillance camera, from the same angle.

A similar thing happened again. With Dr Lawson making his way toward the vehicle, handing something over, and heading straight back to the hospital.

"This footage was filmed a year and a half ago," Roger added.

Paul frowned. "What in heavens is he doing? How many—"

"Thirteen times so far," Susan answered. "There are still six more dates I would like to verify."

"What does all this mean?"

"I don't know, Paul." Susan's face gave nothing away. "After my initial chat with Dr Lawson I felt compelled to do some checking around of my own. Now, I'm not one to defame any one of our staff members. But as you know, Paul, over the years there's been a significant rise in the number of mortalities on the neonatal ward…We cannot pretend these deaths are anything but natural." She sighed and looked over at the frozen images on the screens. "This is very odd. And in my experience, odd is never very good."

"What do we do now? We just can't suspend him for odd behaviour, can we, Susan? We don't know what he's doing. He could be handing over imported cigarettes for all we know!"
"Yes, and what a mighty coincidence that would be," she said with a dissatisfying drawl. "His strange jaunts to this unauthorized vehicle seem to fall on the same days that these natural deaths have occurred. Like I said, I don't want to cast aspersions here," she lowered her voice, "but, bear in mind Dr Lawson is down for deliveries today, tomorrow and Friday..."
There was a long pause. The implication of her words swirled in their minds like a toxic marinade.
"But Susan." Paul said through pursed lips. "We don't have anything concrete. In fact, we don't have anything at all! I don't think we can suspend him on the weight of this."
The sweat from Susan's brow steamed up her lenses. She took off her glasses, brought out her handkerchief and gave them a slow wipe. "Paul. This might be a little out…of our remit. It might be something for the authorities to look into."
It did not need to be articulated. Getting the police involved would be an extreme move for the hospital. Susan knew this, but she didn't let that stop her from putting it out there. She knew the decision was Paul's to make.
The administrator swallowed. He no longer had his hands clasped together in front of him, but was rubbing the back of his neck. He turned to Roger.

"Okay." He nodded. "You can make the call. We'll let the authorities figure it out. But in the meantime everything remains as normal, agreed? Which means Dr Lawson can continue with his duties. After all, we're still in the dark about what is going on here." He looked to the matron. "We'll let the police carry out their investigations. I just hope to god there's a reasonable explanation for all of this, that's all!"

Paul hoped he had made the right decision. First, getting the police involved. And second, allowing Dr Lawson to continue working…of course, the safety of all the residents at the hospital was paramount. But the hospital's reputation was also a big concern of his…*Was he so wrong to feel conflicted about this?* Bleh! What did he care! No one could hear his deepest thoughts.

***

Chapter Twenty-Eight: The Confrontation

<u>Siba</u>

Tobey Daley was light-years away from his soul group, but only in spirit. Regardless, I could hear the little ones chattering amongst themselves. Soul groups are an interesting phenomenon, all the members share a supernatural lifeline. They may not react when the chord has been severed, but they certainly know when it is under attack…

"I'm coming in!" Albert ran then leapt into the majestic waterfall. When he resurfaced his soul mates were all around him.

"I have to admit I do feel bad for Tobey," Li Wei wiped a wet strand of hair away from his eye. "When do you think he'll leave this place, and begin his journey in the world?"

"I don't know," Albert looked down, "nobody seems to know why this is happening to him. I do believe his journey has begun; it just appears to be quite different from everyone else's."

"Did he say there was something the matter?" Nnenna's buoyant face was tinged with concern.

"As a matter of fact Tobey did mention something about babies…being in trouble…"

Albert recalled the last time he and his friend were together. "Even if there is something to be concerned about, I've decided I'm not going to worry about a thing!" He lifted himself off the rocks. He laughed before doing a perfect dive into the water.

Albert's laughter lightened the air and filled his soul group with a burst of energy. Laughter did that. As laughter is a powerful resource—just as it is on earth. But like most of the world's natural resources, it is not utilized as much as it could be…

"Tobey. My brother. I'm coming to be with you soon," Albert whispered into the open waters. "Please don't leave us. We are all coming to be with you soon…"

***

Lydia

Lydia stole a quick glance to the right. Christine looked like how she was feeling inside: a little drained - demoralized. *What now?* They had only just left the hospital five minutes ago. She decided to tell Christine about her odd conversation with Dr Lawson.

"Oh my god! You like him!" Christine accused, "How could you, Lydia? How could you like him?"

"I-I don't know," she didn't need to take a peek in a mirror to see that her cheeks were inflamed like the colour of sunset. "I have no words...I-I don't know how this has happened?"

"You don't know how *this* has happened…?" Christine looked back at her in disbelief. Her ambiguous explanation had likely robbed Christine of speech, and the same could be said for herself, as nothing more was discussed as the two of them made their way back toward the overground station. An awkward silence had crept in, one, which could not so easily be articulated, like most matters of the heart…

Eventually Christine broke the silence. "So what now?" Her eyes were stormy and full of questions. A niggle of despair had crept into her voice. Lydia said nothing for a while. She held her gaze. Very slowly they both began to smile at the situation.

"Unbelievable!" Lydia threw her hands up. "How does that saying go? It's better to have loved and lost, than never to have loved at all!"

"Love? Ha! Please pass me the sick bucket."

Christine spoke in jest, but her relief was palpable. "Seriously, Lydia. I think you may have dodged a bullet there, my friend."

Lydia frowned, "I suppose you might be right about that: 'Sexy. Fit. Debonair' doctor—yes! I'll have some of that. Sexy. Fit. Debonair *'baby-murdering'* doctor. I don't know. Doesn't quite have the same ring to it now, does it?" Lydia said as she nudged Christine,

"No it doesn't. Not even by half!" Christine kissed her teeth.

"You did it again"

"Did what?"

"That thing I said you do with your mouth."

Christine laughed, "I kissed my teeth. And believe me if there ever was a time it is warranted—it is now!"

Lydia looked away with amusement. Her hazel-green eyes rested on the drizzly roads ahead. She wondered when the rain had come in. It probably started when she and Richard were making their way back to the building. Imagine not noticing the rain. *How absorbed in conversation had the two of them been…?* "I'm going to make a call later," she said out loud. And later she did.

After extinguishing the butt of her vogue cigarette, Lydia put in a call to an editor she knew, who worked for one of the tabloid. She alerted his attention to the high number of neonatal mortalities taking place at a reputable hospital in London's East End.

"Keith. I'll see if I can get more information on this. As soon as I have more, you'll have more. But in the meantime, I suggest you have a proper look around. I think this has the potential to be quite a big story…"

Create the story. Make the story. Sell the story! Public Relations was her job—and she *bloody* loved it! Only regrettably, there was very little creativity involved. What was happening at the hospital was all too real, and the consequences had been nothing short of severe.

As customary, before turning in for the night, Lydia poured out her scattered musings in her gold-gilded notebook. A gift she received from her *nana* when she was thirteen years old.

Who told us we grow from our pain—what an egregious lie
Some of us like withered leaves curl up and die...

Dr Richard Lawson—what an odd bod
Damaged goods being dispatched to an unsuspecting public
Are damaged goods—still good...?
Why am I writing this?
Poor Richard
No
Poorer world...

***

Henrietta

"Etta. Any reason why you wanted us to meet here?" The scowl on Richard's face only served to heighten his good looks. Henrietta wanted to humiliate him and hug him at the same time. The internal conflict made her nauseous.

In silence they both stood in the quiet section of the neonatal ward. Henrietta had a quick look through the glass partition. There was nobody around, it was all clear. She turned her attention back to Richard. Henrietta wanted to hurl insults at him, scream at him, thump on his chest—anything! Just to make him see how much of a mess of a man he really was. And yet, despite his flaws she was willing to be there for him. But what was the use? He had no intention of making anything easy for her. How simple it was for him to float around with a stranger out to kill his career. While he stood here grumbling about the few minutes she had just requested of him. But now it was she who had the upper hand. Henrietta was going to do what she should have done from the beginning. She was ready to let him have it!

"Richard. I know what you've been up to over the last two years," she gave him an accusatory stare, "I know what you've been doing."

There was a moment of silence. "What are you talking about, Etta?"

"I'm talking about Diligence. The stem cell project you've been working on with them."

"And what about the project?"

"Have you taken leave of your senses, Richard? You cannot be obtuse about this! This is wrong! It's criminal! It's dangerous! How could you allow yourself to get involved with something like this?"

"Have you finished, Etta? I've got to get back onto the ward." He started to walk past her.

"Richard. I was on your home computer. I've copied most, if not, all your emails with Diligence. I've got it all here on this disc."

Richard spun around. His eyes didn't fall on Etta, but on the blue and white floppy disc she waved in her hand. Richard stared at it. His eyes trailed upwards to rest on hers. More than a minute had passed before anything else was said. "Etta." Richard rubbed his face with his hands. "You have no idea what I've been going through." "Really?" She waited to hear more.

"You're right. This has been my obsession for far too long. It's taken me away from everything." He approached her. "Etta. I don't know what to do any more. I thought I was embarking on a worthy project. Something that would someday provide a viable solution...Etta..." He softly called her name.

"Richard. Oh, Richard, dear..." The hand which didn't hold the disc shot up to stroke his arm.

"What are you going to do?"

"What do you think I should do?" Richard paid close attention to her facial expressions.
Henrietta looked away. She could see that Richard was reaching out to her. He needed help. But she needed something too…she took a deep breath.
"Richard, I'm tired of this, of not knowing where I stand with you." She waited.
Richard looked back at her.
"I'm not happy," she continued. "To be honest, I haven't been for a while, and you're the root cause of it! How can I lie down with you, but wake up hating the world? How is this even possible?" She expelled a bitter laugh. "But this is how I feel when I'm around you. I can't do this anymore!"
"What is it, Etta, what do you want?"
Good question. What did she want? What was she doing? She was begging this man to love her—*begging!*

Henrietta was wrong. She hadn't lost all self-respect; it seemed there was still more she could give. She went for the jugular.

"I just want you to give us…a go…that's all."

Henrietta breathed. Yes. That was her speaking, although it sounded like it came from some far-off place.

Richard still looked at her but there was something else in his eyes. "Etta," he said softly, "I think I need help. I'm not sure what to do."

"Help?" Her face brightened. "I can help you, Richard. Listen. You must distance yourself from Diligence. It sounds like you've climbed into bed with an unethical outfit here."

"I know. I understand what you're saying Etta, really, I do." Richard massaged his temples. "I've realized I've made a colossal mistake. It seems I've been making these crazy decisions for quite some time now. There's no one to blame. I did this under my own volition." He shook his head. "Right now I feel like I can't trust myself anymore, let alone trust…anyone else…" He looked long and hard at her, then shot a quick glance at the disc in her hand.

Henrietta felt terrible. How could she profess to want to help someone, while she blackmailed them at the same time? *That is just insane!*

The floppy disc felt like a lump of burning coal. She looked at it one last time. "Richard, my dear. It's not what you think," she swallowed, "I-I wanted to help you. That was all."

Richard nodded. His eyes never left her face.
"Take it! You should have it!"
Richard quickly did so, and in a swifter move he gathered Henrietta into his arms.
Her deep blue eyes were fixed on his cool grey ones. They searched for hope…for feeling…for anything…but they were soon taken away from her sight, as his mouth descended on hers. She breathed him in.
Oud, Lavender, and a promise of more…
In a moment of clarity Henrietta wondered why she had handed over the disc: Smart Henrietta. Clever Henrietta. *Swore to save lives—Henrietta!* It is not always the rational who are reasonable. *Why the devil did she hand it over?*
Then Henrietta realised why she had done so. She wasn't madly in love—she was *mad* and in love. It was a thin line. She had crossed it. And now she no longer cared…
Although Richard gave a good impression, he didn't actually kiss Henrietta; he just shared the bitter taste in his mouth. Richard had got the disc back—one less thing to worry about. He had to put in a call to Diligence. Whatever was to come, was out of his hands now.

Chapter Twenty-Nine: Professor Florian

Siba

Let me tell you about Professor Elias Dominic Florian—known as 'The Professor' amongst members of his inner circle. Of course, he was the brains behind Diligence Biopharmaceuticals.
Ever since he was a young man The Professor had always kept himself busy. This showed no signs of slowing down, not even when he became the youngest member on the board of directors at the University of Bern—the international leader in scientific research. It was the same institution where he was awarded his doctorate several years prior.
For the Professor, establishing the business was easy to accomplish. However, due to its ongoing relevance in the world, it would not be as simple to dismantle… This is because what had started out as an interesting pastime for The Professor, had mushroomed into an entity which has since been able to wield vast amounts of power and influence in all sectors of society.

The Professor was proud of all his research projects, but like a father of many children, he felt some were more worthy of praise than others: The Alpha Stem Cell Study, being one of them. Years and years of meticulous research had culminated in Diligence finding, and henceforth, isolating the 'weak' gene. The crack team of experts came up with this name to describe their most recent wonder. The gene was referred to as 'weak' in opposition to the vast unknown composition of its greater counterpart, which had yet to be discovered. At the time the discovery of the 'weak' gene was a breakthrough by every stretch of the imagination. And consequently, the patenting of its use reaped huge financial rewards for the blossoming company. But for The Professor, this was not enough…

For you see, many saw Professor Florian as an ambitious man, and he was. But ambition was no drain to the Professor at all. It didn't have to be coaxed out of him like an actor before a performance. Ambition flowed in his blood, his ancestry. The Professor was drawn to ambitious people. A person without ambition to him, was least of all the thing they first claimed to be…Nonetheless, there was something of greater prominence that kept The Professor up at night, and blighted his days. It was buried deep in the heart of all human matters. You see, what propelled The Professor to keep on going till the very end, was his insatiable pride...

Dispensing with the accolades, titles, and distinctions, The Professor was simply Elias Florian. And Elias had lost count the number of times he had been called up by officials from the Nobel Foundation. The directors lauded him for his remarkable findings in Cellular Biology and Biomedical Sciences. But of course The Professor never won, and he could never win, simply, because many of his discoveries worked against the Foundation's core tenets, which stipulated that the recipient of The Nobel Prize had to have created or invented, something that would—first and foremost—be for the greatest benefit to humankind. Suppressing cures and waging biological warfare, through the use of his inventions – although exemplary - was something The Professor had to carry out under a cloak of invisibility…up until now…The Professor, and his special team of experts, were drawing closer to shedding some light on the possible existence of a 'strength' particle: The yin to the yang, the opposite of the 'weak' gene. This particle was a unique strand which embodied all the exceptional qualities inherent in human DNA. What's more, these molecules were rampant in the blood of wholly formed foetuses. All that was needed to ratify the findings, was the last batch of stem cells which due from London any day now. The Professor was proud of this project. Its eventual findings would make him, and Diligence, exceedingly wealthy. But it would also secure him the Nobel Prize, the thing that would give him the recognition he felt he deserved and had systematically been denied. So, one can only imagine The Professor's growing frustrations as talks about the possible termination of his beloved seven-year project, was likely to become a reality.

"What do you mean, Bernard?"

"I mean the doctor," Bernard replied. "The agent we assigned to this project is proving to be a real liability. I don't think he's up to the job. He talks of this task being compromised by a woman who can communicate with newborns. I have no idea what he's going on about. However, it's only just come to my attention that this person's name is being bandied about in the public sphere." He paused. "If details of this project should come out into the open, who knows where it could lead..." The Professor noted the emphasis on the last few words. Bernard cleared his throat. "As I said before, I take full responsibility for this. I had my doubts about this candidate…" He sighed, "I'm still in London for another week. I'll continue to do my own research into this matter."

"And the project?"

There was a long pause. "Even if we agree that the project should be put on hold—not discontinued…but put on hold for the meantime. With everything I've just relayed to you, we're still left with a slight problem. Wouldn't you agree?" The Professor was silent. "Yes," he said eventually. "We are. And what do you propose we do?" "Before it is too late I think we should begin to focus on salvaging whatever we can from this wreckage. We should start making the necessary steps to extract ourselves from the situation."

The Professor breathed in sharply. He was opposed to this outcome, but even in anger rationality needed to always be deployed. Bernard was right, distance was best.

"Alright, Bernard. Salvage away."

"Thank you, Professor, I will be in touch shortly."

Conversation, over with. Problem-solving, enacted. Sometimes you cannot help but admire, the clinical minds of the rational

***

Siba

6:45p.m on a Wednesday evening…

A woman collapses onto her bedroom floor. She writhes on the carpet in abominable pain. "It's not supposed to be like this!" She thumps the ground with a balled fist. And yes, the woman in blatant agony was quite right, as she had lived through the perils of labour three years prior. What is happening to her now was unnatural, because it was as much...

"Oh my god! What is going on?"

Fortunately there is help at hand. Her husband bundles her into the car; ignoring the stunned looks from his neighbours as they rush out to glimpse the owner of those disturbing noises. As fast as he can, he navigates through the city's circuitry roads, praying he will get to the hospital in time. He silently pleads for help. His wife looks like she is ready to die. If this is the case what will become of the little one?

Meanwhile, in a paradise far away, the soul mates had convened again. They were missing another member, but there was no need for alarm. This time it was Albert Simon's turn to make his way to earth, and begin his journey in the big wide world…

***

Richard

Nursing a stiff shoulder and creaking with exhaustion, Richard wrestled out of his theatre-blues and replaced them with a crisp new set. He desperately needed a refreshing drink; something to bolster his energy levels.

A few minutes ago he had delivered a newborn by emergency caesarean. The girl had unwittingly got herself tangled in her own umbilical cord. Rescuing the neonate from the situation was the fun part, attending to the mother who had been in labour for over eleven hours, had been an unwanted ordeal. The biggest drain of his day so far. Skirting past the busy staffroom, he made a brief stop at his workstation. The plan was to take his pills before preparing for his next delivery. He hoped this time it would be the one he had been waiting all week for...

Earlier that day Richard had decided he was going to go ahead and complete his mission for Diligence. If suspicions were raised, what of it? Before they had the chance to figure anything out he'd be long gone. He could always leave the NHS—or Britain for that matter. There were plenty of places he could go to: Australia; South Africa, Singapore. They welcomed British doctors with opened arms. But Diligence offered an opportunity that only came once in a lifetime. No sane person turns their back on success, not if they had worked as hard as he had to attain it. He gulped down the capsules, then he rifled through his inbox. It would be the last check of the day. His phone rang. It was his contact from Diligence.

"Bernard. I was planning to have a chat with you today. I can't talk right now, could I call you later?"

"No." Bernard said abruptly, "This won't take long. Quick as you can, tell me what the current situation is with the arrival of the final specimen," Bernard paused, "…and everything else that has happened so far."

Richard gave a brief report. He outlined everything that had happened up until the point of the phone call. Bernard *ummed,* as though he were verifying the information against his own compilation of facts. Richard did not mention his odd conversation with Lydia; he felt there was no need since they didn't talk about Diligence. However, he debated whether he should inform Bernard about his silly encounter with Henrietta. He decided to go ahead with it. He gave a brusque account of the incident.

"So," Bernard drawled in a soft accent, "she threatened you and mentioned Diligence."

"Yes, that is correct. But I was able to get the disc back, and as soon as I get home I will wipe everything off my computer. Seriously Bernard, there is nothing she can say which cannot be refuted. She is a silly girl—completely neurotic!"

"Okay." Bernard sighed. There was a moment's silence. "Richard. Listen carefully to me. We want you to step away from this project—is that clear? There is no need for you to collect the remaining specimen. Do you understand? We are terminating the project."

"W-what! Why…? Are you sure about this?"

"Yes. One hundred percent. Stop everything, and take care of the matter with your home computer."

"Bernard…has something happened…? I'm sure it's nothing that cannot be sorted out. I can still go ahead—"

"No, Richard. You are relieved of this project. We will inform you of our next step in due course."

Richard was beyond confounded. With steely determination Diligence had set up, and carried out what could only be described as a-near-to-impossible task. And yet, just before its completion, they decide to pull the plug on it.

Had he heard correctly?

Richard was stunned. He fell back in his chair. A cool sensation crept through his chest. It could have been the effect of the drug he had taken, but Richard knew better. It was relief: pure-as-day, god-honest, genuine, relief! Because deep down in that murky well of secrets, Richard wasn't up for the job today.

Because he wasn't quite himself today

Although he kept telling himself otherwise.

Nevertheless the conversation wasn't over, Bernard hadn't finished talking. "So you've told me everything that has happened thus far. Now, tell me everything you know about this baby whisperer..."

***

Lydia

"What time will you be at the hospital tomorrow?" Lydia put the question to Christine. In one hand she held her mobile phone, and with the other she made a hurried attempt to arrange her untidy apartment. Items of clothing were spewed all over her Velvet Italian Mohair suite of chairs, and a pile of used mugs had amassed like a small pyramid in her kitchen sink. She had a cleaner who came in twice a week, yet she still managed to whip up her apartment into a chaotic frenzy. Grimacing, she almost missed Christine's response to her question.

"Did you get that?"

"Sorry—darling, say that again."

Christine repeated, "I said I'll be going to the hospital tomorrow morning, but a bit earlier than usual. Then I'll head back to my office around lunchtime." Christine sighed. "Honestly, Lydia. I'm so surprised work hasn't fired me already. I keep asking if I can leave early or come in later. Or sometimes I call to say I won't be coming in at all!"

Lydia laughed. "I doubt they'd fire you. I'm sure your colleagues are a lot more sympathetic than you think."

"You might be right about that. I thought my work colleagues would be the last people to give a damn, but they've turned out to be the most supportive. I suppose I kind of harboured the fear of being judged, or becoming office gossip."

"Which you are."

"Which I am," Christine chuckled, "but, hey! I guess you can't have it all. Yes, they are a nosey bunch, but I really should appreciate them more."
Lydia tsked. "As I mentioned before, you're very fortunate. I think you're one of the few people I know who can say they appreciate their workplace, or work family, I suppose one should call them. I once worked for a company that ostracized an employee for gaining weight, and then later fired her."
"Oh, Lydia, that's awful! Was it you?"
"Me?" Lydia burst out laughing. "Don't be silly. It wasn't *me!* It happened while I was living in L.A. I interned at one of those high-profile, over-the-top, take themselves *way too seriously* agencies. The cattiness I witnessed there was *unbelievable!* It was the impetus that motivated me to start my own business. I love to work, but I want to do it on my own terms not at the beck and call of some goon on a power trip." Lydia paused. "Are you sure you're going to be alright tomorrow?"
"Yes, I guess so." Christine exhaled. "Tobey said a very close friend of his will be arriving at the hospital, if not this evening then tomorrow for sure. He's dead-worried about his friend's safety."
"This is such a bloody nightmare!" Lydia growled. "Seriously, I don't know what the holdup is. But while Mr Healey continues to drag his feet, I've done some researching of my own." Lydia gave a mischievous chuckle. "I've asked a journalist chum of

mine to meet me at the hospital tomorrow. He said he would be there around four-ish."

"4 o'clock? *Drat!* I'll be back at the office by then."

"Don't sweat it, hun! I'm going to have our pesky reporter take a few photos of *Dr Death* himself."

Lydia could hear the grin on the other end. "Are you serious, Lydia?"

"I'm always serious, darling."

"But isn't that going against some privacy law or something of the sort?"

"Yes, yes, and the rest of it," Lydia said obviously not caring at all.

Christine laughed. "This is crazy! I wish I could be there to see Healey's face."

Lydia stopped talking. "How about I drop by yours tomorrow evening? Then I can tell you all about it."

"Okay, if you don't mind…Oh wait a minute, I'm going to see my mum after work tomorrow. I don't know how long I'll be. But…if it's okay with you - I already know what you're going to say - I keep a spare key under the potted plant outside my front door. If you want to come around tomorrow, feel free to let yourself in. Or you can come meet me at my mum's in Clapton, whichever is easiest for you?"

"Christine!" Lydia shrieked. "Under the plant? That's hardly inventive of you - or *safe!* You may as well drape neon lights around the base along with some complimentary mints."

"I know," Christine laughed pathetically, "but I always keep a spare set under there. I hate the thought of losing my keys and not being able to get back into my apartment. And yes, I think I fear this even more than the possibility of being robbed. That said you still can't get into this block, not without knowing the security code. So, maybe not as reckless as you think, aye!"

"Security code?" Lydia queried. "I bet I could get into your apartment without using it. All I need do is buzz one of your neighbours, they'll let me in. People don't really check these days. How long do you think you'll be at your mother's for?"

"I don't know. I promised I'd check up on her in the week, but really it's her actually checking up on me."

"Okay." Lydia was silent. "Christine. If you can help it, try not to leave your mother's too late. Hopefully we'll catch up tomorrow and I'll let you know how we got—" A lengthy yawn swallowed up the rest of her sentence. "Imagine that. I keep telling you to get some rest, but I think it's me who needs some. See you tomorrow, lovely. Give Tobey a kiss from me."

"I will, and thank you, Lydia. You're a star as always—get some sleep!"

***

Richard

Richard sat facing his home computer. He stared at the lights emanating from the screen as though it were embers in an open fireplace.

As promised, all emails to and from Diligence had been erased from the system. It was as if all their technical findings, discussions, and revelations over the last two years had never happened. But for Richard, they had, and he was nowhere near off the hook, just yet.

Paul Healey was keeping something from him. *What a buffoon!* Earlier that day, after Richard had returned from his break, the administrator could scarcely look him in the eye. Richard also detected a slight quiver in his voice when he spoke to him. *Pathetic!*

Upon seeing that, Richard proceeded to pay closer attention to Susan. As always she gave nothing away. But when he was called in at around 8 p.m. to deliver the Simon's baby, which would have been the last specimen, the matron had crept into the room to oversee proceedings. Richard noticed she had done that a few times on his watch today…

Good thing he was ordered not to collect the specimen. He was very lucky for that phone call indeed…. All the same, whatever Paul and the matron had on him it was inconsequential. He assumed the pair had nothing but their suspicions. He couldn't say that he was at all surprised at their behaviour. Deep down Richard knew there was always a possibility that someone would get suspicious—there were just too many deaths. It was a considerable number to conceal over a short period of time. All, taking place under his watch. Alarm bells were bound to start ringing, the question is: *What can anyone really do about it?* The hospital was over-stretched, and under-resourced. Who could even begin to allocate the time and energy it took to pursue a suspicion? This was, after all, the NHS. Budgets needed to be slashed, quotas filled, and staff members maintained. Honestly, who had the time to care? He shook his head. If he wasn't so tired he would have laughed out loud. If he didn't want to, he didn't have to go anywhere. They had their suspicions and nothing else. Richard picked up his phone. He was *dying* to do something. He thumbed the buttons on his keypad. Round and round he went, circling the digits of her mobile number...He was able to obtain her contact details. He could call her, if he wanted to. *And say what exactly?*

'Hello, Lydia. It's Richard Lawson. I was able to attain your number from a colleague'…No! He couldn't say that. That would be in breach of some personal data act. Maybe he wouldn't mention where he got her number from…
'Hi, Lydia. How are you? It's Richard Lawson. I have two tickets for La bohéme *at the National Opera. Would you like to accompany me…?'* No! What was he thinking? He could no more draw Lydia into his mixed-up world, than he could take back the man he was before the day they had met. Richard couldn't change

the past. Even that was beyond the realms of his capabilities as a life and death maker…
He let his gaze rest on the grainy swirls on his large oak work desk. He followed the light indentations where his pen had punctured the pulpy exterior. He surveyed the phone one last time before tossing it into the top drawer. It was the best place for it. Richard wasn't going to call Lydia. He had a moment of weakness - that was all. For now he'll keep his device in the top drawer. Definitely the best place for it...

***

Chapter Thirty-One: A Fresh Start

Christine

It was bright and early, and as promised I was at the special care nursery waiting to see baby Tobey. The matron sauntered into the waiting area just as I finished my coffee. I shifted in my chair. I didn't want to be seen. I wanted to remove any possible obstructions to my visiting Tobey today. The frosty looks the matron reserved for me and Lydia, let me know that our presence on the ward was far from welcome.

I got up and walked over to the dustbin and disposed of my cup. The matron spoke to the nurses on reception and had her back toward me. I dashed toward the entrance to the neonatal ward. I had just finished pressing the button when the matron called out, "Hello. Christine. Is that you?"

I turned around to face her. "I-I..."

"I gather you're here to see Tobey?"

"Yes...yes I am."

"His parents only arrived a few moments ago, they're with him now." I waited, I perceived the matron wanted to say something else. "Ermm…as I said before, I have no idea what you're doing with the baby, but whatever it is…keep doing it."

I blinked.

Had I heard correctly?

"As you know," the matron looked me squarely in the face, "we've been looking after Tobey for over

year now. Some of the nurses, me included, have grown quite fond of him and his parents.
The Daley's are a really sweet couple; they have a tremendous amount of love for their baby." The matron sighed and looked away. She pushed her glasses further up her nose. "Before you arrived, Kelly and Robert were...well…you can imagine, all hope had gone. But since you've been around their son, they've been able to come to terms with things a bit better. Somehow you've given them peace." It looked like the matron wasn't used to baring her teeth, but just then she managed a small smile for me, "And Christine," she leaned in, "just to let you know the other matter is seriously being looked into, okay?"
I understood. "Thank you, matron." I smiled.
"I best not keep you. Have a good day now."
"You too," I smiled back. *Oh, wow!* I had to stop myself from rushing toward the unit. I couldn't wait to tell Tobey some good news for a change. They believed us! They believed him! Now maybe something was going to be done about it.

***

The Matron

Just before Christine sped off, Susan was about to add something else. She wanted to say: 'And please do say hello to Tobey from all of us…' but the thought didn't quite transpire into words. And just as quickly, she assessed, it would have been a little out of character for her to say as much. For just like the matter of faith, although Susan knew it to be true, she still wasn't quite ready to believe. And so she stood there, for a few minutes more with an awkward looking smile on her face…

***

Christine

"Any more news about your friend?" I asked Tobey when we were alone together. His parents were both out on errands. "I haven't felt anything, and maybe that's a good sign. I presume a lot of babies have arrived at the hospital since yesterday?"

"And they're still coming!" I hoped my optimism would quash any lingering doubts he had. "Your mate may have very-well made it through. I think the hospital is aware that something is amiss, Tobey. I don't think Dr Lawson can continue to work here. Hopefully they will begin to make plans for his dismissal," I drew in a sharp breath, "and - if there is a god - an arrest should swiftly follow."

"I hope so," Tobey muttered. "Christine...it's almost time for my suction." I looked up at the clock and saw it was coming up to the hour. "I guess, I'll see you tomorrow then," Tobey said weakly.

"That's right sweetheart." I made a fuss of tucking him in. "I'll pop in after work. You can tell me another riveting story about one of your great Ancestors." I kissed the crown of his neatly groomed head which smelt of honeysuckle and baby powder. Tobey chuckled. "As a matter of fact, I'm looking forward to hearing all about this sting operation Lydia has set up. I don't think the administrator knows what he's up against. Thank you, Christine. I think we're really going to get him."

"I told you we would," I whispered before pressing the panic button. "That sick bastard is not going to get away with this."

***

"Christine. Correct me if I'm wrong, but did I read somewhere that you have an ability that allows you to communicate with newborns?" Brian leaned back in his chair, he didn't look at me. He seemed to be distracted with the post-it note he twirled in between his fingers.

My sudden laughter even caught me unawares. A few months ago a question like that would have brought me out in hives. But today I was at ease. "Yes, Brian. You did hear correctly." I gave him wide smile, "And whatever you're thinking—it's even more bizarre than you could ever imagine!"
"Really!" He laughed. He sat bolt-upright in his chair, "okay, try me?" He wheeled his chair closer to where I sat. "I've been dying to ask you some questions ever since this news broke out, but we were given strict orders not to say anything to you. You know, because of everything you've been through…I always knew you were special,"

"Oh, Brian, stop that! You're starting to sound like my mother." His chuckle was mingled with relief, "I must point out you've been looking a lot more cheerful of late. What have those babies been telling you?"

"Brian, it's home time. You don't want to hear about this now?"

"I most certainly do."

"Okay, if you insist." I placed my bag to the side. My phone buzzed. I looked down and saw a message from Lydia.

'I've arrived at the hospital with Keith. Tell all l8r'

I reeled off my reply:

'Thx Lyds – knock 'em dead! ;-D'

"Oh, Brian! I totally forgot! I'm seeing my mother later."

"Noooooo," Brian's animated voice boomed across the open-plan office. "I want to hear this!"

"Are you sure? There's an awful lot to take in. I can scarcely make sense of it myself."

"Quite bizarrely, I really do want to know what babies think about. I suggest you get this all down in writing, I see a major publishing deal in the works."

I giggled and shook my head. "Then I will tell all, but it'll have to be another time. Sorry—gotta dash!" I threw him a consolatory smile. I grabbed my bag and said my goodbyes to the rest of the team, before heading towards the exit.

***

Canary Wharf was as busy as usual, with professionals in muted suits scurrying toward their favourite drinking haunts. I had walked halfway across the piazza before I acknowledged my apprehension.

Am I being followed?

A sturdy man wearing aviator sunglasses and a light-blue jacket, headed toward me. But then, he soon passed by and carried on with his wandering.

"Excuse me," said a voice to the right of me. The woman brushed past then proceeded toward the lifts. I scanned my surroundings. Everything seemed as normal.

So why did I feel on edge?

I stepped onto the escalator but stood absolutely still. I allowed the mechanical staircase to glide me to my next destination point.

The train carriage I was cocooned in steadily rocked its way through southeast London. The hypnotic movement almost sunk me into a deep sleep. If it wasn't for the regular announcements I would have missed my stop, which I couldn't afford to do, as I was due to change lines at Bank Station. And much to my annoyance I arrived there, smack-bang, right in the middle of rush hour.

All around me commuters jostled to my left and to my right, and criss-crossing my path ahead. Like everybody else I had no choice but to quicken my steps. I cast a brief look over my shoulder. There didn't appear to be anyone around who had travelled up with me from Canary Wharf. I was on my own, yet I still couldn't shake the uncomfortable feeling I was being followed.

As I soared up another set of escalators I caught a glimpse of myself in the mirrors. My mother was right. I was a shadow of my former self. *What happened to my complexion?* I looked like someone who was on drugs, or at the very least, a person suffering from iron deficiency. However today I had decided to do something different. Instead of snapping my curly hair back into the usual restrictive bun; I decided to let my glossy ringlets run free. I couldn't remember the last time I had worn my hair this way. I looked like a proud lioness—the opposite of how I felt inside. Maybe this was why I wore it this way. Things had to change—and today was the start! I was going to do this for Tobey, and because of Tobey…he said: everyone needs to find happiness in sadness, which was a strange contradiction. But as Tobey pointed out, the world was a sad place, for the mere fact that everything in it was destined to die...

'Why are you afraid when I talk like this?' Tobey had said. His words were gentle, he needed her to understand something. 'Don't you see? Death is all around you. Look at me? It's staring you in the face! There is a flaw to this life, and that flaw is death. It is the huge white elephant in the room. It haunts and

taunts all the peoples of this world; eating away at any shred of peace that could be theirs to have. And this fear drives them in the wrong direction; making them focus on all the wrong things. Don't you see? Something perfected by love can never die...Christine. I wouldn't lose sleep over the imperfect, really, I wouldn't. I came with a burning desire to impart all the wisdom and knowledge that flows in me, to give to the world. But I'm coming away having learnt a very valuable lesson...As you can see, I am dying. But why do I smile, Christine? Why do I smile...?'

It was not the fact that we die, that was of monumental importance, Tobey had later explained to me. But it is how we live...for our life is power: our stories, our struggles, our deeds - are all a glowing testament to that power. A power, which I realised, was harnessed some time before I had entered the world, and one which would follow me after I'd left it.

'It is not the fact that we die, that is of monumental importance, but how we live...it is how we live...'
I took a long hard look at my dimmed reflection. *How many times have I gazed into a mirror without truly seeing myself?* But now I understood what Tobey meant. If the world had nothing to offer but sadness, then happiness could only come from me. I had the power to do something about it, because my life *is* the power...my life...
What could be more exceptional, more profound than my pain...? I remembered asking myself this manifold

question not too long ago. The answer was: *my life…what was I doing with my life…?*
I peered down at the title of the novel I held in my hand: *The God of Small Things*
I was glad I had given into my splurge on the latest bestseller. I book-marked the page and placed it into my tote bag. I didn't know what had brought it on, but I recalled a chain email that had landed in my inbox one afternoon. A gentle chuckle lay hold of my stomach, vibrating as it grew.
The message had read:

Be decisive. Right or wrong, make a decision. The road of life is paved with flat squirrels who couldn't make a decision….

I spent a full minute and a half wrestling with my laughter. *Only god knows what the other commuters are thinking?* I didn't care, which made me chuckle even harder.
Didn't Tobey say laughter was a tonic?
A small part of me looked forward to seeing my mother later. I wondered if it would be visible to see that I had turned a corner. Right then my stomach made a low rumbling sound. *Changes abound.* I do believe that was the stirring of an appetite.
The train suddenly juddered to a halt. The wide steel doors slid open. Two burly men in dark suits stepped into the carriage. I became aware of my apprehension. Three stops later, they were gone.
What is wrong with me today? I needed to eat something.

My mother did warn: if I didn't take care of myself it would catch up with me someday. As soon as I get to my mum's, I'll have a look around her fridge. No doubt she'll be more than happy to see that side of me, if anything.

Flat squirrels? Okay….I really need to stop laughing now…

Chapter Thirty-Two: Visiting Yvonne Shore

Christine

"When my family came over from Sligo in the sixties, I never thought in a *million* years that I'd end up with someone like your father," my mother said with a laughter which was both cheery and unapologetic. She picked up the remote control and placed it on mute, then she turned to face me. "On my soul. I wish he had lived, at least so I could have had more of you."
"More of me?" I pointed to myself.

"Don't be daft! Not y*ou*—exactly, but more children." My mother chuckled. "Imagine, my darling, you came into this world, and just look how you turned out? Look at the special gift that you possess? Alright. I understand you're an exception. But I'm starting to see there are many facets to the human character: shining, beautiful, striking facets—very much like a diamond when held up to the light." My mother's green eyes shone as though she were gazing upon one herself. "As a civilization there is so much more to us than meets the eye, Christine. We are a shining reflection of something, and whatever that thing is," she swallowed. "I believe it's a thing of beauty. Why else were we told to multiply?"

I laughed. "Mum. You know I only believe in the goodness I can see, and I can tell you right now, I'm not seeing much good around." I expelled a bitter sigh. "The other day I met a beautiful girl. She was about nine months old. I was able to have a brief chat with her, as her mother puffed on her cigarette whilst yapping away on her mobile. Sadly, the girl told me she was being abused. She was scared and hungry. I gave her the only thing of substance in my bag at the time; some chocolate mints I took away from a work do. Anyway, she gave me her family details, and as soon as I got home I reported her mother to social services." I turned to glimpse the look of disbelief on my mother's face. "Oh, there's more where that came from. Did I ever tell you I was almost ejected from a house once? The boy I was asked to speak to was eighteen months old. He kept insisting he was fine, but his parents weren't having a bar of it. *'He can't be alright!'* they screamed at me. *'They said he's autistic! Go ahead—talk to him!'* And I did. But the boy gave the same placid response: *'Look! Tell those two to stop with their fussing. I'm fine…and everything is fine…'* I had to relay this to the boy's parents. You should have seen the look on their faces. Honestly Mum. With all the *'talking'* and *'hearing'* that has gone on so far, nothing has changed—has it? How am I making any sort of a difference? If anything, I've become less trusting, more fearful, and paranoid about everything. I could have sworn I was being followed today…I don't feel right. And I realize why that is…life is futile…"

"Good god, Christine!" My mother looked back at me with dismay. "What on earth has gotten into you today? I can't believe you're talking like this."

"Like what?"

"Like…life doesn't matter…I thought..."

"You thought what?"

My mother stared back at me through tired eyes. "I thought we were making progress…Christine, my love. I know you've had your fair share of heartache; I'm not going to pretend I know what you're going through." As she spoke her eyes filled with tears. I hated to see my mother cry, "I agree, life may not always be fair—but it certainly isn't futile. I believe each of us has a purpose, and more than most will go onto fulfil theirs. I didn't say we will be told what that purpose is—who's to say we even need to know? We just need to strive to make sure it is a positive one."

I could hear what my mother was saying, I just couldn't quite comprehend it. I groaned into my balled fists. "I don't understand it, Mum. Tobey is scheduled to die - two days from now, and it's tearing me up just to think about it! Honestly, what is the use? Life is a joke! All we're ever faced with is disappointment and pain. Children let you down. Parents let you down. *People* let you down! This is life, and this is our reality. I don't see any honour in it, do you? I think we should all stop lying to ourselves, especially to the children. We cannot do—what we want to do, or be - whatever we want to be. Sooner or later, we all end up having to do the best our crazy circumstances allow. Which..." I added with derision, "Isn't a great deal for many of us.

A lot of people I know, don't really like their lives, present company included. Life is not a gift—it's tragic. And what? Am I supposed to stand and make a big song and dance about it?"

"That's exactly it," my mother glowered at me, "yes, make a song and dance about it. No matter where you are in this journey, be proud—you possess the gift of life! Whether you're living life as a judge - or a layman; a singer, or a surgeon, we are all important and serve a wonderful purpose."

"A singer or a surgeon? Mum, you've got to be kidding. How are they even comparable?" I would have laughed out loud if I wasn't so full of reproach. "Oh, so you don't think souls need repairing too…?" My mother blinked back at me in a way that said she had never been more serious in her life. "Look Christine, you are part of something great - it's called humanity. It's a journey. Don't look at me like that dear. You can either choose to love it - or hate it, believe in it, or not—just *accept it!* You're a part of it - and it's a part of you. So there's no point in complaining about it child, just go out there and do something great with it!"

"That's so easy for you to say. You don't have this freakish impairment. People are looking at me for answers, but who am I to give it; when I'm still trying to figure out what the question is…?"

"*You* are the answer" My mother's ready-smile did not disappoint. "That is why you are here—I believe that is why we are all here. We are all living answers to prayers, if we would only let it be…"

"Mum," I couldn't find the words I wanted to say. "I'm just so tired..." I turned to face the TV screen, which was now muted. The newsreader said something.

Is it good news? Or bad? I wiped my forehead, realising I didn't care either way. "You'll probably think this is nonsense, but when I was twelve years old I did something that didn't quite sit well with me."

My mother looked surprised. "Oh. And what was that, poppet?"

"I lied to the innocent…do you remember Mason—Ivy's son? I told him I couldn't hear him anymore, knowing full well I could."

"Who? Ivy's boy? That rascal of a son. In and out of prison more times than a sailor in a knocking shop. I don't know what went wrong with him, but he has given his mother nothing but grief ever since I can remember. Is he the one you're talking about?"

I nodded. I was finding it hard to reconcile the good-natured well-intentioned baby, with the dastardly fellow my mother had just described. "Yes. He's the one."

"Darling. You told me about that ages ago. That's not something to feel guilty about—you were nothing but a child yourself for Pete's sake!"

"I know, it's just that…life is funny. There I was not wanting to *'hear'* when Mason urged me to do so. And now here I am with Tobey, eager to *'hear'* so I can help save others." I smiled, "I suppose, in the end, there really is no escaping it. You know what needs to be done—it's just about having the balls to do it!"

My mother's eyes lit up, "Christine. I think that's it! Didn't you say this is what all the babies have when they arrive on earth—courage! To achieve anything in this lifetime it will take nothing, if not sheer bravery to do so. We cannot forget this vital characteristic. Not now, not with the way things are in the world. Be brave my love, have courage, and I can almost guarantee it, you'll come to realise your purpose in life…." My mother paused. "I miss your dad every day, some days more than others. It's a hard one to grapple with, but one of the toughest challenges we'll face in life is learning how to live, without the thing we live for..." I knew my mother was talking about Jerry. "Why?"

"Because I believe this thing called life, holds something far beyond what our small minds and tender hearts can perceive. I think the babies you natter with can tell you a thing or two about this." My mother stared at the rug in the middle of the living room, floor. "You know what, Christine? Life truly is a conundrum: we may not be happy—but we can make someone happy. We may not be rich, but we can make someone rich. We may not have, but we can give - strange, that." She chuckled as she shook her head, "I think you're right sweetheart…we really are gifts…"

***

Christine

"Well, this is a surprise. You've devoured two helpings of my spaghetti bolognaise and half a bottle of red wine. Are you feeling any better?" My mother asked. I smiled coyly and gave my stomach an agreeable pat. "Most definitely." I opted not to share my deep feelings of anxiety that had plagued me all afternoon. I thought about the two men in suits who had stepped onto the train carriage, and the woman in the fluffy gilet who had brushed passed me earlier today. Tobey's impending death had affected me more than I realised.

"Mum, I better get a move on." I rose from my chair.

"Why not take some food home with you?" My mother went over to a side cabinet and brought out a Tupperware dish.

"No thanks, Mum, I'll be okay."

"Are you sure?"

"Absolutely."

I looked out into the night. The light from the hallway lit up the steps below. I scaled down them.

"Call me when you get in." My mother's voice sailed down from the top of the stairs. "Are you sure you don't want me to call you a cab?"

"Mum. I'm going to be fine. Close the door, you'll let the cold in!" Not that there was any about. It was a warm summer evening, and it wasn't quite dark yet. Above me, the sun had exploded into a spectacular crimson and indigo tie-dye work of art. I took a look at my phone. It was 9.22 p.m.

Where did the time go?

I made my way toward the nearest bus stop. In under an hour, I had arrived at Manor House in North London. Some of the Turkish cafes were winding down their shutters. Although it was dark outside it was still quite humid, and the scent of scorched barbeques wafted through the air. I tightened my fingers around my shoulder strap and began my seven-and-a-half-minute walk to my flat.

Tonight I was aware of the long stretch of parkland to the left of me. The dark leafy grounds were fenced by a clustering of shrubberies, which gave the area the feel of an enchanted forest, rather than a municipal park. I shivered as I breathed in the warm night air, while making a concerted effort not to stare into the forest-like void. Besides, if I looked for too long I might spot something I could do without seeing, not that I believed in monsters…but still…

As I advanced up the road I fixed my sights on the ray of lights spilling out from the convenience stores up ahead. Before I arrived at the end of the junction, I turned a sharp corner and cut through an opening, which led into my quiet, but well-lit housing estate that overlooked Clissold Park. I approached my apartment block. After punching in the security code, I yanked open the main doorway; it was a temperamental old thing that had to be handled with force, otherwise the steel door would not open, despite entering every digit in correctly.

My apartment was situated on the top floor. I preferred it this way; I was in seclusion but never alone. Also, from my bedroom window I was presented with a bird's-eye view of The Emirates Stadium. After dark the dazzling flood lights on the field could be seen from miles around. It gave the appearance of a live concert playing to an empty auditorium, or - as I often viewed it - an audience made up of ghosts. That said, on match days, just like the all the other residents, I did not have to switch on my TV to know when the Gunners had scored. The floorboards rumbled, the mirror in the hallway shook, even the top of the sugar pot gave a quick jig. The resonant roar of sixty-thousand voices in unison was felt, as much as it was heard.

As soon as I entered my flat I turned on the lights in the hallway; I kicked off my shoes and hung up my jacket on the coat hanger. My bedroom was ahead of me. The long bus ride home had taken its toll on my weary body. I couldn't wait to change into my night clothes and dive straight under the duvet. Sleep beckoned.

It's amazing what the human eye picks up, even though it seems the brain is far from engaged...

I had passed the kitchen on the right of me, before I realised I had seen something…something...that should not have been there...

I walked back on myself, and just as I thought there was something on top of the kitchen counter. It was small, and I was amazed I had even spotted it in the first place. It was the spare key to the flat.

Lydia! I whirled around. Of course I
was alone—*aren't I?*

I turned in the opposite direction where my lounge was situated. I didn't need to turn on the light as the brightness from the corridor flooded into the room, bringing everything into focus. My living area had a large bay window which overlooked the park. Pushed up against the window, was a petite dining table surrounded by four chairs with piles of magazines arranged on top of the surface. And just before the dining table, a motionless figure lay across the laminated flooring...

"Lydia!" I rushed to the ground and turned my friend over. "Lydia, Lydia..." I cried. There was blood everywhere. It looked like someone had spilt red wine all over the floorboards. It ran down the front of Lydia's jacket, over my hands, and formed a dark puddle in the middle of the living room floor…

"Lydia!" *It really is blood!*

My mind raced: *Run for help! …stop the bleeding...which one first?* My bag was still fastened to my shoulder. I ruffled through it; grabbed my phone, and dialled 999.

"Help. Please. I need an ambulance...there's blood everywhere...my friend...my friend is bleeding…" As soon as I was put through, questions were asked.

"Stay calm, try not to panic, we're sending someone out to you. Can you tell us if she is breathing?"

"I-I don't know."

"Where is the blood coming from?"

"I-I don't know…everywhere!"

"Do you think you can check for a pulse?"

In some way the reel of questions broke through my paralysis. I could feel myself breathe steadily again. And now that I was calm, I was able to answer all the questions being fired my way. "I can't check for a pulse. There is blood everywhere…she is cold…she is not breathing…" I swallowed before ending my sentence, "And her throat has been slashed." I stared in horror at the ferocious wound and repeated, "…her throat has been slashed…"

Chapter Thirty-Three: Bad News Travels Quickly

Siba

Manor House: Murder Mystery!'
'Oscar-Winning Sibling Slain in North London Block'
'Star Tears for Baby Sister'

Before lunchtime the story had weaved its way into news bulletins around the globe. The fervent way in which the news was received, one would have thought it was Hollywood darling—Stephanie Downes—who had met her fateful end, and not Lydia Cartwright-Snowden. An unknown figure, whose life was lost, long before the paramedics had even pulled out of the depot. But as Lydia once riposted: 'Any publicity was good publicity'.

And it would appear the young woman wasn't too wide from the mark. Like a deer caught in headlights,

St Margaret's Hospital Trust fell under the full glare of the world's media. Keith McGuinness, the Fleet Street reporter who had been tipped off by Lydia, had published an in-depth exposé of the high number of baby deaths that had occurred at the infamous London hospital.

On the other hand, there was only a brief mentioning of a certain MD who may, or may not, have had some part to play in the deaths of the newborns. But for legal reasons, no further information could be provided about the staff member in question....

***

Richard

Richard sat at his desk at home overlooking the lab he had put together over the last two years. He wasn't reading the newspaper; he had already gone through it several times that morning. Instead he stared at the grey and white pixelated image of the slain victim: Lydia Cartwright-Snowden.

He didn't go into work today. Paul Healey had called him up earlier to have a brief chat with him. "As you know," the administrator's nervous voice grated on him like a bee in his ear, "f-following hospital procedure, while under investigation, y-you are not permitted to enter the ward or venture onto the premises." Paul Healy stopped talking, or breathing, Richard couldn't care which. "In some cases, and in this case," he coughed, "we would like to see the latter adhered to," he coughed again, "well, at least until after the investigation period, and so on."

If Richard didn't think much of Paul Healy before, he unreservedly detested the man now. For as weakly as the pillock could muster, the administrator waded through a list of supposed set of rights that were afforded to him as a senior member of staff, and the only serving MD on the board of directors. *So…I have rights now?*

"Listen, Richard. You are a highly intelligent and resourceful fellow to the Trust, which has by no means been overlooked. But you must understand the position we are in. The NHS is being dragged into the spotlight. We can sway and appease departmental heads for you, but we're not about to take on the government in regard to this matter. We are going to have to go through these procedures. All that is required at your end is a little patience. I'm sure these outrageous accusations will soon prove to be nothing but a misunderstanding of sorts."

Richard did not share his colleague's sentiment. At that very moment he was wishing Paul Healey would one day grow a pair, keel over, and die!

"Paul. My lawyers will be in touch soon." He ended the call, leaving the hapless administrator to likely gawp at the phone he held in his hand. Of course Richard was lying. He had no intention of seeking legal representation; there was no need. He glanced at the image of a beautiful woman who was killed by an unknown assailant. Other than meeting her, there was something familiar about Lydia. Her death was not an accident, Richard understood. Diligence was out to get Christine, because it was he who had told them where they could find her. He had done it—and he couldn't lie, he knew what he was doing. He'd always known just how ruthless Diligence could be, powerful companies always were. He knew. And just as simple as placing an order, he had told them where they could find Christine Shore, knowing, what they were likely to do. Richard looked at his shaking hands. Although he couldn't see a thing, they were now soaked in Lydia's blood.

Everything you touch…dies...

"I didn't touch her!" he cried. His words rang out into the open air and drowned there…
Richard found there was something more sobering than realising you were the sole cause of someone's death…it's when you know yours is just around the corner. Diligence was not going to go away as he had hoped. He had messed up in *elephantine* proportions, and this mistaken identity killing would only fall harder on him…
Richard had always been a gifted straight-A student all of his life, but underneath it all he was dogged with insecurities, stemming from his struggles with failure. *Only god knows why that is…?* He couldn't blame his old man; he was not a bad person. In fact, his father did the best he could with him. How else was an aging army doctor from Twickenham going to deal with a traumatized pre-teenager who, in under a year, had lost his baby brother—and a few months later—his mother to sudden illnesses? No. He couldn't blame his father. He couldn't blamc anyone for the decisions he made…Maybe the answers Richard sought were buried deep in his childhood, or were embedded somewhere within his genes? Whatever the answer was, it didn't matter now. This character flaw had made his life, and it would soon play a part in ending it…

Richard reclined in his leather chair. For the third time that morning, he counted out two of his treasured pills. Digesting more than three capsules in twenty-four hours was said to be deadly. After placing his phone in the top drawer and clearing away his desk, Richard took down his sixth and final pill... Splayed across the screen on his PC was an excerpt from his favourite novel: *The Lord of the Flies* Richard surprised himself with his laughter. *Ha!* And there he was trying to find the biggest discovery of all time, and it was right there in front of him—the internet! He chuckled like a mad man. If not anything, the information superhighway was truly the most remarkable invention of the twentieth century...*it will change the world…*

He took a deep breath and read his favourite paragraph. It was the part where the young protagonist in the story started to weep for the end of innocence, and for the death of his real friend, *Piggy* Richard closed his eyes. *His friend! His friend!* Richard could see his friend. In a mighty rush all his memories flooded back to him at once…

There they were; laughing and racing each other across a shiny white bridge, which was connected to three separate mountains. It was the same bridge they had built together, not too long ago...oh my goodness! It was so electrifying! So delightful! So euphoric! Richard had never felt so alive in his friends' presence, and the feeling was mutual: his existence empowered her too…they smiled at each other as their glowing hands connected. They were not alone. There was a group of them…all happy…all one…all free…once upon a time in a faraway land...

Richard gasped…*such beauty…such cruelty…*

Aha! So he had met Lydia before. It was a very long time ago. Just before the start…

A wistful smile remained on Richard's lips, even when a stranger in the shadows arrived on the scene. There was nothing for the intruder to do, the job had already been done for him. He crept out as silently as he had come in.

It was the housekeeper who found Richard slumped across his chair. She had made the sign of the cross four times before calling the authorities. She was beside herself. In all her fifty-four years she had never come across a dead body before...

Chapter Thirty-Four: The Journey to the Hospital

Siba

Unlike Lydia's death the report of this mortality did not make the world news. Although, the investigations surrounding the hospital were ramped up by another gear.

`'St Margaret's on its knees as murder probe continues'`
`'Baby-Slayer Suicide'`

Ten minutes after Yvonne Shore had placed the call, a minicab pulled into the side street by her residence. She had ordered the cab for her daughter, who was upstairs getting ready to go out. It was only 9:30 a.m, yet the sun was shining at its midday best.

***

Christine

I put on my sunglasses. I didn't wear them to shield myself from the sun's glare, but rather to keep others from seeing my swollen eyelids. I had spent most of the night in a flood of tears, and the best part of the morning trying to erase the anguish from my face. This morning I had made the decision to wear a black polo neck and a pair of jeans, also the same colour. No one said today was a funeral, but I had attended one a few years ago, and all the emotional cues were in place. This time, however, there was no catharsis to be had. I was not going to see a dead person get buried, I was going to watch a living one die…

"I will eat my hat if this city does not win its bid for the 2012 Summer Olympics," the minicab driver said with a passion. He stole a quick glance at me in his rear-view mirror.

I nodded. I was not in the least bit bothered by the driver's ongoing attempts to fill the void. I had *absolutely* no intention of pondering over the chilling events that had unfolded in my life over the last two days…

"My name is Hassan, and people call me Hassan!" He laughed. "Did you know London is *booming* right now, and property is where it's at. You buy them for a fraction of what they're worth, then you flip them for a good price. It makes good business sense, no?" The driver nodded. "Nonsense!" He barked at the blue car that had pulled up in front of us. "Many people in this city, they don't know how to drive, you see that? They come into this country with their foreign licences which they exchange for British one, just like that!" He clicked his fingers. "And once they get their licence, they drive around like maniacs! No regard for the rules." He brandished a disgruntled look, which he didn't wear for too long, "Crazy drivers everywhere!" Then for some unknown reason, he began to talk about the one topic I did not want to hear about right now. "When I think about the lack of morality in this country, all I can think about is the children, the babies. It's a crying shame, you know that? A crying shame."

I held my breath. I stopped when I realised what I was doing. *Not today. I don't want to hear about children or babies right now.*
I wished the driver would just shut up!
Hassan continued, "When you look around and you see fourteen to sixteen-year-olds killing each other for status. I say who can blame them, right? When their governments do the same in another man's country. What you see is what you do, isn't that correct?" The driver shrugged. He leaned forward and cranked up the air-conditioning. "I don't know what your thoughts are on this war in Iraq, but it's got me asking a lot of questions," he furrowed his brows. "Is this how we end terrorism, by becoming terrorist ourselves? Don't get me wrong, that Saddam is an awful man! Evil incarnate, if you ask me, just like many of these leaders today. But I'm not sure this is the right way to go about this…our children. I couldn't give a damn about religion or the law. The question is: what is *society* teaching our children? There is so much hypocrisy going around. Don't they know? Haven't we learnt? Children never do what you say, they do what they see…" He looked up at me. "Do you have any children?"
"No."
He chuckled, "Neither do I. But my youngest brother in New Jersey has three of them: one girl and two boys. They are being raised like *Americanos*." His laughter rumbled through the car. "All they eat, all day, every day, is that stuff. What do you call it?

Chicken nuggets and fries. However the chickens had never run; the potatoes never saw the sun, and the juice that they drink has no fruit in it! *Allahim!* And it's only *now* they want to address the food we are feeding our children. How was this even allowed to happen in the first place? Before it got to our fridges, *somebody* said this stuff was fit for consumption, no?"
The driver kept on talking, being encouraged, it seemed, by my consistent nods. "They feed our children things they wouldn't *dare* to give to their animals. But the scary thing is, human beings allowed this to happen—*human beings!* And then we have the gall to blame everything on technology, forgetting it is only but a device of our own desires and making…"
The driver fell silent. He poured all his energy into manoeuvring his vehicle around the busy ring road. After veering into smoother lanes he picked up where he left off. "Is it me? Or is it insane to think society should function like technology? Where life is all about being a number, or a nobody; point-scoring—or amassing casualties, rewards, and retribution. This cannot be right? If this is how people want to play, so be it! But it shouldn't be the standards by which we live by…don't get me wrong," he smiled. "There are some games I like to play. Do you like computer games?"
"No. Not really." I almost smiled back. He got ten points for his persistence against my noncommittal stance.

"Well, some of them are quite good fun, but I do believe we've grown lazy. We didn't have computers in our day but learn—did we not? Now we have algorithms and statistics dictating our humanity, even telling us who to love…I fear we have built a matrix and locked ourselves inside it. The question is: who is controlling - who? Let me tell you something." He winked and grinned mischievously. "Corruption always starts at the top, don't let anyone tell you differently."

I smiled. The driver sounded like a conspiracy nut, but he had a point.

The minicab crept up to a zebra crossing, then juddered to a halt. A little girl and her mother stood at the precipice. The girl stared at us with some interest before seeking out her mother's hand. Together they ambled to the other side.

Hassan sighed, he looked like he'd just aged ten years. "It's sad to see, but society is playing Russian roulette with our children's health, education, welfare, and future livelihoods. These little ones don't stand a chance! They'll be swimming in an even bigger pool of stench than the ones we were born into, and somehow, we'll expect them to come up smelling like roses. But I don't think it works that way, I don't think it does. Some of that muck will stick…" The driver stared out of the window as his voice faded into a melancholic haze. When Hassan peered back at me, there was a flicker of humour in his eye. "And that my dear, is the reason why I'm saving up all my hard-earned cash, so I can buy a vast farmhouse which I can run away to," he chuckled, "A nice little *çiftlik* in a remote village in Turkey. So, *Inshallah,* I will not have to see any of this mess, I will just live out the rest of my days in lush surroundings." He then let out a big belly laugh, which I found myself joining in with.

***

Siba

Christine and the minicab driver laughed because the truth really was funny to hear. There wasn't anyone who hadn't entertained the thought of running away from it all. I know, because when I was on earth I often felt the same way...Running to different lands to soak up new ideals, or just to be left alone to preserve the old ones. Running from wars, from anger, from rules, that no longer outline the wrong from the true. Running from corruption, greed, regret. Running to survive, and to survive—you had to run! Run! Run! Run! And that would be anyone's response to the world's ongoing madness. But sure enough, it was nowhere near the answer to it. So I suppose, I could only imagine, that was why Christine and Hassan laughed so deeply…

Christine

"Oh, if it were only that simple," I let out a shaky sigh. I wiped my eyes but left my sunglasses on. "But we can't run away Hassan, we can't run away…" I looked out of the passenger window. A moment passed, "I suppose it's a bit like the Scout's Code of Honour," I said with a sad smile. "The babies being born in these times need to be prepared…so much more prepared." I had uttered this statement more for myself than for Hassan's benefit.

"They sure do!" The driver nodded, agreeing to something he didn't quite understand.

Or maybe he does.

"These babies will need to come out with their eyes *wide* open, for if their leaders are losing their sight—they are sure as hell are going to need theirs! Along with a will of tempered iron." He laughed. "This is a battlefield they're facing, and very confusing times, I must say. Poor souls, it's not their fault—it's our own doing. I'm sure if these little ones could talk, they would let us know as much…"

The driver turned a sharp corner and broke out onto Shoreditch High Street. "Not far to go now."

In the distance, I glimpsed The Gherkin, which was beginning to resemble a large elongated Fabergé egg. I had read somewhere that this much-anticipated building was scheduled to be completed at the end of the year. Change was indeed coming to the East End, I noted with a bleak sense of ambiguity. I glanced at the growing number of construction sites and steel cranes. They bobbed up and down like mechanical dinosaurs grazing on gravel and cement…

***

I handed over my spare key to the senior investigating officer. He oversaw the case now. It was the same key Lydia had used to let herself into the flat. The blood had been cleared from the floor, but the incident tape remained.

'Of course, it is still early on in the investigation,' the officer had said, handing me a clipboard and pen, 'but we suspect your friend might have walked in on a burglary, of sorts. You did later say that you were missing some items: your DVD player and your laptop, I believe?'

'Yes. That's right, but nothing priceless. Not a reason to...kill...'

'Oh, you'd be surprised what people do from the fear of getting caught. There were signs of a struggle…there was some resistance…but don't worry, we'll keep you informed on everything we have.'

The lounge was off-limits. The forensic team was still at work, looking for fingerprints and taking samples for DNA testing... A botched burglary? I raged. This was Manor House, not the slums of Mogadishu! Would a thief violate their victims in such a way? Would a thief do this...? Oh, Lydia.

***

"Here we are! St Margaret's Hospital." The cab pulled up to the curb. I handed over a note, the driver gave me back my change. He looked at me

with some concern. "You have a good day now…take care."
"Thank you Hassan, you too." I stepped onto the pavement and waited as the five-seater eased itself onto the main road before blending in with the growing stream of traffic.
I took a deep breath. I turned around and began to approach the entrance which led to the neonatal intensive care unit.

The Professor

Professor Florian was sat in his study in Geneva. He placed his reading glasses into his right hand and rubbed his dry eyes, as his business partner of twenty years relayed current events to him...

"All evidence of our operation has now been taken care of."

The Professor coughed. "I understand that part. However, correct me if I'm wrong, but didn't the doctor say it was this 'baby-whisperer' who was the problem here?"

"And so it seemed at the time." Bernard cupped his chin and stroked his stubble-free face. "You see, after making my own enquiries into the matter, it turned out it was the other woman who was a bigger threat to our organization."

"Really...?" The Professor did not look satisfied. "Please explain."

Bernard slid a sheet of paper across the glass table. "You see this other woman, Ms Cartwright, was highly connected. And not only was she connected, she was also the proactive type: inquisitive, ambitious—your kind of person in fact." He grinned. "She would stop at nothing until she got answers. Going on the information I had received it was only a matter of time before she would have zeroed-in on our doctor here. I'm surprised she had escaped his notice. Or as we were right to suspect, his attention was not quite as focused to begin with. Either way, with Ms Cartwright and Lawson gone, this matter will soon be heading in the same direction."

"And there's nothing else on Dr Lawson's part?"

"No. Nothing left at his end. It looks like he took care of everything before he took care of himself. Granted, there was the matter with some slighted lover, but the evidence was destroyed, and…if later down the line she were to talk, it's believed she refers to this organisation as Diligence."

"Diligence?" This generated dry sniggers from the pair of them.

Unbeknown to the agents assigned to a project, they were all handed different company names. Hence, Dr Lawson was given Diligence. Although Diligence was in operation, in reality Diligence—as a company name—was no more in existence than money sprouting on trees…

"Why?" Bernard paused. "Should we do something about it?"

"Oh no, there's no need," The Professor shook his head. "It's just a shame. All these losses and still no results."

Dr Marietta stepped into the room. She was followed by a maid wheeling a tray of breakfast pastries and a canister of freshly brewed coffee. The doctor took one look at the frown on her husband's face and scowled her disapproval. "Elias, my dear. Let us not worry about the things we cannot change." She waited until the maid had gone. "I've made arrangements for us to spend a fortnight in the Rift Valley, to take our minds off things for a while. It'll

do you good to get some rest before we start on the next project. Work, we are never short of dear, as you know, but time waits for no man, as you can see."
She squeezed his knee. "Well, not until we find a cure for that." She sat beside her husband. "Listen Elias. We will re-evaluate everything once we get back from Kenya. It really is beautiful this time of year."
The Professor turned to face Bernard, "Isn't she such a thoughtful wife?" he said emitting a smile which made him look ten years younger, "I don't know where I'd be without her."
"That my dear, is because you're such a wealthy husband," Marietta replied, "Sorry, did I say that bit out loud?"
Bernard shook his head, grinning at the pair of them. "Unfortunately I cannot stay for breakfast, I have another meeting to attend." He clicked shut his attaché briefcase, shunting into darkness the 6x4 photographs of the once active, now recently deceased, Persons of Interest. "I believe that is all for now."
"Very well," The Professor accepted the cup that was handed to him. "Just one more thing...this Christine woman - the baby whisperer. It appears she does possess a supernatural gift, does she not?"
"From my investigations, she is authentic," Bernard replied, "and what of it? We've ensured that all trails pointing to our operations have been erased, she can do us no harm."

"No, Bernard. She may be one to watch." The Professor's wizened eyes displayed discomfort and scorn. "If she's the real thing, she is a significant threat going forward. Our investments into cybernetics, bioengineering, and neurology, is threatened by individuals who have these unnatural abilities. My aim is to create a better mortal - an elite species, so that we can control access to the next generation of superhuman beings. With regards to this 'baby-whisperer,' we need to have the hegemony, or neutralize any abnormalities. They threaten the ultimate program."
Bernard nodded. "Let me see what we can do,"
"I know we can rely on you, Bernard," Marietta intervened in good cheer. "But for now let us focus all our energies on our trip ahead." She clapped her hands to signal the end of the discussion.

Ubiquitous as air and vanishes like smoke. That was the last ever mentioned of Diligence…

***

Christine

An air of solemnity had settled on the neonatal ward. It was emanating from a small group of people that had gathered at the far end of the room. They were all close friends and relatives of The Daley's. They had come to provide whatever kind of support they could give to the soon-to-be-bereaved couple….

I was permitted to go into the private ward. I promised myself I would not cry today, however, I could feel my heart wrench into two, as I watched Robert Daley sob into his arms, refusing to be comforted by an older man who appeared to be his father.

Kelly was cradling Tobey. She looked up when I entered the room. "Thanks for coming, Christine." Her face was streaked in tears. "I heard what happened...I..."

"It's okay, Kelly." I nodded, "I wanted to come. I wanted to be here."

I stared at Tobey's greying skin. His small mouth was pulled in a straight line. Even though his eyes were closed, I could tell he was far from asleep. He didn't look restful enough.

The nurse who was hovering around spoke, "As we earlier discussed, we will soon make the move to take Tobey off the respiratory machine." The nurse nodded. "Let me know when you both feel ready to do so." She looked from Kelly to Robert, then left them with their son.

Kelly motioned for me to sit next to her. Robert remained standing by the window with his father, as though the marked distance would act as some kind of barrier from the grim reality he now had to face. "Would you like to talk to him before we do it?" Kelly looked at me.

"Yes, okay." I breathed in. My eyes tingled with tears of helplessness.

Kelly placed Tobey into my arms. I caressed him as I had done so many times before. Tobey sounded groggy, but his relief was audible. "Albert, he's alive! He made it!"

"Yes, he did, thanks to you." I smiled, "All thanks to you..." A solitary tear curved around my face then hovered at the tip of my chin. I looked down at Tobey. "They're going to take you off the machine my darling. Are you ready, Tobey?"

"I am. Remember what I told you. Tell my parents not to worry. I love them now, and I will love them forever."

"I will." I swallowed to allow myself to breathe.

"And Christine. I love you too. You have a rare and beautiful heart. It's much stronger than you think. Good hearts always are...please, no more worries, Christine…no more worries..."

I lost my resolve, I began to weep. I handed Tobey over to his mother, although I wasn't quite ready to let him go. I continued to stroke his hand as Kelly, who was openly shaking, held Tobey close to her chest. She looked down at her baby with all her love pouring out to her son.

The nurse removed one of the tubes in Tobey's mouth, she then dislodged the one attached to his left nostril. All the while, his mother sang
his favourite nursery rhyme as she rocked him back and forth.

'The wheels on the bus go round and round, round and round, round and round…'

It is widely understood the human heart can go on beating without oxygen for one to three minutes, before deprivation kills the brain cells. And that is how it is understood in medical terms…On this occasion, however…

After several minutes had passed Tobey whispered, "It's really quiet around here...so very quiet...can you still hear me Christine?"
My heart leapt. "Yes, Tobey! I can hear you! I can hear you very clearly." Which was true, as he no longer sounded groggy or out of breath.
"I can see something," Tobey said.
"What can you see?"
"I-I-it's a light...it's..."
"What is it, Tobey? Say that again?"
"...it's...t...tt…it's..."
"Tobey...Tobey!" There was silence. I heard no more...

Tobey

"Aha! Tobey you're here!" a loud voice called out. Tobey was hesitant. "You have a question for me?" the voice inquired, full of mirth.
"Yes, I do. I might forget later, so I want to ask you now while it's still fresh in my memory. What happens to those babies that go to The Fears?"

There was a smile nestled in the voice that answered him. "Tobey, my child. I love children, and the children love me. I will not let anything bad happen to them, and fair is fair, right? Where else do you think they go? Why? They come back again of course," the voice chuckled, "they are born again."
"Ah, yes!" Tobey wondered why he hadn't seen the clarity before. "That's right!"

"Are you ready now, Tobey?" Love beamed.

"Yes, I'm coming," Tobey called out, as he ran as fast as he could, to the only light he's ever known. Thus, bringing an end to Tobey's journey here on earth…

Chapter Thirty-Six: Christine Shore: The Baby Whisperer

Christine

My dearest Lydia, so full of life…her body found butchered on my living room floor. Dr Lawson ending it all, whilst reading the story of Lydia's death. The Daley's looking down at their dying son. Seeing Tobey, then hearing him no more…Those harrowing three days—were three days too much for me. Like a kettle on the boil, something inside me peaked at a level then switched off, and two months would pass before I would begin to feel myself again….

In that time I had been invited to funerals, press conferences, and a whole host of engagements. I declined them all, avoiding busy places. I didn't want to hear from any babies or see anyone. I just wanted to be left alone in my flat, watching old movies on my new DVD player…

Three weeks after Lydia's passing, I saw a photo of Stephanie Downes in a glossy magazine. She was dressed in funeral attire: black dress, sunglasses, and a large black hat. The article went on to detail the actress' complete and utter devastation over the loss of her baby sister.

I stopped reading. I thought I couldn't produce any more tears, but they rolled out of me like sweat; setting my cheeks on fire as they coursed down my face. I wondered if the day would ever come when I would cease to hurt.

Oh how I hate grieving! The searing pain, the torment, the sheer unpredictability of it all. *It's hard work!* Such a tremendous yoke we place on ourselves. I could envision Tobey slowly shaking his head as I made provisions to carry it. *But what can I do?* Mourn, I must! The guilt of not grieving is an even greater burden to bear...

The days became weeks, and the weeks slowly turned into months. Then, on one ordinary day, two months after the deaths, I received an unexpected phone call...

The conversation was more surreal to me than the first time I had heard Mason speak out loud, what seemed like all those years ago. I listened to what was being said and made a note of the arrangement.

Once the call had ended, my eyes drifted over to the park outside my living room window. It was a bright day, and everything was still summer green. A crowded bus roared up the highway. A female jogger advanced further into the park. A car screeched. A cat meowed. And I realised I was no longer at that boiling point anymore. I could take in long deep breaths without wanting to be sick. I was back in that state of numbness. The place I had arrived at after my son's passing, and before Lydia and Tobey had blown into my life. I had made it back there - which was good, a little inept, but still better than before.

Putting away my battered jotter, for the first time, in a long time, I began to make plans for the day ahead…

***

Exactly seven days later, on a clear Saturday morning, I was up early. I spent a significant amount of time cleaning up my flat. After I had completed the arduous task, I decided to brew myself a strong pot of coffee. I then decided against it…then I changed my mind again...

A silver hatchback pulled into the estate and entered the visitor's parking bay. A few minutes later someone buzzed my intercom. I pressed the security button to let them in. I took another look around my apartment before heading toward the front door.

As soon as I opened it, I was met with a woman in a red baseball cap. It was pulled so low down her face, I wondered how she managed to get up the stairs. The woman carried a bulky toddler car seat.

I smiled and let them in.

"You recognised me?" Stephanie Downes grinned a little self-consciously. Then in a swifter move, she brought forward the baby seat she held. "And this is my darling, Maybelline, the little nightmare I was telling you about." She handed it over. I caught my breath. Maybelline was the cutest baby girl I had ever seen. She looked like an angel. Stephanie Downes took off her cap and shook out her long scraggly blond hair. The shakedown made little difference.

"I know. I look a right royal mess." She sounded every bit as playful as Lydia did when she made similar remarks of that kind. "Thank you for agreeing to see me." She looked at me sombrely.
"That's okay," I nodded, "I hope you didn't have any trouble getting here. Let's go into the kitchen."
The recently wiped down countertops left a pervading scent of lemon and bleach. I poured my guest a mug of coffee. I didn't add any milk or sugar. I also did my best not to stare, but tried to appear as relaxed as one could, whilst serving an A-list celebrity their morning brew.
"Nice coffee!" Stephanie said with a twang. "I really needed that. I've become more American since I married one." She took another mouthful from her mug. I thanked her.
"I called my sister before…she died. Lydia spoke very highly of you. I know the press have said some unkind things..." She trailed off, "I-I wouldn't have bothered you, except, Maybelline has been crying nonstop—it's driving me crazy! I've been recommended all sorts of new-age techniques. You name it, I've done it! But nothing seems to work. Then I thought of you...I was hoping to meet you at the funeral, but when you didn't show...I-I'm sorry... I…"
"No. It's me who should be apologising. I kind of dropped out of the loop for a while. I guess…now when I think about it, I should have called or something…"

I recalled Lydia's excitement as she relayed the news of her older sister's pregnancy, before rushing off to order her *house-weight* in baby goods from the John Lewis catalogue. No matter how hard Lydia tried to play it down, she really was looking forward to becoming an aunt….

"Well, what do you know?" Stephanie smiled down at her daughter. "She's so quiet now, not even sleeping; just staring up at us like butter wouldn't melt in her mouth."

I peered into the car seat. The baby looked like a cherub with her pale blue eyes and mousy brown hair. She gurgled. "Hello, Christine, finally! It's *soooo* lovely to meet you! I've been wanting to see you for the longest time, but mummy wasn't getting it. I had to keep on screaming and crying and crying, until I got through to her."

I gasped, "I believe you did." I chuckled, "but my darling, I think you've been giving your mummy a lot of grief, and maybe more sleepless nights than she deserves."

"I know, I feel a little bad about that. But I just wanted to meet you that was all. The thing is Christine, I met one of my Ancestors. She said it was very important I pass this message onto you before I forget."

"What was it?"

Maybelline cleared her throat. "My Ancestor said: no matter what has happened in the past—*you,* Christine Shore, should continue to do what you were born to do. The gift that you possess is an accumulation of blessings, but as you are aware—this is not essential. What is, however, is what you decide to do with it." The baby's eyes never left my face. "Although it seems like an age, we are only on earth for a short time, but it is the most important time of all! The world is not how these grownups see it, Christine! They don't understand: *Worldly Knowledge* is no match for *Divine Inspiration*. And this is what we are - inspirations to the world! They can't see it Christine, but these grownups are losing their way. They are replacing hope with apathy. It's being sown into the foundations, and like a cancer - it's set to spread! They don't need to educate us, but liberate us! Free us from this wave of apathy that is being fed to us all. You, Christine, you can see the world through the little ones. You can see what we can do for it and what we can be! We can change it Christine. You won't be alone. Help us, help you, HELP THEM! We can change it! Humanity needn't sail into doom and gloom. We have a choice in this. Let our little voices be heard. Give us that chance Christine. You know we have it in us to change it. Please don't stand by. Don't watch us grow up…to forget that…"

I didn't say anything right away, I only nodded.

"I believe you are wondering if *they* got away with it," Maybelline said. I looked back at her. She continued, "My Ancestor said; just like many others, you now have a piece of the thread. The great tapestry is unravelling..." I detected a smile in Maybelline's voice, "Well, that was what my Ancestor wanted to tell you. I just hope none of this gets in the way of my plans."

Suppressing a smile I enquired, "Oh, and what plans are those?"

"When I grow up, I plan to go into public service. I would like to be a politician."

"A politician?" Her response made me chuckle.

"Yes. I would like to shake things up a bit. You know, create some waves on the political stage. This is what the women in my family have always done. We're a gutsy lot, don't you know? We don't give rubbish, and we don't take any back!"

I burst out laughing, then smiled in admiration, "I believe the women in your family do have this…errr…quality." I leaned forward. "When you see this Ancestor of yours again, tell her I agree with her. I've heard everything, and I'm ready..."

In response to my reply the baby let out great big squeals of laughter.

"Oh my! I've never heard her laugh like that. What did you say to her? What does it mean?"

I was laughing too. I wiped my eyes. "She said the women in your family…have…a thing…you're a gutsy lot, I hear."

Stephanie nodded, looking back at me in bewilderment. "Yes, yes we are," she smiled in awe.

"Stephanie," I turned back to face her. "I don't think you're going to have any more problems with Maybelline crying, I'm quite certain of that. Just one thing, though. You've got to help your baby do what she was born to do. The answer, we may not always know, but the help we can always give. Whatever that potential may be, no matter how daunting or challenging, please help her to fulfil that potential."

"But how will I know what that is?"

"Oh. You don't really need to know," I replied, all-smiles and dry-eyed for a change, "Believe me these babies, they know it for themselves."

"How about you?" Stephanie asked with a warmth very much like Lydia's. "What are you going to do?"

I sighed, I could feel my eyes lighting up like freshly pressed pennies, "I have a gift, I have life. And so long as I have this it means: I have much to learn; I have much to teach," I beamed, as I imagined the cheers of all the babies from around the world and beyond, "so I guess I have much to do..."

With that said, the two of us turned our attention back onto Maybelline. We slowly sipped our coffees, shared pointers on motherhood, and fawned over the baby girl, who was now playing quite contently in her little car seat.

The End

Printed in Great Britain
by Amazon

53346269R00234